D0042026

SPINDLE CITY

JOTHAM BURRELLO

SPINDLE CITY

a Novel

BLACK
STONE
PUBLISHING

Copyright © 2020 by Jotham Burrello
Published in 2020 by Blackstone Publishing
Cover and book design by Kathryn Galloway English

Lyrics to "The Curse of the Aching Heart" supplied by
the Lester S. Levy Collection of Sheet Music,
Sheridan Libraries, Johns Hopkins University

Printed in the United States of America

First edition: 2020
ISBN 978-1-982629-37-3
Fiction / Historical / General

1 3 5 7 9 10 8 6 4 2

CIP data for this book is available
from the Library of Congress

Blackstone Publishing
31 Mistletoe Rd.
Ashland, OR 97520

www.BlackstonePublishing.com

For the past
Mary, Tom, Hiya, and Doc

For the future
Atticus, Miles, and Jotham

We price the cotton.
We spin the yarn.
We weave the fabric.
We dress the world.
Same as it ever was, and as it will always be.
Welcome to Spindle City.

> —Colonel Jefferson Cleveland,
> president of Cleveland Mill, speaking
> to visiting French Trade Council, 1886

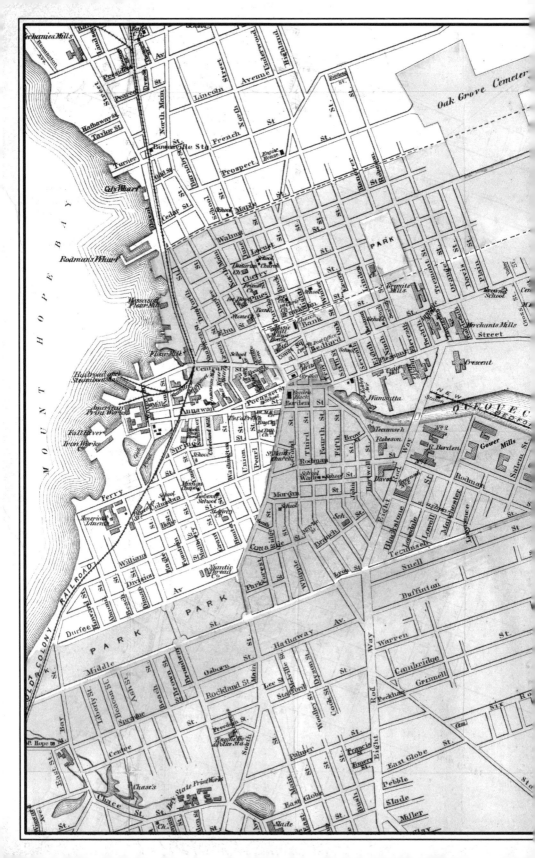

CITY OF

FALL RIVER.

Published by

SAMPSON, DAVENPORT, & C?

Scale 12000' or 1000 Feet to an inch.

NORTH WATUPPA

SOUTH
WATUPPA LAKE

Fall River Water Works

Engine House

Stand Pipe Tower

Reservoir St.

Street

Locust

Oak Grove Av.

Bedford

Stafford

Old Canal St.

Hartford

Bedford

Road

Mason St.

Thomas St.

Fowler

Bassett

Earle St.

St.

St.

Avon St.

Adams St.

May St.

Maple St.

Ardale St.

Smithee St.

Alsop St.

Flint

Jencks

Harrison

Cash St.

Cherry St.

Davis St.

Alden St.

Flint St.

Barnard

Wampanoag

Charlton St.

Boutwell St.

Brevett St.

St. Charles St.

Webster St.

Sch.

Morgan St.

Ferry St.

Brightman St.

Plymouth St.

Borden

Crosdell St.

Campbell St.

Mc Cowan Av.

Morton Mill

Pilgrim

Plymouth

Eastern Av.

East Warren

RIVER R.R.

NEW BEDFORD R.R.

A. R.

School

F.R. Spool & Bobbin Mill

Davis Peck Parking

Variation 10 to 11° Westerly

Magnetic

True

PART I
1911

Invitation Ode
One hundred years ago,
to crude machines we owe
    a tribute grand.
Unfailing progress came,
weaving both cloth and fame,
wafting Fall River's name
    through every land.

Fall River bids you come,
four million spindles hum
    your welcome here.
Join us in rosy June,
come morning, night or noon,
come with your hearts atune
    with festal cheer.

Regatta and parade,
mill goods in pride displayed
    await your call.
A week of merriment,
each day some big event,
a program excellent;
    come one, come all.

          —J. Edmund Estes

PRESIDENTIAL CITY

The kind of day Minister Johns said Jesus had promised. Crisp and sunny, though cool for June. The type of weather, Johns preached last Sunday, that respects a man's daily toil. The paper predicted fifty thousand.

Despite it being Friday, Joseph Bartlett was nowhere near the Cleveland Mill; no, today he was trying to belong, so he stood with the other Cotton Centennial Committee members in the assigned section of the temporary grandstand directly opposite city hall at the assigned time, wearing his assigned straw Milan boater with the blue silk ribbon and his assigned smile—or half smile; he had another bad tooth—waiting for the president of the United States. He glanced at his pocket watch; the *Mayflower*, the president's yacht, was said to have made anchor an hour ago. He wanted to go home to his sick wife, Lizzy. She'd slept through his goodbye kiss. Joseph snapped the gold clasp and sank down on the wooden grandstand that held aloft the portly fathers of Fall River.

The Decoration Committee had gone overboard. The Granite Block, the commercial heart of the city, resembled an exploding firework. Wreaths of red carnations hung from all the office windows. Old Glory fluttered from every building on the block. Red, white, and blue bunting dangled from city hall windows and the bell tower like bats' wings. Suspended from a cross weave of wire down Main Street hung garlands of roses and thousands of incandescent globes. Young female clerks tossed confetti from McWhirr's department store windows; the store's marquee flashed red, white, and blue. Out-of-town revelers, probably stock-owning Bostonians, serenaded the crowd from the street-facing rooms of the Hotel Mohican. To celebrate the city's product, the Cotton Manufacturers' Association had organizers stack five-hundred-pound cotton bales on street corners.

A homespun racket accompanied the patriotic decorations. Screechers, scrapers, rattlers, and croakers filled the spaces between hoarse shouts and whooping calls. Those who couldn't afford the peddlers' noisemakers shook tin cans filled with dried beans or beat coal shovels on frying pans. The policemen's union band marched below playing "Hail to the Chief." Taft's motorcade was close. The Massachusetts militia lined Main Street. BOOM! BOOM! BOOM! The president's naval escort, the battleship *Connecticut*'s eight-inch guns rocked the grandstand with another salute from Mount Hope Bay, and the crowd flinched with each blast. A spooked dray horse galloped wildly past the review stand; police gave chase. Children clutched their mothers' skirts. The roar of the mill's spinning room was peaceful compared to this din, Joseph thought. Main Street was no place for a nervous person.

Young men carried paper signs tucked into the bands of their straw hats. I AM OUT FOR A GOOD TIME. MY HOME IS YOURS. And OH, YOU KID. The ladies got in on the act with slogans like MY HEART IS YOURS and I AM IN LOVE. And Joseph's favorite, MY HEART'S ON FIRE, worn by a red-haired Irish girl with wide hips who reminded him of Mary Sheehan. In the sea of bodies, the suffragettes' yellow VOTES FOR WOMEN pennants popped against the gentlemen's black suit jackets.

A ragtag crew of Portuguese boys wearing their lint-covered work overalls marched back and forth under the Centennial Arch singing the first verse of the "Invitation Ode." No doubt their overseer forced them to memorize it:

> *"One hundred years ago,*
> *to crude machines we owe*
> *a tribute grand.*
> *Unfailing progress came,*
> *weaving both cloth and fame,*
> *wafting Fall River's name*
> *through every land."*

On the horizon, Joseph saw a rare sight: clear sky between the hulking redbrick smokestacks. He smiled. Taft had done it. One hundred and eleven mills were silent. Only a president could close the mills. Anarchists, socialists, suffragists—all stripes of "ists" and "isms" had tried and failed. In Joseph Bartlett's lifetime, textile alley had never ceased to produce cloth. He had half expected Taft would try and fail too.

The president's speech would conclude the Cotton Centennial, a carnival of sorts to celebrate one hundred years of great American innovation in the great American city of Fall River, Massachusetts. Everyone loves a carnival, with the beauty queens, floats, circus animals, parades, contests and games, and rickety, stomach-turning rides whipping through the sweaty aroma of blood sausage and kidneys, cotton candy and hot nuts.

Joseph spotted the checkered hatband of his son in the crush pushing toward the review stand. The boy spun and grabbed the arm of a shopgirl. No, on second glance, it was neither Will nor Hollister; their tickets to the grandstand were tucked away in his breast pocket, had been all week. He touched them now, squeezing the thick cardstock between his thumb and finger. A fellow on the Horse Show Committee slapped Joseph's back, and he bit down hard on his bad tooth. The man shouted something and laughed, but Joseph couldn't make out the joke over the searing pain in his jaw.

* * *

Up in the Highlands, on June Street, the faint strains of the military band in Taft's motorcade reached Evelyn as she worried over the temperature of Elizabeth Bartlett's tomato soup. The poor woman could guess temperature to the degree. Tomato soup must be served between 137 and 139 degrees Fahrenheit. And the soda crackers must be fresh, straight from the tin, and served on a saucer, six per serving. Before Elizabeth's illness, Evelyn had intentionally hardened poached eggs and oversalted beef stews, but now she painstakingly measured, mixed, and stoked in the surefire manner her mother taught her as a girl in Ireland.

She and Elizabeth had dispensed with the usual employee-employer fussiness. They were friends, sort of, given that Highlands society had ceased to visit Elizabeth's parlor after Dr. Boyle imposed twenty-four-hour bed rest. At this stage of the fight, Elizabeth's hollowed bones couldn't support her own weight. *Cored like a bird's bones*, was how Dr. Boyle described the cancer's invasion in a recent note to Joseph. It was Evelyn's idea to move into the small room at the end of the hall; handling Elizabeth's "dirties" had earned her the household's respect. Evelyn believed cleanliness curried favor with the Lord.

Evelyn backed noiselessly into the darkened room. Elizabeth had instructed her to double up the lace curtains during daylight hours to keep her mother's furniture from fading, giving the room the hue of a bruised peach. The trapped air reeked of bedpans and phlegm; it circled the bed like a noose. But before setting to fixing lunch, Evelyn cracked the window, and a salty breeze rolled up the hill from the Taunton River.

Elizabeth's cut-glass animal collection vibrated when the *Connecticut's* big guns fired. The animals were pastured on the oak drop desk cabinet that housed the Minnesota Model A sewing machine Joseph had bought her for their first anniversary. Will had sprinkled straw for the glass animals and arranged them in clusters by species, chickens with other chickens, pigs with pigs, sheep with sheep, and so on up the barnyard hierarchy. Her older boy, the wanton Hollister, attempted to crossbreed the species at every opportunity. Will had balanced the mateless white unicorn on top of the miniature wooden barn. Elizabeth had told him of its magic. *Rub its horn and make a wish.* The boy hadn't the heart to tell his mother that he'd already made hundreds of wishes.

At the foot of the bed, the family's two cats, Bobbin and Thread, snoozed in a pie wedge of sunlight. Evelyn set the lunch tray on the nightstand next to *The Practical Family Doctor*, which leaned against a jar of Pinkham's Vegetable Compound and other half-baked potions and tonics that Elizabeth had put her faith in during her steep decline—all against Dr. Boyle's wishes. Like the rest of her, Elizabeth's face had sunk in on itself as her body gradually shut down. Evelyn believed it an early stage of rigor mortis, though she wasn't sure what rigor mortis was exactly. The term had been tossed about when her little sister wouldn't fit into the coffin her mother had traded her wedding band for.

Evelyn peeled back the sheet and slipped her hand under the embroidered fringe of Elizabeth's nightgown and pressed down lightly. Elizabeth's eyelids fluttered. Her heartbeat was soft, her breaths well spaced. A deep sleep. I know her body better than that silly frog Boyle does, Evelyn thought. She imagined herself Elizabeth's personal physician: Dr. Evelyn Mary Daly. Her surgeon's coat would be the whitest, the finest Egyptian cloth, and her bag made from the softest Italian leather. She rubbed Elizabeth's chest another moment and then did her daily test of how far she could wrap her hand around Elizabeth's bony wrist. She pressed her lips to her patient's hot cheek. Let Saint Peter eat crow, she thought. Then suddenly she choked up. What happens to me if she dies?

Evelyn knelt beside the bed. She made the sign of the cross and mumbled the Lord's Prayer.

* * *

Not far from the grandstand, under a tent erected inside Big Berry Stadium, the local parishes sponsored boys' boxing. Amateur classes only. Hundred-and-fifty-pound limit. The bank of lights hung low over the ring surrounded on four sides by wooden folding chairs. Tunnels of sunlight from the four entries were the only other illumination, each glowing bright like a gateway from a celestial world. When the fights started, the natural light dimmed because of the rubberneckers who blocked it: men who wouldn't, or couldn't, pay the nickel gate. Those who could pay sat thirty rows deep. Each had a relative or bet in every bout.

"Hey, Father," some drunkard, a Protestant most likely, shouted from the cheap seats. "That the blood of God?" The male crowd, all overseers and civil servants, broke into a roar, as Father Maxi, the stout referee with a flattened nose from one too many jabs in his boxing days, bent down on hands and knees to press a towel to the loser's split lip. The victor, Damian Newton, wiped the Yankee boy's blood down his threadbare trousers. His red boxing gloves, like two rotten tomatoes, swayed over his head. Maxi glanced up. Not even the Romans made such a spectacle of victory.

Ringside, Damian's little brother, Patrick, kept a firm grip on his father's belt, hoping the old man didn't blast off. Indeed, as his brother landed the knockout punch, Patrick coiled the belt around his fist like a cowboy might a leather rein.

Pete Newton had used his fists successfully in the general strike of 1904, then again on a granite wall behind Saint Anne's the afternoon of his wife's burial. In the years since, he'd raised the boys on church handouts and his fists, training them in late-night kitchen sparring sessions. Damian pummeled the calcified knots on his old man's back and neck. After each blow, Pete stumbled to his feet, mumbling technique: "More on the jawline," or "Gonna haveta stroke harder to beat a Yankee boy." Patrick always hid under the sink, waiting for the roundhouse that would send his father off to sleep.

As Damian continued his victory dance, Old Pete sat queerly silent, his arms folded over his reed-thin frame, piss drunk, no question, but oddly cool, as if he'd known the fight's outcome before the first bell. Finally, a crooked smile stretched over his scarred face when Maxi announced that Damian's final opponent would be Will Bartlett. Local legend held that Will's grandfather Otis had tossed Pete's father out a second-story window at the Cleveland Mill for barging drunk into the lady weavers' latrine. Old man Cleveland, the patriarch of the company, had investigated the incident, but the weavers said the foulmouthed toper had slipped, breaking both his legs.

A young priest escorted Damian from the ring to change out of his bloody trousers before the title bout. Outside the tent, the Fort Adams marching band played "Onward, Christian Soldiers."

* * *

"How is our dear Elizabeth? Such a dear, dear creature," cooed Mrs. Gower in a syrupy voice. Joseph stared at the enormous ostrich plumes protruding from her head. Mrs. G. was a 78 percent stockholder in the Gower Linen Company and an old family friend of Elizabeth's people, the mill-owning families who lived on the hill. Since taking over the Cleveland Mill six years ago, Joseph equated everyone with his or her share value. If Lizzy died, his would spike, but he'd be free of the Highlands. Her plumes reminded him of bunny ears. He was willing to bet half his meager Cleveland holdings that they were a foot tall, if not longer. Thankfully, Lizzy had never been a fan of such trims on her hats.

Mrs. G. stood above him on the grandstand, fanning a tiny bouquet of white sweet peas and violets tied with white satin ribbon under her nose. All of the committee members' wives waved them, making the entire section of the grandstand smell like a summer garden compared to the stench of manure at street level. The armada of shit wagons the city employed was no match for a week's worth of mounted police, coronation coaches, trade parades, and the Ringling Brothers' caravan of horses, elephants, and zebras.

Mrs. G. had yet to meet his eyes. Perhaps she was really broken up about Lizzy. Dr. Boyle had taken to leaving notes on the state of her condition rather than endure Joseph's long silences. He thought about the inappropriateness of the word "creature." Lizzy isn't a creature. Joseph's throat constricted. The word conjured up an image of Will's pet turtle, Shelly. For a moment, he considered the social consequences of telling Mrs. G. to go to hell, but before he could summon the courage, her white-gloved hand tugged at his black coat sleeve. She repeated, "Such a dear, dear creature. We all miss her so."

"She's holding her own, given the circumstances," he managed. Joseph pinched his tight collar. "No change, really. No improvements since your last visit. Easter, was it?"

"I've been meaning to . . ." Her voice trailed off.

After a long day at the mill, Joseph might not muster much more than a quick peck to Lizzy's forehead. The girl he loved was slowly evaporating, like a bucket of water set out in the sun; each visit to her bedside proved costly to his memory. The porcelain-white feet he'd first laid eyes on that magical summer at Loon Lake were curled and yellowed. The baby-blond hairs on the back of her neck that stood on end when he'd pressed her against her father's boathouse had lost their will. The blue eyes that had matched the lake water had grayed. Who had taken these pleasures from him? The Almighty, Joseph had long ago concluded, was partly to blame.

Mrs. G. latched onto his forearm. The old biddy had quite a grip. He was unsure if she was overcome with emotion for Elizabeth's dire straits or guilt-ridden for not calling in three months.

Slowly she turned to face him, looking much younger than her sixty-five years. Winters spent south are said to preserve youthfulness. "Give her my love, from John and me." She released his arm and patted her gloved wrist against the corner of her eyes.

"Of course."

She glanced to either side of Joseph. "How are the boys getting along?"

"Evelyn can't keep them out of her room." He raised his fists. "They're both entered in the boxing competition. I might sneak off to catch Will's bout."

"Righto." She turned back to her husband, tugging at his sleeve so he'd acknowledge Joseph.

John Gower tipped his boater sternly and then stroked his beard. Gower carried grudges like a camel carries a hump—square in the middle of his back. The old man had not forgiven Joseph for breaking with the Manufacturers' Association during the 1904 strike. The owners told labor they needed a second wage concession in nine months to compete against the Southern menace. Joseph disagreed and raised pay. *Dividends and fair wages can coexist!* During the strike, he transitioned Cleveland toward producing fine goods and odd specialty products like tablecloths that the South couldn't yet manufacture. Cleveland prints were made from high-quality thread, and their colors became known for not running at the first sight of a washboard.

Not getting his long-overdue apology, Gower turned back to the parade. He'd never forget.

Bastard. Joseph rubbed his chin with the stub of his pinkie. Good riddance.

The roar of the *Connecticut's* big guns tore through the Granite Block. Thirty thousand textile workers ducked, screamed, and then leaped to their feet and leaned on the shoulders of the person in front of them. Children cried. Women swooned. Men shouted. *Mr. President! Mr. President! Over here! Over here!* From the review stand, the *Mayflower's* own band struck up "Hail to the Chief." Taft stood in the back of his black Buick touring car, waving his black silk top hat at the crowd. A dozen army regulars from Fort Adams and the president's security detail surrounded the car as the crowd lurched closer. The short route to the review stand was lined with letter carriers waving American flags. Taft plucked a flag from a man's breast pocket. He waved it high above his head. When the crowd roared its approval, the commander in chief smiled, showing his strong teeth. He wobbled toward the review stand. He was wide bodied and stout, resembling a potato with arms and legs. Music blew from all directions. Confetti sailed across the grandstand and down onto the legions in the street. Gobs of the stuff, like colored snow, fluttered into Joseph's ears and mouth. He could already imagine the headline in the late editions: TAFT DECLARES FALL RIVER PRESIDENTIAL CITY. The guns continued, *BOOM! BOOM! BOOM!* Twenty-one shots rocked the grandstand. Noisemakers squealed. Children were hoisted onto shoulders. The hatband slogans and pennants blurred and the crowd surged forward as Taft mounted the podium stairs. *There he is! There's the president!—I can't see!—There! On the stage!—I see him! I see him!* A man on the Parade Committee knocked Joseph's shoulder; he shouted into Joseph's ear, "We did it! A red-letter day. The goddamn president in Fall River."

Joseph forced a smile. "Heck of a day," he said. But the man shook his head and pointed to his ear and then looked back to Taft, still waving the miniature flag.

* * *

The carnival midway ran down the length of Pleasant Street. The commotion from city hall rolled past the dunking booth, the three-hundred-pound woman, and the incredible shrinking man, past pigs on spits and puddles of ale, past mounds of lemon rinds and elephant dung. At the end of the midway, the roar of the *Connecticut's* big guns was reduced to a faint tremor deep within the bowels of the fun house.

Hollister Bartlett, Joseph's oldest son, pushed his palm up his runny nose and then wiped his hand down his trouser leg. The touch of the flu he had woken up with that morning would be a worthy excuse for dropping out of the boxing competition. He sat on an upended mop bucket nestled in a fluffy bed of work rags and burlap that filled the cramped space with the smell of oil and straw. The closet was pitch black, reminding him of his mother's room. The ride operator, already in his cups, had given Hollister a key and three minutes to find the storage closet hidden in the Hall of Mirrors. "Behind the famine panel," the operator had joked, pocketing Hollister's dollar bribe. Hollister pressed his ear to the back of the warped mirror and smiled. "Famine panel," he said, just now getting it. The mirror squeezed the life from you.

Out of habit, Hollister snapped open his grandfather's pocket watch but couldn't decipher the hands. When he had handed his girl-of-the-month the two-cent admission, he'd instructed her to enter alone. Maria was the oldest yet—nearly twenty, a good four years older than himself. Their code word was "spider."

Hollister worked after school managing all the women's accounts in his father's mill store. Maria got hired in the card room beside her mother when her father lost his job on a New Bedford fishing boat. In two weeks, Hollister's eraser had worn her charge sheet thin in places. Two yards of cloth had become three yards. A quarter pound of sugar became a half. And unluckily for Maria, her account swelled even when she wasn't shopping. Hollister had gone out of his way midmonth to inform her of her cash deficit, something he told her he "didn't do for all the girls." Maria understood the word "deficit" because the landlord spoke of her father's debt each month. Hollister pulled her to the end of the counter and said, "There are other ways, creative ways, to pay off the debt." Hollister's pride and ambition were matched only by his ability to spot weakness.

"Spider. Spider." Maria inched into the Hall of Mirrors, tiptoeing forward as if bracing for a blow. "Spider. Spider." The first mirror gave her three heads. The next blew up her pencil-thin frame like a soaked sponge.

Hollister set his hand on the latch to open the panel, then sat back down. He still hadn't figured what he was going to do with her. She was the prettiest of the five he'd outwitted. Unlike the pampered Highlands girls who still believed storks delivered babies, the immigrant girls knew hard knocks and a woman's obligation. His previous four "dates" hadn't uttered a word while he'd squeezed their small breasts and spastically humped their bare legs, and only one actually spoke. Her name was Viva, and she had asked him if he was proud of himself as she stepped out of the women's latrine, adjusting her stockings one morning before the mill opened. Viva gave Hollister pause, and if she had pushed him further, asked him what his mother thought of him or why he couldn't get a regular girl, he might have stopped altogether. But she hadn't, or couldn't, given she spoke little English.

"Spider. Spider."

Only a freak would bother with these stupid girls, Hollister thought. Silly Highlands girls gave thrills if you bought them treats. And the dumb Irish, they charged a nickel a feel. The hell with Maria. Is it *my* fault her father couldn't bait a hook? I could get her better jobs, but she has no imagination, no future.

"Spider. Spider." Maria's voice faded as she walked deeper into the fun house.

Let her die in the card room with her stupid mother. Freak.

* * *

Back on June Street, Bobbin, the more brazen of the Bartletts' two cats, flopped down on a pillow, sticking her rear end in Elizabeth's face. She rolled over for Evelyn to scratch her tummy. Instead, Evelyn deposited the cat on the foot of the bed, then jabbed her finger into the beast's nose. "What have I said?" Evelyn hissed. "No sitting on the pillows." Bobbin scrammed. Evelyn pulled the starched sheet over Elizabeth's shoulder and laid her silky hair across the pillow. Streaks of gray dated the forty-three-year-old Elizabeth.

Evelyn thought she ought not wake her patient for tomato soup. She set the lunch tray on the nightstand and took up the Dickens novel she'd been reading aloud to Elizabeth. Instead of a day off to attend the carnival, as Evelyn had been promised but secretly dreaded, knowing she'd either be stuck tending her sister's children or be paraded past would-be suitors (squeaky-wheeled Irishmen from the Globe neighborhood) by her matchmaking mother, Evelyn chose to lounge in the cozy window seat of her small room with *Oliver Twist*. She made a mental note to tell Elizabeth about the two goldfinches that had taken up in the old oak outside the kitchen window, and then remembered she must tell Albert to refill the feeder. Momentarily, but only momentarily, she listed the household chores left to finish: laundry, floors, ice to order. Luckily, Mr. Bartlett had been too preoccupied with the centennial to notice her falling off lately. She cursed the second girl, Leah, for leaving the washing unfinished. Evelyn heard a streetcar pass down the hill and wondered what mischief Leah would get into on the dirty carnival midway. It was no place for a lady. The hall clock struck three bells. A roar rolled up the hill. Elizabeth slept on.

* * *

By Helen Sheehan's count, the president owed her ninety cents in lost tips and wages. She sat on Mrs. O'Donnell's back stoop, tossing stones into an enamel dinner pail, waiting for the old biddy to fetch her wages. Usually Helen made two dinner runs between the mills and Mrs. O'Donnell's. Eight pails to Anawan and eight to Cleveland; that's sixteen pails. At a nickel a pop, that's eighty cents, plus tips. But on account of Taft's damn speech, and the party the owners were throwing for themselves, they had done the unheard of—closed shop—and the last shift of the week tipped the largest.

Pie tins crashed in the pantry.

"Oh, cherries!" the old lady shouted, followed by "Peaches." Pitted fruits were Mrs. O's curses.

Helen called, "You okay, Mrs. O?"

"Another minute, sugarplum."

Sweet old witch, Helen thought. But why store your loot on the highest shelf if you can't reach it? She had a right mind to pack up and fetch the week's wages on Monday, but the last time she did that, her mother had ripped on her. The fight had ended with Helen shouting, "All you care about is my money," to which her widowed mother replied, "When the money stops coming, you die."

Helen liked money—liked it fine—but her jobs stunk. They were the best-paying sidelines for a girl whose mother forbade her to work in the mills. She lifted the right leg of her brown trousers and scratched the dry skin on her calf. She was tall for her age, and fast. Taut muscles stretched over her thin bones. She kept her hair closely cropped around her heart-shaped face like the modern women she admired in magazines she nicked from Elizabeth Bartlett. As a young girl, her aunts and uncles had fawned over her comely looks. But Helen thought only people with money could afford to be beautiful, and dismissed her relatives as she did the boys' whistles. Beauty meant being idle, and Helen was a worker. She had no time for stupid boys. And her brother Ray beat the lazy Irish boys who dared cast a lingering eye on his baby sister.

"How's it coming, Mrs. O?"

When Helen really wanted something only a Highlands girl could afford, which was most everything, she stole it. She demanded honesty from everyone but herself. If her father hadn't gotten himself killed at the mill, she would have had gooey licorice candies and baby dolls whose eyes shut when you laid them down to sleep. Her stealing kept her from getting angry at the world. The coins she managed to squirrel away from her mother were hidden under a warped floorboard in the hall closet, wrapped in her dead father's linen handkerchief. Every Sunday after Communion she listed the junk she'd pinched for God. She was owed twice as much, given the circumstances. And besides, didn't Mr. Bartlett always say everything came out in the wash?

After her father's death, Helen hid most everything. The Highlands girls teased her for wearing trousers and her father's old work shirts. The sons and daughters of mill workers were sympathetic on account of her father's death. A third group theorized she just craved attention because her mother and brothers were all too busy to mind her, given their own jobs. Young Will Bartlett's gang couldn't figure Helen out for nothing. She was what the kids called "peculiar." But he wanted to know her secrets.

By the end of the day, they'd have at least one thing in common.

* * *

Joseph spotted Massachusetts governor Foss on the review stand, sitting with Senator Crane among the president's entourage of secretaries and centennial dignitaries. Congressman Greene stood a few feet to the side, straightening his blue silk bow tie. Mayor Higgins, flush from his introduction of the commander in chief, waved to friends in the wings.

Phrases like "largest cotton manufacturing city in the country" and "many races, more cosmopolitan than many other large cities" and "men never possessed by a selfish or sordid motive" flew from his double-sided mouth, hot with civic pride.

The last boast seared Joseph's skin. He looked over the grandstand to see if anyone else noted the irony of the statement, but no man met his eye. The other mill owners respected his intellect and work ethic, but the tragic mill fire that led to his running Cleveland Mill cast a long shadow. Few remembered his father, Otis. These men spun gold from cotton, or so they believed. Joseph sat down on the hard wood bleacher and slumped his long, thin frame forward over his knees; his youthful face could not hide the dark circles under his eyes.

Joseph recognized Matt Borden's voice and lumbered to his feet. He quickly spotted the great man smack-dab in the center of the grandstand chatting with his son, Howard. Borden dabbed a white handkerchief to his bald pate and scratched his walrus mustache. He was well fed, like Taft. Howard checked his watch and whispered something to his father, who nodded in agreement. Matt Borden lived in New York, in part to keep his extended family of hangers-on at a distance. He had gone to considerable trouble and expense to erect a forty-five-foot mast atop his formidable American Printing Company to fly the Stars and Stripes. The flag greeted the *Mayflower*. Too much had been made of it. To the mill owners seated near Joseph, the flag wasn't a symbol of America or Taft, but of Borden watching over the Manufacturers' Association. Borden brushed confetti from his son's shoulder as he peered into the swarm of newspapermen in the press section. Joseph couldn't maneuver between the ladies' hats to see who was catching Borden's eye. More than one smut peddler had been rumored to be on Borden's payroll.

Joseph heard rather clearly the Lancashire growl of George Pierce, the undersecretary of the United Textile Council, shouting something about the dissolution of Standard Oil, a topic sure to boil Yankee blood. Joseph smirked. He liked Pierce's gall despite the fact that it might lead to Fall River's downfall. Blackballed by British mills, Pierce came to America looking for a new fight, shouting or punching whatever itched his brain. Owners were "cockwinders," and workers "builders." Pierce's arrogance, when mixed with the owner's sense of entitlement, led to strikes and lockouts.

On the review stand, Taft set his silk hat on the podium and cleared his throat. "I esteem it a great privilege to be here to help you celebrate the one hundredth anniversary of the founding of the great textile industry. When your committee, headed by your congressman, Mr. Greene, invited me to come here, I ventured to inquire whether any speech-making was necessary. I was told that was not important. All that was necessary was that you should see me." Taft stepped back from the podium and the crowd roared. "I venture to think that if there is any street in Fall River that I have not traversed, it was because the committee forgot it."

Standing between Matt Borden and George Pierce, Joseph realized that like the red section rope that divided owners from workers, he straddled two worlds but belonged to neither: the Protestant boardrooms of Matt Borden and the Lancashire toil of Pierce's Episcopalian brothers with their lodges, clubs, and unions. Jefferson Cleveland and Otis were probably the last two men—owner and laborer, Protestant and Episcopalian—whose relationship wasn't predicated on deceit. As a cotton agent and then mill owner, Joseph had tried to appease the Yankees—converted to their church, frequented the Q Club, learned golf; for God's sake, he'd married a Yankee—but he would never be one of them.

Taft continued, "Therefore, I think I have had the pleasure of seeing most of the people of Fall River, as they have had the pleasure of seeing most of me." The crowd erupted in laughter and applause. Men waved their straw and felt hats. Sunlight reflected off the president's big teeth.

* * *

From his corner of the boxing ring, Will Bartlett searched for his father and Helen Sheehan in the graduated darkness. Men pointed to each corner and then exchanged handshakes or money. Others smacked a rolled program over their knee and chomped Henry Clays the city had imported from Cuba with the centennial seal on the band. The burning tobacco filled Will's nostrils more than his own stinking sweat. He tried to think of a greater accomplishment in his young life than getting to this boxing final. Years of getting teased for his meager size—his mother promised he was a late bloomer—and look at him now, nearly the height of his brother and twice as strong. No high mark in school or mill chore had ever generated a crowd like this. And Hollister? Jerk.

Will squinted into the crowd. Of course, he had given up on his mother years ago, but his dad and Helen had promised. Stupid mill. Stupid cancer. Stupid Fall River.

Helen's older brother Tommy worked Will's corner, a towel draped over his neck. He snapped, "What you looking at?" He twisted the boy's head forward.

Will avoided eye contact with him, had since the day Tommy got popped for welshing on a bet. The trauma had messed up his right eye, turning the white all soupy red around his iris—a real bloody blinker.

Tommy craned backward to survey the crowd. He still had one good eye. His pal from the newspaper flashed a thumbs-up and waved the list of bets he'd taken on Will. He rubbed his thumb across his index and middle fingers. Tommy saw green.

Tommy slapped Will's sweaty back with his open palm. The crack turned heads. "The fight's right here. They'll be here. Focus on the madman."

Damian paced the west end of the ring like a caged bull, reeling punches into the air, his hunched back extending his reach a few inches. Father Maxi called his name, and the boy pounded a combination off his own head. But he was running off the energy in the tent and off fear—the fear that no matter how hard he socked his old man, the bastard got up. Damian released another flurry off his own skull. The Highlands chancer was leaving in an eternity box.

The opening bell rang, and the boys shuffled to the center of the ring.

After three matches each, their movement was confined to the upper half of their torsos. Their feet rocked forward and back. The fatigue fogged their minds; technique was discarded. The crowd chanted, propelling their rubbery arms. Jabs gave way to wild roundhouse punches. The crowd jumped to their feet, cheering the boys' wildness. Grown men shadow-boxed in the aisles. In the ring, misguided palms and wrists caromed off shoulders and hips. By midround, Will's neck was rubbed raw by the laces of Damian's left glove. Maxi danced a two-step, up then back, separating the two. He shouted "fight" and "break up" in quick succession. Tommy shouted too—instructions he'd pounded into the boy's head—but Will heard only his beating heart. Damian's arms whirled as if he were clawing through a swarm of hornets. At the bell, he clawed faster. Will covered up. Separating the two, Father Maxi caught a punch square on the jaw.

The boxing judge, Father Croix, sucked on the tip of his blue scoring pencil between rounds. His subjective powers hadn't had much work. The majority of matches ended in one of three ways: with one boy cowering under Maxi's long wingspan, with a spectacular nose and eyeball explosion of blood and mucus, or with a knockout. None of these required Croix's crisp numbers to separate the winners from the losers. He was encouraged by the stamina of these two boys. Poise and enthusiasm weighed heavily in Croix's scoring, as did making the sign of the cross prior to each round, though the latter didn't appear on the official scorecard. After one round, Damian, the Catholic, held a slight edge.

Will couldn't catch his breath. Like his grandfather Otis, he suffered from shallow lungs. Between rounds, Tommy rubbed out his arms and poured water down his gullet, but Will gagged, spitting most of it out. "Where's Helen? Where's—"

Tommy pulled Will's chin forward; their two foreheads touched. "Concentrate, or he'll knock your block clean off." Tommy pointed across the ring.

Will gasped, "If no one sees, it never happened." Will peered over his shoulder, and Tommy pinched and twisted the younger boy's right nipple. Will slapped Tommy's arm and squinted into the dark recesses of the tent.

Tommy couldn't believe his baby sister stood between him and fifty dollars. "He's over there," he shouted, and then, "She said she'd be by after running dinner pails." Will snapped back around. "And you better be whipping him when your girlfriend arrives. She'd kick his ass."

Tommy spat out instructions for the next round, and Will rubbed his gloves down his hairless twelve-year-old legs to stop his thin calf muscles from quivering.

Damian didn't lift his head between rounds. The young priest working his corner repeated the command, "Punch, move, punch, move," and attempted to get Damian to take some water.

When the boy pushed the water away, Pete Newton exploded off the bleachers, his ruddy cheeks burning their usual crimson. Rumbling down the aisle, he forearmed the popcorn vendor into a row of spectators. Pete hung onto the ropes to steady himself. His cup of beer sloshed over the canvas. "What kind of sissy did God deliver me?"

The young priest said, "Knock it off, Pete."

"Sissy," Pete hissed.

Little Patrick dangled off his father's belt. "Stop," he called. "Leave him be."

"Sissy."

Father Croix shouted, "That's enough, Pete."

"He's pissed." The popcorn man marched toward the ring.

"Don't come home if ya loses."

"Find him a seat," a spectator shouted. Others start throwing cups and programs.

The popcorn man and a parishioner from Saint Anne's dislodged Pete from the ropes.

"Kick him out!"

Pete threw his cup at the ring hitting the young priest square in the chest. "Orphanage for you, boy."

* * *

Taft continued: "I congratulate you on your city. It is a city of enterprise, happy with the hum of industry. It is a city with men at the head of it with energy and foresight, so that when the textile industry was threatened with competition in other parts of the country, they devoted their brains and their skill and their keenness of intellect to improving the industry and devoted themselves to its higher branches."

* * *

Joseph peeled away from the grandstand, disappearing into the throng, all shoving forward to get a glimpse of Taft. In the street, boys who usually swept floors or collected discarded tin raced up the block, weaving between gaps in the crowd. Ladies shouted at them to slow down. Many didn't earn enough to enjoy the carnival rides or eat the vendors' fried dough balls, so Joseph was pleased to see them enjoying themselves just the same. On North Main Street, he looped back to City Hall Square and dipped under the canvas tarp draped around the grandstand. Joseph nearly tripped over a mound of seaweed and rocks for that afternoon's clambake. Flies buzzed past his face then returned to the seaweed pile. Wooden scaffolding poles rose from square blocks like a line of toy soldiers. The stifling hot air choked him, and he began to retch. Joseph nuzzled a handkerchief to his mouth and glanced up at the stressed bleachers that bent toward him each time the crowd moved. Shafts of light shot between the gaps in people's legs as if beamed from the projector at the Savoy Theater. The president's voice was muffled, but Joseph could still make it out. He spotted Matt Borden's soft leather heels.

"Over here, Captain." Joseph turned to see George Pierce standing ten spaces up in a sea of fallen confetti, crepe paper, and empty bottles of King Philip lager, licking a swirl of cotton candy off a wooden stick. Pierce wore two buttons on his lapel: a Taft campaign button from the previous election and a souvenir keepsake printed with the carnival's slogan, FALL RIVER LOOMS UP. Years of police batons rapping against his knees and shoulders had taken their toll on the fifty-eight-year-old. He walked mechanically and sloppily, like a windup toy soldier missing a part. His shock of white hair and wide, thin smile ever present. He was the happiest foulmouthed anarchist Joseph had ever met.

"Enjoying yourself?"

"Bingo bingo." Pierce licked cotton candy off his thumb. "Want some?"

"Got a bad tooth." Joseph wondered how Pierce managed to keep all *his* teeth. His tongue gingerly explored the far reaches of his mouth, the tip wedging between the gum and root of his top left wisdom tooth. His mouth was full of salty spit.

"I got a piece of string."

Joseph snorted, and then arced a bloody glob over his shoulder. He said, "I hear your parade float won the union division."

"I hear Cleveland's was dead last."

"We'll get them at the next centennial."

Pierce narrowed his eyes and then choked on some cotton candy, getting the joke. "Yes, the next great one hundred years of cloth in Fall River." The irony of the statement was greeted with a wave of applause in the grandstand. Joseph, Pierce, and perhaps Borden were the only ones who could imagine an end to Fall River's textile dynasty. Joseph flinched when the crowd stood; at any moment the weight of his well-fed competitors and their bejeweled wives might crush him.

Pierce said, "These fat cockwinders won't last another twenty."

"My boy, he's boxing. What do you want?"

Pierce handed Joseph a leather-bound book. The binding was sticky. The name Cummings Mill was embossed on the cover.

"How did you . . ."

"We stole it."

Joseph raised his hand. "I don't want to know."

"Cummings announced that he'll be putting more looms on the idle list and shutting down for four weeks this summer—a vacation my union doesn't need—because the price of goods in the market was below the cost of production."

"Prices are down. That's no secret." Joseph ran his fingers down the rows. He couldn't tell someone how to run a business—"independence," another Cleveland mantra—but he was pleased to see Cummings paid a few cents more for his dye.

Pierce tapped his cotton candy against the ledger and said, "Look at the advanced sales figures, lines ten through twenty-five. The brokers are paying far above the costs of production. The association is going to produce to the deadline, then sit on inventory for four weeks to raise prices for inflated profits."

"You can deduce this all from one ledger, from one of the smallest mills in the association?"

"No, my friend. History foretold the scenario. This is just concrete intelligence. Bingo bingo. No more lectures about temperance with operatives living in rat cellars."

Joseph snapped the ledger shut. He didn't need a history lesson from Pierce. "The twenty-five percent curtailment may be extended. I told you that months ago."

"The spinners and others are already running low of curtailment benefits. The loom fixers and weavers are in dire straits."

Joseph tapped the ledger against his thigh. He had grown tired of being the go-between for Pierce. And right here, right under the other agents' noses. Pierce's ego had no bounds. Bingo bingo up his ass.

Joseph said, "You should unite all workers. Cause a real ruckus." In Fall River, the powerful Manufacturers' Association only worked with the United Textile Council, Pierce's council, and its five established craft unions. The unskilled workers—weaker, less organized—weren't recognized. Joseph's small operation wasn't immune to union troubles, but years ago Jefferson Cleveland had stuck his nose up at the Fall River system and made sure the Cleveland Mill worked with labor. The association carried antiquated mills and spendthrift treasurers on its back. Their board's crossed bloodlines had given birth to deformities. Heck, Borden lived in New York to stay away from his bumbling clan.

Pierce repeated the council's mantra concerning wages: "The weaver for the weaver and the spinner for the spinner."

The grandstand crowd cheered. A few men stomped their feet. The entire structure shook above them. Joseph hoped the Planning Committee hadn't cut corners on construction. A wax hot dog wrapper floated down from above. Pierce stepped closer to Joseph to be heard over the racket.

"We can handle another ten percent, short term, but nothing more. And no shutdown."

"Borden won't shut down. I won't."

"Don't speak for Borden."

Joseph removed his hat and wiped his eyebrows with his handkerchief. When had it gotten so goddamn warm?

Pierce said, "The association will. We'll strike before allowing them to build up rich inventory on our backs."

"Then a wage concession."

"No."

"Where's your compromise?"

"Just arrange a meeting."

"This could have waited."

"Do it today. The owners are buoyant. You'd think it was dividend day. If they can entertain a president, then they won't worry much over one little labor—"

"Agitator."

"They'll want to pound their chests in my face. They think they created all this cotton candy on their own."

Joseph said, "I'm headed to the boxing tent."

"That's another way to settle matters."

Joseph gave Pierce a sideways glance.

Pierce licked the cotton candy. "Then a little heat. Inventory burns so eas—"

"Never another fire."

"You're right. Sorry. Then perhaps a kidnapping will get their attention?" He licked the pink corners of his mouth and winked. "Send word by the end of day. Bingo bin—"

"Just shut up." Joseph clenched his jaw and grimaced. "Now, my boy, he's boxing." He stepped to the edge of the tarp. "He's a champion."

"If only we were all Highlands boys," Pierce said, tossing his cotton candy to the flies. "If only."

* * *

Hollister pressed his ear to the wooden door. Freak. He jumped to his feet. A broom handle smacked a tin bucket. The floorboards rattled outside.

"Spider. Spider." Maria pressed her face against the famine panel.

Hollister braced his hands against the jamb.

"Please. Spider. Spider."

Her breath dampened Hollister's palm.

Hollister fingered the latch, paused, and then leaned his shoulder into the door. He could wait all day.

Maria tapped her forehead against the mirror. Near tears, she whispered, "Spider. Spider."

Hollister sniffed his palm. He frowned, and then wiped it down his trousers.

"Someone comes." Her voice cracked. "I'll tell."

Hollister snapped the latch up, yanked the door open, and grabbed Maria's forearm, jerking her into the storeroom. She gasped at the darkness. The door latch dropped as a gang of kids stomped into the Hall of Mirrors laughing and spitting insults. *Fatso. Pumpkin Head. Two-face.* They ran through the entire litany of names the mirrors encouraged.

Hollister spoke through his teeth, "Why didn't you go away? You're so stup—"

Maria cupped his mouth. "Shhhhhhh."

Hollister grabbed her wrist and bent it back. "Stupid, stupid, stupid."

Maria took a deep breath but didn't scream. He twisted her arm, and Maria's knees buckled. She clutched two fists full of his trousers above the knee, began to hiccup.

"Quit that." He pressed his palm over her mouth.

Hollister double-checked the latch, and they both froze, as the gang stopped at the famine panel. *Pencil neck. Pinhead. Flat butt.*

* * *

"You're late." The priest manning the east door waved Helen through.

"Work," Helen said. She tossed him a bag of roasted nuts she'd nicked on the street. She leaned close to his ear. "Who's Will Bartlett's next victim?"

But the priest didn't flinch or wave his finger and say, *Now now, Helen. Boxing is for exercise.* He smiled and said sarcastically, as if Helen was the last person on earth to know, "Damian."

Helen coughed up a nut. The Damian who bit off Billy O'Brian's earlobe last summer at Bliffin's Beach? The Damian who dragged a coffin from the undertaker's motorcar? The Damian who urinated in Sister Mary's pea soup?

The priest popped a hot nut into his mouth.

* * *

"Who's there?" Evelyn jolted awake, *Oliver Twist* smacking the floor as the cats scurried under the bed. She wiped a trickle of drool with her sleeve. She glanced at the window. The cats had overturned the soup, and her patient still slept. The lukewarm soup was sprayed across the hardwood. Dirty fur balls, she thought. They washed with their own spit, for Ham's sake.

Evelyn righted the bowl with her toe and wet a towel in the china bowl on the washstand. She knelt to slop up the mess. Shiny eyes followed her movements from under the bed. "Bad girls," she scolded. "No more fish for dinner. Bad girls." At a minimum, Evelyn thought, they could kill mice like the tabby at the apothecary. Evelyn crawled toward them, wiping up their radish-colored paw prints. Suddenly she was a big-game hunter stalking prey on the Dark Continent. Or rather, leading the mercy killing of a wounded beast. She, and Elizabeth, and the adventurer Margaret Bullock sporting mosquito-net hats and khaki trousers cinched at the waist with large leather belts—three sisters of adventure—leading a band of shirtless natives deep into the bush.

Evelyn sighed and then hoisted her knees up in two labored motions. She wanted everything perfect. Standing, she saw a trail of crimson paw prints leading over the sheets to Elizabeth's pillow. She paused. The word "queer" zipped across her mind. Lifting her skirt, she shuffled quickly around the bed, and the cats raced out of the room.

"*No!*"

There was a streak of blood under Elizabeth's nose. Evelyn covered her mouth. They'd attacked her sister! "I'll kill them!"

She snorted back tears and cradled Elizabeth's chin in her palm. She said, "Elizabeth, dear," dabbing Elizabeth's nose and lips. Evelyn grimaced, half expecting to see a scrape on Elizabeth's porcelain skin, but there was no gash.

Evelyn sighed; she replaced the pillow with the fresh one she kept nearby. Elizabeth's head flopped to the opposite side. A bitter smell filled the room. Evelyn crouched down and slipped her hand under the sheet and mattress pad. It was wet. Criminy. Joseph would be livid. Evelyn tapped Elizabeth's shoulder. She had to move her to the divan.

"Dearie," she began. "Come on, droopy eyes." Elizabeth was still. Evelyn knotted her fingers together to suppress the shakes. She squinted. Another shallow pool of redness had collected under her patient's nose. As Evelyn reached to wipe it away two canals of blood burst from Elizabeth's nostrils.

Evelyn screamed.

* * *

In the dark, Hollister licked the moist hand that had covered Maria's mouth. She smelled nice—something soapy, something peppermint. But she was a freak, like the others. He clutched her thick black hair and massaged her head. Her cheek brushed his thigh as he pressed his nails into her scalp. "Nothing to fear," he said and eased up the pressure.

She jerked, pushing against his knees, but he chopped down on her shoulder blades with both hands, and her body collapsed as if suddenly punctured. Her head fell into his groin; he smothered it against the beating shaft of his penis. Maria stiffened. He rose up on tiptoes as his body shuddered. Maria's arms dangled at her sides. As his heels lowered to the floor, he released her head, and they both exhaled.

Hollister pinched his damp trouser leg. Far off, a marching band played. Voices outside passed through the Hall of Mirrors. He whispered, "Maria," and began pressing down her hair with both hands as if she were a doll.

He could now make out the outline of her small figure. Her head swiveled in his hands; he squeezed her earlobes. By touch, he straightened the seams of her blouse directly over her shoulder blades. When his fingernail caught on a tear in the cotton, he stopped to pinch the two ends together. "There," he said, thinking he'd mended the rip. "You can be my secret girlfriend." She was as pretty as the girls on the postcards hidden under his mattress. He thought of buying her something expensive on the midway—a hand-painted cameo perhaps. It'll be the most expensive thing she's ever owned. He cupped her face in his hands. "Hey," he whispered, "I'm talking to you."

Maria's heel tapped a bucket as she stood. Her breathing filled the space, then stopped. He sensed her mouth near his ear and dipped down. "You pig!" she shouted, and he stumbled backward. "Proud now?"

Her hand fumbled for the door. The latch released, but Hollister jumped, blocking her way.

"You proud?" she repeated, louder.

Suddenly, Hollister remembered Viva. She had said the same thing, hadn't she? Could the two be partners? He was always careful to pick girls in separate departments. Most had been Portagee, but he'd never seen any of them together. He'd scouted them as if they were ballplayers. What if they were scheming against him, hidden outside the door ready to pounce, Maria the star of their revenge?

"Freak!" Maria spat in his eye.

Hollister slapped her face. No, he thought, I didn't just do that.

She whirled back around. "Freak!"

He punched and Maria toppled backward, upsetting the bucket and brooms. He hovered over her. "Shut up."

A voice outside said, "You hear that?" Feet shuffled. The voice was now right outside the mirror. "Is it part of the ride?"

Maria screamed.

Hollister clamped his hand over her mouth. He pressed his knee into her chest. "Be quiet, and they'll go away."

The voice outside moved to the crack in the secret door's frame. "Who's there? You hurt?" The voice turned away. "Get the man."

Another boy, farther off, shouted, "Right!" Feet thumped off the wooden planks.

Hollister eased his weight off her as the footfalls faded. He released his hand from Maria's mouth and wiped it across his chest. "That was close," he whispered conspiratorially.

Maria jammed her knee into his crotch and knifed her nails into his neck. Hollister fell backward, and Maria scurried toward the door. Two loggerheads of pain crashed in the middle of his spine, and then his brain, already disturbed from a touch of the flu, exploded. He staggered, unsure which wound to grasp hold of. His foot landed in a bucket. The far-off marching band seemed to pass right through his head.

Maria's hand was frantic on the latch. "Help me," she cried.

"Who's there?" the voice outside called.

"Help me!"

"I'll save you. I will."

Save? The word gathered force in Hollister's bowels and reached his brain as he grabbed a knot of Maria's hair and yanked. Her scream was cut short as his elbow connected with something fleshy near her throat. She collapsed to the floor. Turning, he stepped on her knee and his ankle rolled.

"Shut up," he growled.

"Who's that?" the boy outside yelled.

Everyone just shut up. Hollister leaned on a broomstick. The pain in his ankle calmed him. Slowly he began to separate the sounds: the approaching footsteps, the trumpet from the tuba, the boy's warm breath through the crack, Maria's whimpering. Her groveling was maddening. She wouldn't shut her hole. *She'll never be my girl. None of them know how to please a man.* Hollister zeroed in on her crying. He smashed the broom handle down on the noise.

* * *

The postal messenger had lost his hat, and now his six-button blue jacket was spread open, fluttering behind him like a cape. He was running full bore toward City Hall Square, worming between the merrymakers. He ducked under arms and around tent poles. A woman stepped on his foot and fell, but he had no time to stop—others would help her. He clutched an unsealed note. "Of grave importance," the dispatch had said, knowing the boy would recognize Joseph Bartlett on sight.

"Mr. Bartlett!" the boy shouted when he saw Joseph walking near the grandstand. It was Henry Daly, Evelyn's younger brother. He was really hustling. Blooms of confetti, an inch thick on the sidewalk, exploded under his feet. Not more than ten years old and already a worker. But the boy ought to be in school. Henry called louder. Joseph smiled weakly to passersby. His throat constricted. He wondered if anyone had spotted him with Pierce. He glanced around for any of the local smut peddlers, but all eyes were on Taft. Henry stopped before him and doubled over, out of breath.

"Easy, Hank Daly," Joseph said. "Where's the fire?"

"Sir," Henry started but broke into a coughing fit. Another boy arrived with Henry's black cap. Neither would meet Joseph's eyes. Joseph patted Henry's back. A man nearby asked if the boy was going to be sick. Taft's voice boomed from the plaza.

Joseph forced another nervous smile. He squeezed Henry's elbow. "Speak up, son." The crowd surged forward, carrying them with it. Joseph crouched down. Henry held out the note, his face a mat of tears.

Before succumbing to another coughing fit, he managed, "Mrs. Bartlett, sir. She's . . . she's dead, sir."

* * *

A cloud of cigar smoke floated beneath the bank of lights as the bettors belted hot air into the sweltering canvas tent. Tommy held a paper bag over Will's mouth and instructed him to breathe. Father Croix's score card had the match all square. He motioned to Father Maxi, who twirled a finger to the bell ringer to start the last round. Maxi wanted a scotch. The boys hadn't trained hard enough. Perhaps four fights in one day was too much.

Helen huddled next to Tommy, her forehead pressed against the bottom rung of the ring, hands clasped in prayer. "I know it's been, like, forever," she whispered, "but your girl needs a favor . . ."

Taft said, "And now, my friends, I did not come to make a speech."

Joseph pulled Henry Daly into his arms. He wanted to tell the boy that it was all a mistake, that the mill fire that killed Thomas Sheehan and Stanton Cleveland was not his fault, that none of this was supposed to happen: not the silly parade float or stolen mill ledgers or an overstuffed Georgian mansion on the hill. Lizzy and a New Hampshire lake—that was all he had ever wanted. But how do you define devastation? How could he tell a boy what he'd only experienced by living?

Taft said, "And I did not come to get squashed by gigantic cotton bales."

Maxi waved the boxers to the center of the ring. He held their wrists up so their gloves touched. "Last round, boys," he said. "Everyone's a winner." Maxi dropped their wrists, and Damian's gloves fell to his knees. Maxi shouted, "Fight!" but Damian didn't move. Tommy yelled for Will to get his dukes up. "Be steady! Watch out!" But Damian was no magician. Pete ran toward the ring, cursing. He pushed a large man down in the aisle, and a scuffle broke out in the seats. Damian stretched his chin as far out as it would go and shut his eyes.

"Deck 'im!" Tommy called. "Around the house and through the barn." Fifty bucks would pay off a boatload of debts.

Will closed his eyes as he whipped his arm around his body. The glove slammed into the side of Damian's head, the laces slicing open the soft skin behind his left ear. Damian crumpled to the canvas. Will whirled in a circle, his feet tangled in Damian's splayed limbs. Falling, he spotted his father marching toward the ring.

Taft said, "Nor did I come to shake hands and make long speeches."

Maria's hand fell from Hollister's leg. He whispered, "Stop fooling," and nudged her ribs with his heel. The scrape on his neck throbbed against his collar. He unbuttoned his shirt and felt a sticky wetness. "Quit. Someone's coming. Get up." He knelt down. "Maria?" He jostled her shoulder. His hand slid over her chin then her nose and forehead. He licked his finger.

"Open the door," the ride operator called. A second later he rammed his shoulder into the famine panel, popping the latch.

Taft said, "I only came to see you, to say howdy-do."

Will met his father's eye between sunken chins and pumping fists. Joseph's bow tie was cockeyed and his slicked-back hair mussed. The straw boater he was clutching had a fist-sized dent in the top. Pete Newton stormed up the opposite aisle with little Patrick twisting from his belt like the tail of a kite.

Taft said, "And to congratulate you on the wonderful prosperity and on the wonderful progress that you have made."

Dr. Boyle measured out one gram of head powder and stirred it into a glass of tepid water, but Evelyn couldn't lift her head to drink. Boyle pushed aside the cut-glass animals and set the glass down. He lifted Evelyn from the divan, stepping on the unicorn as he left the room.

"To congratulate you even more on the happiness of the individual in Fall River, of which there is evidence on every side."

Will dove under the ropes, landing on all fours on the cement floor and skinning his knees. He juked under his father's grasp and sprinted toward the hazy light shooting between the bettors' heads. Half the crowd turned for a glimpse of pig-eyed Pete; the other half twisted to catch Will's gymnastics. Father Croix snapped his blue scoring pencil in half. Maxi lifted Damian's limp body from the ring.

Will ran up June Street, ripping the gloves' laces free with his teeth. His left eye was purple, the other nearly swollen shut. Ladies out walking screamed at the sight of him. He stopped at the house gate. Dr. Boyle sat hunched over on the front stoop. He looked up and shook his head, and without a word, Will ran farther up into the Highlands. Joseph's automobile jumped the curb. The engine roared as he leapt into the lawn. "Will!" he shouted. "Will, come back!"

Helen rounded the corner, her legs pumping like pistons. "Which way?" she stammered. "Which way did he go?" Joseph pointed, she pointed, and then she sprinted down the sidewalk.

Tommy appeared at the corner, doubled over, gasping. Joseph met his eye. "Find Hollister," he called. "Go find my son." Tommy slowly pivoted back down the hill. Joseph ripped the committee badge from his lapel and spun his boater down the street. He snapped his jaw shut and ground his teeth. His eyes welled up. He inhaled deeply and then spat his rotten wisdom tooth into the grass.

"And to wish you Godspeed in making greater steps forward in the next hundred years."

Thunderous applause and cheering swept Taft from the review stand, with many in the crowd believing they'd see the next hundred years. Taft encouraged them by flashing his presidential chops. They stood four and five deep down Main Street and hovered on rooftops waving red, white, and blue streamers and rattling noisemakers. All bounced on tiptoes to catch a lasting glimpse of the man who had helped them, for one afternoon, forget everything but their pride.

Far out in Mount Hope Bay, the *Connecticut*'s big guns fired, and the crowd, momentarily stunned, flinched. The boom rumbled up June Street and then echoed eastward down into the Globe neighborhood, rattling tenement windows in the Flint and Mechanicsville, disturbing the water in Bleachery Ponds—its rumble recorded as far as the town of Westport, five miles to the east.

Before the *Connecticut* lifted anchor, the special editions of the *Herald* and the *Evening News* hit street corners. Newsies shouted, "President declares Fall River presidential city! Read all about it! Next hundred years to rival the last! Historic edition! Here today, gone tomorrow! Two bits buys you immortality! Read it here! It's all here!"

A BOUNTY IT WILL BE

João Rose sat in the window seat of the Westport-bound trolley cradling his little cousins, five-year-old Pearl and seven-year-old Michael, in his ropy arms, thinking he had blown his only chance to see a president. Once a politician from Lisbon had visited São Miguel, but João had been too sick with fever to watch the senator's landing party tour the island. His neighbor on the farm, Kitty, had thought him crazy to miss the last day of the Cotton Centennial, but his uncle Manuel believed the centennial a perfect excuse to avoid the city. Crowds of English speakers made him nervous. With everyone in the city ogling Taft, the river would be deserted. The trolley reflected this fact. It was full not of beachcombers, but of blurry-eyed Irish housekeepers heading down to their Highlands employers' summer cottages. João was proud to see a few Portuguese in the service class. Most summers, the Highlands wives arrived in the country after the Memorial Day parades and stayed through Labor Day. Everything was delivered from Fall River, including their husbands on weekends. But the centennial celebration had altered routines, forcing the housekeepers to act as advance parties. Tasks such as receiving food and ice deliveries, preparing menus, sobering up the gardeners and drivers, doling out chores to the second girls, all had to be supervised by someone trustworthy. So they traveled back and forth the two weeks of the centennial. Thankfully, things would return to normal after the president sailed that afternoon.

Tomorrow, summer restarted in the country, and all amenities and food-stuffs must line the pantry shelves.

Though people were standing, Manuel took up two seats with his quahog gear: teeth, poles, burlap sacks. The handles of the long wooden poles slanted out the open window. He had forged the quahog teeth, the razor-sharp iron hooks that scraped the hard clams off the ocean floor, at his own blacksmith and machine shop on Columbia Street. In the Azores, he had made mostly farming tools, but in Fall River he forged damn fine replacement parts for mill machinery, and the occasional anchor or harpoon. He could replicate any part or tool once he'd handled it. Today he hoped to clear three bushels of quahogs—two to sell, one for himself and his neighbors. The extra money was put in his special home-buying account at the Five Cents Savings Bank—a bank that accepted five-cent deposits. Who had invented such a thing? Only in America.

Manuel looked over his shoulder at his strong nephew, thinking the boy might pull in a fourth bushel if they made low tide. He rolled his bulbous nose in his palm then spat out the trolley window. Though he didn't see João as much as he'd like, the boy had come through with money to save his business, so Manuel didn't meddle in his nephew's affairs. João had worked in Manuel's shop while attending night classes at the Durfee Textile School, then took a job in the Cleveland Mill as a loom fixer. He was promoted. He courted a girl from the neighborhood. Neither lasted; Manuel didn't know why. Soon after the tragic Cleveland Mill fire, João took over the management of the mill owner's dairy farm in Rhode Island. The boy worked hard—too hard Manuel thought. But Rose Butter sold well, making João a handsome profit. Only in America could farmers make profits.

They hailed from the village of Ponta Delgada on São Miguel, an island part of the Azorean archipelago. New England whaling ships first called on the islands in the early eighteenth century. Local sailors hopped ships for the New World. Nonmariners followed. Manuel was the first of his family to believe the promises of upstart America. His first letter home caused quite a stir in the village. He told the story of an irate Irish customs inspector on Ellis Island who had shortened his name from Rosario to Rose.

Damn Portuguese have the penmanship of a squirrel. He bounced through a half-dozen towns and even more ideas. He wrote home, *Some speak badly of America, but never in public. America has hidden costs.* (This line resonated with João's father, who promptly sold an additional cow for his son's journey.) Manuel lived for two years on Cape Cod before settling in Fall River, where he fell in at a foundry in the seedy Mechanicsville neighborhood. He found cheap lodging north of the city in Steep Brook. There was land there, and Manuel worked it with other Portuguese families. He rented a room from a farmer and soon proposed to one of his daughters. He planted her a hedge of blue hydrangeas as a wedding gift. A year later Manuel invited his brother's family to join him in the New World.

* * *

The trolley stopped in the village of Westport, and the four hitched a ride southwest on the back of a farm wagon to Adamsville, Rhode Island. The road to Adamsville was lined with dairy farms and large plots of squash, corn, and tomatoes. The outcroppings of rock reminded João of his father's land on São Miguel. João counted no fewer than fifty head, a number his father could only imagine. At the duck pond bridge in the village center they passed a gristmill, and farther up the Fo'c's'le tavern and a baseball field marked by a metal plaque shaped like a rooster that commemorated the town's founding in 1867. At the ball field, they hopped off the farm wagon and headed south toward the ocean on foot, walking back into Massachusetts. Locals called the harbor area of Westport by its Indian name, Acoaxet, while the Fall River summer residents simply called it the Harbor. From June through August, the city invaders owned the sandy beaches. The local farmers swam in the Westport River.

Just inside the Rhode Island side of the state line was the house of mill owner John Gower. An enormous forsythia bush, allowed to grow wild to a height of ten feet, fronted the Gower property. The Fo'c's'le regulars spread a rumor that Gower was afraid of the ocean, so he'd chosen a spot at the head of the river. Highlands gossip countered that Gower didn't want to pay the higher taxes in Massachusetts. Most of his peers owned homes right on the high tide line. Replacing water-damaged floors or a wind-damaged shutter was an annual expense they didn't consider an inconvenience.

The west branch of the river contained Manuel's lucky quahog spot: a sandbar called Lions Tongue. It was a tidal river that ran four miles inland between wooden banks. Except to local fisherman, the lower half was not navigable, on account of the salt marshes and sandbars. Lions Tongue was up near the mouth of the harbor. They would start digging on the tip and work their way inland as the tide came in.

The path to the river cut through a briar patch that had been beaten down into a U-shape by local fishermen dragging small skiffs to the water. The wet green terrain was wildly different from dry São Miguel, but the two shared the salty Atlantic. At a crest in the river path, João noticed the lobster trap buoys were slack in the channel, pushing neither in nor out. The tide was changing. The medium tide created a sliver of a path up the shoreline to Lions Tongue that varied from marsh to sand to slippery crags of barnacled rock. Green and blue eelgrass floated on the water. One swoop of a net would deliver an assortment of crabs and perhaps a bluefish. João carried Pearl on his back while Michael wandered behind, stopping to poke at crabs or skip stones. Manuel hauled their quahog equipment over a wooded path farther inland, where the footing was better, though he had to stop at each property line to climb stone walls grown over with raspberry vines spun with poison ivy. On his first visit to the river, he had spotted a deer in a clearing surrounded by a flock of gulls. This contrast was confounding. He'd never seen a deer before. He took cover behind an uprooted oak tree trunk and readied his quahog teeth but, in preparing his defense, cracked a twig with his heel. The snap drove the deer into a retreat that churned the gulls into a cyclone of white. Manuel was curious about the creature, as he was about the first deer tick he found sucking the soft skin behind his knee. So much of the land was a mystery: tightly clustered scotch pines, the cattails' brown heads that darted in the wind like minnows, and hungry osprey, circling two hundred feet above the channel in winding figure eights.

The few homes on the river were perched up for the view across the channel. Some had long stairs built to the water. Others had docks installed on high wooden pylons. Above the homes, a patchwork of stone walls divided pastures and fields. Teams of buggies and taxis ferried the housekeepers to the beach homes on a single paved road that bisected the fields. The road, paid for by the Fall River summer people, allowed the men to come and go as they pleased. For the first year it reached only as far as the golf club. Hopefully, a man in a car would stop and offer to take the extra bushels off Manuel's hands at a fair price.

Walking behind his uncle, João felt Pearl slipping off his back. Her pinkie nail nicked him behind the ear as she made a spastic swing at his neck. He felt a sudden pressure on his larynx and then heard a popping sound as his gold necklace snapped. Pearl sat up on the sand with the necklace limp in her palm like a dead minnow. She looked up wide-eyed, blinked, and then wailed, screaming for her mother.

Manuel charged, shedding quahog tools as he ran. He scooped up Pearl and cradled her like a baby doll, pressing her face to his chest. Once he saw she wasn't hurt, he jiggled her in his arms and tickled her armpits until they were both laughing hysterically, as if the accident had been a big joke.

Michael hooked the end of the necklace from the sand with his stick. João rubbed his neck.

Manuel shrugged. "Not bad news," he said, then seeing Pearl's owl-eyes moisten at the sight of the broken links, he added, "I can easily fuse the ringlets together in my shop."

"That's a girl necklace," Michael teased his older cousin.

"Girls aren't so bad," João said as he tousled Pearl's hair.

"Whose is it?" Pearl asked.

João tugged the necklace off the stick slowly, as if removing a ribbon from Pearl's hair. A few years back he'd given it to a Yankee girl he was courting. But her Irish father found João, a Portagee working the mill floor, undesirable and made her return the gift.

He'd won it on a sandbar six months before he had left for the New World. Locals called it Parrot Beach for the bright rainbow of coral that lined the ocean floor. Each afternoon, João gathered there with his friends to dive for mussels and shells. One day Lourdes, the prettiest girl in his group, challenged the boys to a contest. She unclasped her grandmother's gold necklace from her neck and tossed it underhand into the lagoon. The boys scampered to the edge of the sandbar as the necklace danced and quivered through depths of thickening light. The refracted rays warped the links and shrank the necklace bit by bit until it was lost on the shimmering sea floor some thirty feet below.

Lourdes stepped to the ledge. "I will marry the one that brings up my grandmother's necklace." She raised both her arms high over her head. "Ready?" She dropped them. "Dive."

Ten boys jumped into the lagoon. Two scrambled out, remembering their fear of the water. Lourdes and the other girls dropped to their hands and knees and peered over the ledge at the tangle of kicking feet, their soles the palest patch of skin after a hot summer. Their brown bodies shrank and then were lost in the sparkle of the coral and fish. A trail of air bubbles burst on the surface, blocking the view completely. After ten seconds three heads bobbed above the waterline, each boy complaining of sore ribs and cuts from sharp elbows and nails. The girls on the beach laughed and threw sand at the boys. Lourdes's eyes widened as she dipped her face to the water. She knew only three boys could hold their breath long enough to find the necklace. Two boys shot up on either side of her. They beached themselves half out of the water, heaving for air. One promised to buy Lourdes a million gold necklaces if she married him. The other vomited.

At fifteen feet, the water temperature dropped ten degrees. At twenty the ocean floor lost its golden shimmer. At twenty-five the colors muted. Schools of silvery minnows zoomed at the three boys, turned away at right angles, then whipped back around. A tall boy with angular limbs held a slight lead over João and his best friend, Julio. The pressure built in their ears. Their lungs burned. They knew how to extend their strokes, to slow down and glide, but what if the tall boy beat them to the bottom? João stopped to clear his ears. Julio too. The tall boy continued a few feet and then faced them, thinking he'd won. Suddenly he seized up. His hands gripped his ears. Blood seeped from his nose and rolled up his face. Their pressure equalized, João and Julio passed the tall boy as he shot toward the surface. Fish darted in his bloody wake. João had pegged the necklace near an outcropping of red coral, but now he wasn't so sure. A cloud obstructed the sun, and everything went gray. The boys hovered over the sea floor. Their legs parted above them, bent at the knee. With one arm each they frantically swam down, while the other flipped over rocks and shells. Small explosions of sand clouded the water.

Julio scurried over the rocks rubbing his eyes after each stroke as ribbons of blood seeped from the barnacle cuts across his knuckles. João swam toward a shiny patch of sand as Julio hovered over a crevice between two rocks; his arm plunged down and he pulled out a pearly oyster shell. He grimaced, and then smashed the shell down on the rocks, slicing his palm. The sunlight returned. João grabbed Julio's arm and the boy jerked around.

Lourdes's necklace hung from João's neck. Julio tossed the shards of shell at his friend. They floated an inch then tumbled down to the sand. Julio pinched off a rope of snot and then squatted down to the sea floor and rocketed topside, his left arm out ahead of him. João peered up at the squirming legs on the surface. Water now flowed freely in and out of his mouth. He felt a constriction in his throat and then a sharp pain seized him. Lourdes was promised to one of the boys above. His family owned five fishing boats; the boy would inherit the fleet. No dairy farmer's son working borrowed land, no matter how many books he could read, had such a future. But now she was his. He urinated. The yellow stream blew through the fabric of his trunks, forming a jellyfish-like sac. He put the necklace in his mouth. He'd stay under forever, with Lourdes, growing gills, living among the coral and shellfish. We can live in underwater caves. The children will have flippers. Flippers, yes, flippers.

João lost his grip on the rocks; buoyed by the little air swirling in his lungs, his body ascended. An updraft of current propelled him, then the warmer water triggered something. His legs kicked, but his arms trailed at his sides. He felt the sun and peered up. Black spots blotted the sky. A silvery trail of bubbles tickled his groin. His throat opened, and a rush of salt water flowed down his throat. Fifteen feet from the surface he stopped kicking. His body suspended, arms and legs splayed out like a frog preserved in formaldehyde. He didn't feel the hands around his waist or the fingers pinching his armpits.

Lourdes screamed when his face broke the surface. João's head rolled forward; a boy pulled his hair to keep his face out of the water. The tall boy clasped João's swim trunks and hoisted him to the sandbar. He rolled João on his side and drummed his back with two fists. Julio was doubled over, shouting at his friend to breathe. After a few seconds of pounding, João vomited up two puddles of water.

"João?" Lourdes sucked the back of her hand.

The tall boy flipped him flat and blew into João's mouth. His chest heaved as he choked down gargantuan breaths. The girls broke their huddle when they saw João was breathing. Two choked back tears; others treated the boys.

João opened his eyes and the crowd hollered. His bloodshot eyeballs rolled and he blinked hard, convulsed. He made a start to sit up, and the tall boy pushed him down. He felt something fall against his throat and remembered Lourdes, the contest, the silvery minnows like knife blades. João fingered the necklace. He took a shallow breath and coughed. He rolled onto his side. Lourdes knelt close, her soft knees touching his silky chest. Her lips fell on his upturned ear. She rubbed smooth João's back. In a low voice, she whispered, "I'm yours."

A tingling sensation rolled his stomach. Slowly his friends came into focus. A steamer hummed in the distance. A flock of gulls flew passed. Then Lourdes's face blocked the light. She smiled and whispered, "You won." João seized the back of Lourdes's head and pulled her face to his. Their friends hollered. The kiss lasted a single beat before João's brown body jerked, and she fell on her back beside him on the sand. She squeezed his hand as he coughed and coughed.

Years later on the Westport River, Pearl said, "The next girl who wears it you'll marry."

João rolled the necklace between his hands. I should have married, he thought, should have swum down inside Lourdes and died on the sand.

Lourdes's father forbade her to see João after he heard the story. He punished Lourdes's mother the entire fall by slamming doors and making threats. In November he threw an andiron through a picture window. "She will marry the fisherman's son. It is arranged." After six months of begging and crying Lourdes's tears dried up, and she sent João a note rolled in a glass bottle: *A fisherman's wife I will be.* Once the fisherman's son returned from military service, they would marry. Heartbroken, unable to concentrate in school, and fearing military service, João approached his father about joining his uncle Manuel in America. His father had wanted it too. And so he began selling cows.

The fisherman's son was sent to João's house the day of his departure for America to ask after the gold necklace of Lourdes's grandmother.

"I threw it back into the lagoon," João said. He gave the boy a bitter smile. "You can fish it out since you don't have the lungs to dive for it." The fisherman's son shrugged. João returned to his packing.

"I never wanted it," the boy said. "The necklace." He nudged João's trunk with his toe. "But America. America," he repeated.

"What of it?" João said.

"Don't you know?" João shook his head. "You won, you dummy. You won."

Years ago, the old village healer had told João's grandmother that if she didn't bless others, she would suffer from a long illness. Soon after giving this warning, the old healer died, leaving João's grandmother to bless her neighbors—only she could rid one of *mau olhado*, or the evil eye. It was said João shared his grandmother's healing power. The morning he set sail for America, she called him to her room in his father's house. On the floor she set a clay bowl with dried rosemary, bay leaves, and garlic, and struck a match. All the shutters were pushed wide open. João's grandmother feared that a *quebranto*, or curse, threatened her grandson's trip because so many of the boys in their village were jealous.

"Jealousy breeds bad fortune," she said and instructed João to sit cross-legged with the bowl between his legs. She stood over him as he inhaled the burning herbs and cloves until God told her that the quebranto had flown out a window.

On the carriage ride to the boat dock, the grandmother shared a recent dream. She had seen a large tract of black soil and many animals. She said she saw João standing on a porch overlooking it all.

"But how? I will be in a city," he asked, remembering that his uncle's letter spoke of cotton mills.

The old woman shook her head and yawned. Her powers had limits. She said, "You will pay dearly for this bounty, but a bounty it will be. I have seen it." She kissed her grandson's cheek, and fell asleep.

* * *

The lobster trap buoys and channel markers had begun to drift downriver by the time they reached Lions Tongue. Manuel hurried to assemble the quahog poles while João squatted at the water's edge. The drop was steep: twenty feet in two steps. João imagined the fun of running off the sandbar into the water. He wet the surface of his right hand and licked it. The incoming tide was saltier than the outgoing. The water was cool, a good ten to fifteen degrees cooler than in São Miguel for this time of year. And not as blue, rather shades of green and gray.

"Jeez! Look at that one." Little Pearl pointed to an enormous house under construction above the tree line. The third story observation deck would offer a commanding view of Cuttyhunk Island, and on a clear day, possibly Martha's Vineyard. The summer people owned the best views of the river. Most homes were carved out of farmers' corn and alfalfa fields, though nothing grew within fifty yards of the homes. The bloated summer cottages had somehow poisoned the soil for the native farmers.

Pearl pulled her cousin's trouser leg. "Buy me that house?"

João looked back up the hill. His face lit up. There were mahogany decks facing east to the river and south to the ocean, and behind them, large plate glass picture windows. Michael dropped a handful of periwinkles and then turned and waited for his cousin's answer, though the boy's expression soured as João hedged. Ever since they had seen the house where João lived on the Bartlett farm, they had figured he owned it, and all the surrounding farmland. He knew he should have nipped this fantasy in the bud—*No, I work for the man who owns the farm, Joseph Bartlett*—but at the time, he had selfishly wanted anyone, even two children, to believe he could be the kind of man to own such a property.

"No," João said. "I'd never buy such a house." He spun Pearl in the air. "I'll buy one ten times as big. But there, on the water." He pointed toward the southern stretch of beach. "Wake up and swim. Like I did back home." João lowered Pearl to the sandbar, and she and Michael raced down the water's edge after a gull. João's mouth went dry. Someday Pearl would stop believing his lies. He peered up at the large house. The voice inside his head amplified. *A home ten times as big.* His neighbors would seek his opinion on important affairs. He imagined a woman, his wife, with porcelain skin like Elizabeth Bartlett, waving to him from the patio and then laughing as he chased her with a watering can. His new butter business would lead to a fleet of delivery trucks, customers in New York, a great bounty—just as his grandmother had predicted.

Manuel belched. João winked at his uncle than turned back to the looming castle. He lowered his arm, unsure whether or not he had been waving back at his imaginary wife. Manuel preferred to chew his tongue than shape it around words; in America, Manuel spoke with his hammer and anvil. It seemed the only thing his uncle had changed in coming to America had been his address. More Portuguese inhabited the neighborhood of his blacksmith shop than lived in São Miguel. Manuel's pockmarked cheeks caved in, triggering a wet snort and hock that produced a gargantuan glob of yellow, snot-filled mucus that somersaulted to the sand. Whether it was a direct comment on the house or simply his usual phlegmatic housecleaning, João wasn't sure. Manuel was a spitter, but it also meant *Get to work.*

"We're the Portuguese pilgrims. We made the Cape. We built it up," Manual said in Portuguese. João froze at the sound of his uncle's deep voice. Manual leaned against his wooden pole. "Then the artists come down. They must paint a hundred miles of nets and boats and docks. And then the writers heard about it, and the summer people. But we started it. Fishermen up and down the Cape. The Grand Banks is a gold mine."

"You work with Yankees?"

Manuel grunted, spat again, and said, "In the city, Portuguese and Yankees don't always get on so good. But on the water, we all square. Out there, the same rules for everybody." He thrust a pole into João's chest and set to work.

They fished for three hours before stopping for lunch. Michael filled the burlap bags. A bored Pearl wandered into the woods to collect wild raspberries for her mother. Sloops appeared in the channel. The sailors waved and shouted out greetings. Seven years ago on a blustery day, much rougher than this one, João had saved Hollister Bartlett's life after his father's sailboat had capsized. Joseph Bartlett had used the word "hero" repeatedly that day, but talk didn't impress João. The runaway boat and child would have sooner or later gotten caught in a salt marsh or simply run aground. João had saved the boy only from nightmares, but João was new to America, so he didn't argue with the mill owner's choice of words. "Hero" it was. João parlayed the accolade into a job at the Cleveland Mill and work for Manuel's fix-anything business.

After a lunch of *chouriço* and sweetbread, Manuel was back at it. João followed him into the water, raking the quahog teeth through mudflats and eelgrass. They needed to keep one step ahead of the creeping tide. In three more hours Lions Tongue would be gone.

When it vanished shortly before three, the men hauled four bags of quahogs up to the single-lane road. They waited twenty minutes before a driver from one of the Atlantic Avenue mansions offered to buy the three bushels for a clambake his boss was having, a sort of post-centennial celebration. He mentioned his boss had chaired the Automobile Parade Committee. This meant nothing to Manuel. But João made a mental note of the man's name, thinking Joseph would probably attend the bake. And for a fleeting second he wondered how he might get himself invited. On the near-empty trolley home, Pearl snuggled under her brother's armpit. Slobber leaked from Michael's open mouth. Raspberry stains covered their skin like a poison ivy rash. João always rode home in a back-facing seat so he could look toward the sea. He closed his eyes to listen to the caw of gulls over the clatter of the train, though he, too, soon dozed off.

On his drive back to Middletown, João stopped by a Columbia Street tavern to hear news of the president's visit and arrived home on the farm after midnight slightly drunk. If not for the morning milking, he would have stayed later to listen to more stories of Taft's speech and the battleship *Connecticut*'s booming guns. He found a note tacked to the front door, its four short black sentences written on the back of a Rose Butter label:

Elizabeth Bartlett died today. The service is in three days. Join me in praying for our friend. He won't weather this blow gracefully.

Kitty

João wedged the tack from the door with his thumbnail and folded the note in half. Inside, he set his hand on the light switch but then dropped it and sat down on the mudroom bench. He removed his boots and sat in the dark. He had first met Elizabeth Bartlett at the Cleveland company picnic at Lincoln Park. She'd extended her hand, and foolishly he'd bent at the knee and bowed before the queen of Cleveland Mill, but she'd hoisted him up. Called him a "hero" for saving Hollister. She said his future was bright.

João walked through the dark house, opening all the windows. From the mantel he collected a clay bowl and set it on the hearth. He sprinkled dried rosemary, bay leaf, and garlic in the basin; he struck a match. He sat cross-legged with the burning herbs between his legs waiting for a sign that the quebranto hanging over the Bartlett house had lifted. He would wait all night if necessary. Joseph Bartlett deserved as much.

BRUISES, SOME OF THEM DEEP

Joseph pressed the ice pack to his jaw between sips of whiskey. The left side of his face was frozen blue, but the pain burrowed deep in his jaw; the rest of him was numb. Usually, the third glass of rye removed all the pain. At least the salty taste from the pus had passed. God damn this day. Joseph kicked the porch wall, cracking a clapboard. He stood up and paced the screened rectangle, alternating between the whiskey and a cigar from the cedar box Hannah Cleveland had presented him when he took over running the mill. "You're one of us now," she'd whispered, still bleary-eyed from her son Stanton's death. The tobacco was brittle and stung his throat. He clicked his tongue over the remaining twenty-nine teeth, stopping to wedge the tip between the gaps. Another enameled soldier was sure to exit. But what did he expect? They'd served him well for forty-two years. The collateral damage from his last abscessed tooth hadn't been pretty. Dr. Boyle had prattled on about silk floss, but it was no use. Taft's pearly chompers were surely falsies, a man his age. Otis had favored a seahorse ivory denture. Joseph extinguished the dry cigar. Perhaps it was just his time.

The house was quiet, save for Evelyn muttering prayers over his Elizabeth's body. Hollister and Will were gone, bunking at the Sheehans' while their mother lay in the front parlor. A nice cross-breeze swept through the porch, cutting the stifling heat. Earlier he could make out a long stripe of moonlight down the Taunton River, but now low-flying clouds draped the city. An occasional motorcar or horse carriage passed below. It had been an exhausting day of preparations, house calls, and a long conversation with Matt Borden, who'd sailed back to New York before the *Mayflower* lifted anchor. Lizzy's death had set certain arrangements in motion, such as stock transfers and grave purchases—tidbits that Joseph had thought his boys would take care of after he passed.

This was his punishment, he decided. The center had finally come undone. Never again would he be able to blame Lizzy, or her people, for his failings. But the weight of her family's wealth cut deep. Borden had suggested New York bankers, encouraged Joseph to move the lot of it out of Fall River investments. "The next frontier," he called it, as if his niece's death was a footnote in a quarterly report. The cemetery caretaker appealed to Joseph's thriftiness by suggesting that investing in a large family plot made fiscal sense, so Joseph had begrudgingly anted up hundreds for himself and the boys and the boys' wives, if they so chose to join the Bartlett family for eternity. And if they were ungrateful, the caretaker assured, this meant "more space for you and the missus." Space for what, Joseph wondered. His library? Lizzy's antiques? A tomb for his crazy maid to lament at? Knowing a patch of earth sat ready for his demise made him uneasy. Joseph's last task of the day was approving the outfit Mary Sheehan and Evelyn had selected for Lizzy, a brown handkerchief-linen gown with inset lace he'd purchased in New York last winter. It wasn't what he'd have chosen; he wanted something sunnier, the lavender silk piece he'd recently picked up. But he was too weary to object. No, the ladies should select the gown, given that they were going to have to maneuver poor Lizzy's stiffening limbs.

Joseph poured another dram of rye. He set the crystal decanter on the sideboard, then held his glass up to the light. It was now his property. Along with the bone china, divan, Persian rugs, and Dunning still lifes. All the accoutrements a Highlands household required. Everything Lizzy had wanted. Like June Street itself. But Highlands women don't usually marry Irishmen. He'd backed into a life he'd gladly return, as if it were a fine mohair overcoat he'd worn around the store: yes, it looked good, but seemed off, no thanks. No, now it was his, wrinkles and all. And the boys. Perhaps, without a Yankee in the household, the Ladies Auxiliary would pressure him to sell.

Evelyn wandered onto the porch rubbing her doughy cheeks and blinking rapidly to wake from her Catholic trance. She looked around the room and then knelt down to rub a spot from the carpet with the corner of her apron.

Joseph toed the spot. "Can I help you?" he snapped.

"Sir?" She scrambled to her feet. "There's a man at the door." She pointed over her shoulder. "He wants a word."

Joseph smacked the decanter against his thigh.

"They've come to evict us already?"

"Sir?"

If it was a man from the mill, he would fire him on the spot. Joseph turned to the vestibule.

Evelyn tapped his elbow. "The back door, sir."

"Who is it then?" He handed her the ice pack and decanter.

"Didn't say." Evelyn narrowed her eyes. "Said, you'd 'understand.'" She knew of her boss's involvement with union rabble-rousers.

It was probably one of George Pierce's idiots in training; he'd grab his gun, scare the crap out of the dope. Curse this day. "'Howdy-do' to you, Mr. President, you fat walrus."

"Sir?"

"Move." He brushed past Evelyn, cursing the time he had to wait until Hollister took over the mill.

Before Joseph stepped down the stoop he sensed a shift in the weather— dampness up from the water weighing down the air. The heat had broken. Smelled like rain. He opened his mouth and inhaled. The cool air soothed his mouth. Evelyn must drop the windows.

A figure and horse-drawn carriage stood just outside the arc of light cast by the kitchen fixture.

"Who's there?"

João Rose stepped into the light. He was dressed in black, a virtual shadow. Joseph scanned the neighbors' for prying eyes. João knew the rules about house visits.

Joseph said, "It's a bad time, João. Lizzy—"

"I'm sorry." João stepped closer. "I have something to show."

"The farm?"

"No." Joseph had been putting off their quarterly state-of-the-farm meeting. And now he had the boys to manage. He'd never get straight again.

João turned toward the farm carriage, motioning Joseph to follow. Rain began to fall.

João set his hand on the door handle. He put on his black hat, made a start to speak, then paused and released his hand from the handle. "Not good events."

"It's been an unpleasant few days." Joseph's tongue explored the soft pit in the back of his mouth.

João said something in Portuguese, and the latch inside the cab unlocked. The door opened on two slim legs wrapped in plain black cotton stockings.

João said, "Come forward. It's okay." The woman's legs shuffled. A moment later her left hand clutched the doorframe and the leather seat creaked. The left side of her face inched into the weak light. Her skin was light brown and beautiful, though swollen; the eye, black and focused on the carriage floor. Joseph glanced down to see what caught her attention. Rain pooled on the running board. João mumbled something and she sat up, and turned her shoulders to face them.

"Jesus." Joseph whipped his wet bangs off his forehead.

Her right cheek was bruised, nearly black. A cloth bandage covered the eye, and the thin slope of the nose took a funny bend near the tip. Her rich, dark hair was pulled back in a scarf, revealing a shaved patch above the right eyebrow and, there again, a dressing dotted with blood. This one snaked into her hairline.

Joseph stumbled back from the carriage.

"*Obrigado*," João said, his voice barely audible, and the girl fell back. He shut the door. The lock snapped closed a second later.

"Who is she?"

"Maria. She sews for Cleveland. So does her *mãe*. The *pai* is out of work. A fisherman."

"She get hit by a truck?"

"Her *pai* spoke with Manuel. Also from Santo Cristo." João paused.

He sucked his teeth. Surveyed the yard as if pitching a price for its care. He took a step toward Joseph, his voice low. "You have heard lies."

Joseph shook his head. "I don't know that girl."

"Hollister does."

"You mean the fun house incident?" Joseph said, startled. "The police called. Said they'd stop by after the funeral. My boy was attacked."

"No, no, no." João removed his black hat and slapped it against his leg. His eyes narrowed. He said, "Your boy attack Maria. Your boy in trouble with my people."

"Nonsense!" Joseph remembered clutching his son to his chest when Tommy had brought him home. His oldest son. Motherless and bloodied. Hollister had run the block after hearing the news. They found him later that afternoon in the tree fort the boys had built years ago with Wiggins. Mary Sheehan had set a dinner tray at the base of the old oak. Joseph had wondered what the boy was hiding from. Was that the word he'd used, "hiding"? No, he thought, this girl's face set the word in my head.

Joseph said, "Hollister said a girl slipped in the fun house. A drunken operator hit him." João's expression didn't change. "*Slipped*, João. Not anything like this."

"No, no, no," João said. "She *with* Hollister. He beat her. Glass boom when the man forced door. Shards cut her legs."

"And Hollister's neck."

"No, no, no. She cut him."

"You're talking about my son."

"He cheated her in the mill store—"

"Impossible!" Joseph clutched his stomach. The pain in his jaw had fallen to his gut.

"He forced her to . . . how do you say?"

"Not another word." Joseph paced behind the carriage. He spied the light in the parlor and Evelyn's shadow moving about the coffin. There was no place for him to store this new information in his full head. He flung his hands over his head, walked a few paces, stopped, and walked back. His right arm shot up, and he made a start to speak, but then lowered the arm to his side. He nodded for João to continue.

"The police protect him, not her." João paused, glanced at the neighbor's house, and walked to Joseph. "Stories involving you people always lost in translation."

Joseph tapped his toe in the puddle encircling his feet like a noose. *You people.* He now understood the police chief's courtesy call the day after the incident. The up-and-coming mill owner sympathetic to labor, the death of his middle-aged wife, a Durfee no less, mother of two young boys, took precedent over the mild disfigurement of the daughter of an unemployed Portuguese fisherman in the Flint. The chief saw an opportunity; Joseph would have to repay the favor.

"What does she want?"

"To cut her throat with a razor." He dragged a finger across his throat, then glanced at the granite house. "Boy here?"

"No."

"You do something, Joseph." João touched his boss's elbow. He'd had never spoken Joseph's Christian name.

"I'm sorry, João."

"Sorry don't make it hurt no less."

João stared at the carriage. Joseph stared at João. Yankees for the Yankees. Irish for the Irish. French for the French. Portuguese for the Portuguese.

"I'll make it right."

"No." João shook his head. "Never right. Never."

"What now then?"

João brushed a twig off the carriage. "I take her to Middletown. Kitty help her heal. The apothecary give me all we need."

"I'll send Dr. Boyle out."

"That paper man, Connelly, been asking around Columbia Street."

"I'll deal with him," Joseph said. "What's her father's name?"

"Francisco Medeiros."

"I have shares in some boats." He spoke in a flat voice. "Have him come to the mill store."

"They cheer you in the neighborhood," João said. Perhaps he couldn't hurt his old friend any longer. Joseph appreciated the effort, but what Hollister had done was his failure as much as the boy's.

"But not under my own roof." Joseph's wet shirt clung to his long torso. His wet trousers began to constrict around his legs. He seemed to be expanding in the rain.

João watched a motorcar pause at the corner. It cruised on. A gust of wind loosened the upstairs shutters, and they clapped against the house.

Joseph said, "This is the second time you've saved Hollister."

"Next time I let him drown." João looked up at the house again, his eyes landing on each window. Joseph knew the wiry farmer could scale the building.

João said, "I will plant a tree for Ms. Bartlett."

Joseph extended his hand and João took it. "Godspeed."

Joseph stood in the rain until the carriage turned down the hill. He removed his wet shirt and stood for a moment half-naked. He bent backward and closed his eyes, letting the rain cleanse his face. When his heartbeat slowed he righted himself, a tad dizzy, and peered up at Hollister's bedroom window. Oh Lizzy, he thought, how are we to survive without you?

Approaching the kitchen door, he paused and turned back to the yard. What was clanging? On a low-hanging crabapple branch, at the back of the yard, Lizzy's seashell wind chime twisted sideways in the wind and rain. Every Highlands housewife had a garden full of beach-inspired crafts from summers spent in Westport. The kitchen light reflected up off the wet grass and brightened the strands of white shells. Lizzy thought the chimes gave voice to the spirits.

* * *

Joseph poured another healthy standard of rye and followed the smell of vanilla to the parlor, hoping Evelyn wouldn't burn down the house with the candles. She sat slumped, snoring in his leather armchair beside Lizzy's open walnut coffin. He considered the two of them. There is a peacefulness to the dead, pristine for their eternal sleep, but the longer Joseph studied Lizzy, the more he became aware of the haunting stillness of her chest, her eyelids, her waxy hands. And the chilling pallor. Evelyn's light freckles glowed compared to Lizzy's whitening cheeks that no amount of rouge could warm. The few strands of strawberry hair were all that remained from her youth. Their youth—it seemed so very far away. He couldn't call up one memory. *Hollister. Hollister. Hollister.* The boy's name pounded between his ears. He tucked a loose strand behind his wife's head. "Lizzy, there is so much to talk about." He stepped away from the coffin and raised the lip of his tumbler below his nose hoping a liquor-induced sleep might help him forget that his son had sexually assaulted that poor girl in the fun house. The previous night, drinking had helped, at least for a few hours. His increased tolerance made it harder to forget, but easier to summon the courage to beat the fear of God into the boy.

A motorcar turned up June Street, and the passing headlamps filled the room. The light reflected off the gilded picture frames on the desk: photographs of her father and mother in South Park, the family portrait from last Christmas. Above the desk in an oval frame hung an oil painting of Joseph's father, Otis. God, how she'd loved the old taskmaster. They were cut from the same hard cloth. The artist had captured a brooding expression, a disapproving frown—or that's how Joseph read it now. The expression changed each time Joseph had sought its approval in the years since the old man's death. The artist had taken some liberty in smoothing out the scar on his neck and muting eyes bloodshot from chronic insomnia. Joseph was developing similar eyes. Otis's investments had taken care of everything. Rents from his real estate holdings in Newport had allowed Joseph to buy waterfront buildings. Money from the Middletown farm Otis had purchased paid his sister's yearly allowances. The man had been a peer to men like John Flint, farmer turned tin peddler turned real estate speculator turned mill owner—men who had made something out of nothing. Joseph looked into his father's eyes. The old man worked tooth and nail to afford the type of privilege Hollister now took for granted. Otis would have beaten the boy and thrown him into the Taunton River.

Joseph stepped to the windowsill and dumped the glass of rye into a potted germanium. He wouldn't forgive what the boy had done, but he wouldn't lay a hand on him either. There had to be a third way.

He jostled Evelyn. "I'm going up, dear. You come too."

"Yes, Mr. Bartlett," his half-asleep maid yawned.

"Tomorrow will be a long day."

"Right behind you, sir." But she turned her back to him and stood over the coffin. When Evelyn had finished fussing with Lizzy's hair, she moved on to the dress and shoes and then knelt down and bowed her head. Her hands clasped.

Joseph's chest fell. He'd never had the heart to deny a person their passion. "You'll stop and change the candles?"

"Very soon, sir."

Joseph left Lizzy in the care of his impossible maid and mounted the stairs on heavy legs. He lay in bed smoking, something Lizzy had forbidden, the ashtray balanced on his chest. He was exhausted, and a tad drunk, but sleep didn't come—hadn't since the move from Snell Street. This was only the second time in eight months that he'd slept in the big bed—after Lizzy's last turn he'd bunked in the spare bedroom. A misty rain streaked down the windowpane. He heard the faint rattle of Lizzy's wind chime. He extended his arm across the bed; the sheet was cold. He snubbed the cigarette and pulled on his trousers, fresh shirt, and hat and slipped out the kitchen door at half past one. In the misty fog the streetlamps returned a murky glow. He kept to the shadows as he walked down the hill. He stopped across the street from the house, unbelieving the desk lamp in his old office was on. But Mary had a sixth sense about such things. The lamp had been their signal after Thomas had died. Their rendezvous were less frequent after Pete had arrived, the lamp dark since Elizabeth's illness. Years later, standing on the deck of the steamship *Priscilla* as he left Fall River for the last time, Joseph would remember Mary's kindness as he wept. He'd cling to the deck rail as the boat steamed down the Taunton River. The red light on the Borden Flats Lighthouse another beacon on a foggy night.

The light in the front hall fired on then off as he turned up the slate path. He stopped to steady himself, and then that poor Portuguese girl's face hit him between the eyes.

Mary Sheehan's face appeared between the front curtains, fogging the window glass. She sighed, released a small smile, and then nodded her head, as if he were a lost traveler she'd been expecting for hours.

Joseph smiled. "I saw the light."

"Seems about time."

A sense of relief coursed through him, and he fell to his knees.

She cradled his head against her flour-stained skirt. The house smelled of fresh bread. She massaged his scalp with her thick fingers, bits of dough stuck between them, and slowly Joseph relaxed. Mary repeated the refrain "Think of the boys" but kept a lookout for movement at the top of the stairs.

"No," Joseph moaned. He leapt to his feet, punching the vestibule chandelier with his outstretched hand. Mary let out a quick shout. She covered her mouth. Joseph grimaced as he lowered the bloody fingers. A shot of pain seized the hand and wrist that had knocked the silver base. The pain continued up his forearm and into his shoulder. It shot down his spine, encircled his stomach and groin, and then nestled in his knees. A flash of heat gripped his chest. He fell forward into Mary's arms, driving both of them across the room into his old study. She dumped him on Otis's old couch and removed his soggy shoes and socks. She washed the wound on his hand and bandaged it. She retrieved a water pitcher on the desk and poured him a glass, hoping to flush the liquor from his blood. Satisfied he could drink no more, she set his head in her lap and took to massaging his scalp. As his temperature fell, Joseph spoke—first of Elizabeth, and then of João. When describing Maria's face, he felt Mary's abdomen tighten against his cheek and stopped the story. Soon, he drifted off to sleep.

He woke to chimes from the Remington grandfather clock. Outside, the sky was blackish-gray. He remembered coming to the Snell Street house, but not into his old study. Mary was sprawled across the old leather easy chair. Joseph leaned over to lace his shoes, and a shot of pain gripped his forearm. There was a bandage wrapped around his knuckles. *The chandelier.* He figured he hadn't slept more than an hour. He licked the dots of blood on either side of the bandage, then rolled on his damp socks with his left hand and tucked the shoelaces under his heel.

He pulled a couch pillow and propped it between Mary's head and shoulder. He caressed Mary's cheek with the back of his hand. He resisted the urge to carry her upstairs, to slip in beside her. She'd been the one who'd challenged him to confront Stanton Cleveland. And then, in the aftermath of the fire, had put her own grief aside to challenge him again to run a fair business. How could he have missed Hollister's abuse? He kissed her fore-head, and stepped toward the study door. A stair creaked, or was it the wind? He paused for a second, heard nothing, and then slipped out the back.

At five minutes to five on the morning of his wife's burial, an ex-hausted Joseph Bartlett entered his dark home to find Evelyn lying on the floor next to his wife's casket. The smell of a body beginning to sour cut through his hangover. Feeling ill-equipped physically to handle the sight, he shut the pocket doors to the parlor and retreated to the vesti-bule, where he hung his now-shapeless hat on its silver peg and peeled off his wrinkled raincoat. He rubbed his stomach. The vat of water Mary Sheehan had forced him to drink hours earlier lapped against the walls of his bladder. He took a deep breath through his mouth and then slid the pocket doors down their tracks. Lizzy and Evelyn were unchanged, but now his eyes had adjusted to the light and he saw the wax. White wax spiraled down the iron stands the church had provided. It burrowed into the carpet. Wax pooled on the stone pedestals of the plant stands, run-ning over their wooden lips and down the legs like icicles. It had run off the end tables and onto the divan, the easy chair, and the footstool. Every candle Joseph had left in Evelyn's care to change had burned down to its wick's end. Joseph exhaled. He snapped off a corner of the petrified wax from the chair cushion, pressed the chip against his upper lip, and took a deep breath—vanilla bean. He whispered Evelyn's name, but she didn't stir. He tried again. Nothing. After he'd vetoed Evelyn's request to have nuns from St. Patrick's sit with the body (*We're not Catholic, Evelyn*), she had taken the task upon herself. Evelyn's idea of observing meant sleeping on the parlor floor. She hadn't even removed her dust cap, and her ging-ham bib apron was cockeyed, covering her round hip. But she had moved the flower arrangements to the breezeway to afford herself more space to stretch out. He hadn't the strength to deal with this now, so he closed the pocket doors and slipped the hallway Oriental under the bottom gap, hoping to contain the smell for a few more hours.

He set his hand on the banister and mounted the stairs for the second time in six hours in hopes of finding sleep by the top landing. He lay in the spare bedroom, but again sleep eluded him. Finally the pressure in his bladder demanded his attention, and he went down the hall to relieve himself. He drew a bath. Waiting for it to fill, he sat on the toilet and watched the first light peek over the horizon. The dreaded day had begun.

He dressed in the dark suit Evelyn had left out. Henry Daly had shined his shoes. In the hall, he peeled back the black drape from the mirror to check the straightness of his tie. The knot pinched his neck, and he redid it twice. Joseph decided he wanted to spend the final morning of the final day of his married life alone with his wife, reading the paper as they always had before the boys woke. He figured such an attempt at normalcy was silly, but he must try. Tomorrow his wedding band would lose the little luster it had left.

At the foot of the stairs, Joseph paused to consider stepping over Evelyn and begin reading his paper. Thankfully, the boys would not wake to a similar sight. He added this inconvenience to the long list of events he knowingly denied about his life. He'd leave the boys at Mary's until the house was scrubbed and aired. Joseph waited on the last step for the six o'clock chimes, but when none came he kicked away the Oriental and threw open the pocket doors to the parlor. He quickly backpedaled to the porch and threw those doors open in hopes of creating cross-breeze. Let the fumigation begin. As he measured the morning coffee, he remembered Dr. Boyle had stopped the clocks at 1:35 on June 23. A baking tin soaked in the sink basin. A frosted chocolate cake sat under glass on the butcher block. Joseph zipped through family birthdays and anniversaries. When he could think of none, he removed the glass top and burrowed his finger through the icing to the sponge cake. Chocolate cake with chocolate icing—Lizzy's favorite. Crazy Evelyn had made a funeral cake for the reception. What had he done that was special? He smoothed over the deep crater in the cake and replaced the glass dome. He whispered a small apology to Evelyn, wishing Lizzy hadn't encouraged the poor girl so much.

He balanced the cup of coffee under his nose, stopping at the liquor cabinet to add a dash of whiskey. He decided to pull the ladder-back rocker from the vestibule and sit beside his wife, looking out into her garden as the sun rose in the east. One of the few duties Evelyn had been able to perform in her present state was opening the window shutters. Lizzy's hypersensitivity to the cold, plus her mad insistence that sunlight would fade her family furniture, was one of the few household rules Joseph did take issue with. Somehow the illness had brought on this queer preoccupation, as if she were afraid the items would ruin before her death. He couldn't make heads or tails of it, but now that the parlor was actually *acting* as a morgue, he didn't want it to *look* like a morgue. He wanted light. He'd said something overly sentimental like "The garden view will be a constant reminder of her beauty." Evelyn had finally unsheathed the windows in a full cry. Jesus, he didn't understand that woman. And if he had to hear another story about some youthful Irish uncle or cousin dying from dysentery or typhoid, there'd be another funeral to prep the house for. The idea of Evelyn flitting around the house setting wreaths and such, contacting the Sisters for her *own* funeral, before her *actual* death, gave Joseph a chuckle, but his face quickly hardened when he reentered the parlor to find the pathetic sot still belly-up on the floor, and surrounded on four sides by puddles of candle wax, one hand gripping a leg of the table that supported his dead wife.

Joseph dragged the rocker across the room cracking the hardened wax and releasing the scent of vanilla bean into the stale air. He positioned it next to the head of the coffin, but a tad forward so he wasn't head-to-head with Lizzy. He slid the window up and sat back. The first sip of coffee, the most potent, pooled in the hole where his molar had formerly resided. His jaw clenched as the whiskey burned off the live nerve endings. Now only his bandaged hand ached. Outside, a row of shrub roses swayed over the porch railing. Clusters of rose hips were hardened and brown, their moisture sucked dry by aphids he hadn't taken the time to spray. In past summers, Lizzy's tweezer-like fingers had destroyed such pests before they'd had a chance to multiply. She had a planter's luck. Everything she nurtured grew. Joseph would have Wiggins deadhead the roses tomorrow.

Yesterday's *Herald* was where he'd left it, tucked into his father's old rolltop desk, now Lizzy's writing desk, or was. He broke off a wax tendril clinging to it and rubbed it under his nose. It had hardened within an inch of the oxblood leather blotter, though a separate channel had snaked its way down the curve of the twisted molding. There it froze sheets of Lizzy's personal stationery into a brick of wax and paper. He flipped the *Herald* to page seventeen to reread her obituary. He objected to the words "industrialist's wife" and found the term "society philanthropist" a bit hyperbolic, but the picture had reproduced well. A photograph from a series he'd commissioned last summer, before her final spiral. Today, on the morning of her funeral, the picture gave him a chill, and he quickly tucked the paper back into the desk. His chest seized up. How could that same smiling woman now lay a foot away dried up like a raisin, her cheeks fallen in, fingers like dried sticks? He felt the sensation of standing in a pocket of rain showers with sunny skies all around. How could one exist within or outside of the other? In that instant he wanted all of the photographs destroyed, but without them he feared the boys would remember their mother as a shriveled shell. Her slow deterioration was the reason he'd worked late at the mill these last few months. It was the reason he had allowed Hollister to stay out at night, sometimes skipping dinner. It was the reason—

He heard a purring and looked down as the cats scratched themselves against the rope molding that wound up the sides of the desk. They looped between his legs and then hopped on the sills. A squirrel scurried across the lawn, and Bobbin scratched at the screen.

Joseph pulled out the thick wads of letters that were stuffed in the top pigeonholes of the desk. Most were invitations or announcements, some unopened, from Lizzy's many affiliates and family friends. Though bedridden, the cards kept her up on society—her one tether to the bustling world. The mail delivery had been one of the highlights of her day, though bittersweet since each bundle of letters served as a reminder of her once-active life. Many of the organizations kept her on their mailing lists for this reason—now they can save themselves the two-cent postage, Joseph thought. These people knew she'd never attend another Young People's Society meeting, or the Truesdale Hospital nurses' graduation, or Monty and Genny Duval's Fourth of July party at Goosewing Beach. Another card announced a special lecture on modernism by Reverend Sperry. The Metacomet Bank was sponsoring an exhibition of Chapin's and Dunning's work. He thumbed through a thick stack of cards. He had no idea she was so civic minded. His mail had been set aside by the time he came home, and the business or boys had dominated their remaining conversation. He opened an envelope from the Fall River orphanage. The letter included minutes from the board's last meeting about their annual picnic. As he read, Joseph choked up. Printed at the top of the stationery was Lizzy's name—she'd been on the steering committee—*Elizabeth Durfee Bartlett, Decorations.*

For a moment, he allowed himself to admire how his lonely maid clung to Lizzy. She had met Lizzy with an illness and only knew her with an illness. He blew his nose, then dabbed his eyes. Sick Lizzy was enough for Evelyn to love.

"Mr. Bartlett?" Evelyn sat up on the carpet, an island in an ocean of white wax. The carpet crunched as she moved, the sound like shifting sheets of ice.

Joseph turned from the window. Evelyn snapped off a corner of wax and raised it to her face to examine it. Her eyes danced around the parlor stopping on the other reservoirs.

"Sir?" she said hesitantly. She raked her fingers down her face stretching her eyelids so wide Joseph could see the swollen red capillaries lining the rim of her sockets.

He broke off another wedge from the rolltop, frowned, and then tossed it at Evelyn's knees. She was near tears. "You have two hours, Evelyn. The family arrives at ten. Put out the coffee. The muffins are at the back door already. There are flowers too. The man delivered the ice while you were sleeping. Please bathe. And make this mess presentable. Evelyn? Are you listening? Wear your black sateen apron for coffee." The poor girl was suddenly in a fever, on all fours collecting wax. As she crawled below Joseph, he leaned forward on the rocker to block her path.

"It's fine, dear. Now go find the other candles Minister Johns delivered and light them. I don't want the boys' last olfactory memory of their mother to be one of sour milk." Joseph moved to his left, forcing Evelyn to make a wide loop away from Lizzy. "Stand up, woman!" She hopped to her feet. "Now go!"

As her footsteps faded, he inched the rocker to the head of the coffin and stroked Lizzy's hair. It still had some spring, some life. Evelyn called from the other room, but Joseph didn't acknowledge it. He focused on the red roots, not wanting to see the rest of her deflated body. He freed a knot of hair tucked behind her ears. From the desk, he got a pair of scissors and cut off the lock dangling over his thumb. He rolled the fibers into a ball and deposited it in one of the many reply cards on the desk.

"Mr. Bartlett." Evelyn's footfalls rounded the staircase, and Joseph scooted the rocker forward.

"I can't find the candles."

"In a box on the cellar stairs."

Evelyn stepped into the room, scrutinizing the coffin. He followed her gaze to Lizzy's hair.

"Sir?"

Joseph opened his mouth, but his voice caught in his throat. He stared at Elizabeth's strawberry hair, remembering it floating on the surface of Loon Lake, and later that same year, its brilliant strawberry color fanned across white pillows in the honeymoon suite at the Knickerbocker Hotel. Strands of it got wedged between the motorcar seats, frozen in the bath soap, baked into birthday cakes, and matted against his chest on hot summer nights.

Evelyn pointed at Lizzy's head. Her voice cracked. "Mr. Bartlett!"

"Goddamn it, Evelyn!" Joseph jumped to his feet. One wrinkle in this day was going to be his way. "It's the way I like it. Do you hear me?" Evelyn cowered. "It's how I want it later."

"But, sir—"

Joseph ran his fingers through his hair. "Will you please, please, please allow me this last morning with my wife?"

Evelyn bowed her head. She paused, then mumbled some sort of reply and backed out of the room. Joseph pulled the paper out from the desk and sipped his coffee. The desk chair creaked as he leaned back. As a matter of habit he checked the cotton prices in New York first. As he scanned the box score of yesterday's Red Sox game, a dentist's advertisement caught his eye. TEETH FIXED. AFFORDABLE. WHY SUFFER ANY LONGER? Why indeed! He reached for the scissors and snipped it out.

SNELL STREET

"If you nip that roast again, you're gonna lose a finger," Mary Sheehan said to Hollister as she shook out a yellow cotton napkin and set it across her lap. She laid her hands flat on the dining room table. The chandelier hung low over the center. The blinds were drawn. Mary caught the eye of her older boys, Ray and Tommy, and nodded. "Everyone hold hands." Mary bowed, and her children followed. The Bartlett boys stared at one another over the canned peaches. Hollister kicked his brother under the table, and then both fell forward.

"Dear Lord, bless our food. Thank you for the guests at our table. We know Your wisdom will help us over these troubled waters. Everyone pray for His blessing." Mary took a deep breath; she imagined her dead husband, Tom, sitting in Ray's chair at the head of the table, and what her stillborn baby girl, Annie, might have accomplished in this changing world. Her chest ached. Joseph Bartlett deserved better. Earlier that afternoon at the burial she'd clutched his elbow as he'd wept.

Ray cleared his throat. "I'm blessed."

"You're hungry," Tommy said.

"Silence," Mary snapped. Losing a father was one thing, but a mother—a child! The elder Mrs. Bartlett, Joseph's mother, had taken her dinner early and retired upstairs. Indeed, she'd fallen asleep at the brunch, upsetting a pot of coffee. That woman knew mourning. She'd been at it for the better part of ten years.

"It is in Your name we pray, the Father, Son, and Holy Ghost. Amen."
Mary crossed herself. "Okay, now." She paused to yawn. She hadn't slept
well on the easy chair. "Ray, carve the roast."

Hollister let out a small cheer and rubbed his hands together. Cousin Pete
licked his lips. The boy had been living with the family since Mary's sister died.
Mary winked at Helen sitting beside Will. Her daughter's eyes were devoid of
their usual mischief. Tommy sat in the last chair on the right so he could see everyone at the table with his good eye. Dr. Boyle called the condition "hyphema,"
the result of head trauma, but the family simply referred to it as "strawberry
eye," the result of a Louisville Slugger. Tommy still bet twice what he had in his
pocket. He had long ago given up Boyle's suggested remedies of bed rest, ice
packs, elevated pillows, and—his favorite—not to strain during bowel movements or sex. The latter of which Tommy wished was a problem. Each morning
his mother set out a clean, warm cloth to wash away the gunk and puss that collected overnight. If his vision was impaired, Tommy never said, but Helen knew
better: she'd been exploiting his blind spots since the accident.

Mary turned to Will. "You can let go of my hand now, sweetie." The
child had an iron grip. She'd set a washcloth out for him these last three
mornings. Boxing was barbaric. He might have clobbered that Newton
boy, but to look at his swollen face, you'd think he'd lost the fight.

"Sorry, Mrs. Sheehan," Will mumbled. Helen offered a weak smile
and squeezed Will's hand under the table.

"Pass plates." Ray clanged the knife off the china platter. Though
cursed with lazy eye and a simple disposition, Ray was Mary's favorite.
Her first. The gentle giant. Hands the size of a dinner plate and a jaw as
strong as oak. He held up the crusty end cut. "Who wants first?"

Pete raised his plate and shouted, "I do."

"It's a monster." Ray furrowed his brow as he heaved the slice of meat
up and down on the fork, exaggerating its heft.

"I can tame it," Pete said with a laugh.

Ray slapped the meat on Pete's plate.

Mary said, "Will, honey, pick your face up off the plate." The boy's
ears turned a shade of red that reminded Mary of tomato slices. Helen
scratched his back. The little lamb did care about something.

"I got one for ya," Helen whispered in Will's ear. "Why are elephants' feet flat?"

Ray called, "Who wants second from the end?"

Will pushed his chair back and ran from the room. Everyone froze. Ray hovered the next slice over Tommy's plate as Will's feet pattered up the stairs. The family looked up, following the footfalls down the hallway. A beat later the four corners of Tommy's bed scraped across the floor.

"He's blubbering," Hollister said.

"Shut it," Tommy snapped.

Mary glanced at Hollister licking peach syrup off his fingers. "Not a word when he returns." Mary pointed at her oldest son. "Ray?"

"What did I do?"

"Who raised you?"

"You did."

"Watch it."

"What? You did."

"Serve your sister first. You know better." Manners were forgotten when such a spread was prepared. Mary had popped a quart of elderberry wine, two cans of peaches, and some spinach. Helen had baked the potatoes herself and prepared the roast so her mother could take a nap—worn down by nerves, she explained. Cooking was a point of pride for young Helen. The girl had learned to cook the time Mary had traveled to Ireland to tend to her sick, pregnant sister. The swaddled Cousin Pete accompanied her on the crossing back, her sister having died during labor.

"Pass your plate, small fry," Ray said. "This beast could feed the neighborhood."

Indeed it could. The money Joseph had sent her to take the boys for a few days covered the roast and more. She'd prepared corned beef, baked chicken with potatoes, and now the roast beef. She wouldn't allow his boys to let their appetites go like her children had when their father died; the Lord needed his servants strong at times like these. As for the money, she'd long given up trying to convince Joseph that the weekly stipend for his mother was far too high. He knew the price of food and that his mother ate like a bird. The weekly check covered the entire family's food bills. And with the three children working, and now Ray's promotion, the family's income had never been higher; Mary was even considering raising Ray's weekly allowance so he could spoil a girl. She collected all the checks and doled out the spending money. She knew Tommy hadn't quit the gambling. His wardrobe alone suggested something fishy. But Helen reported he was more careful since his accident. Besides, he would marry soon and move out; he needed to learn to handle money. With the house coming rent-free, Mary, for the first time in her life, no longer needed to work. Joseph now insisted Cousin Pete should attend college; Helen, normal school. The girl had already passed Mary in formal schooling. Joseph discouraged her from taking jobs, but Helen was hardheaded, like her father. At six she'd told her mother she no longer needed to be tucked in; at ten she was having her tea and toast while reading the first editions before her brothers had even risen from bed. There was already talk of another summer stint ushering at the Savoy. And just last week Her Highness had brought home smoked salmon packaged in a tin—from Oregon, no less. Mary had searched for her daughter's secret stash. Helen hated parting with her earnings and had told her mother so on many occasions, and weekly called her grown brothers nitwits for turning over their salaries. Mary let her daughter's opinions pass with the breeze. Helen was thirteen. She didn't know how good she had it.

Mary passed a plate over her daughter's head to Tommy. Poor Helen folded her napkin in squares, nibbling her bottom lip. The gravy on her plate congealed around the beef. "Eat," Mary said.

Helen wound her foot around the leg of Will's empty chair pulling it toward her.

Tom and his only daughter had been as thick as thieves. The funeral had churned up the past. She'd bitten the priest who dragged her from Tom's burial. And who could forget drunken Ray rowing far out into the South Watuppa to sob? Mary hoped, and yet didn't, that Elizabeth's death might toughen Will's Highlands skin. She admired his softness. The Bartletts would not suffer the material losses of the Sheehans, but she knew Will would now have a hole in his childhood armor, and that the hole would metastasize unless he devised methods to disguise it. Helen was a master of disguise.

Mary said, "You remember how hard it was." Helen nodded. "Let's give him a minute."

Suddenly Helen burst into tears. Mary caught Tommy's good eye as she brushed her daughter's cheek with the back of her hand. She whispered, "I'll go." She winked at Tommy as she rose from the table. She spot-checked plates. "Pete, Hollister, eat your vegetables."

"They will," Tommy said.

When Mary's footfalls reached the staircase, Hollister asked Tommy, "So where's the dance tonight?" He jabbed his fork into the beef and sawed off another block of meat. Chewing, he scratched at the long scab running from his clavicle to his jaw and swallowed in one quick motion. "Any girls gonna be there?"

"Of course, you dummy!" Helen barked, eager to take Hollister down a peg. "It wouldn't be a dance without girls."

"You don't say."

She shot him one of her "I'm smarter than you and always will be" looks.

Ray said, "Wouldn't that be something?" He examined the end of his knife and licked it. "A bunch of fellas dancing together."

Cousin Pete put his left arm out and his right hand to his chest and swayed.

Ray pointed his knife. "Something like that, yeah."

Pete fell into a bag of giggles. He had the Bartlett habit of biting his lower lip when he laughed.

"Put those fellas in the loony bin," Hollister said, his brow furrowed.

"I've seen *you* dance with a boy in the pavilion," Helen said, learning forward in her chair. "*You* seemed to enjoy it."

"That was a gas, a joke on the dumb music." Hollister shrugged and popped a wad of bread in his mouth.

"Was not!" she barked, waving her folk at Hollister. "I saw *you* do it!"

"You saw nothing."

"Goof."

"Dingbat."

Tommy smacked the table. "Enough!"

Ray scratched the back of his head. "I danced with a girl named Paula at the academy once." Ray's attendance at dances had dwindled along with his success rate with girls, though his recent promotion to supervisor in the female-dominated spinning room had helped his confidence. "She was like, like . . ."

"Like what?" Pete asked, nearly jumping out of his chair.

Ray dragged the carving knife across the red center of the roast. "Like, like, beautiful."

Tommy caught Hollister's eye, and the boy cough-laughed into his napkin. Ray didn't notice either way. Tommy leaned back in his chair. He'd left his tie, jacket, and hat on the hook by the door so as not to bring attention to his evening plans—it was work, after all. He booked acts, did promotion, and took tickets for Mr. Giles in Tiverton and for Mr. Dubois at the Sandy Beach Pavilion. He'd had the jobs for years, and he couldn't imagine giving them up. But tonight he hadn't much of a stomach for the event, the last of the postcentennial dances. Earlier that day he'd stood with Helen near Elizabeth Bartlett's grave and been one of the first to place a flower on her casket. Mrs. Bartlett had encouraged his writing and helped him latch on at the newspaper. She used to read and correct the short copy he wrote for the community newsletters—pieces about fishing parties on the South Watuppa Pond, inclement weather on the islands, beauty pageants on the Cape, or regatta races in Newport (he loved the races)—filler columns mostly, but she took the time. When his first piece came out in the *Globe,* she clipped and framed it. It still hung over his bed.

Tommy tossed his napkin on his plate. He looked around the table. They don't get it, he thought. None of them do, except Helen.

The table chatter turned to roller coasters. "I rode it five times in one day," Hollister bragged.

"Really?" Pete said.

"The operator is my pal," Ray said. "Told me to come by anytime. No charge. That's free."

"Really?"

"And at Lincoln Park this summer—"

Helen drummed her fork against the side of her plate.

Ray blinked.

"What?" Tommy snapped. She stared at her older brother. He'd been steamed up for weeks. He was figuring something. Something big. But he'd kept his trap shut.

Tommy leaned forward in his chair, his strawberry eye glistening. "You got something to say, twerp?"

She gripped both ends of her fork. Her arms stiffened but it wouldn't bend. "Damn it!" She heaved it over Hollister's head into the wall. Ray took a bite of roast; his jaw slowly churning.

"That's all you got?" Tommy chirped.

Helen jumped up. "Enough. All of you. Chattering like a women's knitting circle. Nothing will ever be the same. Not never ever. Mrs. Bartlett is dead! Will's more bruised than the roast! And that fool"—pointing at Hollister—"did something screwy. But you half-wits chatter on about dance halls, baseball, and now, the Lincoln Park coaster. What is it with you pudding heads? Will's mom croaked!"

"She's my ma too."

"Shut up!"

Helen snapped up her knife and raised it above her head. The boys ducked. She had just learned the word "puerile," reading *Pride and Prejudice*. The word came to her now.

"Such puerility!" The boys exchanged puzzled glances. "Look it up!" she shouted, hurling the knife into the wall, tearing the rose-colored paper. This was her mother's doing; this faux normalcy was for the benefit of the Bartlett boys, but Helen knew it would only delay the mad sadness until they were home with their mute father, alone in their rooms with their mother's ghost.

"You have quite an arm," Tommy said, breaking the silence. The boys laughed. "Red Sox should have signed you instead of the Kansas Cyclone."

Helen slumped down in her chair, burying her face in her napkin.

Ray held up the last slice of roast. "Who wants the butt?" Bloody juice and white knots of grease pooled into the recesses of the carving platter. Tommy said to save the charred end for his mother. They all knew one of her guilty pleasures was gnawing on the crusty end. Helen wondered what her mother had done to always get the butt end. She smirked at the thought, then hardened as she remembered the previous night. What was he doing here?

Passing the balustrade on her return from the toilet last night, Helen had heard voices and hid in the shadows. She'd caught a glimpse of her mother embracing Mr. Bartlett. Actually, Mr. Bartlett was kneeling in a puddle of rainwater he'd tracked in, weeping into her mother's skirt. Helen's first thought was that he'd come to take the boys home, but given the late hour, she knew that was silly. Her mother had stroked his head and whispered. Suddenly he'd sprung to his feet and hissed something that caused her mother's face to blanch. His arm shot to the ceiling, knocking the chandelier over the door. The crystals rang out and the light flickered. He'd shown up drunk to make demands of her mother. All men bowed before the bottle. But booze dealt a final blow, and he collapsed into Momma's arms. She led him into his old study. The door swung back, but the humidity had warped it, and the latch didn't take. From the balcony, Helen heard the springs on Otis Bartlett's old leather couch whine. Helen waited for shouts, but none came. Helen knew adults did things in the dark. She wasn't sure what exactly, but she'd seen the couples at the Savoy touch and coo when the actors got fresh on the screen. When the picture ended, they were all in a big hurry to get home and turn the lights out. And with Mrs. Bartlett barely cold! Helen thought to wake Ray and Tommy to investigate, but what then? Did the household really need another crisis? She decided to man her post; if her mother called, she would be Johnny-on-the-spot.

Helen had woken to the creaky hinges on the front door. She blinked in time to catch Joseph Bartlett's heels. She waited for her mother to exit the study. Nothing. What had he done? Helen wanted to slide down the banister and burst into the room, but her legs hadn't woken up yet. She heard rumblings down the hall. No doubt old lady Bartlett was hoisting herself out of bed for one of her frequent trips to the lav. If the old granny saw her, she'd have to lift her from the seat, so Helen tiptoed back to her bedroom. She thought her mother deserved what she got for not fighting back. What kind of spell had he cast on her? No man would ever own *her*.

She'd lain in bed replaying the scene. There were obstacles to saving her mother. First, who would believe her word over Mr. Bartlett's? And second, did her mother want saving? She had seen the old gal handle herself fine when Tommy stumbled home drunk. Surely Mr. Bartlett was no match for a woman as stout and cunning. All this guessing had her head spinning.

Tommy tapped her plate. "Eat up, sport."

Helen glared at her big brother. Feed the damn roast to the dogs. A good biscuit, like the English rounds she'd stolen from the corner grocery, and a cup of Earl Grey were all she required to balance herself.

Tommy poured himself another glass of wine. "You boys go easy on Will," he said. "Not a word about his black eyes. Remember, he's a killer."

"How much you make on the fight?" Ray nudged his brother with his elbow.

The simp didn't know when to shut up, Tommy thought. If his mother found out he'd wagered on Will's match, he'd have to forfeit the dough to the church and go visit the Father. The little smoke had battled his heart out. That Damian kid was the odds-on favorite. Tommy wasn't pleased to hear that Pete Newton wouldn't let the poor kid back in the house—he'd been living with the family downstairs since the fight—but old Pete was likely to get gassed some night soon and forget the whole thing.

"Yeah, you know." Tommy shrugged. "Enough to buy new choir books." He winked at his sister.

"I still can't figure how the pip-squeak did it," Hollister said. "Damian would give me trouble."

"He'd smash you," Helen said.

"Buzz off."

"Cretin. Clown. Crud."

"Watch it." Hollister raised his fist.

Ray clapped his hands. "More," he shouted.

"Loon. Lout. Loser."

"Why you little—" Hollister pushed back his chair.

Ray lunged past Cousin Pete and grabbed Hollister's chin in his meaty hand. "You're gonna have a heck of scar." He squeezed Hollister's cheeks together a few times as if checking the pressure in a bicycle tire. "How big was that piece of glass?"

"About this long." Hollister held his hands shoulder-width apart.

"Lucky it didn't cut your head off," Helen mused.

"Now sit down," Tommy said.

"The operator just went nuts, huh?" Ray knocked Hollister's chin with his fist and hunched over his plate shoveling home mounds of spinach. The man was muscle bound like their father.

"Crazy as a cornered rat." Hollister rubbed his chin.

When has *he* ever seen a cornered rat? Helen wondered. What a liar.

She'd gone to investigate, to find this deranged ride operator, and discover all this glass, but the carnival had left town the day after Taft's speech. Before going to the Sheehans', Hollister had spent the better part of the morning sequestered in his father's study. At one point, Tommy disappeared inside only to exit an hour later with a scowl running across his face as long as the Quequechan River. Hollister had hovered around Will's room acting queerly earnest. Since climbing down from the old oak in the yard, he had dried his tears and stood stoically at his father's side. He had even assisted Evelyn with the chores; this was something Helen had never seen.

By today, the stoic, helpful Hollister had regressed into the spoiled Highlands brat she knew well. He'd started calling Will "pig face" on account of his black eyes and swollen cheek, and more than once shouted at Helen to get out of his grandmother's house. Luckily, Joseph had stopped by and fetched Hollister for a follow-up with Dr. Boyle. She sensed whatever mischief Hollister had cooked up in the fun house would end badly for him. The Bartletts were cursed.

"You hear that?" Ray said.

"What?" Hollister said.

"Shh." Helen raised a finger. "Footsteps."

They eyeballed the creaking boards across the upstairs hallway, down the stairs and through the breezeway. Ray dumped warm juices on Will's and his mother's cold meat. He held each plate up as Helen dished peaches, Tommy scooped spinach from the nearly full bowl, and Cousin Pete tossed slices of bread. As the door swung open, each made eating noises. Forks scraped on plates. Will scurried to his seat. Mary stopped, glanced at the flatware on the carpet, but continued to the head of the table.

"Well, now." Mary snapped her napkin. "How's the dinner?" Ray and Pete spoke at once, their mouths full of roast. "Who's being stingy with their spinach?"

"Hollister didn't have any," Helen offered, sticking out her tongue.

"Pass it over." Mary dished out the limp greens and looked at Tommy. "Before you leave, help your brother close the windows."

"There's no rain up there," Ray objected, always one to avoid the simplest household chores. He would refit the pipes, but not lift a dish. Just like his father.

Mary set her fork down. How old had Tommy Sr. been when he'd proposed? Nineteen? Twenty? It was high time Ray married. There had to be some ugly duckling out there for the misfit. "My ankles are throbbing. A rainstorm is coming . . . Tommy, you tell Little Doc to drive easy to the dance. No showboating for the gals. It's gonna be slippery. And you're in early. I need you in the morning."

"I'm just taking tickets tonight."

"Take Ray along. Introduce him to a nice girl."

"*Mother.*" Ray groaned.

"Who's having pie?"

Hollister took a deep breath, then gulped down a forkful of spinach. He nodded at Helen and then kicked his brother under the table. Will clutched his shin. "You got something in your eye, little brother?"

"Hollister, that's enough," Mary said.

"What'd I do?"

Will's eyes welled up. Cousin Pete snickered. The older boys excused themselves to take care of the windows. Walking past, Tommy smacked Hollister in the back of the head.

"Thomas Francis Sheehan!"

"What?"

Ray clutched Tommy in a headlock. "Want me to take care of him, Ma?"

Mary jumped to her feet. "RAY, OUT! TOMMY, OUT! HOLLISTER, OUT!" She threw her napkin into her chair. "Pete, stop that laughing. Nothing's funny." She slapped Ray's arm to release Tommy. "I want those windows down in ten minutes."

"What about the pie?" Hollister protested.

"Out!" Mary shooed them from the room.

"More pie for us," Helen whispered. She found Will's hand under the table and squeezed.

ORANGE REVOLUTION

Joseph sat alone under the South Park shelter, drumming a tall brown envelope off his kneecaps. He picked at Hannah Cleveland's orange wax seal with his thumb. It was Joseph's routine to stroll in South Park on Sunday afternoons. Since Lizzy's death in June, one of the boys or Mary Sheehan would accompany him. He sat in a shady corner away from families and the August sun. There was no breeze off the bay. It was promising to be a scorcher.

He had just come from his annual state-of-the-mill brunch with Hannah Cleveland, the matriarch and largest stockholder of the Cleveland Mill. He'd known Hannah his entire life but could never shake the feeling that she was always testing him, waiting for him to slip up. He visited her house often as a boy. With her son, Stanton, away at boarding school most of the year, Joseph became his surrogate. While Otis and the colonel talked shop in the study, Joseph would sit on his hands, scared stiff that he might break something valuable. And there were many valuable pieces to break. She claimed to possess the largest collection of hand-painted porcelain waterfowl outside England. Waiting, Hannah would quiz Joseph on his studies. On one visit she went so far as to deprive him of cookies for failing to know the capital of Indiana. She gave birthday gifts but derived fiendish pleasure from hiding them somewhere in the fifteen-room High Street mansion. Joseph spent the better part of each birthday tiptoeing through rooms whose items he dared not touch.

Though always eccentric, in recent years her behavior had become erratic. "Crazy" was what Lizzy had called it the time Hannah came for Christmas dinner bearing Easter baskets.

The state-of-the-mill brunch was held, as it was every year, in the atrium. Jefferson Cleveland had built it for Hannah's fortieth birthday and stocked it with exotic tropical plants and golden pear and orange trees. The luncheon was mostly ceremonial, like the English prime minster receiving the queen's blessing on the government's annual budget, but then again, all queens have their pet projects, and Hannah announced hers before the coffee cooled. Last year she'd grown incensed after reading newspaper reports on the living conditions of female workers in Bangor. The papers were thick with testimonials from fourteen-year-old girls during the strike, and Hannah ate them up. She became convinced that Cleveland could do more for its women. Joseph agreed. Hannah had announced that, yes, she was pleased with her 14 percent return but was willing, in the short term, to earn perhaps 10 percent for the sake of "her girls." She instructed Joseph to expand the mill library, serve free milk in the lunchroom, devote more money to college scholarships, and provide free medical care for company children. When Joseph reminded her that those were proposals he'd made in the past but that the figures showed returns more like 8 percent, she brushed him away with a wave of her hand. "Make it real," she'd barked. (The free milk perk received positive coverage in the workers' publication *Labor Standard*—a rarity for owners—and Hannah read it enthusiastically, though it drew the ire of other Highlands families who now had to provide free milk of their own.)

But today's meeting had not followed the usual script of proposal, caveat, food. This was unsettling, like watching a three-legged dog run. Coffee, muffins, salmon, eggs, all served and picked over, and still, no new pet project on the table. She just sat opposite him, displaying a knowing grin. She wore her usual home uniform, a tea gown of orange china silk with satin trim and the gold chain of her Italian handbag coiled around her elbow—no doubt stuffed with hundreds of dollars. *Just in case!* she liked to say. Was she angry with him? Wasn't production up? Hadn't she approved of the recent wage hikes? Did he forget to deliver her invitation to the Prairie Sponsors dinner? Did she not approve of Lizzy's funeral arrangements? What did Matt Borden say to her in the cemetery?

Hannah rang her bell, and Perkins brought out two cups of orange sorbet and then set a thick envelope at Joseph's feet. Now she was ready.

"Joseph, I've never liked the textile business. It itches," she began, licking her spoon clean. "I can't sew. Wool makes me sneeze. All that lint in the factory; it's bad for the lungs. Your father—" she blurted out, surprising herself, then matter-of-factly continued, "Lint. That's what killed the man." She paused to take a scoop of sorbet. She pointed her spoon at something down the hill. "My people were whalers, rather chilly people, but fearless. They owned shares in New Bedford boats. No crazy Ahabs in the bunch. When I met Jefferson, he was an average-looking man—liked clementines, ate fish. His father made nice shirts. He was suitable to Daddy because he wasn't going to move us into *his* house, and so we married. He improved himself, took risks, became a rich man. Fine. But he loved cotton more than me, Joseph. He loved his looms more than me. He loved ring-spinning frames more than his own son. He knew Eli Whitney's middle name but not my sister Jackie's. And his favorite color of dye: blue."

"Mrs. Cleveland, please." Joseph coiled his napkin around his left wrist.

Hannah raised her palm. "Young man, shush," she piped.

Joseph was not prepared for any kind of widow-to-widower regret fest with batty Hannah Cleveland. He knew he'd made mistakes—they happen—but he loved Lizzy. And damn it, Lizzy loved textiles.

What old Hannah really disliked was living like so many of her Victorian Highlands sisters: stinking rich and no one to enjoy it with. Her arthritic fingers had undermined her last joy: the ladies bridge circle. But who decides which women get to live so damn long while others die in their prime? Joseph tightened the napkin.

Hannah paused to consider her sorbet. Orange was her favorite flavor and color. In fact, Cleveland had a whole line of orange fabric named after her. Joseph noticed that the tablecloth was orange, and the centerpiece orange yarrow. Come to think of it, they'd enjoyed orange juice, apricot muffins, smoked salmon, runny fired eggs, and even cantaloupe. Could she be suffering from some sort of orange overload?

"I may be as nutty as Ahab now, Joseph, but I'm done with textiles for good. And I'm done living in this hollow castle."

Keep going, Joseph thought. He unwound the napkin and color returned to his hand. Sell the mill and set me free.

"I've broken the trust holding Stanton's stock. In three months this house will be sold and I will be living with my sister on an orange grove in Saint Augustine." Her white-gloved finger pointed to the envelope at Joseph's feet. "You are now the majority owner of Cleveland. She's yours. When I go, my twenty-five percent will transfer to you as well." She paused for him to speak. Her eyes narrowed. "You going to be sick? Take a drink, son." She lifted his water glass. "There now, take a moment," she said.

He gulped the water. Sweat glistened on his brow.

"Just remember, while I'm still alive, don't mess up." She caught him glancing at the envelope. "Go ahead, take a peek."

Joseph cut the orange seal with his butter knife. Indeed, there was a letter from her Boston attorney certifying the dissolution of the trust and the transfer of Stanton's stock. He scratched his chin with the stub of his pinkie finger. He tasted his breakfast in his throat. He wanted to move to Middletown, run the dairy farm. Though he knew he'd never had a choice, until now he could kid himself that he was just another one of Hannah's employees, like Perkins here: Perkins delivered orange sorbet; Joseph delivered 14 percent returns.

"So? What do you think?" Hannah set her chin in her palms like a little girl. The early onset of cataracts had begun to cloud her blue eyes.

Joseph mopped his brow and stared down at his plate, at a hardening pool of yellow egg yolk. He took a deep breath and held the air in his chest to keep from collapsing.

"Now, I know what you're noodling, dear boy," she said, standing. "You're noodling, How can I repay such a generous gift? Well, I'll tell you: orange patterns." She snapped her fingers. "Perkins!"

The butler came forward holding sheets of fabric that had been ripped into strips and then pinned back together in alternating color schemes: orange and white, orange and blue, orange and yellow, and on and on.

"Take these to my designers and see what they come up with."—*my designers*; they would always be her designers—"Questions?"

Joseph shook his head.

"Good. Perkins, put these in his automobile." Hannah picked up her cane and stood. "Now, give me your arm, dear boy. Walk with me."

Joseph escorted her into the heart of the steamy atrium. He ducked under its green leaves, the air sweet and earthy. He had a sudden urge to dig his hands into soil, to fill his nostrils with the scent of turned earth. How was it that a man who did nothing but produce never felt like he produced anything?

Hannah sat down on an iron bench under an orange tree. The back of the bench was forged to resemble grape vines. Tiny fruit hung off the ends of the finely crafted leaves. She scratched the space beside her. "Sit with me?" she asked, more a plea than a command.

The ironwork dug into Joseph's back. Hannah reached up and picked a ripe orange off a branch. She held it up for Joseph to sniff and then deposited it in his jacket pocket. She nuzzled her head under his long arm.

He set his hand over hers. He whispered, "Please forgive me."

"I love oranges, Joseph," she mooned. "I love all things orange."

* * *

A family at one end of the South Park shelter packed their picnic and left. Joseph took a lap around the perimeter. Satisfied he knew no one was hiding in the shrubbery, he slid the stock certificates into the light. A crazy woman had just given him two million dollars. Part of him felt liberated—now he was running *his* business and *not* Stanton's—but then why did he felt so trapped? When he'd finally told Lizzy about his involvement in the fire, she'd quoted scripture: "By mercy and truth iniquity is purged: and by the fear of the Lord men depart from evil." For six years he had lived faithfully by the words "mercy," "truth," and "fear." He softly fingered the certificates. Perhaps she'd been right.

"Shouldn't those be in a safe?"

Joseph sprung off the bench as if a bee had stung his behind. The certificates scattered over the cement.

"Look what I caused." A slim woman stepped forward. The shadow cast by her enormous wide-brimmed straw hat swallowed Joseph. "Can I help?"

"No." He blocked her view of the certificates. "It's nothing. Something for my son. School honor certificates. He's a wonderful speller. A math whiz." He scrambled on all fours shuffling the sheets. He rolled them into a cylinder and crawled forward to retrieve his errant straw boater, thinking such a woman had probably never seen a stock certificate—she dressed too simply: straight blue broadcloth walking skirt, plain tucked blouse with three-quarter sleeves and a simple flat collar, chiffon with frayed satin bow. Her white canvas high-top boots were beaten like a boxer's nose. No, she'd never seen a stock certificate in her life.

"Hollister or Will?"

"Pardon?" Joseph dusted off his hat.

"Who is the math whiz? Hollister or Will?"

Joseph looked around to see if anyone else had heard. He realized he was still on his knees and jumped to his feet. He smiled in case any of the Sunday regulars recognized him speaking with this pushy woman. Slowly he came to the conclusion he'd never laid eyes on her before. It was none of her damn business what was in the envelope. Though, was she a teacher? When was the last time he'd been to their school? Had he ever been to their school? He stepped back into the shadow of the corner. She was tall. She had a round face with sparkling blue eyes and a toothy grin. Her hands were thick; a band of tiny scars wound over her left knuckle. She'd spent some time outside in the sun. Rather an attractive schoolteacher. He said, "Hollister in math. Will in spelling." He bounced the certificates off his knee and tucked them back in the envelope.

"Nice try, Mr. Bartlett." She playfully poked the nose of her parasol into his shoulder as she backed down the shelter steps toward the water. Two small boys raced past chasing a ball. "But this girl knows a stock certificate when she sees one."

Joseph followed her down the grassy slope thankful the afternoon heat had kept the regulars indoors or at the beach.

She stopped and extended her hand like a man and Joseph took it. He met her eye; a strained expression came over her face. She squeezed his hand. *Who is she?*

"Mr. Bartlett, I've been meaning to call, but that, as you will soon learn, isn't possible for a girl like me."

No, it wasn't. Not even now, whoever she was. Joseph felt the eyes of passersby pinned to his back. He eased his grip on her hand, but she held tight.

She turned her wrist down to inspect his hand. "They say you lost a section of your pinkie finger. I figured it was in a boating accident."

Joseph pulled his hand away. "A cotton bale crushed it." He itched his chin with the stub. "My first day. A long time ago."

"So you rode in with the cotton."

"My father made me work in each department when I came back to Fall River."

"And you didn't mind going from Matt Borden's buying house to the shop floor."

"Otis knew which way the wind blew before the clouds."

"Oh, your famous father. A dying breed of man. I'd have liked to have met him."

Sensing more eyes on his back, Joseph began to walk away from the shelter. In the distance, he saw the colored flags blowing on top of the supports of the Sandy Beach toboggan ride. Molten clouds hung over the beach. Will and Helen had taken the trolley down to the amusement park earlier that afternoon. They were surely in the water by now.

"What do you want, Miss . . ."

"Strong. Sarah Strong." She smiled.

Joseph took another step and then stopped and stared at her. He rolled his eyes and shook his head. Sarah Strong—socialist, suffragist, sociopath—dubbed Sarah the Strangler by the Bangor, Maine, mill owners for her ability to choke production and stir violence. Otis had warned him of women like Sarah Strong: greyhounds with wolves' teeth. His mother called them man-haters. Strong worked for a splinter group of the International Workers of the World, a militant union-organizing machine whose basic tenet was to desecrate capitalism. A skilled orator, she helped the IWW convince Bangor's skilled workers—weavers, loom fixers, dyers, and spinners, plus scabs—to join the unskilled in their strike last year. Something George Pierce would die before letting happen in Fall River.

That move had proved a difference-maker, and the owners finally agreed to wage increases, though Bangor would never be the same. Seven years earlier, in 1904, Fall River had seen a similar walkout. Eighty-five mills, sans Cleveland and Borden's Iron Works, locked out their workers, refusing to negotiate wages. After six months on bread and water, the workers, many near destitute, returned not more than a nickel richer. To replace the thousands who had moved away, the owners found a new wave of immigrant dreamers. But each generation took the work out of necessity, and each swore their children would never slave before a deafening machine. The Yankees who had worked for Jefferson Cleveland were replaced by the English, then the Irish; since then, waves of French-Canadians and Portuguese had arrived to sweat and die in the textile mills of Fall River.

"Good day, Ms. Strong." Joseph turned east and hurriedly made tracks for his motorcar.

Strong lost the grin and gave chase. "I want just a moment, Mr. Bartlett. And if you refuse to hear me out, I will scream at the top of my lungs and swear to each man in this park that I am your whore."

Joseph stopped and took out his handkerchief and patted down his brow and neck. He'd hit a trifecta of crazy: Evelyn, Hannah, and now this Sarah character. But the first two were benign. This one could exile him from every decent circle in town, even the few he actually enjoyed. He'd read about her in the *Globe*: a New Hampshire farm girl is forced to work in Nashua mills. At seventeen her mother dies and she uses their savings to attend Mount Holyoke College. When she graduates with honors to limited career options, a cousin in Manchester writes with news of an impending strike and bossy male overseers, and Strong reads this as a message from above to devote her every breath to labor terrorism.

Joseph eyed her up and down. The most feared agitator in all New England twirled her parasol like an innocent virgin. A real outlaw. The Robin Hood or Jesse James of union organizing, depending on your point of view. Outwardly she looked sane, showing no signs of forced famine, excessive clubbing, or hours of Chinese water torture. She had approached Joseph on a sunny August day in front of the whole town as if they were school chums. Normally, she wouldn't be allowed to come within fifty yards of a man like him. But picking a Sunday, knowing he was alone, that he was even in the city on an August weekend and not in the country—she'd been watching him.

Joseph felt the charge he got during his clandestine meetings with George Pierce. Coming off her victory in Bangor, he guessed Strong wanted to sniff out allies and brew trouble before the IWW organizers picked their next town to persecute. Lawrence was also rumored to be making strike preparations. But he didn't sit at the association's table. He was no good to her.

"Walk behind me, Ms. Strong. I will listen, but stay behind me—understand?" Joseph walked toward the toboggan ride.

She nipped at his heels. "Fall River women demand better wages."

"Who says? You?"

"You know as well as I the hardships these women face, Mr. Bartlett."

"Do I? My operatives enjoy many benefits."

"That's why I'm contacting *you*, sir. You understand, unlike your peers, that these hardships don't need to be endured. I came to Fall River to record their grievances. I'll submit my report to my friends to see if the time is again ripe to challenge the owners."

"Your friends? Agitators in the IWW?"

"They are fighters for justice."

Joseph wondered if she was always this self-righteous. It was like talking to Matt Borden about the value of a dollar. Joseph tapped the stock certificates against his leg. The value of a dollar. What do I know?

"What do you want with me? The association doesn't listen to me."

"But you belong to their club. I'm asking nicely for you to consider my proposal."

Asking nicely. Joseph smiled broadly. He considered disappearing into the crowd filing into Sandy Beach, meeting Will and Helen at the circle swing as they'd planned, and then changing into his swimming trunks. The chalkboard at the entrance listed the water temperature at seventy degrees. Boys on roller skates clamored passed on the boardwalk, the last boy unsteady, his arms flapping like a gull. "Bend your knees," Joseph called. "Now push, don't run. That's it. Good." Joseph couldn't remember the last time he'd taken the boys figure skating on the South Watuppa.

Sarah Strong leaned toward him. "I was a fast skater once."

Joseph hated this position, the middleman to get to the bigger fish. When would he wash his hands of all this backdoor dealing? What had it ever gotten him? But he was curious. He'd heard only rumors about these fiery women. Last year in Bangor, one had stolen a police badge and ticket pad and then patrolled the streets in a homespun uniform, issuing citations to mill agents' motorcars. But left unchecked, Sarah Strong and her cronies would bring more than high jinks to Fall River. They'd bring picket signs, hate mongering, scab baiting, and perhaps, the dynamite stolen from the Bangor armory last year. There'd been bombings in New York. For all the Fall River system's faults, Joseph wouldn't trade it for a riot. Apparently, Sarah Strong was too stupid to realize her actions only made the owners stronger.

He leaned over the white picket fence that surrounded the wooden maze of supports that was the toboggan ride. Helen's favorite. The downslope of the last hill lay within arm's reach. Strong stood a dozen pickets away. She opened the parasol she'd been carrying. The shade of it created a large shadow around her. A toboggan car jittered up the first hill. The tow chain clackity-clacked between the two-by-four wooden crossbeams. Another car zoomed down the last slope. Screams rose above the chattering, then subsided. At the top of the first hill, the riders raised their arms.

"Your proposal, Ms. Strong. I'm waiting."

"I want to show you something you've never seen, Joseph." Already she was using his first name. He wondered what about his demeanor put women at ease so quickly. He waved to one of his mill clerks walking inside the park. "If you saw the living conditions. It's inhuman. The boardinghouses are unsanitary."

"They can find other work."

"No, they can't. They're slaves to the loom. Standing all day, and then home to cook, mend clothes, and nurse sick children. The men leave for a pub, or worse. It's an endless cycle. Have you ever been to the edge of the Flint? To the worst ones?"

"I know of it."

"Aren't you a bit curious?"

"I have other business."

"Come see them with me and I'll make my proposal. You can leave or join us."

Join? Joseph smiled again. The woman was indeed crazy as a cornered rat. Join her in what? His own suicide? Though he was curious to see if the exaggerated reports in the *Labor Standard* were to be believed. Children playing in sewage? Girls as young as fourteen prostituting themselves? He'd once asked Evelyn if she thought such stories were to be believed. "When the Irish lived in those units, there was no problems," she'd said. "Those dirty Portuguese thrive in the grime." Just once, Joseph wanted to ask Evelyn why, if Irish were so great, did she live at his house?

"If I don't agree to your offer, what then? Another screaming fit?" Joseph kneaded the handkerchief in his wet palm.

"No." She moved down the fence toward him. She slipped her fingers under the top of her blouse. "I'll rip my blouse and run to the first policeman I find, screaming, *'Rapist, rapist!'*" A toboggan car rocketed past.

Joseph scratched his chin and scanned the crowd for Mary Sheehan—she'd save him.

"Five seconds."

"You're crazy."

"Three."

"Where?"

"Ever been to the Drovers Café in the Flint?"

"I'll find it."

"In one hour, then. I'll be waiting." She winked at Joseph and then spun on her heel, almost poking out his eye with the point of the parasol.

He dabbed his forehead. No woman had ever winked at him.

* * *

Joseph found his green Pope-Hartford right where he'd left it, though Wiggins had raised the top to keep the sun off his fair Irish skin. Most of the other mill agents drove large touring cars or Overlands, but Joseph preferred the tight ride of the Pope. Lizzy had been clamoring for a Cadillac. Of course, he thought. Otis would have driven a Cadillac too.

Wiggins was snoring.

"All up, old man," Joseph shouted. Wiggins pinched his bulbous nose and blinked himself awake. Albert Wiggins was a cousin of Evelyn's and known affectionately as Minimum Al for his paltry work habits. Joseph grabbed the flask teetering on the dashboard. He screwed on the cap and wedged it under the passenger seat. Joseph ditched his cap and tie and told Wiggins he was going to the beach. "If I miss Will, tell him I'll see him for dinner." Wiggins wore a flop cap popular with the men from abroad. Joseph told him to hand it over. Joseph had intentionally stepped in dog shit on the walk over and now explained to Wiggins he needed his shoes also. Joseph's shiny Johnston & Murphy leather loafers would be a sure giveaway in the Flint. Wiggins, still groggy, handed over the items. He took Joseph's envelope and puttered up the hill.

Joseph took a trolley up President Avenue, then walked to Drovers. It being Sunday, and hot as hell, there was a lazy mood in the streets. Families bought foodstuffs from peddlers' carts and the few open shops. Young men under awnings passed cigarettes. A middle-aged man in a red vest eyed Joseph suspiciously. They rubbed shoulders as Joseph passed. Down the block a woman leaned against a lamppost licking an ice cream. She caught Joseph's eye and followed him into Drovers. Inside, he passed by Sarah Strong's table, knocking it with his foot, and then turned back outside. He glanced at the lamppost and caught sight of a young man guiding the ice cream woman down the block.

Across the street were four identical triple-deckers with mansard roofs and clapboard siding with narrow corner boards. Each had a type of handcrafted ornamentation at the cornice and doorframes not seen in recent years. Piano music stopped and started; Will was learning similar songs. The small yards were well tended. Herbs and tomato plants were cut into small beds out back. These were the homes of civil servants and overseers, not unskilled workers. The sun dipped, but the heat was still oppressive. The windows were thrown open. In one, a woman pulled a thread from between her lips and eased it through the eye of a needle. In another, a bare-chested boy shined a row of shoes, the tips hanging over the street. A man handed Joseph a flyer for a concert at the local parish.

Sarah Strong stood beside him. "I didn't recognize you." Again with the wink. Hopefully she was the only one not fooled. No one would believe it if they saw them together. "These aren't what I want to show you. Let's walk."

"Where to?"

"The edge of the Flint. Cogsworth country."

The Cogsworth Mill's boardinghouses and tenements were routinely singled out in the labor's papers for health violations. Cogsworth Sr. was among the first mill owners to stroll through Quebec offering carrots of salvation to desperate farmhands. For a month's pay, the wagoner would deliver the novices to a Cogsworth boardinghouse and then to the mill, where a supervisor would note the novice's name and impose a weekly garnish, usually twice the agreed amount, to pay back the mill for advancing the wagoner his fee. This neighborhood, Sarah explained, was one of five she'd been researching. It appeared she'd rented rooms nearby.

"Among the unhappiest of the unhappy," Joseph said. "Your mission won't prove to be much of a tussle."

"The mostly Irish police force, whose fathers and mothers toiled in the mills a generation before, rarely come to these streets. They wait till the noise of rebellion swells to their triple-decker apartments in Corky Row."

"I know all this."

Sarah shook her head at him. She ended the travelogue with a short historical summary that Joseph had no desire to be reminded of: "At first, the mill owners supplied the rooms to house workers who had no rent money or transportation. Villages sprung up around the mill for the workers. Now they trap them."

He had to admit, mill owners did not make very good landlords. Jefferson Cleveland had built houses in the 1870s and shortly thereafter sold them to his workers at cost.

Nearing the Cogsworth area, the scenery changed. So did the smell.

"See how the buildings are clustered close on both sides so they loom over the street, affording no relief from the stench of garbage," Sarah said, and spit into the street. "Each tenement houses four to six families. The yards, or dirt piles, breed dust and more garbage. The granite bedrock foundations made service pipes impossibly expensive, the owners never pressured the mayor, so anything built before 1880 has either no plumbing or a poorly rigged system." Communal privies stood in clustered courtyards. Some families rigged pipes down windows.

In the front of the next tenement, a square section of lawn had been cordoned off with stakes and black ribbon. Funny, Joseph thought, the dirt in the squared area was the color of cinnamon.

"Now that is queer," he said aloud, observing that in the center of the plot the grass was green, or well, sort of green, and brown. And wet. He turned to Sarah. "Water in this heat?"

"Cesspool burps," Sarah said. "They haven't seen the honey wagon in six months." Sarah dipped her toe into a creeping stream of black muck lining the gutter. "Cogsworth had mastered every legal maneuver to make even the most ardent statehouse representative weary. These drains are not far from their water source." She wiped her toe on a piece of paper in the street. "Dysentery, anyone?" She kicked the shit paper at Joseph, and he leapt backward, nearly tripping.

A boy in overalls and a dirty undershirt passed, pulling a dog missing a hind leg and towing, in turn, a cart of iron scrapes. "Move out," the boy shouted, as he marched up on folks, who split and came back without looking at him or his cargo. Joseph stopped in the road when he passed.

Sarah pulled his sleeve. "That boy is a few years younger than Will. Probably never been to school. His mother is a prostitute." Joseph continued walking. How did she know so much? He could see where standing water had evaporated in the dips in the road, leaving behind a dirty green fungus. Mosquitoes swarmed around bits of rotten fruit in the gutter. In the distance, a rooster crowed.

Every few blocks, a ground-floor door was missing. In its place hung a curtain of tobacco smoke. Crowds of men stood inside carousing, their laughter and curses reaching the street. Men in rough clothes smoking clay pipes climbed up the cellar stairs hauling pails of ale. Watching the exchanges, Joseph bumped shoulders with a woman wrapped in a dark shawl. Ale sloshed out from under the shawl, splattering his shoes.

"Kitchen bars. Rum houses. The dealers distribute too," Sarah said. "All in violation of the boardinghouse rules. Want to go enforce your owner friends' rules?" At a distinct disadvantage, Joseph kept moving from one grossity to another instead of challenging Sarah. She'd continue to bait him no matter what he said. He had no answer. He was not the savior of Fall River.

"You oppose wealth made in any way?"

"Abject wealth leads to abject poverty. Damned if you do, damned if you don't. We wouldn't have the former without the latter." Joseph flipped over this logic, thinking there must be some way to compromise. But why tolerate even a little poverty if it can be avoided? Could capitalism exist without poverty? What was enough wealth? Two million? Lizzy's people, the Durfees, were always pressing for more. But what of the mantra Kindness, Piety, and Fear? He'd been hoping to save his soul from eternal damnation, and instead, he'd just become a millionaire. He wanted to believe there was still time for salvation. He kept walking.

The man in the red vest he'd seen earlier turned the corner. He came at them, staring intently at Sarah. He kept a thick mustache and wore fine tailored clothes. She didn't, or wouldn't, acknowledge him as he closed. Closer, Joseph could see lines behind his spectacles. The man was older than Joseph first guessed. He carried a black satchel. Joseph turned his shoulder as they passed but they hit anyway. Something in the satchel rattled.

"Pardon me," the man intoned, tipping his derby to Sarah. Joseph turned to catch him disappearing into a tavern called Lizzie's Axe.

They overtook a knot of ashen, needle-thin women. Their hair was parted down the center and wound into braids or tied with lifeless red ribbons. Joseph had expected more activity in the street, given the weather.

"Fifty-six hours in the mill taps the strength," she said.

"They do get paid," he said.

"A subsistence wage."

Joseph caught one woman's eye. She smiled. He smiled back. She was Portuguese. Perhaps he could help a few of them if business picked up. A man passed Sarah and put his arm around the woman. Her husband, Joseph guessed. She'd been smiling at him. The man kissed her, his lips covered in red sores.

Sarah sighed. "Shuttle-mouth."

Joseph nodded. He knew many of the mills had yet to adopt the perfected shuttle on their looms. Without it, weavers drew thread from the bobbin by puckering their lips against the loom and sucking the thread through the hole. The man had probably taken over the shuttles of a sick coworker.

They passed a half-dozen women—girls really—chasing their puny children. A few were missing locks of hair. And each left a most foul-smelling wake.

Sarah wrinkled her nose. "The meek shall *not* inherit the earth."

Joseph fixed on a woman with red markings on her forehead and ears. Sarah explained that she dyed red yarn without proper clothes. "The heat in the rooms makes for wicked perspiration. Their faces get marked wiping the sweat, but the real damage is here," she said, thumping her chest.

He said sarcastically, "I think choir practice is about over."

"But I'm just heading to the pulpit." Sarah winked at Joseph.

He crossed his arms so as not to strangle her.

A middle-aged woman was dealing out coins to a bread peddler. She could barely pick them up with her twisted fingers. To be heard, the man shouted the price into her ear.

Sarah approached the woman and helped her count the coins so she wasn't cheated. Watching the scene, Joseph determined she had a good heart but a sick brain. She turned back, jabbing her finger in the air. "Your machines are killing them slowly. The deafening machines take their hearing; their eyes go inspecting cloth."

Joseph chopped her arm away from his face and continued to walk. He stopped outside a building on a dusty corner lot. Joseph recognized Father James Curley, Mary Sheehan's priest at Saints Peter and Paul, distributing fruit from a parish cart. During the 1904 strike he'd sided with the operatives.

"This way," Sarah said, ducking into the apartment doorway. "We can talk in my rooms." She explained that she'd chosen a building occupied by a mix of French-Canadians, Poles, and Italians, though they were still separated by floor. They stopped on the first landing, waiting for a group of four adults and six children, two families, to unlock a door. The boys carried picnic baskets. Joseph's foot slid across the stair. The embedded grime was as slippery as the oil-soaked pine floors in the mill. The men said hello to Sarah, and she replied in French. The boys eyed Joseph suspiciously.

"Ten people in three rooms," she whispered as they passed. "The children speak little English. No schooling."

The next apartment door swung open to a very pregnant woman sipping a glass of water. Her two children lunged at Joseph, dragging him into her single room. The children's hold weakened as Sarah spoke. "*Il n'est pas le docteur. Je vais envoyer Missy en bas. Nous aiderons.*"

"Any minute now." Sarah gave the woman a thumbs-up. "They thought you were the doctor."

"The father?"

"Works in the dye room."

"Someone should fetch him."

"In Bangor we nursed pregnant girls."

"Girls?"

"Abused by their bosses. When they announce they're pregnant, they get dumped, and blackballed. The men already have families." Sarah stopped on the stairs. For the first time all day her tone softened. "That's my aunt's story. But she tried her luck with the abortionist and lost."

The next floor was Italian. The landing smelled of urine. Sarah, of course, knew the story. "Enrico came home drunk last night and Concetta locked him out. When he tired of banging, he pissed on the door."

There were three doors, all open in search of a cross-breeze. A woman sat nursing an infant, her swollen breast hanging out for all to see. Her olive-skinned neighbor stood bare-chested except for the suspenders supporting his trousers, fiddling with the spring motor of a battered phonograph; his wife stood over a washboard in a closet sink. Behind door number three a sewing machine sat in the middle of the room. Two youngsters—no more than six, Joseph guessed—wrestled over a blackened ball on the rag rug beneath the machine. The smaller of the two, painfully thin. Their mother straddled the windowsill; she sucked a cigarette and exhaled through her nose. She wore a calico house gown, obviously homespun, the fabric bunched in her lap. She caught Joseph staring at her thigh and smiled.

There was one door at the top landing—the attic apartment. Sarah tapped the door and walked in. "Those are the pens your peers condemn their workers to. It's a cycle of poverty that few can claw out of."

Joseph paused on the threshold. The setting sun overwhelmed the space and his vision, but the air smelled of a workroom, of ink and paper, more than a ladies' quarters. Two single beds were pushed together in the center of the room. There was one dark wood chest of drawers with a yellowing mirror. A wooden pole wedged between two corner walls served as a closet. Surprisingly, there was a washroom with decent light and working plumbing; it housed a sink and toilet. There was no kitchen, just a closet sink and washboard. Three geraniums in moss-covered pots sat on the unpainted windowsill, their green tendrils snaking down it and across the floor. The plants gave off a tinny odor that Joseph could taste.

A young blond woman sat at a round table in the corner of the room. She hunched over an open journal scribbling lines of numbers with a yellow pencil. The table was cluttered with posters, papers, ink stamps, and books. An Egyptian brand cigarette burned in a clamshell ashtray. She didn't even glance up at Joseph. It was as if she'd expected him. Above the table hung a photograph of labor crusader Jennie Collins addressing women operatives. Joseph recognized the Gower Mill in the background. There was a handwritten caption across the bottom of the photo: *A strike requires courage to face starvation for the sake of justice. The traitorous behavior of a few shall not defeat the purpose of the many.*

The younger woman finished her writing, closed the journal, and jumped to her feet. She took a drag from the cigarette and shot Sarah a glance. She wore men's trousers and a white cotton blouse; a gold pinkie ring, similar to the one Sarah wore, dangled from a silver chain around her neck. She turned to Joseph and looked him and up and down. Exhaling gray smoke through her nose, she said, "I thought you'd be taller."

"And you are?"

"Missy."

"Sorry to disappoint you, Missy."

"Oh, I'm not disappointed, Mr. Bartlett." Missy set the cigarette in the clamshell. "Sarah has been looking forward to meeting you."

"I bet she has."

"I'll leave you to it."

Sarah motioned Missy behind a tall blind. The fabric panels were embroidered with peacocks standing on mangrove branches; yellow and white fish swam beneath them. Joseph heard the women whispering. He flipped through the books on the table. There was Marx's *Communist Manifesto, Progress and Poverty*, and other socialist-loving garbage. Among the trove of papers, he spotted a month-by-month forecast from the New York futures cotton market and a slip noting the price of printcloth. Another paper predicted a bumper cotton crop for 1912. Nothing too difficult to get, but why would she study it? For the same reason he had when he'd found out about Stanton's nefarious bookkeeping: to see if the owners were keeping two sets of books—one for themselves, and one to show the operatives. When the agents could show that the price of production exceeded the price of their goods, wage cuts could be justified. Perhaps he'd underestimated this Sarah Strong. A newspaper clipping taped to the wall quoted a suffragist's speech at the recent New York State Fair. The phrases "by any means necessary" and "to the death" caught his eye.

Missy stepped out from behind the blind, holding a tray with a washbasin, towels, and a blue porcelain teacup.

"Call me when she's crowning," Sarah said.

"Door," Missy said to Joseph, cocking an eyebrow.

"Where are my manners." He held it open. "How will we get on without you."

"You're really much shorter than I imagined."

"You two should have an act in the circus," Sarah said.

Missy winked at Joseph. "Come find me when she's done."

"Don't forget this." Sarah shook a tall mason jar of dried straw. She set it on the tray and kissed Missy full on the mouth. Missy trotted down the stairs. She called, "Coming, Mrs. Chevalier."

Joseph shut the door. "What's the straw for?"

"Leave it open," Sarah said. "It's dried poppy straw to make tea. Helps with the pain."

Joseph whistled.

"Do you know the mortality rate for babies born in a slum?"

"I bet you're gonna tell me."

"I overestimated you, Mr. Bartlett."

"Time for my countdown. Five minutes to make your proposal, after which I am leaving. And you can scream *rape* or *bloody murder*, but I am leaving." Joseph reached for his pocket watch. He checked the opposite vest pocket. He shook his head. "Son of a bitch."

Sarah laughed. "The man in the red vest."

"You know the scoundrel?"

"Just recently. He's an abortionist."

"Isn't that poetic, a pickpocketing abortionist. If I wasn't so cross, I might laugh at the absurdity of it." He couldn't wait to tell Mary—she would make sense of this. "Four minutes."

Suddenly Verdi's opera *La Traviata* filled the building. The Italian had fixed the phonograph.

Sarah went behind the blind. "Fitting performance for this neighborhood?"

"How so?"

"It ends in death." Sarah tossed her blouse, skirt, corset, and garter belt over the top of the blind.

"Ms. Strong, if you please."

"Relax, Mr. Bartlett," she called. "You're not my flavor."

She emerged wearing a pair of men's denim jeans, khaki safari shirt, and black leather boots. She brushed past Joseph, muttering "Time to work," and hovered over the top banister. "Anything, Missy?"

"Nothing," Missy shouted back.

Sarah bustled passed him, cradled the still-burning cigarette, and took a long drag. She leaned her head back and exhaled a thick cyclone of gray smoke.

"Bastard owners exploit workers in Fall River. This isn't news," Joseph said. "I can do nothing to change it."

"What can you tell me about George Pierce?" She snubbed out the butt.

"Unskilled workers weaken his bargaining position. He won't talk to you."

"We'll see about that." Sarah stacked the papers on the desk. "I have nothing on you, Mr. Bartlett. But this is your town, not mine. Your citizens dying. Not mine. Remember that."

"You have no idea what I have done for this city."

"Here or Lawrence, we'll organize unskilled operatives to protest for a wage hike and shorter hours."

"And get folks killed, like in Bangor? Is that your aim?"

"And the owners will lock them out, call out the militia, and then hire scabs. But my plan is to enlist mill agents sympathetic to labor to publicly support the strikers. Newspaper tours of your mill will follow. Open your books. It will put pressure on the others to follow suit. Improving the conditions of all workers, not just Cleveland operatives, will be your legacy, Joseph Bartlett."

The unions had tried the same strategy of divide and conquer in 1904, and it had failed. Was she so naive? Had she really no idea of the owners' power? Cleveland printcloth couldn't be given away to the Salvation Army if he aligned with her. And the city's greatest capitalist—a man who once said, "I believe in the accumulation of wealth without any limit"—Joseph's mentor, Matt Borden, would disown him. There was one thing Joseph would put above an operative's welfare: his family. He doubted Karl Marx himself could talk sense into the silly woman.

Sarah placed a gold ring on table. "Wear this in solidarity."

"You're crazy." He tasted bile in the back of his throat. "I do all I can."

"Nonsense!" She slammed down the papers; the ring skittered across the floor.

"You bring guns and dynamite into Fall River, and they'll hunt you down."

"You and I have seen it all, Mr. Bartlett. But the difference is I've seen enough."

The chant, "BABY! BABY!" blew up the stairwell. Sarah shoved Joseph into the doorjamb and vaulted down the stairs.

The first-floor landing was crowded with the extended French family rubbernecking into the apartment. They parted so Joseph could enter; it smelled faintly of blood and cigarette ash. The red blind was lowered on the hood to block the setting sun. The air sparkled with floating dust. Mrs. Chevalier lay splayed on a blanket in the middle of the floor; Missy knelt behind her, holding up her head and shoulders. The two small Chevalier children, a boy and girl of perhaps four and six, crouched under the kitchen table.

"*Une pression supplémentaire*," Missy said.

"You're witnessing a miracle, Joseph Bartlett," Sarah said over her shoulder, then to Mrs. Chavalier, "*Je vois ce bébé.*"

The baby's head and shoulders emerged. Mrs. Chevalier's cheeks blew in and out.

"*Poussez!*"

Mrs. Chevalier screamed as Sarah eased the baby from the womb, untangled the cord, and wrapped the child in the towel on Mrs. Chevalier's belly. "*Bébé en pleine santé. Toutes nos félicitations.*"

Mrs. Chevalier wept. Her children crawled across the floor to touch their baby brother. Missy held the teacup to Mrs. Chevalier's lips.

"*Chevalier* is French for *knight*, Mr. Bartlett. This boy will one day slay the kings of Fall River."

"So the meek shall inherit the earth," Joseph said, backing out of the room.

"Immigrants will shape America in this century."

"And I will cheer their ascent."

Sarah wiped her hands on a the corner of the towel. "Here comes the rest, Missy. Hand me that bowl. *Poussez!*"

I will pray for them all, Joseph thought. May this brick tenement be his castle. The fields of refuse his bounty. The street urchins his army.

"You can save them all," Sarah called. "Time to stand tall."

Joseph dropped Hannah Cleveland's orange on the kitchen table and slipped out of the room and down the stairs. As he reached the curb, Mrs. Chevalier's screams accompanied Verdi's courtesan, Violetta, filling the tenement with sadness and joy.

THE NARROWS

Joseph baited Will's hook with the night crawlers he'd just purchased from Fontaine's. George Pierce wasn't due till eight thirty and was sure to needle him about the recent curtailment at the association's mills.

"Cast it out there." Joseph pointed at the horizon. "Just like last time."

"We didn't catch anything last time."

Joseph snapped the *Herald* across the fold and sat back, reading. "Today we will. I promise."

Will whipped the rod over his shoulder, the sinker smashed into the newspaper then cartwheeled forward, but jerked to a stop when the line caught on the reel. Hook plopped into the water five feet from the end of the dock.

"Sorry."

"You'll get the hang of it."

"Should I recast?"

Joseph ruffled the paper back into form. "Just be patient."

The Bartlett men sat on a rickety boat dock belonging to the Watuppa boat club, facing the south pond. They'd come early to stake out a secluded spot, but the Narrows, a thin strip of land dividing the North and South Watuppa Ponds, didn't offer much cover from the people walking along beach, out enjoying the late August morning. The trolley tracks to New Bedford and beyond filled the middle of the land. Stilt cottages and businesses like Fontaine's that lent paddleboats and ice skates lined the southern strip, while the northern side was the property of the Watuppa Water Board, which forbade boating and fishing and skating and ice harvesting. Fishermen from up the Flint ignored the no-trespassing postings and filled their wicker baskets with perch and black bass. Most anglers dropped lines from the stone causeway or tossed out from the marshy beach, and the northern shore was littered with discarded rods and tackle from men who had been caught in the act.

Far out in the water, a steamboat skimmed the water. He could just make out rows of legs draped over the top deck. The boat reminded Joseph of the family clambakes Lizzy's people used to throw on the eastern shore at a placed called Adirondack Grove. He hadn't spoken to any of them since the funeral.

A cluster of seagulls crept down the dock. Will tossed them a worm. The lead bird snatched it out of the air.

"Don't encourage them," Joseph said.

"Everybody's gotta eat, isn't that what you always say?"

"People. Not thieving gulls."

"I wish I could fly."

Joseph peered over the paper. "Really? And where would you go?"

"Just see the world. Pyramids. Great Wall. Deserts. But from up there." Will pointed the tip of the rod.

"If you pull that off, I'll be your chaperone gull. I'd like to see those things."

"We won't be gulls. They have no stamina for where we're going."

"What's it gonna be then? Osprey?"

"Nah. Not any birds from around here. We need to be seaworthy. Long flyers. Albatross is the ticket. Saw a picture in *National Geo*. Longest wingspan going. Takes us anywhere we wanna go." Will turned, blocked the light with his hand. "You really coming with?"

"Someday." Joseph drummed his fingers over the paper. "But you go with or without me."

The gulls squawked and scattered off the dock.

"Flying rats is what they are," George Pierce shouted, whipping his rod before him like a sword. He dropped his tackle on the dock and scrubbed

Will's head. "Top of the morning to you, young William. Paper says it's gonna be another scorcher."

"What's news?"

"The weather. A real lobster boil." Pierce mopped his ruddy face with a cotton hankie. "Sorry about your wife. I assume you received the card from the union?"

Will turned to his father. "Thank you and yes." Joseph brushed his son's cheek. "Watch the line."

Pierce lifted his rod to the boy. "Good fishing at this hour."

"So, what's the news?" Damn my father, Joseph thought. Otis had had a special relationship with Pierce's father. While Otis's independence won respect in some circles, he was never accepted as true Yankee blue, and the closer Otis worked with Jefferson, the more his fellow mule spinners, men who had known *his* father in England, felt betrayed. Now, years later, Joseph had risen higher than any of them.

"Funny how we never discuss anything but those deafening mills."

Joseph glanced at the hulking Randall mill on the western shore, near the mouth of the Quequechan River. "That's why we're here, George."

"There—you used my first name. I heard it. Now that is something friends do, right? Ain't I right? Aren't we friends, Joseph?" Pierce extended his right hand to Joseph.

Joseph lowered the paper. Who were his friends? This was a difficult question.

Pierce dropped his hand. Scratched his jaw. "So, how's the mouth? Any more loose teeth?"

Joseph skimmed his tongue around the inside of his mouth settling on a creaky molar at the back of his jaw. He gave it three weeks, maybe four. He pushed the tooth with the tip of his tongue and tasted blood. "You fish—" he began, and then stopped, waiting for the green New Bedford trolley to clatter past. "You fish, George. I pretend to fish."

"You know we sometimes have union meetings in the pub?"

"Just like on the island." That was probably one reason why they'd never negotiated a major wage concession from the association, Joseph thought.

"A good pub builds community."

"Anything else on your mind?"

Pierce brushed Will's shoulder. "Getting any bites?"

Joseph turned to Will, surprised. He'd forgotten about him. Wasn't this meeting the start of his grooming process? The heir apparent, like it or not.

"Answer him, Will."

"But you said—"

"William."

Pierce knelt down on one knee. His tone softened, "You like to fish, Will?"

"Some," Will mumbled.

"What's the biggest fish you ever caught?"

Will shrugged.

Pierce licked his line and threaded a hook. He made a knot with his tongue and pulled it tight with his teeth. "You know the cotton business like your daddy?"

Again, Will shrugged. Joseph said, "He knows the finest silks to the cheapest cotton. Can run a mule spinner and balance books. He'll run this town someday."

"That so?"

Joseph pinched Will's shoulder.

"Yes, sir," Will barked, jerking his shoulder free.

Pierce turned to Joseph. "Just like old Otis taught you. Makes me miss my boy." Pierce reeled up his line. "You know, Will, we'll always need another straight-shooting Bartlett." Pierce launched a long cast into the water. "Now, Will, you need to throw out away from the dock. There's nothing biting that shallow."

Will looked over his shoulder at his father. Joseph nodded. Will reeled in.

Pierce pointed. "The ornery bastards are near those rocks. Let me help."

Pierce handed his rod to Joseph and stepped over him, knocking Joseph's boater to the dock. He lifted the boy by the arm, and reaching around him, set his hand over Will's. They rocked to and fro, practicing the casting motion.

"That's it." Pierce released Will and stepped back. "Now let it fly."

Will took two steps back and skipped into the throw. The line spun high into the air falling just short of Pierce's float.

Joseph shot up, nearly dropping Pierce's reel into the water. "Nice throw, son." Will beamed.

Pierce winked at the boy. "Maybe the cotton business ain't for him."

"And what is, fishing?"

"Or boxing." Pierce sat down on the dock. "I heard about that whipping."

"He'll settle on mill work."

"The fish might outlast the cotton."

"I doubt it," Joseph snapped. He tossed the rod at Pierce and reached for his hat. "What's news?"

Pierce pointed at the newspaper. "Did you read my quote on the production goals?"

"I haven't gotten to the funny pages yet."

"Those controlled fires saved us." A week after the centennial, two fires had ruined the inventories of the Gower and Pocasset mills, forcing the Manufacturers' Association to pull back from their threatened summer curtailment. And Globe Yarn lost two months of thread to a broken water main.

"If you have to rely on luck like that fire, you'll never beat the owners. I've told you before: you're better off teaming up with the unskilled workers. The craft unions could stomach the company. Give them half a vote; who the hell cares? Cause a real ruckus."

"Must we do this dance every time?"

Enlarging the union would mean the council might lose its special status with the association. "Then you could really milk those old men—like in Bangor: your members broke ranks and won wage increases for everyone."

"The weaver for the weaver and the spinner for the spinner." Pierce hummed the refrain.

"It's a quaint old ditty. But times are changing." As always, the council was behind the pitch. "And the women—they need stronger representation in negotiations. Again, you saw what they contributed in Bangor: picketing, parades, pestering scabs. Your kind, my friend, is a dying breed."

Pierce whipped in his line, the tone of his voice hot. "Are we in Bangor, Joseph? No. Do you see any of those Wobblies here? No. The day I sit at a table with a radical bitch like Sarah Strong, I'll cut off me own prick."

"She got results."

"Rumor is she's coming to Fall River."

"And targeting the union."

Pierce shouted, "Never. Their equal rights slogan is poppycock."

Fishermen surfcasting on the shore stopped to stare at Pierce.

Joseph raised his newspaper. "Easy, George."

Pierce glared at Joseph. "Unskilled immigrants aren't worth the trouble. My men make almost twice as much—and deservedly so."

"As a matter of fact, our fathers weren't born on President Avenue, either." Joseph snapped his fingers in that aw-shucks kind of way and tipped his hat back to feel the sun on his face. "All right. I didn't convince you." In Otis's heyday, the unions didn't represent any immigrants—skilled or unskilled—so some inroads had been made.

"I hear rumors that the Elephant Man is coming after you. You know, he still can't sleep over missing his chance to get Cleveland into the association. Before the fire, Stanton was a shoo-in there." Pierce reeled in his line frantically, but nothing was at the end but his bait. He cut the line with his pocketknife and began tying on a larger hook. "When Borden dies you'll lose some security. The Elephant Man wants Cleveland, Joseph. He wants the entire city under the association."

"We're too small to cause a hassle."

"Who said anything about size? It's about controlling it all. Please, don't make me lecture you on the Fall River system."

Joseph wondered why he had allowed himself to be a conduit for the unions, as he did at every clandestine meeting with Pierce. Joseph enjoyed knowing the scoop early, but it wasn't critical to the operation of the Cleveland. And with Sarah Strong loose, Joseph thought, where was his out?

"I've got one!" Will's line tightened and he yanked back on the rod, setting the hook. The fish jumped out of the water.

"Nice size too," Pierce shouted.

Joseph readied the net in the water and then lowered the fish on the dock. The fish's gills gaped open and shut. A trail of blood leaked from its mouth.

"It's a monster." Will danced around the thrashing fish. "Get him, Dad."

"He's like our friend here, Will," Joseph said, nodding toward Pierce. "A dying animal."

"The thing about your father," Pierce said, "is that he never can bag the big ones."

Will flinched at the flopping fish.

"Let me show you." Pierce stepped on the tail and handed his pliers to Will. "Just reach in his gullet and twist the hook out . . . That's it. Off the lip. Easy."

Will raised the hook, beaming. "What is it?" The fish heaved on the dock.

"A perch." Pierce lifted the fish by the mouth and dropped it into their basket.

"Your line!" Will shouted.

"They're biting today." Pierce reeled in a black bass. Joseph lowered the net and scooped the fish to the dock. Pierce grabbed the fish in his hand and pried the hook free. He sized up the fish, fingering it below the belly, and then moved to tossed it back into the water.

"Keep it," Will said excitedly.

"Females that size go back," Pierce said as the fish hit the water. "Keep too many of those, and there's nothing to catch."

As Pierce rebaited his hook, Joseph unfolded the newspaper and skimmed the article that quoted the labor leader. Pierce helped Will cast his line. Setting the paper down, Joseph said, "What did you mean, the fire was 'controlled'?"

"What did you hear?"

"What the fire marshal reported: spontaneous combustion of fine dust saturated with oil smoldering in a mechanic's repair wagon. Smoke damage alone ruined Gower's thread."

"Funny place to park a wagon, ain't it?"

"Why are you telling me this?"

"We're mates."

"And the water main rupture?"

"Dumb luck. But it made the other less fishy."

"And you think you're better than—"

"Sarah Strong and her International Workers of the World radicals are high from their Bangor success. They'll be looking for sympathizers in the owners. You're a target."

"Will, pack it up," Joseph snapped. "We're leaving."

"Got another." Pierce said. He'd hooked another bass, but this one was much larger, and male.

Will handed his rod to his father and grabbed the net. His thin arms bulged lifting the fish to the dock.

Pierce knelt down on the wooden planks next to the glistening black bass, the line disappearing between its gaping lips. It had swallowed the hook. Pierce whispered something to the fish. Looking up at Will, he said, "You know what we call this one?"

"No, sir."

"Lunch!" Pierce wiggled the line and gave it a sharp tug; the fish jerked forward, but the hook didn't budge. He pointed at the tail. "Step on that." Will did, and Pierce released some line from the reel and wrapped it around the toe of his shoe. "Get ready, boy," he said. His eyes narrowed. "One, two, three." He jerked his foot back, ripping the hook free. The sound was like a sheet of paper being torn in half. The fish's bloody innards slopped onto the dock. The worm dangled from the hook. Pierce lifted the disemboweled fish by the gills and dangled it before Joseph, whose face flushed three shades of green. "Fire talk turn your stomach?" Pierce chuckled. "You're no stranger to it. What was Cleveland's mishap? A broken lantern?"

Joseph squeezed Will's shoulder. He whispered, "Let's go, son. Grab your rod."

"Sometimes you're lucky." Pierce raised the fish higher still. "Sometimes you're not."

Before Will could finish stowing his gear, Joseph yanked his son to his feet and started down the dock. The boy shouldered his rod and the basket. A hook and float swung wildly over his shoulder.

Pierce called, "I'll be in touch."

Joseph remembered the reason he had few friends: loyalty.

* * *

Later that evening Joseph battled his demons alone on the rear stoop of his Highlands mansion. He knew his friends and competitors were just as weak after a day of pretending. They were probably crying in the bath this very Saturday, reliving their own moments of regret. Joseph put little faith in any sort of atonement, believing even a religious cleansing did not completely erase the memory of an ill-spoken word or wanton act. Tragic memories buzzed above one's head, just out of reach at a low but persistent frequency. And no philanthropy or hushed prayers could rewrite the past. He wished a large tree limb or the gutters would crash down on him. He would gladly exchange a bale of good memories for a thimble-full of nightmares. And now he had Lizzy to mourn.

As the humid air tightened around him, Joseph crawled into the house, collapsing on the screened porch. Mary Sheehan found him in a similar position, but asleep, sprawled across the chaise, when she arrived with a dinner of corn chowder, homemade wheat bread, and a strawberry pie. She had sent word that morning to expect dinner, though she knew how hard he worked and figured it best to let him nap. Earlier that afternoon, without her adult children loitering about the house (something she was determined to remedy with an arranged marriage if necessary), she had taken a long walk down to the Narrows; she had even dipped her feet in the South Watuppa. After Saturday Mass at Saints Peter and Paul, she had visited the cemetery where Tom was buried, but instead of going in, as was her custom, she had set flowers against the wrought-iron gate nearest his plot and hurried home to pick berries.

She set the dinner basket in the kitchen and went to find the boys. Hollister's room was empty. She discovered young Will asleep in the drawing room, a half-finished model dinosaur was splayed on the table where his mother had lain a few weeks before. She scooped the boy into her arms and carried him to bed.

Downstairs, she unpacked the dinner basket in the kitchen and then lit the range to warm the chowder. She found a blanket for Joseph, pulled a chair up next to the wicker chaise, and took out her knitting. She paused the needles every few minutes to listen to Joseph's deep breathing. She had grown used to such stillness from Joseph. On their Sunday walks in South Park, they strolled side by side, occasionally brushing elbows but not speaking, much like a husband and wife who felt content and unafraid of long silences. When they did speak, it was of the children or events in town and very rarely about his work at the mill and never of the past. "Let us never speak of what we might have done differently," Joseph had told her once. And although she thought such bottling-up might kill a man, she respected his wishes.

She shooed a fly from his cheek. The last trolley of the night rumbled in the distance. She set her empty chowder cup on the tray and went to the kitchen. She cleaned the dishes and began straightening up. Evelyn's work had fallen off after the funeral. On the porch she fetched Joseph's shoes and hat. Folding his jacket, she spotted a shiny rectangular piece of glass in the breast pocket. She smiled at the sight of it, and then, after re-checking he was soundly asleep, she peeled back the fine glass limbs of the object until it was fully extended. Even under the weak porch fix-ture the glass reflected the light. As she twirled it between her hands, tiny tornadoes of color burst inside each arm. Mary giggled. She pressed a hand to her open mouth. Was it magic? Only Highlands men owned such whatchamacallits. Where do the rich find such wondrous things? she wondered. And what kind of man might invent it?

PART II
1905

The difference between a moral man and a man of honor is that the latter regrets a discreditable act, even when it has worked and he has not been caught.

—H. L. Mencken

WHEN SPARKS FLY

Joseph knew that Stanton Cleveland was keeping a second set of books when he agreed to a union demand to allow the local clergy to examine the ledgers. Once the men of the cloth signed off on the numbers, the planned production curtailment was agreed to by the spinners and weavers. CLEVELAND IN DIRE STRAITS, read the headline in the *Evening News*, OTHERS WILL FOLLOW. But Joseph had no proof. The battles between the two men began after Otis's death and Jefferson Cleveland's retirement. First Stanton started overcharging operatives in the mill store, and then he fined them for meeting with George Pierce. Joseph knew he'd lost Stanton in 1904 during the showdown between Borden and the Manufacturers' Association. Borden needed gray cloth for his American Printing Company, and the association's mills refused to sell. When Borden's agents told him that Stanton Cleveland had refused to sell him the cloth he wanted, he summoned Joseph to a secret meeting aboard the steamer *Commonwealth*.

Joseph hopped a train to New York to catch the boat back to Fall River. At Pier 19, he found his ticket under a false name, as Borden's man, Sullivan, had instructed. In his six-dollar stateroom (Borden's party had taken all four seven-dollar rooms), he found a note instructing him to wait until he was summoned. Joseph removed his tie and jacket and read the *Times*. At eight o'clock the opening march of the boat's evening orchestra concert floated down the corridor. He had made the trip dozens of times and could pinpoint the boat's location by the passing lighthouses. When he saw Little Gull Island out the porthole, he knew it was near midnight. He ordered a Horlicks malted milk and fig pudding. He knew Borden conducted business on the boat, but it was really getting on. The old man had something up his sleeve. To calm his nerves, Joseph washed his face and damp armpits and then rang the purser for a bourbon. When the man arrived, Joseph bought the bottle. He hadn't seen Borden since Otis's funeral, and there only briefly to exchange condolences, and Borden's usual mantra: "Call if you need anything, dear boy."

Call if you need anything. Joseph wondered how many men Matt Borden had thrown that line to. He had heard the phrase a handful of times while learning the selling side of the business from Borden at J. and E. Wright and Company, the largest commission house in New York. Borden saw two threats to the manufacturing and selling of textiles: the Fall River system and the Southern menace. The Fall River agents believed that control of the competition was best achieved by dominance through their vast productive capacity. Their bare-knuckle business model relied on strikes, lockouts, political hardball, and mandatory vacations for operatives to deal with price fluctuations and pesky unions. The Southern assault, Borden explained, was the antithesis of this model, a capitalist's dream, there were virtually no barriers to profit: weak unions, poverty wages, small or nonexistent municipal taxes, and no workday regulation. "This lovely combination," Borden prophesized, "will someday close Northern mills and push grass up Plymouth Avenue. And, dear boy, I plan to be in the thick of it." In New York, Joseph grew frustrated by the work stoppages and strikes back home. He was forced to break contracts with printers and commission houses. The Fall River system killed profits and relationships. The vast capacity of Borden's Iron Works and American Printing Company and the staunch independence his New York base afforded him made him few friends in Fall River. When you worked for Matt Borden, you just didn't give a damn what others thought, because deep down you knew they wanted your job.

At Point Judith, Joseph ordered a pot of coffee and a slice of sponge cake. He reread an article in the boat magazine about the decline of New Bedford whaling.

In August of 1894, Joseph and Borden had worked their last bit of magic. The Southern menace had driven prices on printcloth to a low of two and a half cents a yard. When Fall River mills refused to sell to Borden, he went to his contacts in New York and Philadelphia to buy cloth for his American Printing Company. His triumph was reported in the *Fall River Globe*. Borden "shipped prints enough to supply customers' demand out the front door, sold cloth in the gray from the back door and made money on both deals." While the markets in Fall River and Providence scrambled to sell off their cloth before the season ended, Joseph accepted Borden's offer to vacation with him in New Hampshire. It was there that he first met the niece of Borden's sister-in-law: Elizabeth Durfee. Six months later, they were married at the First Congregational Church on Rock Street. Their reception at the Quequechan Club was followed by a weeklong honeymoon in New York, courtesy of Uncle Matt. The wedding guests stood on the wharf under the shadow of the Iron Works as the *Commonwealth*'s paddlewheels made waves into Mount Hope Bay. The following week, Joseph had started as the Cleveland secretary, working alongside his father. Everything had gone as Otis had envisioned.

A loud knock woke Joseph. He wasn't sure how long he'd been asleep. He slid the blue porcelain washbowl under the bed with his bare foot and took a deep breath. He called, "I almost swam ashore in New London." He paused beside the porthole as the Goat Island lighthouse signal swept across his face. It was two-thirty in the morning.

Before Joseph reached the door, it sprung open.

Borden marched past, elegantly dressed in his silk bedclothes and smoking a cigar as if this appointment was just another in the long queue that filled the day of a textile king. His hair was coiffed, and his handlebar mustache looked recently waxed. "Money problems in Philly, dear boy. Sorry to rob your sleep." The steward who had shown Joseph his room shut the door. He had changed into a business suit, and his hair was combed back, exposing a foreboding brow. He held a thick ring of bronze stateroom keys. They must have weighed five pounds. Joseph smiled. Of course. The man was Borden's. He called them lookouts, but they were spies.

"The man is a bad seed," Borden began, starting right in on Stanton. He stood by the open porthole and pointed his cigar at Joseph.

Joseph cleared his throat. He nodded toward the steward turned cotton mole.

"Don't mind Sullivan."

"I'd prefer."

"Sully, wait in the room. Have the girl heat up some warm milk. I won't be long."

When Sullivan's footsteps were out of earshot, Joseph said, "He's changing our relationship with the association. I found out from the colonel that he canceled an order for new looms and will instead recycle Gower's old ones and received a kickback. The operatives are clamoring." Joseph paced the room. "He pulled a trick on the clergy with those books. I'm convinced of it. There's a second set."

"He thinks you played Otis and his father when you worked for me."

"Played?"

"Tossed them bones but never any meat. And though this is a poor excuse, he enjoys the company of those dimwitted owners. Those are the boys he rode ponies with at birthday parties."

"I've noticed their agents don't trust me as before."

"They trust the mighty dollar and only the mighty dollar."

"It's bigger than that."

"Hogwash."

"At Cleveland, Otis . . . he considered our workers' welf—"

"Double hogwash."

"Uncle Matt, I'll stop Stanton for everyone's welfare."

"As you wish, dear boy. Just find the goddamn books."

"I know." Joseph clucked his tongue.

"Where does he keep things? He's not very bright. You can wait until he pays you a handsome dividend and buys your silence, or attack and use them against him." Borden threw his cigar out the porthole and sat down. His voice rising, "I'll never deal with him again. Shutting me out. Your father would have flattened him. I threw an ink blotter across the office when they told me he wouldn't sell. I worked with Jefferson for thirty years. Outlandish!" Borden coughed, struggling to catch his breath. He set one hand on the side table and placed the other to his chest. His flushed cheeks puffed. Joseph poured a glass of water and Borden drained it.

"Do me a favor, dear boy," Borden said in a raspy voice. "Look after my boys. I fear they'll get caught up in their own hubris like Stanton when I am gone." He wiggled the glass.

"If they'll listen," Joseph said, refilling the glass.

"Fine." Borden sipped his drink and stood up. "You must distract Stanton somehow. When he's in Newport this summer. No, this must be done sooner. When he goes to take a crap, ransack his office; when he goes to bed, ransack his house. Find those books, Joseph, and you'll run Cleveland Mill. Your way. Understand?" Borden clapped his hands. "I knew I could count on you."

"And if I can't find them?"

"If you can't"—Borden gripped Joseph's shoulder—"then those workers you care so much about will lose everything." Borden winked. "Time for my milk. Keep in touch." Borden disappeared out the stateroom door.

Joseph poured himself another bourbon and slumped on the bed. He scratched his chin; his tongue lapped his mouth. Borden's plan was seriously half-cooked, but the yarn began to spin. At the Hog Island light, Joseph picked up a pen and outlined his plan to break into Stanton's office the night Cleveland installed the new Corliss steam engine. He knew just the man for the job. It was four-thirty in the morning. The *Commonwealth* would make the Fall River wharf within the hour.

* * *

It was just past suppertime. A good breeze crept up the granite hills of the city. The rain had held off another day, but the gray overcast sky, thick and brooding, held out the promise of the first good drenching of spring. The green nubbies of Elizabeth's first crocuses had just broken the surface of the black dirt in the front garden. Soon the daffodils would follow, then the dogwood would bloom, then the lilac, and the chives in her kitchen garden. Then a parade of perennials: bleeding heart, peony, shasta daisies, monkshood, phlox, Japanese lantern, and into chrysanthemum. During the growing season, Elizabeth attempted to teach Joseph each plant's botanical name. *Candytuft is* Iberis. *Doesn't it look like candy? Just try saying it. Is it sweet? Eye-beer-is.* Why couldn't everything be as intuitive as bleeding heart? From May till September he could approximate the date by looking at what was blooming. To participate in his wife's hobby, he tended the rose beds. But now, in early April, roses were months away. Only the crocuses took a chance against a late frost. He moved between the mounds of manure he'd dumped over the roses' root balls the previous November, careful not to topple the petrified globs of shit.

Joseph steadied himself on the garden bench. The extra whiskey had settled his nerves but upset his balance. He'd give João Rose another minute to get into place.

Joseph knew safe combinations, which key fit which hole, the number of stairs between landings, the time it took to run from the front gate to the road, the carelessness of Stanton Cleveland, the black cover of a moonless sky, that the night watchman sweetened his coffee with bourbon. Even with all this intelligence, Joseph realized his plan was pretty bush league.

Stanton had kept him busy in Newport and Providence brokering cotton and fine cloth goods for the better part of the year. Actually asked Joseph to stay out of the office so Joseph's business at the mill was confined to one morning every other week, usually in Stanton's office, where he'd leave signed contracts for the safe. Like his father, Stanton scribbled the combination in his desk drawer.

Joseph had purchased a similar safe from the Troy Store. One weekend, with Lizzy and the boys in Boston, he instructed João to break into his own house and steal books from the safe. The first night Joseph fell asleep at two in the morning on the parlor divan. When he woke at seven he twirled the dial of the safe: 9-13-16. The books were gone. There was no sign of a break-in. His first thought was that João had lied about his farming past. The next night, he fell off at ten o'clock. At five the next morning, the books were back in the safe in the same order, aligned at the same angle but for the movement of the bookmarks. The boy was made of smoke. Operation Magellan was planned for the night of the Corliss installation.

Joseph walked down the dimly lit walk to the corner where his carriage waited. He asked Wiggins if there'd been any mishap at the stable, and Wiggins gave him a funny look.

"No, sir," Wiggins finally answered, surprised. "I've been waiting *for you* for ten minutes." Joseph stood below the coach expecting Wiggins to extend a hand; when none came he hoisted himself up. Wiggins snapped the reins.

Joseph tapped his heel on the floorboard. Immediately João lightly reciprocated from below. Not only was the boy made of smoke but he was also a contortionist. Joseph slumped back into the leather bench and released a long sigh and dozed off. This was an ugly business.

"Wake up!"

Joseph opened his eyes expecting the police. It was only Wiggins.

"Why are we stopped?"

"Show him your face." Joseph leaned out from under the carriage awning so the light from the gas lamp struck his face. With union bandits threatening unrest, all the mills employed twenty-four-hour security.

"Good evening. Here to see the new machine? They say it's a wonder."

"They're sure making a racket, Mr. Bartlett."

Joseph slid a bottle of bourbon to the man. "It must get cold on such a raw night."

The man tipped the throat of the bottle against his forehead in a salute. "Not tonight, sir." He pulled the gate open and stood aside. Joseph heard the chain rattle behind them.

Wiggins tied off at the office tower while Joseph walked across to the mill buildings. The office tower had formerly been a fix-it shop, and the subflooring was saturated with oil like the hardwoods in all the mills.

Joseph called back to Wiggins, "When you're done, take a walk to the guard. That's good Kentucky bourbon."

"I brought my cup," Wiggins said, already making tracks toward the gate.

At the factory door, Joseph turned back to the carriage. He made out a figure scurrying across the lawn, but as soon as he zeroed in on it, it disappeared in the shadow of the office tower. He checked his pocket watch. João had twenty minutes.

The new turbine generator was the largest investment Cleveland had ever made, and Stanton wanted to be on hand when Tom Sheehan and his boys installed the beast. The two-thousand-horsepower Corliss steam engine wasn't the largest in Fall River (a larger one ran Matt Borden's looms), but it was by far the largest in the Cleveland Mill. Like Borden's, the giant steel crankshaft had been forged by the Bethlehem Iron Works in Pennsylvania. Stanton had thought to plan a celebration, but the fun went out of the idea when Joseph reminded him of the hoopla Borden made when he threw the switch on his first steam engine in 1895. He had chartered the Fall River Line's flagship steamboat, the *Priscilla*, for his New York and Philadelphia business associates. Otis Bartlett and Jefferson Cleveland were two of only five Fall River men at the champagne lunch to dine on littlenecks, oysters, beef filet, and capon with truffles. Phrases like "Boss Borden" and "Fall River's greatest son" were tossed around like cigars between tables. Mayor Greene ruffled when one Philly banker questioned who'd be dumb enough to rebel against Borden's princely rule. Nearing the end of the lunch, the usually taciturn Borden addressed his admirers. He removed a check from his vest pocket as he spoke.

"Gentlemen," he began. "I believe in success—"

"Hear, hear!" a man shouted.

"—the greater the better."

The crowd roared.

"I believe in the accumulation of wealth without any limit. But unusual success in the accumulation of wealth brings with it extraordinary responsibilities. Mr. Mayor, would you please come up here." Necks craned to Mayor Greene's far table. "It is with great honor, Mr. Mayor, that I can live up to my great responsibility. Today I present you a check for one hundred thousand dollars to be distributed amongst Fall River charities."

The men at Otis's table jumped up to their feet with cheers. Cigars hung from every lip. It was a thunderous sound and kept on for a bit. No man wanted to be the first to quit flapping his wings for the Boss.

Instead of a party, Stanton had chilled a case of champagne at his mother's house for a brunch on Sunday for the company officers. Tom Sheehan would be the only exception in attendance. Sheehan was Cleveland's lead engineer. While most carried slide rules and wore cotton shirts and ties, Sheehan preferred the dress of his men: leather boots, rough cloth trousers and blouses, and over it all he wore the operative's black apron. And the men copied his style by hiking their trouser cuffs up over their ankles and knotting their shirt sleeves above the elbow with short cuts of thread so the fabric didn't catch in any of the whirling belts. Sheehan's men were easily recognizable on the shop floor. Most were broad-chested, with arms as hard as iron. Some joked that they'd follow Sheehan into battle. In the last three years, Cleveland Mill had suffered only one shutdown due to machinery failure. A stray cat had birthed a litter of kittens atop a warm generator. Sheehan brought one of the three that had survived the fan's blades home to his daughter, Helen.

Bright light and the echoes of clanging wrenches and machine parts filled the shop floor. The air was heavy and smelled of cowhide. Joseph walked to the edge of the assembly area and stood next to the old power supply and a mountain of worn leather belts. For a moment, no one acknowledged him. A team of men, mostly skilled Frenchies, worked a winch as another group bolted the Corliss to the reinforced floorboards. The new hardwood shined next to the old oil-soaked floors. Joseph noticed that one of the newly hired security guards had removed his coat and cap and joined the men at the winch. That left one guard unaccounted for. A man shouted that the bottom was secure and motioned for a ladder. Then the man climbed up above the new steam engine to unbolt the winch's cables. When the man was down, the group stopped to admire the new device. A silence followed. None of them had ever seen such a machine. A few stepped forward and ran their hands over it. Joseph craned his neck up and down. The future had arrived.

A voice called down from temporary wooden scaffolding towering above the engine: "Now put the damn thing together." And the men began phase two of the installation. "Keep us on schedule, Tom."

Tom Sheehan gave Stanton a half-salute. He spotted Joseph at the foot of the scaffolding and waved. Joseph felt Stanton Cleveland's eyes upon him. Purchasing the Corliss, the mother of all steam engines, had been the first significant step Stanton had taken without Otis's or Jefferson's counsel. And unlike the majority of his decisions, this one appeared not to be guided by caprice. Joseph knew the old boy reveled in such sweeping changes, but this would be his last success before the company's correction.

Their eyes met between the swinging cables. Stanton proudly surveyed the giant device and then returned to Joseph. After a beat, Stanton slowly nodded his head and flashed a wide grin.

Joseph tiptoed across the floor and stood under his boss. "How goes the fight, Stanton?"

"This is a historic day for us. No longer in Borden's shadow are we. No, sir."

Joseph didn't know exactly what Stanton meant by that. It was like comparing the Boston Red Sox to Saint Anne's baseball team. Borden still had five thousand more employees than Cleveland. His output was quadruple theirs. His agents numbered ten to Cleveland's two. Ordering automatic Northrop looms, keeping wages high, thinking without the association's blessing—that's the ticket.

"There's light burning in the offices," Joseph said.

"Been going back and forth. It'll be a late night. But Sheehan promises we'll be up by morning. I'm staying for the assembly. The fifth biggest part Corliss has ever sold."

"I've come with news from suppliers in Chicago. My man there—"

"Not now, Joseph. I can't think of that. But perhaps you should go there. To Chicago and Saint Louis. Find us some markets. Take Elizabeth and the boys."

"I was actually thinking of pitching an office in the tower. Managing accounts from here."

"Won't do. That won't do at all. A man wants a warm handshake after inking a deal. You're our representative to the customer." Stanton turned from the activity on the shop floor to Joseph. He winked. "My man out there"— Stanton pointed at some imaginary horizon—"needs to be out there."

There was so much of this business Stanton had never stopped to understand, and Joseph couldn't help but admire the man's total lack of concern for anyone but himself. The status of the Corliss excited him more than its output. But all it meant was that Stanton could write a check with many zeros. Joseph looked at him closely. Scared he'd end up with a woman like his mother, Stanton had never married, preferring the company of spinsters in Boston and New York. His stomach hung over his belt, and an extra roll grew under his chin. The corner office suited Stanton. Chops and whiskey lunches too. As boys, they'd once smashed up old farmer Bud's weather vane with rocks. Under interrogation, Joseph spilled his guts. But Stanton produced a cousin who vouched for him—a real actor that cousin—and said they'd been fishing in Richmond Pond. Joseph had always wanted to be the boy who got away with something. Hollister was such a boy. In this moment of triumph, Joseph envied Stanton, standing on the scaffolding like some king on his balcony. But this is a tragic play, Joseph thought. The emperor had no clothes. A strand of lint hovering in the air lodged in his throat, and he turned and gagged. He checked his watch. He coughed. Stanton tossed down a flask, and Joseph took a swig.

"You there," Stanton shouted at a workman. "That's a year's wages. Be careful." Tom Sheehan raced over to help the man set down a piece meant to be handled by three, then lit into him.

"Take it all in, Joseph. Take a deep one." Stanton took back the flask and swigged. He surveyed the complex matrix of new leather belts that the new engine would power to drive the looms. "I'll leave a mark regardless of what happens now," Stanton said. "Tomorrow we jump headlong into the industrial revolution."

Joseph cracked the lid of his pocket watch again. "It's actually been going for some time now."

"You know what I mean," Stanton barked.

Joseph had heard Stanton's spiel at board meetings and billiard clubs for the past six months. Stanton's ambition had no memory. This was what made the man dangerous. Let the competition wade in the past, he told Joseph. The past was always someone else's mistake.

The men began hammering two metal joints of the Corliss. Joseph shouted over the racket. "When can we talk about the high inventories we're sitting on?" When Stanton didn't respond, he repeated the question. Still nothing. He walked over and stood beneath the scaffolding. He tugged Stanton's trousers. "What's the bin for?"

"What's that, Joseph?"

"I heard you're building a new storage bin."

"Heard right."

"Extra inventory. I must not be selling well enough."

"So Chicago must be a sign."

"Unless you're stockpiling to weather a lockout."

"Lockout?" Stanton climbed down from his perch.

"A bird told me."

"Never been a lockout at Cleveland and won't ever be one. But . . ." Stanton turned back to the floor. "But if the operatives strike, who's to stop it?" He climbed back up onto his throne. "You not staying?"

"What?"

"You keep checking your watch."

"It's not keeping good time."

"New?"

"What?"

"The watch, Joseph. Is the watch new?"

Joseph nodded. "A gift from Elizabeth."

Stanton pointed at the Corliss. "My father is planning a visit down tomorrow. He still can't believe it. Old Otis would have loved to see this."

Yes, Joseph thought. Since Borden's party in 1895, he had encouraged Jefferson to make a similar purchase.

"I'll see you in the morning. To throw the switch, as they say," Joseph said. "If I'm allowed."

"The whole town is invited." Stanton marched to the far side the scaffolding and barked at a man.

Joseph called to Tom, "Don't break the man's new toy." Sheehan waved for him to hold up and came jogging over.

"The secret project, Joseph. I've made it," he said, and removed a clear-glass rectangle the length of a pocket prayer book from his apron. "A glass pointer for your presentations. One of a kind. Remember? You gave me the idea." Sheehan unwound the glass arms. They were fused together by tiny brass hinges. It measured two feet unfurled. He snapped it in the air like a conductor with a baton to demonstrate its durability. His smile glowed brighter with each swipe of his new contraption. He set it in Joseph's hand.

Stanton peered down on them, eavesdropping. "It's a bit opulent."

"It's so light," Joseph said.

"I blew the glass myself. Each arm is hollow. That took a while. See how it catches the color of the light."

"Like a prism."

"Yes. The Mechanicsville foundry made the hinges. They're the smallest parts ever made. Give it a try."

Joseph whipped the pointer through the air.

"I'm making one now for little Helen's birthday."

"I'll pay for it all."

"Just show it off on the road. Tell 'em it's one of a kind. I figure twenty-five bucks apiece. Stanton helped with the paperwork. My patent is pending."

"Whoa," Stanton grunted. "Until you make that kind of money, get back out there. They're lost without you."

Tom Sheehan winked at Joseph. Backing toward his men he said, "One of kind, Joseph. Make me a rich man."

Joseph snapped the pointer in the air.

Stanton said, "The man's brain is in the clouds. He's an engineer, not an inventor."

"Engineers are inventors." Joseph twirled the pointer, catching the light. He watched Stanton shout to Sheehan's assistants, but they paid him scant attention.

"Well, we can't make do without him. Just look at him. He's a brute." Stanton paused to watch Sheehan instruct a group of men. He turned suddenly, studied Joseph for a moment, and said, "Big changes start tomorrow, my friend. We have much to talk about."

"I couldn't agree more." I'll catch the greedy rat and call a truce. Joseph checked his watch. "See you in the morning then. Nine?"

"That's fine." Stanton peered out over the construction. "She's a beaut."

Joseph tipped his hat to Stanton and walked out of the mill, collapsing Tom Sheehan's wonderful new creation. "I couldn't agree more."

* * *

Joseph tapped the floor of the carriage. "Magellan? Magellan?" He ran his hand under the seat and then back over the leather a third time. No ledger books. No João.

"You lose a melon, sir?" Wiggins turned his head upside down.

"What? No." Joseph sat on the seat. "Just dropped my hat that's all."

"It's on your head, sir."

"I just found it. You ready to go, or you too drunk?"

"It takes more than a couple of pulls to lay me out."

Joseph nodded. "Then suit up."

"As you wish." Wiggins unhitched old Molly and walked her around. Seated, he said, "Hold on to your hat, sir. Yah." He whipped the horse into action. The guard at the gate waved the bourbon bottle as they left.

João wasn't under the carriage, nor was he waiting at the house. The boy made of smoke had been snuffed out. Joseph figured the police would call before morning. He searched the garden, whispering for João. Finding no trace, he slumped in a chaise longue on the sun porch nursing a drink. Another bottle of Kentucky bourbon stood guard on the end table beside him.

A metallic scratching came from behind the hydrangea bushes.

"Magellan. Magellan." João dragged his nails down the porch screen.

Joseph sat up. "João?"

"I start accident."

"Come to the door." Joseph pulled the screen. In the dim candlelight, Joseph could make out the scratches across João's face and chest. His hair was charred. His bloody fingers wrapped in scraps torn from his shirt. "What happened?"

João lifted his shirt and pulled two red leather-bound ledgers from his waistband and set them on the first step at Joseph's feet.

"You smell of fire."

"I start accident."

"Speak." Joseph scooped up the ledgers and tucked them under the chaise longue cushion. When he turned back, he saw João had backed out of the light. The neighbor's German shepard barked, and the boy jumped. Joseph gestured him to sit. "Those cuts. Come here. What happened?"

"Glass. The mill fence. I climb over to escape."

"Wait here." Joseph returned with a bowl of water and a roll of gauze. The two men sat side by side on the stoop. Joseph set João's hand over his knee.

"Now take it slow, João. What happened in the tower?"

"They chased me from floor to floor. But the fire fast. It jump from the man's lamp. Ate the office. Leapt around us. Boards snap. Glass melt behind me when I jump."

"Raise your hand." Joseph had seen fires in the mills before. Buildings lit up like a torch. Firemen feared the oil-soaked floors. "Did the men chasing you get out?"

João shrugged. "I see only men run in. All them shouting."

"Damn Matt Borden."

João dropped his head down. "I ruin everything."

"You didn't," Joseph said. His eyes welled up, and he wiped his face across his sleeve. "I did. Raise the hand again." Joseph soaked another bandage in the water. "No one got out?"

João shrugged again.

Joseph squeezed João's forearm to reassure him; the boy winced. Joseph wiped another cut. The bowl of water turned red. An immigrant's life was one of short childhoods. Joseph wrapped the last bandage around his chest. "Change those tomorrow," he said and dumped the water into the grass.

João yawned. The first rays of light pierced the horizon. A wet, fog-like mist hung over the lawn. Lizzy's seashell wind chime rattled.

"Now, João, think. Did anyone recognize you?" Joseph's mind clicked into a defensive mode.

João looked down at the strips of fabric encasing each of his fingers. Shook his head.

"Did you come right here?"

João nodded.

"You'll go to Kitty's in Middletown. I have a farm there. You've had an accident at the foundry. Working with Manuel. Understand?"

João nodded again.

"Did you take all the books in the safe?"

João nodded.

"Was there anything else?"

João stood. "This." He pulled papers from the back of his waistband. They were damp with sweat.

Joseph saw the seal of the US Patent Office in Washington, DC, and then read a brief description of Tom Sheehan's glass pointer, followed by the long number it had been assigned. The patent holder was listed as Stanton Cleveland.

"Whom are you talking to?" Lizzy stood in the archway that connected the sun porch to the house.

Joseph jumped up. "The bunnies. You've seen them around. I was talking to the bunnies." Joseph put his fingers behind his head to mimic bunny ears.

Lizzy laughed. "I know what bunnies are, dear."

Joseph turned back to the stoop, but João was gone. So were the bowl and bandages.

"What's that?"

"What?"

"Those papers."

"Some work." Joseph folded the patent in half and set it under a planter.

"Stomach upset again?" She held the bottle of digestive powder and a glass of water.

Unlike his tender digestion, her Durfee stomach could handle any shellfish or bad news. Joseph had an inclination to tell her what had happened, but resisted. No need to worry her. The boy could be wrong. A simple fire could be gotten over. It's what insurance was for.

"Yes?" she began, anticipating he had something to share.

This was one thing he'd always enjoyed about marriage: the sense of knowing someone better than oneself, and of course, being sympathetic because the one who screwed up wasn't you. Perhaps he would tell her. She was too deep into her life to want to start over. Then he broke into a cold sweat thinking of her humiliation if he were arrested.

Lizzy stepped forward. "Have you been crying?"

Something rustled in the hallway.

"Who's there?" Joseph snapped.

"Come in, sweetie," Lizzy whispered, then turned to Joseph. "That's enough. You've scared the boy." Lizzy moved aside to reveal Will clinging to his mother's nightgown. "What has gotten into you?"

"Nothing."

"Perhaps a cold shower would do you better than that powder."

Will walked past his mother and sat on the chaise, rubbing his eyes.

The moment to share his crisis with Lizzy had passed. Joseph noticed the crickets had quit, and the light had begun to raise the dark cape hanging over the city. A new day.

"Come here." Joseph kissed Will's drooping head, then fell back on the chaise with the boy in his arms. He smelled of sleep. "I'm gonna steal your hotness."

Lizzy set the glass on the wicker end table and stirred the digestive powder into the water. The spoon clanged against the glass. "Really, Joseph," she whispered. "What has gotten into you? You act as if someone has died."

* * *

Months after the fire, Joseph was dispirited and pale. None of his clothes fit properly. His teeth hurt. He'd sent his family to Westport for the summer to give himself space to think over what to do next. As the hot months passed, he slowly reversed the majority of Stanton's plans—a glass of digestive powder always within reach—worker privileges were reinstituted, the Manufacturers' Association's emissaries politely rebuffed. His health had improved, but then talk of a move had reaggravated his weak stomach. His longtime neighbors on Snell Street wanted him to move. When you ran a mill in Fall River, you lived in the Highlands. It was that simple. Lizzy understood this. And in September, she returned to the city with a lead on a fashionable address on June Street.

The night before the move, Joseph hesitated outside the dining room door, smelling the rubber of balloons and his cousin's Turkish pipe tobacco. He'd already caught a whiff of Lizzy's famous pumpkin pie cooling in the kitchen. His back stiffened. What was she up to? A moving party?

There was a rustling inside; the hoarse breathing of his sick boy, Will; the mousy squeaks of Lizzy's cousins. The Durfees knew how to celebrate good fortune. Someone shushed the group. A chair creaked.

"Elizabeth?"

"Come in." Her tone was gay. Oh no.

"Surprise!"

The door had not swung back to center before Joseph switched direction and marched into the hall, almost breaking his neck on a stack of packing crates. He pushed straight into the parlor only to find his mother, Constance, wrapping a gift in purple and yellow tissue paper. She held a crystal ashtray in one hand. Startled, she didn't rush to cover the other pieces: a letter opener, penholder, a leather-covered writing tablet. The gift had taken planning. And his mother rarely spent money on this scale. It was probably English crystal that had required a special outing to Boston or Providence. Her shock softened into pride as she approached Joseph with the ashtray.

"Won't that look handsome on your new desk?"

"Why?" He shook his head, then threw up his arms. What weren't they hearing? He bowed his head.

"It's time to celebrate, Joseph. If your father was—"

Joseph cut her off with his raised hand and exited the room. He stopped in the vestibule to dislodge a strand of royal-blue ribbon from his ankle. The children's noisemakers still rattled in the dining room. He stepped through doorway after doorway until it seemed to him he was crossing hundreds as he wound his way through walls he had knocked down to make this former three-flat into a single-family house. There were nooks he'd never set foot in. He had given Elizabeth almost three thousand square feet, for heaven's sake. What number would please her? He'd grown up in one of the original apartments—five people competing for oxygen in little more than eight hundred square feet.

In a dark alcove at the base of the stairs, Otis was packed and ready to move. He'd always had nothing but contempt for the Highlands. The portrait, commissioned a year before his death, sat half out of a wooden packing crate stuffed with straw. The old man's stare sent chills down Joseph's back. There was just no pleasing the man.

Joseph stuffed the portrait into the crate and stepped to the glass panes framing the front door, stopping momentarily to press his hand to the glass. The cold rain pounded the garden into a soggy gray mud pool, all except for the last blooming roses, a cluster of orange teas called Sutter's Gold, which Elizabeth had told him not to cut back. But the cold had won. The flower heads were frozen. In years past, by this time, the bush would be pruned and smothered in manure, but she'd wanted it to keep blooming until they moved. She'd almost gotten her wish.

Inside his study, he stopped to listen for the pattering of feet, but all was quiet save the wind. What didn't they understand? Had he not made his wishes clear? Now they shall know what I mean, he thought. He heard someone calling his name from deep within the house. He slammed the study door shut.

The study smelled of smoldering wood smoke and the cedarwood cigar box that Hannah Cleveland had presented him when he took over the mill. The Cuban cigars inside had gone untouched. His study would be the last room packed. The bookcases lining the walls held the volumes of books he'd shipped home during his brokering years in New York. After work, he would wander eastside bookshops, then dine alone with a new purchase. He'd read each once, his favorites twice. He wanted Elizabeth or the boys to get the bug so they could discuss them, though now, running the mill, his time was limited. He missed the adventure books most, and the stories of the sea. As a boy he'd imagined himself a famous navigator: da Gama, Cortés, Drake, Cartier. Each time he stepped on a Fall River Line boat for home, he wanted to ask the captain to make for the open sea. To be free.

Immediately after the fire, he had been stoic, then humble, receiving Jefferson Cleveland's blessing with modesty and shock. To Elizabeth's dismay, he'd turned him down at first. The money scared him, he said, though he had handled vast amounts for Borden in New York. Then the responsibility, he confided one night in bed. But he knew the cloth business. She knew the cloth business. Otis had made sure he had learned everything. Borden's call convinced him to take over the mill. Elizabeth had tracked her uncle Matt down in Chicago. He called Joseph the following day. Borden stated three reasons why Joseph was the man to lead

Cleveland: for the stockholders, for the operatives, and yes, Uncle Matt conceded, for Otis. *Wasn't that what we decided on the steamer?* Borden pledged his support against the Manufacturers' Association, *but decisions must be made. Others are waiting in the wings.* The second set of books had shown all the crookedness Joseph had feared; of course, they were worthless now, but he had kept them anyway, for some reason, locked in the gun cabinet—Otis's gun cabinet. The old man had been something of a collector. Joseph didn't have shells for half of them. There was a pearl-handled Colt Peacemaker, Winchester and Remington rifles, a Luger semiautomatic, a Smith & Wesson hammerless, plus an assortment of single-barrel shotguns. No doubles. Otis liked to give the pheasants a sporting chance.

He found the cabinet key in his desk and unlocked it. He set two rifles on his desk to get at the red leather ledgers. The paper still smelled of smoke. Joseph picked through the books, stopping occasionally to compute Stanton's neat figures at the end of their orderly columns and rows. Jefferson's blessing worried Joseph. He had his own ideas. Fine goods were the future. The Southern menace already controlled half the coarse-cloth market. Soon they'd own it all. Cleveland Mill would diversify and upgrade equipment. He'd projected lower stockholder returns for three years to offset capital investments. He'd hear the flack. With Jefferson's voting stock he could win any battle, though that wasn't Joseph's style. But Borden was right: decisions had to be made.

In the hallway outside, Lizzy tiptoed past her mother-in-law, with Will and Hollister and her cousins in tow. His mother trampled into the vestibule, her skirts ruffling, prodding her grandsons for information. Joseph's cousins-in-law brought up the rear, pulling up their wool overcoats. The boys raced halfway up the staircase and wedged their faces between the balustrades as their mother eased the study door open, entered, and shut it without a sound.

The fire didn't throw much light, so it took Lizzy a moment to spot the tall outline of her husband across the room. In the weak light, his face appeared bruised. She crossed the room and struck the desk lamp. Joseph stood near the open gun cabinet fingering a book. His willingness to show his anguish over Stanton's death made her love him more. But eight months? Her own sister's death hadn't taken more than four out of her. Oh, Joseph. What shall I do with you? Perhaps I don't understand the depth of this man, she thought. They'd been practically brothers.

His depression had returned the day they bought the house on June Street, and the talk of moving had only exacerbated his blue mood. He'd fought with the bankers and the movers, and then suddenly—recently, in fact—he'd dumped whole affair on Lizzy.

She crept behind him and slid the ledger out of his hand and set it on the desk. She then set about replacing the guns in their carved slots in the cabinet.

Joseph watched her do this, thinking how much he loved his wife. Uncle Matt's endorsement had broken down all barriers to their marriage, but for the first few years, Joseph had found himself the odd man out at family gatherings. Joseph had put on airs for her people by studying up on the Fall River School of Art and chasing golf balls with her brothers on steamy summer beach days. He had lived among the New Yorkers, as the Fall River elite fancied themselves, and still he found himself lowering his voice when his parents' Lancashire brogue slipped out while cheering at a ballgame or singing holiday carols.

Lizzy found his efforts endearing, and let them continue, not wanting to displease her father. But when the old man died, she told Joseph to stop trying so hard. She'd said, "You're stuck with me, Bartlett, so you can quit losing golf balls. It's costing us a small fortune." Joseph knew shooting par could not change his birthright, but he had kept trying until Lizzy released him. She'd had to. With the old man gone, she was totally dependent on her husband.

She locked the gun cabinet, tucked the key in her waistband, and then led him to his leather reading chair. She unlaced his black wingtips and set to rubbing his feet. Where has my brave man gone? she thought. Why such remorse for an accident?

She'd questioned her relatives' mean-spiritedness their first years of marriage, going so far as to reproach her sister-in-law when she overheard her say Joseph would only make Lizzy common. He had carried her higher than most of her cousins. They would now frequent *her* parlor. A full-time cook would follow, a second girl to clean during the day, a touring car for Joseph.

He didn't disapprove of Elizabeth wanting the spoils of her cousins. For this reason, he neglected to tell her that Jefferson Cleveland had not transferred Stanton's shares to him; instead they were put in a revocable trust until his wife Hannah's death. So when Lizzy called him the new majority stockholder of the Cleveland Mill, he didn't correct her. His considerable raise would offset any doubts. He would provide Lizzy with the means to be active in society, but with one caveat: he would not always be at her side. Respecting each other's personal foibles and biases had been an unspoken arrangement since the first year of their marriage, and periodically each added his or her own amendments to this contract.

"Darling." She lifted his feet to her lap.

Her silky red hair was pulled straight up on the sides into a thick knot stuck through with ivory combs. He remembered the shopgirl who had sold him the combs at Bloomingdale's. She was lovely girl—a reader too. That had been in New York, after he'd first met Elizabeth Bartlett at her uncle Matt's lake home in New Hampshire. Then, as now, Lizzy looked up at him with her blue eyes, making him a bigger man.

The wind beat against the windowpanes. Did she say something? He felt her hands rolling his socks off. She laced her fingers between his toes. The wind died.

"The party was for all of us. To say goodbye to Snell Street. This is the only home the boys have known."

Joseph pulled his feet off her lap and stood up. He saw his reflection in the glass of the gun cabinet and shut off the desk lamp. He poked at the fire. He hated his behavior and ground his teeth so hard his jaw ached. Blood pumped under his temples. Shadows shifted under the door sweep. He'd done right by the Sheehans by allowing them to move rent-free into the house to care for his mother. And it was his idea that the mill complex would bear Stanton's name. It's a start, he thought, a retreat from perdition.

"There was nothing you could have done." Elizabeth stood facing her husband. For all her love, she couldn't take much more. She had waited too long for this ascension. She held Joseph's chin in her palm. "This will stop at June Street." She stepped to the door. Young Will's wooden toy train set lay in heap in the corner.

Joseph said, "I'm responsible."

"Rubbish." She threw up her hands.

Joseph shook his head. "It was an accident, but one I caused," he continued, his voice barely audible. "There's blood on my hands."

Elizabeth turned to the fire. Her shoulders fell. Impossible. Suddenly she didn't trust her legs and sat down on the leather ottoman. "No," she said. The tightness of her corset was suffocating.

"Yes." The pounding in Joseph's head abated. His toes released the carpet. "Stanton kept crooked books. The red ledgers. On that night—"

"Stop talking." Elizabeth put her hands over her ears. A second set of books? Fires? Four men dead. Four wives abandoned. Eight children. And her Joseph at the center of it? Not possible. But what of her boys? June Street?

"Oh, Lizzy. How I've wanted to tell you."

The Durfee blood in Lizzy thumped from her chest as it had never before. She said, "Now you have." She stood. All the light in the room seemed to emanate from her eyes. "The die has been cast. As Minister Johns might say, 'By mercy and truth iniquity is purged: and by the fear of the Lord men depart from evil.'"

Joseph hated when Holy Rollers used the Bible as an index, simply flipping to an obtuse passage that justified their every thought or action. But alas, Joseph replied with a scripture passage of his own: "The labor of the righteous tendeth to life: the fruit of the wicked to sin."

She countered, "The lot is cast into the lap; but the whole disposing thereof is of the Lord."

"Oh, Lizzy." Joseph slumped in the chair. "How I have prayed."

"Put trust in Him." She knelt before her husband. "And come with me." She waited for him to look up.

Minutes passed. He began to weep.

Elizabeth crossed her arms. "You have this night. Tomorrow we reshuffle our cards. The boys and I are leaving with or without you. What's done is done." The room began to spin. Another word and she would collapse to the floor. She steadied herself on the ottoman and walked to his desk and picked at the ledgers with her middle finger, swiping the yellowed pages to and fro. She looked at her husband slumped on the couch. Her heart beat faster. No bogus arithmetic, she thought, is taking my family down. She thumped the ledgers closed and tucked them under her arm. She stepped to the hearth and tossed one then the other into the fire, and then marched across the room.

"Lizzy?" She stopped at the door but did not turn. In three weeks they'd be married ten years.

"Yes, Joseph."

"Oh, Lizzy." He wept. "What can I do?"

"I'll be waiting outside this door." She paused and turned to the hearth. The fire raged, filling the room with red light. "You have the night." As she turned the doorknob the shadows lurking beneath it scattered.

Joseph heard a balloon pop followed by laughter. The wood smoke mixed with the smell of pumpkin pie and coffee. The moving party went off as planned.

PART III
1912

You made me what I am today,
I should hope you're satisfied,
You dragged and dragged me down until
My soul within me died.

You've shattered each and every dream,
You fooled me right from the start,
And though you're not true, may God bless you,
That's the curse of an aching heart.

—"The Curse of an Aching Heart"
(You Made Me What I Am Today)
Henry Fink, Lyrics / Al Piantadosi, Composer

YOUNG SOLDIER

Despite changing out of his gabardine suit and into a light blazer and cotton slacks, Joseph perspired the entire drive. North of Boston, the high clouds lost their sinister blackness and the driving rain decreased, but the persistent drizzle was enough to keep the windows sealed and the breeze out. It was an unseasonably warm April day, the hottest Patriots' Day in recent memory. Thankfully, young Will had dozed most of the trip after a sleepless night anticipating seeing his brother for the first time in nine months.

As Joseph pulled through the gates of the White Mountain Military Academy, his palms moistened. When he had told Will that they were going to visit his brother, Will ran screaming to his room, shouting he was sorry for whatever wrong he'd done. "Please don't dump me, too, Daddy," he sobbed. Joseph's heart broke.

Joseph had yet to hear from his older son. He assumed he had not escaped or shot an instructor, but a letter from the boy was long overdue. Joseph expected a long rant. This lack of news made Joseph more skeptical that the academy, regardless of its reputation for saving "problem boys," could rehabilitate Hollister. What Joseph didn't know was that Hollister's letter writing had been prolific. The campus postmaster gave the first letter to the school's commandant, retired Major General Darby Blunt, who after reading the beginning salutation, *Dear Jailer*, knew the letter was headed, not to Joseph, but into Hollister's already thick file, which he kept under lock and key. After Labor Day, he sent Hollister another envelope with instructions to try again. Blunt commandeered that effort, too, in which Hollister compared his father's backbone to that of a slug's penis.

Hollister thrived at White Mountain. He demonstrated superior aptitude in mathematics, science, military history, and strategy, though his instructors warned Blunt that in war games designed to reenact scenes from the Spanish-American War, Hollister had a tendency to replace the San Juan Heights with Fall River, decimating his hometown on paper. In a report on modern warfare he estimated the damage land- and sea-based artillery might inflict on a certain house on June Street. It was exacting work to be sure, and Hollister's painstaking detail—including work camps in the mills, and a floating prison on the South Wattupa—was what troubled the commandant, though the military man in Blunt thought the work showed promise. He wrote to Joseph, saying the boy had a real aptitude for warfare but suggested he keep him sequestered for the holidays, and for Joseph to delay his planned visit until the next term. For Christmas, Blunt gave his new protégé Sun Tzu's *The Art of War*. In the winter term, Blunt extended the boy's privileges, keeping him out of only one activity: the shooting range. During live-fire exercises, Hollister was summoned to Blunt's office, where the two discussed historical battles over games of chess. Blunt spoke in a circular manner that began and ended with a story about his father, another decorated soldier, and the importance of his family in his military career. Hollister knew what the old man was up to, but listened quietly, not wanting to ruin their time with the nonsense he threw at the younger instructors. If Blunt wanted to believe he could make a soldier out of the boy, then he'd let him dream. In spite of himself, Hollister was fascinated by the stories, particularly Blunt's taking San Juan Hill with Teddy Roosevelt's Rough Riders. As winter thawed into spring, Hollister came to realize that the military might be his route out of Fall River forever.

* * *

Joseph parked the Pope-Hartford next to the large touring cars and Cadillacs near the administration building. Across the lot, rusted carriages and tired steeds idled in the shade. Patriots' Day brought the rich and scholarship families together at the school. Joseph hoped his tuition dollars supported a few good boys as he and Will fell in with the crowd. The drizzle had momentarily stopped. The trees on the woody campus had just begun to bud. A mild winter and soggy spring had turned the grounds a lush green.

Wooden bleachers had been erected on either side of the main road that ran through the campus. In the ball field at the far end, the student regiments stood in full parade uniform. The school band led the procession, the skins of their drums read WHITE MOUNTAIN INF. REGT. in red ink. The drum major lifted his baton, and the drummers began tapping out "Hail, Columbia." The crowd sang as the horns blew. Following the band, four old gray mules pulled the school's only mobile firepower: two decommissioned Civil War cannons. Four cadets rode atop the guns. Red, white, and blue bunting fluttered off the rear of their wagons.

The youngsters, the nine- and ten-year-olds, followed the cannons, their heels tapping out a synchronized beat. Wooden rifles rested on their shoulders. Parents stood and pointed as their boys passed. Each cluster of boys turned and saluted Commandant Blunt, their stout leader, and the academy instructors sitting on the review stand opposite their parents. Blunt stiffly saluted each passing unit. Joseph was surprised to see a few women in the teaching ranks, though they were not in uniform, and all rather dreary looking—English teachers, he surmised. He wouldn't mind if Helen were sent to such a place. As far away from Will as possible.

"Where's Hollister?" Will stood on the bleachers squinting into the crowd. "They all look the same."

In Blunt's invitation to the event, he had mentioned that Joseph might not recognize his son; and indeed, as much as he craned his neck scanning cadets, Hollister had vanished. I am a horrible man, he thought. The boy couldn't be motivated to participate in team sports in Fall River, thinking that he could be won over by this type of discipline was ludicrous. Will soon gave up searching for his brother. He pulled his coat tight over his shoulders, bracing against the drizzle. Joseph wrapped his arm around him.

"We'll find him," he said as a bolt of lightning flashed across the darkening sky. "Perhaps he's won a special commendation and is waiting for his introduction."

When the drizzle turned to a downpour, Blunt announced they were cutting the parade and speeches short and the families should head to the cafeteria. The cadets lined each side of the brick walk holding black umbrellas for their guests. Inside, another set of cadets handed each mother a scarlet carnation as she entered the mess hall. The room was long and white with state flags hanging from the rafters. At the far end there was a stage. Old Glory hung from the ceiling over the pulled navy drapes. White tablecloths covered the mess tables. Joseph sent Will off to the seating chart to find their place. Mothers held their boys by the hand, many speechless at how clean their boys looked, though a few weren't satisfied and began applying wet thumbs to errant hairs. The fathers who hadn't served told their sons how girls went weak in the knees over a bloke in uniform. Others stood back-to-back with their boys, impressed how much they'd grown, as if the school had altered their biology as well as their attitude. The military fathers stood silently behind their wives, never taking their proud eyes off the miniature versions of themselves. Joseph recognized a few of the men from the photos that hung in the administrative office.

"Over here," Will shouted above the din. Joseph spotted him next to a table set near the kitchen. Each time one of the student waiters swung through the doors a blast of warm air followed, carrying with it the smell of roasted beef and potatoes. "Have you found him?"

"Not yet." Joseph was surprised to find himself and Will seated near Blunt's table, but then all the staff had been mixed with the cadets. A student stood near the table with his back toward Joseph. "May we sit anywhere, young man?" Joseph asked.

"Yes, sir," the tall boy said, his voice deep. He waved to a cadet across the cafeteria.

"We enjoyed the parade," Joseph remarked, thinking the boy was much thicker in the shoulders than his son.

"Thank you, sir." Another clipped response. Joseph wondered if they were allowed to string two sentences together.

Joseph said, "Is it something you practice?"

"We march every day."

"You do it very well."

The cadets stood at attention and saluted when Blunt entered the cafeteria. Not knowing any better, Will jumped to his feet, and Joseph followed. A smattering of applause greeted Blunt, but he waved it off; from his thin smile, Joseph could tell he had expected nothing less. He was a tall, thick-bodied man with a bushy sponge of white hair and confident stride; though he walked briskly, his head and shoulders moved stiffly, and Joseph detected a slight grimace when he turned his head. His wore a dress uniform that didn't appear very army. Joseph noticed it wasn't made from the coarse wool of the students' uniforms, but from a superior linen fabric.

"Yes," the student standing before Joseph smirked. "We are swell marchers." The boy fell forward over a chair, laughing hysterically.

"Hollister?"

"Hollister!" Will raced around the table and vaulted into his brother's ropy arms. Hollister lifted him into the air, kissed his cheek, and then playfully rapped his knuckles against his younger brother's head. Will clung to his brother's neck and Hollister held him against his chest.

"I knew I could fool you. I knew it." Hollister's face lit up. The light reflected off his white scalp through his closely cropped hair.

Joseph sank into his chair and watched his sons, mouth agape. It was his boy, but a larger, stronger version, with a fine coating of fuzz over his lip. But unmistakably a Bartlett. He was struck by the sudden tenderness he felt for Hollister; he'd expected the boy to take a swing at him. And poor Will. Not until this moment did Joseph realize how lonely he was on June Street. Joseph blinked. He looked around the room at the family reunions occurring across the shiny parquet floor. He was unsure how he had gotten to this sad place in his life, seated on the most rigid wooden chair he had ever encountered, under the flat light of a military school cafeteria in the middle of New Hampshire. How far the Bartlett name had fallen in the last two years. Oh Lizzy, he thought. I've failed miserably.

Joseph rolled his tongue over his teeth. He looked down and caught his reflection in the china place setting. His pale complexion looked ashen. Was it possible that this place and Commandant Blunt were the elixir to

cure the family's ills? How could a crude alchemy of discipline and isolation change his wild child into a young soldier? Joseph watched his sons'
horseplay. Was such a metamorphosis possible?

The mother seated next to him squeezed his forearm. She said, "That
tall one's the spitting image of his father."

Joseph smiled at the woman and sipped his water. She winked. He was
content to sit the entire afternoon and listen to the music of his boys' laughter.

"I told the guys you wouldn't recognize me." Hollister turned to his
father. "Sir?"

"Call me Dad."

"Commandant insists we respect—"

"Then, Father."

"I fooled you too."

"What's in the water?"

"It's the uniform."

Joseph stood quickly, knocking his knee against the table. Water
sloshed over the rim of his glass onto the ironed tablecloth. "And you've
grown. And look at your face—that fuzzy lip of yours."

Hollister lowered Will and stroked his chin. His back stiffened. "That's
my mustache."

"Of course," Joseph said, rubbing his sore knee. "And a damn fine
one." Over the edge of Hollister's tight collar, Joseph spotted thin, gauzy
scars from last summer's accident. That was the gutless euphemism he'd
used when describing Maria's assault and near rape to Mary Sheehan:
"Hollister's accident."

Standing toe to toe, Hollister's nose came to Joseph's chin. Soon he'd
surpass his old man's six feet.

"And you've just had a birthday. Did you get my card?"

"Yes, sir."

"We've got something for you in the Pope."

"I saw you checking out my regiment."

"I spied each group, but couldn't make you out."

Joseph was waiting for an outburst, a roundhouse. He set his hand
on Hollister's shoulder, rubbed the thick wool between his thumb and

forefinger. Quality stuff. Hollister's face was flushed. His eyes sparkled. Could he be genuinely happy to see me? Blunt may have carved a soldier from a block of wood in less than a year, but Joseph still remembered the scheming little boy he had dropped off nine months ago. All the crooked edges couldn't have been whittled down in that time, could they?

Hollister extended his hand, and Joseph pulled him into a hug. Hollister pressed his hands into Joseph's back. As Joseph relaxed his embrace, Hollister pulled tighter. A father seated at their table snapped at his son to stop staring. Will's face flushed. He tugged at his father's sleeve.

Hollister turned his mouth to his father's ear and whispered, "Mother always said you were weak. And it was your weakness that destroyed this family."

The cafeteria door opened, followed by the clanging of pots and pans. As the crowd whirled, Joseph jabbed his thumbs into Hollister's armpits releasing the boy's iron grip.

"I'm still your father," Joseph hissed. Hollister turned away and Joseph clutched Hollister's elbow. "You'll do as I say."

Will weaseled his shoulders between his father and brother. Joseph clutched the boy to his side and kissed the top of his head. Hollister busied himself pressing down his suit pants and jacket.

"Ladies and gentlemen," a cadet announced from kitchen doors, "lunch is served."

* * *

The Bartlett family waited outside Blunt's office in the dimly lit administrative building, seated on yet another trio of ridged wooden chairs, waiting for their name to be called. Will sat between his father and brother.

A cadet with a clipboard appeared at the end of the hallway. "Bartlett!"

Joseph set his hand on Will's shoulder. "Wait here." Joseph shuffled through a table full of magazines and handed his youngest a *National Geographic* instead of one with a gun on the cover.

Blunt stood behind a large oak desk. "Welcome." Blunt pointed to the chair opposite the desk. "Please." Hollister stood at attention inside the door, his khaki cap tucked under his arm.

A large painting of William Tecumseh Sherman followed Joseph across the large rectangular office. The room was carpeted with Persian rugs and oxblood leather chairs. Two tall glass cabinets held military books and trinkets such as a miniature cannon cigarette lighter and a collection of hand-painted Revolutionary War soldiers. A rosewood corner table held a whalebone chess set. Joseph paused before the fireplace. He'd expected a spartan office, but this matched the man's taste in fabrics.

"We finally meet, Mr. Bartlett." Blunt extended a hand across the desk.

"Your letters are brief," Joseph said. He shook Blunt's thick hand and froze. Blunt's chin was dotted with shallow-pitted wounds, and his neck burnt red. The raised tendril-like scars fanned out from his collar like sucker shoots from an oak tree. Joseph imagined a white-hot cannonball exploding on a dusty Puerto Rican hill. Was this why he quit the regular army? Blunt's square jaw turned up and he smiled, stretching the scars on his neck, their bloody hue softening to a warm salmon.

"War souvenir," Blunt said, pumping Joseph's hand three times. "I hope the luncheon was satisfactory?"

After a moment, Joseph squeezed back. "Yes, fine, of course," Joseph stumbled.

"You know, I found our cook in Cuba and paid the freight for her pots and pans. Can you imagine? She wouldn't come unless I brought her cooking utensils."

"Now I see why my son is getting so strong."

Blunt shifted his weight and Joseph glimpsed a silk-wrapped saber mounted behind the desk.

"Yes, our boy." Blunt stopped, his eyes taking in Hollister. "We've made some strides. Haven't we?"

"Yes, sir," Hollister snapped.

"And there are more to come. Mr. Bartlett, I have friends in Washington, in the military, who rely on me to identify promising soldiers." Blunt stood up straight, crossing his arms. "Spots are held for me to fill at West Point."

"The military academy?"

"The very one."

"You're not implying . . ."

"I thought he might tell you over lunch."

"There was no time, sir," Hollister said.

"Of course."

Joseph looked at Blunt and then to Hollister. "When would this be?"

"Next fall. Hollister would stay on and take summer school until then."

"Nine months can't make a man." Joseph gestured toward the door, but Hollister kept his eyes forward.

"We had good raw material," Blunt said.

"I've spoken to Trinity College in Hartford, plus there is a summer job waiting. You'll learn the cotton business with a clearinghouse. I've had it all arranged."

"Thank you, sir. But I prefer the first option." Hollister's eyes burned a hole in the window behind Blunt. He'd somehow gotten stiffer standing in the office.

"That's all you have to say? You prefer? This really isn't your decision." Joseph turned, eyeballing his son. Then to Blunt. "Or yours, Mr. Blunt."

A wiry smile crept across Blunt's face. "Of course not, Mr. Bartlett. You're in charge."

"Certain actions have limited the boy's options." Joseph hated to bring up Maria, but he needed to take back control. Did they call this rehabilitation or brainwashing? "Last summer the boy wept in a tree fort after the death of his mother, and today he's ready to lead a skirmish line in some far-flung Indian campaign?"

Blunt came around his desk and leaned against the corner.

"He is no longer a boy, Mr. Bartlett. White Mountain has taught him discipline and responsibility and given him a sense of duty to something besides his own hide."

Joseph pictured Maria's dented face. He pushed back the leather armchair and sat. He was tired of standing between these two.

Blunt turned to Hollister. "Your father has made you a good offer, son. College. A job in the family business." Blunt was offering the boy cover like he would a fellow soldier on the battlefield.

"I'm an army man now, sir," Hollister said, looking at Blunt, but Joseph knew to whom the comment was directed. "Cotton is not my future."

Joseph glared at the painting of Sherman. *You* went there. Is my boy West Point material? Damn. Will is my only hope.

Blunt said, "Son, why don't you take your brother on the tour of the campus. I want to speak to your father alone."

"Yes, sir." Hollister saluted Blunt, snapped his heels, and spun around.

When the door shut, Joseph jumped out of the chair. He raised his arm, but thought better of it. He looked right, left, then back to Sherman's portrait. His arms settled on his hips. "I want my son back, Mr. Blunt."

"He's a real leader, that boy. A real strategist. He took the older boys' guff and proved his worth." Blunt walked over to the chessboard and snapped up a knight. "The army would hate to lose a leader like that. He might turn the tide of a battle someday."

"He's a manipulator. He knows the path of least resistance. Always has."

"I think we've broken him of that."

"He's coming home."

"You must let go, Mr. Bartlett." He turned to the chessboard. "Knight takes pawn. Hollister is strong, smart; he's a young man now."

"A young man who may be a threat to others—and you want to give him a gun."

"Let the army educate him a tad longer. We're in the business of changing boys into men. There is prestige associated with these academy appointments. Much more than a bought admission to Trinity College."

"I don't like what you're insinuating, Mr. Blunt."

"Insinuating? Oh hell. Am I not being direct, Mr. Bartlett? The boy will fail in Hartford without the discipline of the military, and you know it. Nine months ago he might have killed the next girl he seduced, but—"

"Mr. Blunt, *if you please.*" Joseph slowly removed his bowler and ran his hand through his thinning hair.

"The army will teach him to respect his fellow man."

"And women?" Joseph interjected.

"Of course." Blunt walked back around his desk and ran his finger down a roster of names. He glanced at a wall clock. "When you first called, you asked me if I could find something your son is good at. 'If you find that,' you said, 'then he has a chance.' Well, Mr. Bartlett, it is not buying cotton for one of your mills. The boy has a mind for military strategy like I've never seen before. And a gift for mapmaking. He can glance at a battlefield and re-create the terrain in minutes."

Joseph clicked his tongue over his teeth. Elizabeth had purchased an easel and paints for the boy one Christmas, but Joseph had never given more than a cursory glance at the portraits.

"Are you saying my boy is good at the mechanics of war?"

Blunt snapped and pointed at Joseph. "Exactly."

Joseph ground his teeth. No movement.

"Please let me know your decision." Blunt marched to the door. "I need to write my friends in Washington in the next few weeks. It's complicated." Blunt opened the door. "Sir, I have other parents waiting."

Joseph zeroed in on the flecks and folds of black oil paint in Sherman's eyes. Are you watching this charade? Do you judge me like old man Otis? He set his hand on the mantel. He glanced at Blunt then back at the portrait. Otis would have dealt with the boy at home. He whispered, "But times have changed, old man."

"Sir?" Blunt said.

Joseph whipped back his hair and dropped his bowler over the crown of his head.

"No need to wait," he said, and extended his hand. "The boy can do as he wishes."

"Excellent. Excellent." Blunt gripped Joseph's shoulder, guiding him into the hallway. "Good day, Mr. Bartlett."

Joseph stopped on the threshold. "You'll watch out for him?"

Blunt replied loudly so the others would hear. "I watch out for all my boys."

The parents in the hallway set down their magazines; the women smiled awkwardly to one another; the fathers continued to pace.

* * *

Beside the car Will handed Hollister his present, a balsa wood plane model.

"I'll fly a real one someday," he said, handing the model back to Will. "You build it."

Will hugged his brother. Other families walked past. The air was wet. Car engines roared.

"Will, wait in the car," Joseph said over his shoulder.

"Sir." Hollister extended a hand.

Joseph searched his son's eyes for some sign of recognition of what he'd done, some sign of the scared boy he'd dropped off nine months ago. He said, "You've hurt people." He squeezed Hollister's hand. "What do you say to that?" Joseph crunched his son's hand, gnashing his knuckles. Hollister swayed but refused to buckle.

"I say nothing."

"Nothing?"

"I say sorry." Joseph released Hollister's hand. Two classmates walked past. One brushed his shoulder.

"I told Blunt he could make you a soldier. Fall River can wait."

"I'm not coming back," Hollister said, rubbing his palm.

"Everyone returns home. And when you do, you'll face what you've done."

"I won't fail."

"Just survive." Joseph squeezed Hollister's shoulders. "And pray."

"To Mother every day."

"I love you, son."

"Sir." Hollister swiveled on his heel and fell in with the other boys.

* * *

On the drive back, Will spoke excitedly about dorm rooms with gun racks built into the walls, though the guns were only wooden models. He said Hollister was sure Joseph would demand he go to Hartford and that that would have just caused a huge fight because there was no way he was going.

Joseph brushed his son's head and sighed. "Yep, we have an army man in the family now."

Will flew the model plane box across the dash, making engine noises.

"After we check in with the cotton agents tonight, we'll stay in Boston. See if the Red Sox are in town. Whaddaya say?"

"Yeah, Dad. Great."

Joseph cracked his window when the drizzle stopped. At a break in the clouds, a large rainbow appeared, and he veered off the motorway to a muddy dirt lane for a better look. When Will ran off to urinate behind some budding forsythia, he pulled out his handkerchief to shine the bell-shaped grill of the Pope. Wiggins needed a speaking to about car maintenance. The man's binges were legendary. Joseph caught himself smiling in the shiny chrome. Hollister was as obstinate and reckless as ever. A West Point appointment! Huh! Amazing! There was no job in Hartford, no admission to Trinity College. He'd made it all up to see what Hollister would choose: the easy street in Hartford or the rigid army way. White Mountain had indeed taught him something. And now they could take responsibility for his actions, Joseph thought. I'm sorry, Lizzy. He kissed his knuckle and rubbed his chest.

"Looking good, Dad," Will said, buttoning his trousers.

Joseph stepped back and snapped the hankie against the grill. "Spic and span like your brother."

"Can't believe he's a soldier."

"Indeed," Joseph whispered. And God help the poor bastards that have to fight him.

LAND BETWEEN MY HANDS

Joseph left June Street at three-thirty, motoring down Main Road in Tiverton. He crossed Stone Bridge and entered Portsmouth, passing Island Park near four that afternoon. Middletown was a short distance farther. He drove slower than usual, hoping he'd run out of gas or a gale might blow up from Mount Hope Bay and him an excuse to turn back home. But Wiggins had filled the tank for the weekend, and the Lord had delivered another brilliant late-summer day. In the months following his Patriots' Day visit to White Mountain, Joseph had replayed his altercation with Hollister in the cafeteria. He'd begun to question his abandonment of the boy. All summer this poisonous stew simmered, and now, going to see Maria for the first time since the accident, the pot boiled over.

Otis Bartlett had bought the Middletown farm as a real estate investment, not for its rich black soil. Before Hannah Cleveland had handed Joseph the mill, he'd planned to quit and set about making the farm a profitable business. João turned a profit now, but a substantial infrastructure investment was necessary to sell large quantities of his butter and milk out of state. In their state-of-the-farm meeting last year, when João said distributors could handle sales, Joseph expressed his fears about putting too many middlemen between the farm and its customers. João's other brainstorm, to add cattle to the dairy operation, was swiftly vetoed.

The sweet honeysuckle that rimmed the eastern edge of the property brought a smile to Joseph. It had been Lizzy's idea to plant it, and though her nursery and greenhouse plan never grew out of its small plot near the house, Kitty maintained it religiously. At the turnoff he honked at Kitty packing up her vegetable and flower stand. She was a short, stout woman with muscular arms and deeply tanned skin from another summer spent working outdoors. Joseph had always been fond of Kitty. She'd been widowed some ten years, but with João's help, she kept up her family's vegetable operation. She and her two daughters managed the stand from June through September, selling out most days to day-trippers and summer residents of Newport.

Kitty stood and waved fruit flies off the tomatoes when the car stopped. She turned the bruised patches down. When she didn't hear a car door slam, she stood and raised her hand to block the sun.

"Well, Mr. Bartlett, you are a welcome sight for lonely eyes." Though she was a few years older than Joseph, she insisted on calling him Mr. Bartlett out of respect for Otis. The old man had allowed her family to stay on the farm after the foreclosure, though he'd politely asked the brother who had run it into the ground to leave. "What brings you out to the country on a late Sunday?"

"Some business with the boss," Joseph called over the engine's hum.

"Been a time since you been out this way."

"Want a ride to the house?" Joseph pointed up the road. "You can remind me of the way."

"Can you wait a minute? I'm just packing up. Mostly crickets today."

Joseph pulled the brake and got out and helped her load wooden crates of tomatoes and melons and corn into the back of the car. Kitty set the flower bucket between her legs in the passenger's side. Each dime bundle was tied with red ribbon.

"Hand me one of those."

Joseph ran his hand up the bunch of flowers and then pressed his palm to his nose. Besides the hybrid tea roses, Lizzy's garden in the city had gone to seed. He plucked out a yellow begonia and tucked it in the band of his hat.

"Lizzy loved flowers." He handed Kitty a black-eyed Susan.

"I know," Kitty said. She squeezed his forearm and then wove the flower stem through her coiled hair. As the car gained speed, the earthy smell of the vegetables circulated between the seats.

Kitty said, "I thought the big farm meeting was never going to happen."

"Is that what it is called?"

"João asked me to put in our wish list a month ago."

"You have a real democracy here." João's diplomacy always tickled Joseph. He wished he had such a luxury at the mill. Before Kitty began to lobby him directly, he asked, "So, Kitty, how has the new girl worked out?"

"New girl?"

He played dumb. "What's her name? Maria?"

"She's not so new anymore." Kitty adjusted the flower bucket between her legs. The shine went out of her eyes. "She lives with me and the girls. Had night terrors at first but now sleeps most nights. A little weak in the right eye but don't complain none."

Kitty looked out her window and removed her hairpins. The cool breeze swept her hair back. In the rearview mirror, Joseph watched the black-eyed Susan tumble down the middle of the dirt lane. He braced for questions about Hollister or what he'd done for Maria's family. None came. He had endured such silences. Evelyn and Mary Sheehan—heck, even his own mother—had had similar reactions at the mention of the girl's name. The greatest isolation over the long winter came at night, alone in bed. Joseph had imagined their tight lips were a result of not wanting the conversation to lead to their opinions of his poor parenting or, worse, Lizzy's. He feared what they said about him in private.

"She up at your place?"

"Sundays she's at the big house, João's teaching her to read." Kitty lifted the flower bucket to her lap. "Oh, there was something: a fire in one of the outbuildings. A lamp fell, but João smothered it. Burnt his hands, though."

"Badly?"

"Bad enough. Maria made an aloe salve for the burns."

Joseph removed the begonia from his hatband and laid it on the dash. He turned to Kitty. "Thank you for minding her."

Kitty had the last word on the matter. "She's a quiet girl," she offered, "but industrious."

At the house, Kitty called to one of the boys to unload the vegetables and flower bucket. She waved goodbye to Joseph, thanking him for the lift, her tight smile telling him what she really thought of him.

* * *

João sat in the front parlor, going over the sales figures, Expanding the sweet corn was the next project, then, God willing, a cranberry bog. The low rumble of Joseph's car filled the house. João lowered the ledger book and folded his reading glasses. The car horn moaned twice, and Maria looked up, startled from her book. She had taken to reading Otis's books to learn English, just as João had years before. Today she'd complained of chills, and João had draped a brown afghan over her shoulders. When the car engine cut, João resisted the urge to go to her. He caught her eye. Her pupils widened. They both looked at the clock on the mantel. Joseph was right on time. Turning back to the ledger in his lap, João could not recall the figure he'd just computed for the cost of excavating a bog. The clock's ticking filled the room.

Kitty had been encouraging Maria for a week now to start readying herself for going back to the city. Her family said a year was enough recuperation. They needed an extra hand with the small children or for her to earn a higher wage on a factory floor.

"It's time." João walked to the door. He wore gray-striped overalls under a denim vest and a white cotton shirt with cutoff sleeves. His thick black hair stood on end. (He ran a hand through it when calculating figures.) He paused to tuck his reading glasses in the breast pocket of the vest, hoping Maria would respond, but she hadn't spoken much the past year, and she didn't now, just kept her eyes trained on the window.

João set her bags near the door. Since she'd come with so little, there wasn't much to pack. He crossed his long brown arms. "Here are your things."

He walked in front of the window to make sure she understood.

Her gaze seemed to go through him. It was a look that had confounded him these last months. It occupied a state somewhere between coma and comprehension. But he hadn't seen it in the two weeks since the reunion dance.

Lately his eyes hadn't been zooming directly to the anchor-shaped scar on the bridge of her nose where the broomstick had struck. She had caught him staring more than once. The summer sun and time had muted the scar to a mere smudge. A stranger would notice the bend of her nose, but not the scar—not unless they had seen her in the month after the accident. Luckily, her mother had pinched the skin tight in the hours after the blow. But it saddened him to think that every calm pool or glass window she looked into would remind her of the horrid event. And then the screaming nightmares that had kept Kitty and her girls up nights would return. João wondered, as he often did, what sort of disfigurement Hollister carried. He had often dreamt of the deep scars he would someday inflict on the boy. He looked out the window.

Joseph waved to João.

The younger man nodded. He turned back to Maria, then pointed to her bags. "He won't wait long."

She blinked, their code that she understood.

"Thirty minutes."

* * *

The men sat on a stone bench between two large hydrangeas, the acidic soil produced brilliant blue flowers. João's gardens produced Kitty's dime bouquets. Joseph had removed his jacket and rolled up his sleeves. The farm brought roughness out in men. João's ropy limbs mocked Joseph's smooth forearms.

He said, "How's that new tractor working out?"

"That new engine, she's beautiful. Raises our profit. More of that in the future."

"I like hearing you talk about the future."

João squinted into the fading sun. "The sun's my friend—and the rain. I feel at home. If I can't feel the land between my hands, I want to die."

Joseph removed his hat to fan his face. "Kitty said something about a fire?"

"In the tool shed. Small, but straw burn terrible."

"You burnt?"

"Jeez, hands hurt pretty bad." João raised his scarred hands and shrugged. "But I don't think she'll leave no pain."

There's a slight change in the boy, Joseph thought. João kept smiling at his hands. But there was something else—something off, something missing. Joseph, suddenly irritated, changed the subject. They both knew why he was there. "So how is she?"

"She hardly speaks," João said, his smile widening. "But she a good worker from barn to field."

She'd spoken no more than a handful of words, preferring instead to nod at João's farm chore demonstrations or wave to his dinner suggestions or exhale an exasperated moan when a cow kicked over a milking pail. Though at first unnerved by her reluctance to speak, João had come to find this arrangement agreeable; it required he make eye contact with Maria to assure her understanding. Like Maria's relocation, he hadn't had much of a choice in the matter of his own. But after nearly six years he had accepted his fate. It wasn't the life he'd dreamed of on his crossing— the point had been to *get off* the farm. But this wasn't his father's arid soil. He could produce here. And lately, he'd seen its potential and begun to spend more time in the farm office than in the barn. He only milked in the morning—and that was because he liked watching the sunrise. Maria, too, had taken a liking to the early morning rhythms of farm life and insisted on taking on more chores, though João had told her to ease into it. She started on with the butter girls, making Rose Butter—*Extra Alfalfa Makes It Super Creamy*—but when two men left without notice, he pulled her to the milking barn. She'd taken to the job. He enjoyed having someone around who understood Portuguese, and had assumed they'd discuss life in the Azores, given she was from a nearby island, but she showed little interest in their homeland. Mostly, they sat quietly in the musty barn listening to streams of milk ping off the sides of their tin pails. Still, he was happy for the company on cold winter mornings. But as winter turned to spring he began to fear she'd lost any joy in life except tending the animals.

One early morning he told her one of his grandmother's folktales, thinking Maria's relatives had told similar stories.

"To be beautiful is to have blue eyes, blond hair, and skin as white as milk. The island princess was beautiful," João began. The horizon burned a brilliant mix of copper and gold. João sat on a short wooden stool so Maria could see him between the cow's hind legs. The barn cats wound between his boots. A milky mist rose from his pail. "The island princess wanted to marry a simple-minded prince to rule his kingdom. But the simple-minded prince spent his days on horseback, traveling over his lands. One day he came upon a country girl with nothing more than a mule to her name and a fat bump on her forehead. The prince began to spend time in the girl's village. The island princess became madly jealous of this country girl. And soon the island princess's blue eyes faded to black, and her blond hair turned brown, and her pearly skin tanned. The island princess set out a magic picnic for the prince of fine jellies and exotic fruits that would make the prince love her instead of the country girl, but being that the simple-minded prince was simple, he did not like fine jellies and exotic fruits, so he fed the picnic to his horse. The next day, at the king's festival, the horse broke free from his lead when he saw the island princess and trampled her to death. Later, the simple-minded prince set to marry the country girl. When she raised her veil at the church the crowd gasped. The country girl's eyes had turned blue, her black hair blond, and her dark skin was white as milk. Now she, too, was beautiful."

João stopped milking. Grandmother told it better, he thought. She painted pictures with her hands. Maria paused and turned toward him bleary-eyed. I scared her, he thought. Had she stopped listening after the word "trampled"? Or perhaps, he hoped, the words "princess," "beautiful," and "marry" circled her brain like dobby horses on a carousel.

Maria slowly scooted the wide-lipped pail across the dirt floor with her foot and emptied it into the aluminum tub and sat down under the next cow. She dabbed her eyes on her sleeve. João knew America could crush one's spirit to the point where you no longer believed that a peasant could marry a prince. Even on the islands, the peasants rarely won the ring.

When he could no longer stand her silence, he stood up and then flung open all the windows and doors in the barn to flush out evil spirits. She stopped milking. He stood over her and extended a hand. She set her chin in his palm. After a moment, he said, "The princess fell under the mau olhado." He waved his free hand over the crown of her head. "I bless you against it." He waited for what seemed like an hour for a reaction. But none followed. Finally he dropped her chin and emptied his bucket.

After a few minutes she stood and emptied her pail into the tub. She stepped beside João and said, "I fear you are too late," then shuffled off to the next cow in the row.

* * *

Through the front window of the house, João saw Maria going between rooms. Smoke came from the chimney. She's making traveling tea, João thought. He wondered if she'd packed the hair combs and lavender silk party dress he'd bought her for the reunion. Far away, her shadow seemed to dance like she had in his arms the one time she had agreed to leave the farm. Actually, she'd had no choice. In late June, Kitty's relatives held a reunion in Westerly. João had tagged along the last few years to organize the clam boil. Neither João nor Kitty thought it a good idea to leave the girl unattended. Besides, a weekend of organized games, hiking, at least one christening, and a dance with music provided by Kitty's cousins would be restorative to the girl's soul. In an effort to explain Maria's presence at the party, Kitty told her family João was bringing his sweetheart.

In his arms on the trampled grass dance floor, João heard Maria laugh for the first time. She seemed in a trance, spinning under the sparkling white lights. And soon João lost track of the movement of his limbs, preferring to concentrate on the rich scent of her hair. He insisted they dance to each tune. Kitty and the others left them in their own orbit, but she watched them like a proud mother. Maria understood the music's spell better than João thought, for before the band's last songs she pulled him to a corner of the tent. The front of her lavender dress was damp. Wisps of hair clung to her temples.

"What is it?" João asked, looking over his shoulder as the band tuned up for the last song. Her face beamed, but she didn't speak. When he tried pulling her to the dance floor, she resisted. "What?"

Yawning, she glanced over her shoulder to her room in the main house.

"You want to sleep?"

She nodded.

He cursed himself for thinking the night would never end. Plus, he'd hogged her, there were probably younger, more handsome men she'd wanted to dance with. What an *idiot*. He should have continued at the textile school, or started his own business with Manuel. He buried his nails into his coarse, chapped palms.

When he wouldn't meet her eye she squeezed his wrist.

"We'll dance again?"

"Yes," she whispered.

"The music, the band."

"Yes."

"They play all night."

She squeezed his wrist again.

For the first time João was the one without a voice.

She blinked a few times to reassure him and then kissed his cheek. "Thank you, João," she said. "For all the cows."

They both laughed, and she released his wrist and whirled out of his reach, running out of the tent toward the main house. He watched her go, hoping she'd stop and look back, but she disappeared into the dark night.

João slumped in a chair near the edge of the tent, refiguring what she'd said and what he had forgotten to say. He sat there for hours, nursing tall mugs of stout that Kitty's brothers kept replenishing. The next morning one of the cousins found him asleep in the grass near the bandstand. He fetched João a cup of coffee and then asked him to help dismantle the tent.

* * *

Joseph and João leaned over the paddock gate, watching a cow drink from a bathtub trough. "Kitty said the girl has been pretty tight-lipped," Joseph said.

João nodded.

Joseph blocked the sun with his hat. "She could talk, though. Correct?"

"Yes."

"Is she going to?"

João wanted to ease his friend's concern about his son's fate, but he could only guess at the venom that Maria kept inside.

The girl speaking to the authorities—or worse, the press—was the only angle Joseph hadn't covered. And really, he didn't want to, but now, after all this time, he worried more for her than for Hollister. It had been a point of pride with him that he would never lie about what had happened, but then, no one had asked him directly. There were rumors in the mill, but none stuck. One had her married off to a New Bedford angler. When Billy Connelly from the *Gazette* came sniffing around the mill, Joseph had braced himself for an attack. Instead, the girls in the cloth room clammed up; they hid Maria's mother in the latrine, and the trail went cold. But the stress of that event caused another of his teeth to fall out.

In the past year Joseph had spent countless nights hunched over the mill store account ledger trying to decipher Hollister's figures and eraser marks. After the incident, Hollister had said there were other girls but refused to name them or rather, if he was to be believed, that he couldn't remember their names. So Joseph spent nights refiguring purchases and double-checking prices to see where his son had begun to overcharge the girl operatives. After two months, he'd narrowed down the suspect accounts to ten, though judging by the eraser marks, there could have been as many as fifteen. (Joseph's first note in the margin was a reminder to fire Hollister's supervisor.) Unsure which girls had been wronged by his son, he decided to list a ten-dollar credit for all fifteen suspect accounts. After that, Joseph set about figuring a larger credit for Maria's mother. Since the girl could no longer collect it herself, he decided to give the woman fifty dollars. He wrote the number and shut the ledger. After a minute, he flipped the ledger back open and employed the eraser himself. He removed the fifty dollars and put down twenty-five. Fifty dollars sounded too much like a payoff. *No, sir, I am paying compensation to an employee who had been wronged by the Cleveland Mill.* Given the woman only made twenty-eight dollars a month, fifty would look like hush money. Joseph reopened the ledger a third time and again turned up his eraser. He changed the two to a three, giving Maria's mother thirty-five dollars in credit. He tapped his pencil against his son's nameplate. The boy was lucky that Otis wasn't alive. He slumped back in his son's old chair and slowly shut the leather ledger with the tip of the pencil. Joseph pressed his palms into his eye sockets. A chill shook his body. Fifty dollars. One hundred. A thousand. No matter. He still couldn't sleep through the night.

* * *

Joseph turned back toward the house, and João fell in beside him. Usually when Joseph visited the farm, João seemed buoyed by some great invisible balloon. But not today. João fidgeted with his reading glasses and failed to hold Joseph's eye.

Joseph pulled an envelope from his jacket pocket. "Deposit this in the farm account. There's enough for the fall improvements and one of your new projects." He raised his hand to stop João from speaking. "It doesn't matter what it is. Circumstances have changed. Just make sure it can turn a profit in two to three years. Also, I need to postpone our state-of-the-farm meeting." Joseph spun his hand in a circle. "There are some things I need to wind up first. But before then, ask old man Pennywich what he wants for his acreage over yonder there. His boys aren't coming home to work it. But play dumb. Make up some cock-and-bull story about you wanting your own lands. Bad-mouth me. He'll come running to the city to squeal on you. When he tells me he doesn't want the land falling into Portagee hands, I'll offer him half of what he told you it was worth. He should have sold out years ago. His river access will make for a nice cranberry bog. Don't you think?"

João smiled, though he was unsure if it was because he was angry at Joseph's presumption that he *didn't* want his own land or because his boss always seemed to be a beat ahead of him. He had not shared his bog idea with anyone.

"I got ideas," João offered.

"Then we'll discuss them in the fall."

Suddenly Joseph was upbeat. Farm business was an excellent tonic for his family woes, just as the mill had provided him a distraction during Lizzy's demise. He told João to draw up a new five-year plan, taking Pennywich's land into account. Joseph had already figured a plan in his head, but it had included him running the show. He'd shape João's figures, but he knew for the plan to succeed it had to come from João. Joseph would get to work on a ten-year plan. By then Hollister could run the mills. *Hollister run the mills?* Joseph rolled a pebble under his shoe. That would be the day. Joseph resisted pegging his dreams to Will. He kicked the pebble. But he would have to see Maria before prognosticating any further. One look in her eyes, and he'd know if he could ever trust Hollister with the family's legacy.

Joseph scratched his chin with his stub pinkie. "All right, João. It's time." He took the younger man's hand and squeezed. "You've done me a great service this past year."

"We all even now," João said. He held Joseph's hand fast, waiting for a gleam of recognition in the older man's eyes. When he was sure Joseph understood what he meant, he pulled his hand away, believing he'd gained too much from his friend's misfortunes.

The light had fallen in the west. The sun kissed the horizon beyond the cornfield. Joseph turned his back on the blazing sunset and then paused to admire the shadow of his head and shoulders cut out in the gravel. He turned his head to see his profile. João did the same. The young man's chin was a perfect square, while Joseph's resembled the curve of a baseball. Joseph squinted into the sun. He wondered if folks in western Rhode Island shared the same sunset. At what longitude did the sun kick up a degree? He imagined a day when a man could travel between time zones—take his salad in Massachusetts and dessert in California.

João stepped between Joseph and California. His bushy black hair blocked the sun. "So?" he said, wanting an instruction.

"I'll wait in the car." Joseph pointed to the horizon. "When the sun goes, we go."

João sucked his teeth. He glanced at the horizon, and then turned and jogged to the house.

The smell of fresh meat and olive oil filled his nostrils before the door was half-open. A casserole of rabbit pieces and bacon and chopped yellow onion browned on the range. A cup of rice stood near a tub of Rose Butter.

Maria stood over the wooden chop-block cutting round angel muffins from a roll of sweet dough with a tin cup, her cheeks flush from standing over the hot oven. She stroked her neck as she spoke. "I don't feel cold no more," she said in English.

The shadow João had seen through the window had not been Maria making tea but rather her pacing between the kitchen and the tree stump out back used to slaughter small game. Far off, he heard the dogs barking. No doubt fighting over rabbit guts. But the time for a Portuguese meal had long passed.

She spoke his name for only the second time. "I'm no leaving, João."

João stumbled to the chopping block as if cut down at the knees.

She spoke fast. A smudge of white flour gleamed on her dark cheek. "My people was farm folks too. Maybe I wouldn't do so good with a city job. I stay here with the simple-minded prince."

João stood up straight. His heart flipped. He opened his mouth, but she raised the tin cup.

"After supper you'll help me back to Kitty's. And in two weeks, if you are willing, on a Sunday, we marry. I ask Kitty's cousins to play our music."

He slowly nodded as a smile stretched across his face.

"Again we dance. And after—"

Maria stopped talking suddenly and slumped to the floor, out of breath. Her almond face lost its hue. It was more than she had spoken in the past year.

"Head down," he instructed. As he caressed her warm back, his hands shook. "Breathe. Good. Breathe it in."

He glanced at the open window. The evil eye had lifted.

By the time João finished explaining Maria's decision to Joseph, his voice had reached a fever pitch. Panting, he waited for a reaction, but the older man didn't speak. In fact, a complete lack of recognition seemed to glaze over Joseph's face, as if he'd been coldcocked. João persisted, "May we have your blessing?"

Joseph wondered what had transpired in the short time João had been in the house alone with Maria. Or had João known all along of the girl's intentions? Or had it in fact been *her* intention at all? He spotted Maria's twisted nose pressed against the glass of the kitchen window. Her eyes darted between the two men. Even from such a distance, Joseph could see the gap in the hairline where the broomstick had split her scalp. He should have been relieved. Indeed, her staying on the farm meant Hollister could return to Fall River. The army wouldn't pay him forever. But Joseph wasn't relieved; rather, he was anxious, fearing another confrontation with his son. But he was just a boy, a boy with an adult's strength. The father in Joseph wanted to bring Hollister home, while the man in him wanted to beat him with that same broomstick. His glimpse of her the night after the accident had not been a dream.

"Hi ho," Kitty called, trotting down the lane toward the car. "Forgot my kerchief."

Sensing she had interrupted, Kitty simply waved the hankie to indicate she had found it on the passenger seat. She jogged back up the lane, but her appearance had changed the mood, and Joseph knew the moment for sharing his deeper feelings had passed. He tugged at his collar and pinched the seat of his pants. Lately none of his clothes seemed to fit properly.

João had not taken his eyes off Joseph. He expected an answer.

"So if you marry, she won't be leaving the farm?" It was a silly question, but Joseph wanted to be clear, and João answered straight-faced, understanding his friend's need to bury the past.

"She never be happy without some land under her." João turned back to the house, his face suddenly flushed with pride.

Joseph extended his hand a second time, and João took it, knowing this gesture was how Americans made deals. But it also signified he had his friend's blessing.

"What gift for the bride and groom?"

João shook his head. "Otis outfitted the house well. More levers and machines than I understand."

"For the girl then."

João's grin widened as he remembered the reunion in Westerly. "She likes to dance."

So did Lizzy, Joseph thought. "You've given me an idea," he said, picturing the Victrola in his parlor. He'd have the Troy Store deliver a new model to the farm next week.

Joseph looked at the house, then back to João. "Wishing you a blessed life together."

Walking up the dirt road to his car, Joseph stopped. He snapped his fingers. "The gold chain." He'd heard the story of Lourdes and the fisherman's son and the dive at Parrot Beach. The chain was missing from João's neck. He heard the house door sweep open then slam shut. He turned. Tiny dust devils swirled a path to the house. In the kitchen window two silhouettes danced. The sun dipped below the horizon. Far off, a cowbell rang.

THE LESSONS OF TROY

Will squeezed his butt cheeks, but the noxious gas continued to escape. The glass of water he'd gulped down to wet his dry mouth was also working against him, but he feared that if he redistributed pressure from his bowels to his bladder, he'd surely crap his pants. And on anyone's embarrassment meter, someone urinating himself would register as forgettable, while exploding in diarrhea would become a tale retold by Troy Store employees well into the 1920s.

The Troy manager, Mr. Knipper, busied himself with paperwork across his large mahogany desk. At first he relished hearing the poor boy's stomach churn—a big point of holding the boy was to scare him—so when he caught a drift of the boy's flatulence, he ignored it, wanting the kid to pine a tad longer, but after sustained putrid volleys, his nostrils began to burn, then drip. He pressed his palms into his deep-set eye sockets and let out a long breath that sent a shiver over his corpulent frame.

He pointed his ink pen at Will and then to the door. "Lavatory: through the door, then a left. Back in three minutes, or I send the dogs."

Of course he had no dogs, but Will didn't even notice the threat. In fact, so much of his concentration was focused on the emergency in the lower half of his torso that when he left the office, he forgot which way the manager had said to turn. The faint strains of rushing water pulled him to the left. And just in time. Instead of a series of gates opening along the track of his bowel like so many locks along a canal, it was as if a stopper had been removed from a drain. His body emptied in one giant whoosh, and he took his first deep breath in some hours as a stream of urine splashed against the porcelain lip of the bowl. A powerful ache filled the pit of his empty belly. He wiped and pulled the chain, and then he fell forward, resting his elbows on his knees. He clutched his pinched pale face between his open hands and sat for the remaining two minutes thirty-four seconds wondering why Helen hadn't come to his aid. And what in the world would he tell his father?

* * *

That morning, when she woke to overcast skies, Helen sent Will a picture postcard with instructions to meet her at the Troy Store at three o'clock that afternoon, and to wear his father's largest overcoat with the sleeves rolled up. Troy's selection couldn't be matched. After one recent walkabout, Helen brought home knitting needles, Nottingham lace, and smoked codfish. Usually the first item was what she was after. The others just presented themselves as she floated department to department, making sure not to linger. In summer, only foul-weather days made the trip worthwhile.

She smirked when they passed a sign painted with the Troy Store motto, YOU PAY LESS HERE—she paid nothing. They strolled through the robin-egg-blue rooms past fine china and glass to the reassuring commotion of the fashion departments. She told Will to browse men's fashions. She hit the ladies. She ran her fingers down a row of hanging corsets, thinking her mother would never get her into one of those. Next came outdated gingham skirts on discount. Even the operatives in the mills demanded finer cloth. Helen hovered around the silks. They were compact enough to hide easily and made good gifts. She rubbed a slippery bathrobe right off its hanger. She bunched it into her gaping pocket and browsed on.

Inviting Will into her secret world had been a great risk, but after he'd told her why Hollister was sent away to military school, she felt obligated to reveal a secret of her own. When Will called her a liar, she produced a porcelain sugar bowl and Swiss chocolate. The Troy Store, she said boastfully, was where her sordid double life had flourished the summer her mother was abroad.

Helen had discovered the joys of stealing by accident in Mr. Mongie's corner store. Ray's overcoat made her do it. It was soggy day. Tommy sent her out in the rain to buy a pack of Chesterfields. She bought candy with the few remaining pennies he'd left her for the effort. At the candy rack, a Mary Jane toffee dropped into the rolled-over folds of the coat sleeve when she reached for a chocolate bar. As she went to fish out the Mary Jane, Mr. Mongie lowered his newspaper. "That all, Helen? Any licorice fish?" he'd said over his half-moon reading glasses, peering down at her like the retired policeman that he was. Could he send her to jail? Her mother said in some countries cheats and stealers got their hands cut off. Though when pressed, Mary Sheehan couldn't come up with *specific* countries where the punishment was practiced. No, Mr. Mongie wasn't the amputation type. No one had seen the Mary Jane fall. Was there anyone else in the store? Helen's smile stiffened as the seconds passed. Mr. Mongie folded the paper and stood up from his stool. Now she was too embarrassed to put the Mary Jane back, surely he would think she was stealing, so she smiled harder.

"Cigarettes and the chocolate then," he said, ringing up the sale.

She gave Tommy the Mary Jane, and he said she was all right, even offered to take her to Lincoln Park to ride the coaster. She nicked him a Mary Jane on each subsequent visit to the store.

Helen stood under the South Park shelter, her brother Ray's old overcoat laid out on the cement to dry. Aside from some bum asleep on a far bench, she was alone. The promised rain had kept the crowds indoors. Crime taught Helen that men held low expectations of pretty young girls, a fact she exploited. The male store clerk actually smiled at her before nabbing Will. (For this, she stole a tie.)

When did boys corner the market on bravery? she thought. They're all boneheads. Will's a wimp, Hollister an ass, Tommy unlucky, Ray a half-wit, Mr. B a fake. Daddy would have invented the world twice over by now. She reached under her blouse to remove the silk tie; she draped it delicately across her lap and pressed the wrinkles out with her palms. It was Italian, a handsome new fashion, ocean blue with white strips going crossways. She held it up under her chin and caught the reflection in a splash of rainwater, imagining her father wearing it.

The bum rolled over and grunted. She wound the tie around her fist and resisted the urge to punch the stuffing out of the old toper.

What would Will Bartlett blubber on about when his father arrived? She had felt the bond between them grow over the summer, and she'd lowered her guard, so wanting a true friend. He would never get past this. She cursed herself for being so foolish. A dozen city blocks would forever separate their destinies.

She removed from the waist of her skirt a bundle of white cotton dinner napkins with ugly pee-colored seashells embroidered in the corners. She had snagged them from a sale table during her retreat—she couldn't help herself; they were so ugly she felt sorry for them. She used the napkins to wipe off the wet plank of the bench. She tossed them at the bum. Seated, she tried to think if there was a lesson to be learned in Will's capture, but couldn't figure one, except that she had broken her only rule: Crime and Partners Don't Mix. Given that her first pupil was going to end up in the brig, it was a rule she'd never violate again.

Poor Will. She had overestimated him. The cool confidence she'd witnessed in school and Highland parlors was absent under real pressure. The sweat coming off his forehead could have filled a canteen. She'd chosen the gold earrings on the hunch that he'd probably steal for her but not himself. If he'd taken the time, he would have noticed she didn't even wear the stupid things. Men. She had to teach Will it wasn't the cost of things, but the rush you received when you got away with something in your pocket. Of course, this wasn't a hard and fast rule. Helen stole many things for their sheer beauty, and unless she did, she'd never own them. Will's pockets were always silly with allowance money—his weekly chores, a joke. She'd grown up too fast since her father's passing not to understand the economics of her family. In fact, years ago when her mother took her trip to Ireland, it was young Helen who stepped in as the family banker, collecting checks and disbursing spending money to her doting brothers. She even shortchanged Ray once just to see if he was paying attention. He wasn't. True, most items she stole had to be kept secret, but she didn't care. There were hers. They had value. When the money goes, you die. Enough said.

* * *

Joseph parked on Pleasant Street beside the Troy Store, waiting for his strength to return. Young Will's latest transgression, while not near the level Hollister's folly, hurt Joseph more. Joseph knew the boy was over his bouts of self-pity and the acting out that followed Lizzy's death, so he surmised this latest episode had its roots in the murkiest of pots: adolescence.

Since Lizzy's death Joseph had come to know many things about his family. First, he found out just how much of his sons' development had been guided by their mother. She had filtered everything they read, ate, saw, felt, and heard. Second, he discovered that the years of her illness meant years the boys suffered without her guiding light; God knows he was in no shape to fill the void, what with his nagging denial and then unyielding grief. Luckily, Will's tender age required him to stay close to home, usually playing peggyball with his friends, but Hollister, poor Hollister came untethered. And last, and perhaps most painful to Joseph, he realized just how much of his involvement in the boys' lives had been scripted by his wife. She spoiled them in return for accompanying Joseph on Saturday afternoon driving trips to New Bedford or Yarmouth. The feigned interest the boys exhibited in his workday was a direct result of a threat of no dessert after supper. Only when he was forced to raise his hand did the boys *really* pay attention to him. He prayed—oh God he prayed—that a paper cutout of himself might not have done a superior job fathering them. Each day he regretted his decision to write off Hollister. Perhaps he'd make a good soldier.

With Lizzy not four weeks gone, he had told Hollister a fishing trip was in order. *Just the two of us on the Merrimack River.* The cycle seemed to have no end. Hollister spent days assembling rods, reels, provisions, and even researched the types of tackle New Hampshire fish favored. The boys weren't used to a summer in the city. And though Joseph didn't approve,

Will took a job as a soda jerk at Randall Apothecary. Jobless and home-bound, Hollister hung around June Street until the fishing trip.

Joseph's sweaty hand had slipped over the steering wheel as he drove between the academy's iron gates. He told Hollister about the cabins the school rented in the summer to fishermen like themselves. His instructions, as spelled out during his brief phone conversation with Commandant Blunt, were as simple as they were hard to stomach: "Lead the boy into the administrative building, and then lie about forgetting your billfold in the car. Don't turn around. Don't look back. Just get in your automobile and go. He won't need anything—no clothes, no teddy bears, no kiss goodbye. He'll thank you for this someday."

"And when can I come get him?" Joseph had asked.

"From what you described, this may take some time."

"Christmas?" When Blunt didn't respond, Joseph said. "When will I hear news?"

"I'll send word. He's part of our family now. We've broken plenty of mustangs."

"That's it?" Christ. The boy had not been orphaned, or had he?

"Goodbye, Mr. Bartlett."

On the street a black carriage passed, and Joseph glanced at his gaunt image in the window glass. He was resigned to the fact that he might burn in hell for suppressing Maria's attack. Thank God João was going to marry the poor girl. But still, Joseph imagined the two of them at their kitchen table swapping stories of how they might ruin him. He would keep them well stocked in new music for the Victrola. Of course, João's butter business was slowly making him a rich man. (And the rest of the operation was making Joseph an even richer one.) It had taken him six years to completely trust João. Maria had many more to go.

Joseph stood on the sidewalk outside the Troy Store, buttoning and unbuttoning his suit coat. He decided to circle the block. Haven't I minded the boy well? Joseph thought. With Mary Sheehan's help, of course. He left the mill promptly at six to dine with his son. On his trips to New York he arranged for Will to tag along. Only at the mill or with his son did he keep his feelings in check. Of course he loved his son, but did he really love spending time with children? He was never one for nursery rhymes or make-believe. Thankfully, Will showed a genuine interest in the cotton business, and Joseph relished teaching the boy the basics so that, perhaps, he might continue the family's run.

* * *

Two minutes to the dogs.

Will's first guess was that they had Helen in another room and her mother was coming to fetch her. But that didn't wash. She had been too smooth going about her business. The only time she dared meet his eye was when she pointed him toward the unmanned jewelry counter. He smiled as he remembered the silk tie that sucked up her sleeve as if her arm were a straw. She'd made it look so easy. Will's face stiffened, then flushed; he couldn't fathom what he'd say to her after he was released from house arrest. Was there anything Helen hadn't done? Could he be a friend to someone who was always right? Always the boss of him? Perhaps it was like his mother had said, that they'd just been assigned to different ends of the pretzel, but eventually, they'd meet at the knot in the middle. The end-of-the-season dance was in two weeks. Would she boss him around the dance floor? Fetch the punch? Walk *him* home?

One minute to the dogs.

He whispered, "She made it look so easy. Really, Dad, Helen's a pro." I won't rat on Helen, he thought. She'd kill me. I'll throw myself at the mercy of the court.

Will worked hard to keep his old man from feeling like such a failure. He enjoyed New York taxi rides and ordering chocolate malts to the stateroom on the boats; he looked forward to skimming cranberries from the bogs. But he had grown tired of the forced questions about his school days, the buddy trips to Fenway. Even baseball seasons end.

Will was humored by his father bending over backward to suggest that mill work was only one of *many* career options; he did this even while explaining the intricacies of the new Northrop looms. Will learned to name the parts of a Moscrop single-thread yarn tester and the capacity of a

Rhoades-Chandler separator. The man from the Draper Corporation in Hopedale began sending Will birthday presents. The young boy had been grandfathered into a post without ever applying. Even Hannah Cleveland talked shop with the boy in hopes of keeping her many orange-inspired cloth lines alive when she was eventually discontinued. But Will hadn't accounted for the watchful eyes of his grandfather. Otis haunted Will from his hook in the hallway. The dead man's gaze spoke of the obligation Will was under after Hollister had gotten himself exiled. It was getting to the point where the simple act of wearing soft Cleveland fabrics reminded Will of what he must do. Getting dressed he would count the years between now and the end of college. Perhaps he'd obtain an apprenticeship in New York or Philadelphia, but after that, he was stuck in Fall River, stuck at the Cleveland Mill.

Will stood in front of the mirror, buckling his trousers. He was already thirty seconds overdue. He ran cold water over his rosy cheeks. His face was still fleshy and smooth. Bartlett men grew weak beards. He straightened his shirt and smoothed down his trousers. He took a deep breath. I don't have the face of thief, he thought, nor the guts.

* * *

Joseph turned the corner back onto Pleasant Street. He tried to remember his own teenage life, but it was so far removed. Scooting his mattress closer to the radiator was one memory. The other was the temptation of girls. And not having enough to buy candy. He had dropped the receiver when the store manager told him the price of the earrings. One dollar and ten cents. Gold painted, costume trinkets with a matching charm bracelet. Will earned five times that amount in spending money. The manager said he'd hold the boy until Joseph arrived and then in passing mentioned there was no reason to get the law involved. This comment boiled Joseph's blood, for it was an obvious allusion to this being a favor that would require payback. Both men knew the police would simply call Joseph and issue a reprimand. But calling the law in would also mean a paper trail— one that would be picked up by muckrakers like Billy Connelly or his network of narcs. The manager surely read the Highlands gossip rags.

Inside the store, Joseph passed the jewelry department and stopped to stare at the shiny assortment of gems and metals. He stepped to the counter and fingered the costume jewelry, finding a set of earrings similar to those the manager had described over the phone. There was nothing spectacular about them. Nothing at all. Just two simple studs. Joseph smacked his fist against the glass counter, rattling the rack of jewelry. Was the boy's taste also on the fritz?

"May I help you, sir?" A saleswoman steadied the clanging rack of trinkets.

"Do you like these?" Joseph held the studs up to the woman's earlobe.

The woman blushed. "Really, sir," she began. She shot a glance at a coworker dusting the opposite end of the counter. The saleswoman set her hand on Joseph's wrist and lowered his arm. "That's not for me to say."

"They're the most god-awful things in the store."

"Then, perhaps there is something in the case that interests you?"

"Why would he want these?" Joseph hung the earrings back on the rack and spread his arms wide. "Of all the thousands of items in this place, why would anyone take these?" Joseph dropped his arms to his sides making a loud clapping sound. "Helen." He shook his head. "Where did I go wrong?"

"Sir?"

"Which way to Mr. Knipper's office?"

She pointed over her shoulder. "That way."

Joseph nodded. He trudged around the jewelry counter toward the distant offices. Of all the poor influences he had steered his boys away from—immigrant gangs, spoiled Highlands riffraff—he never imagined a young girl living under one of his own roofs could be the cause of such calamity. Mary had no control of the girl—or her sassy mouth—but given Hollister's path, he'd never raised the issue of child rearing. Mary was one of only a handful that knew what had happened in the fun house. In fact, Joseph had no real proof that Helen had led Will astray, and Lord knows, he'd never get either of them to admit it, though the earrings were surely a present for Mary's wild child. He must stimulate the boy before he made a tragic error in judgment. He couldn't lose another boy. The Lord was cruel, but not that cruel. Or was he?

FIREWORKS

Mary Sheehan and her widowed neighbor Rita crouched low and pressed their noses against the parlor window of the Snell Street house. On the porch Will and Helen waited on the swing. Will sat sideways staring at his date, his eyes traveling head to foot and back. Helen crossed her ankles, her left toe dragging across the wood planks as the swing swayed in the late afternoon breeze.

"Yes, it's really me," Helen said. "I wore a dress to your mom's funeral. Remember?"

"Yeah, but . . ." Will rubbed the fabric between his fingers. "Choice stuff."

"One more minute of gawking, and then I'm gonna slug you."

"Does that hurt?" He patted the coils of her French twist.

"It's all the rage in Paris, don't ya know."

"You don't know squat."

"But it's fun to say."

He tapped his index finger on the emerald cameo pinned at her neck. "Old lady Rita make this too?"

"I stole that." She touched it. "Saw one like it once in one of your mother's magazines."

"You could be in one of those magazines." His eyes settled on her round breasts.

"I even let Rita wash my face with lemon."

"I wondered what that smell was."

"It's my first dance." She gave him a sideways glance. "Got Highlands boys to impress."

"I'm a Highlands boy."

"Halvies."

"I asked ya."

She followed his gaze. "You can touch them if you like."

"Don't say that."

"Time's up." Helen stood as a car pulled up to the curb. "My chariot has arrived."

Inside, Tommy called, "You seen my hat?" He galloped down the stairs and stuck his head in the parlor. "What are you doing?"

"Nothing." Mary and Rita whipped around, pinching the curtains closed behind them. "Hat's on your head."

"Oh." Tommy turned the front corner down over his strawberry eye. He smiled. "I'll spy on those two all night. Don't worry."

A car horn squeaked.

"What's the hurry?" Mary said. "Have Little Doc come in." Big Doc, Little Doc's father, was one of the few veterinarians in southern Massachusetts, and the first vet to own an automobile.

"Gotta go." Tommy winked and ducked out. Mary and Rita gave chase.

"Tell Little Doc to turn those lights on," Mary called from the porch.

Tommy squinted into the setting sun. "Go inside, Ma."

"Helen, you mind that new dress."

Helen waved off her mother as she climbed into the back seat. Tommy slammed the door. "Hit it!" Little Doc shifted, all the kids waved, and they were gone.

Rita patted Mary's shoulder. "It'll be fine," she said. "I can always make another dress."

Nellie Zorra, Little Doc's girl (or rather, he was hoping to make her his girl), sat up front on Tommy's lap. She had large green eyes and finely coiffed black hair with turquoise combs that complemented her olive skin. She reminded Will of the actress Florence La Badie. Will and Helen crammed into the back of the Buick with another couple. Will squeezed her hand. She smelled like lemonade. Will had suggested they take the trolley, not wanting to wait for Tommy to set up the dance, but Helen insisted she arrive like the Highlands girls, in a chauffeured motorcar. The summer dances at the pavilion were one of the few places where all of Fall River's classes mixed—at least those that could afford the price of admission.

At the top of Pleasant Street, Little Doc stopped and pointed toward the barges anchored in the river. "There's fireworks at nine. We can see them from the beach."

"Look." Helen pointed to the sun setting over Somerset. The clouds were breaking up and the sun reflected off their underbellies in rich coppers and reds. Good fireworks weather.

Helen had counted down the days to her first dance. Tommy's work for the dance promoters kept the topic swirling all summer. Mary Sheehan called it the Summer of Nag, and it wore her down. Rita conspired against her neighbor by sewing a linen dancing dress. Queerly, Helen had had her hair done—a first. The conical tube pinned to the back of Helen's head batted Will between the eyes the entire drive to the beach. Helen knew full well Tommy couldn't be trusted to look after her for more than an hour. He would make sure she arrived with two shoes and sound bones and returned at the assigned time with two shoes and sound bones. But supervising what transpired between going and coming was where Will Bartlett figured in to her plan.

Little Doc parked in the row outside the Sandy Beach Pavilion, and Tommy dispensed free tickets on the veranda. "If anybody asks, you paid full price," he whispered, then hurried off to set up the bandstand, move the chairs around, and mix the punch. "Official junk," he assured the crew, though Will had seen him showing off a new set of dice to Little Doc on the drive. Other cars started arriving. The Labor Day dance was always a sellout. Tommy expected close to five hundred. For tonight only, the usual dime tickets were upped to a quarter. The band came from Boston. On the boardwalk Will heard the last runs of the toboggan ride rumble in the distance. Children's shrill screams carried from the giant circle swing as their mothers packed up picnic dinners in the nearby elm grove. Will and Helen traipsed down to the water's edge. There was little wind, so the chop in the bay was small. The tide trickled in.

Little Doc and Nellie and the other couples talked on the picnic tables under the awning of the boardwalk, licking their ice creams. The boys smoked. After a time, Little Doc and Nellie hopped down the beach in front of the bathhouses and took a turn dancing. Will watched them between skipping stones with Helen. Between Tommy and Doc, Nellie was sure to have sore feet. Will figured to tire Helen's with the new dances he'd learned over a year ago in his mother's parlor. He remembered her advice on how to treat a lady in public: how to hold her hand, make small talk, and compliment her wardrobe. *And don't ever, ever,* she drilled, *leave your date alone. Women don't function well alone; it rattles the confidence.*

Helen smacked his arm. "Did you know Nellie's father died of brown lung, just like old man Otis?" Helen had a knack for taking girls down a peg. Her information was usually correct, cobbled together from eavesdropping on operatives gossiping when she delivered dinner pails. Rumor had it Nellie wasn't too well liked by the other girls in her boardinghouse. Helen continued, "You want to know a secret?"

Will smiled. "Do I have a choice?"

"I heard that dumb Nellie wants to change her name now that her pop can't stop her. Something that doesn't sound *Portuguese.* What do you think of Nellie Zero?"

"Quit it."

"Or Nellie Zilch?"

"I figured you'd give her a break."

"Cuz my dad died?"

"A job shouldn't kill you."

"That's our lot, Will Bartlett." She skipped a stone and Will handed her another. "She's a social-climbing numbskull."

Every girl that showed interest in Little Doc or Tommy or any of the gang was out for something. Granted, Helen's intelligence on Nellie didn't put the girl in the best light, but brown lung? And besides, she sure was pretty. Prettier than Florence La Badie on account of her tan skin. Nothing like the pale ghosts that haunted the Highlands mansions. So what if she wanted out of the mill before her lungs and hearing went? Couldn't blame her for that.

Helen peered down the beach at Little Doc and Nellie. He spun her around in the sand. "She's falling for him because of the car. But Tommy makes just as much at the paper. More, counting the dances."

"And the gambling."

"He could bury Little Doc in money."

"Perhaps Tommy has another girl."

Will thought this might trip Helen up, but she knew the skinny on his love life too. "Not unless she's a card dealer."

Will knocked her shoulder. "Leave her be."

"Look at that. They can't be a couple. She's an Amazon." There was another reason for the nickname Little Doc. He was short, and at nineteen, already losing his hair. He had grown a beard to make up for the deficiency topside. "They shouldn't be doing that. You just watch. Her ankle will twist like a screw through butter." Helen smacked sand from her hands as if that was the last word on the matter, and then added, in further defense of her brother's taste, "She's too daft for Tommy."

"Who says she's Tommy's to be had? She's Little Doc's girl."

Helen placed her fists on her hips. "I stopped being that foolish the day my father croaked." Will froze, wishing he could utter such airtight declarations. "Everything is up for grabs," she added, scratching her French twist.

"I like your hair."

"Yeah, well, it's okay."

"And that dress is the best here."

Helen lifted the hem high and watched the soft fabric float back over her knees. "Rita sure made a fuss. Don't make a big deal about it inside." She punched his arm. "My reputation."

"As a foulmouthed, thieving—"

"I'm planning a big job."

"Really?"

"Bank job. Big. Gonna need a good nickname for the papers." She stood on her toes and pretended to moon for the cameras.

"The Fall River bandit," Will said.

"Good one. But that's a guy's name." Helen kicked the sand. "The world needs more girl outlaws."

"Sounds good, Calamity Jane, but the banks are closed now. You can steal something tomorrow." He extended a hand. "Come here." All those dance lessons in Will's mother's parlor had been leading to this night. They were alone, without parents, and yet, like adults, clean and fine smelling—and smartly dressed at their first big shindig. He said, "Guys were peppering me about you."

"About being in my gang?" Helen teased. She stepped back on the sand, and sized him up like a stubborn bank vault. Will tipped his boater back, catching the sunset on his cheeks. Helen straightened up shaking her head. "Boys are so stupid."

Will fell back against a rock formation and slid down to the sand. Helen tiptoed forward, holding her long skirt as if crossing a puddle. She slumped down beside him. Three sloops cruised across Mount Hope Bay. Sounds of the orchestra warming their instruments drowned out the voices of couples passing above them on the boardwalk. Will hoped Helen hadn't seen Sunny Brayton roll up with a carload of Highlands kids. But of course she had. That's why she'd run so far down the beach. Sunny was Fall River royalty. Not much in the looks department—Helen beat her hands down with a little scrubbing—but Sunny was the queen. And what Sunny lacked in looks, she made up for in meanness.

He glanced at the faded scribble of scars on Helen's neck. "I know you saw her."

"The witch?" Helen splayed her legs and poured sand between her hands. "She bragged about going to dances for a year, though she's been too young till this summer. Tommy should have tossed her out by the ear."

"Could he do that?"

"Not if he wants a job in Fall River." She scooped another handful of sand. "If she so much as steps on my foot, I'm going to let her have it."

"Forget about her." Will knocked her elbow.

Helen dropped her head on his shoulder. She tapped her toes on the sand. Will recognized the waltz and mimicked her steps. She sped up and he kept pace, grasping her hand for balance. The music quit and Helen stopped. "We make quite a pair," Helen said, and turned toward Will. "So, what's it gonna be, Will Bartlett?"

"Hey!" A tall boy dragging a barefoot girl by the wrist came running up the beach. "Doors open in ten minutes," he shouted. He broke into a wide grin and saluted Will and Helen. The music started up again, and Helen hoisted herself up, dusting off the sand. "You got the tickets?"

"I got 'em." Will rolled over on all fours and slowly stood. Now or never, he thought. "Listen you—"

A cry echoed down the beach. Will and Helen spun as Little Doc caught Nellie in his arms. Other boys jumped down to the sand to help carry her up to the patio and lay her across one of the picnic tables. Helen sprinted toward the action. Little Doc sent one boy to fetch some ice; he unstrapped Nellie's shoe and cradled her ankle in his palm. More couples rubbernecked a view. Nellie said something in Portuguese, and one of the girls pulled her dress below her calves. Helen and Will wedged to the front. He winked at Nellie. Little Doc handed his suit jacket to Will and got down on one knee. Little Doc's status as a veterinarian's son had blessed him with medicinal powers. Will noted such status allowed a man to clutch a woman's calf.

He said, "How's it looking?"

"Hard telling just yet," Little Doc said. He turned her leg. "Can you wiggle your toes?" Nellie did. "It ain't broken."

Everyone leaned closer as he led Nellie through a battery of tests. A poke to her heel produced a grimace; she could spin the ankle with pain.

"Strained ligament," Little Doc concluded, and the crowd nodded their agreement with the diagnosis.

"That serious?" Nellie asked.

"For a racehorse. But no dancing tonight." A boy returned with a cotton sack holding a crush of ice from the snow cone man. Little Doc set a rock under her heel and pulled a handkerchief from his pocket to tie the ice to her ankle. "That will keep the swelling down. Better take you home."

Nellie crossed her arms and began to cry.

"Just have Tommy get her a chair," Helen said. "You can watch, right?"

Nellie sniffled.

"Okay," Little Doc said. He dipped down and whispered something into her ear.

Nellie wiped away her tears and smiled.

"Doors open!" a tall boy shouted. And the couples turned toward the pavilion. Tommy stood at the door waving for folks to get in line. A sign over his head read, SOLD OUT.

Will and Little Doc stood on either side of Nellie and guided her to the door.

Tommy saw them coming and cleared a path to the front of the line. "Let 'em through. Clear the way," he shouted, waving his arms. He tipped his head to Little Doc. "She okay?"

Little Doc caught Nellie's eye. "We're just gonna dance the slow songs." Nellie's face bloomed.

"Good man," Tommy said. "I roped two chairs on the side." He pointed to the spot. "Next." Tommy ripped the tickets he'd slipped Will an hour ago and waved them through. Helen stopped in the entry, squeezing Will's hand. White string lights roped across the rafters; three spinning glass globes hung over the dance floor. A trumpeter blew spit from his horn. A boy chased his date across the dance floor; the line for the ladies' toilet was already three deep. The couple next in line shoved Will, and Tommy said, "You're in, kid," as if he didn't know his name.

"Come on." Helen ran into the crowd.

The octagonal hall had windows facing the water, a raised bandstand at the far end, a corner set up with punch and snacks, three walls of cocktail tables and chairs. The kids from the different neighborhoods pulled clusters of chairs together into circles. Each clique represented a parish. The older boys hovered around the seated girls like lookouts, watching the other camps; between the door and Helen's posse Will heard three different languages. He stopped once to chat with the boys from his neighborhood. Like his father, he would mix between groups, also keeping a wary eye out for Damian Newton's crew.

Crossing the floor back to Helen, John Gower Jr., of the Gower Linen Company Gowers, smacked Will's shoulder. "They make Hollister a general yet?" Gower had large ears like his father, and a memory to match. He hovered over Will.

Rumors had been swirling about why Hollister had left town. One had the boy killing a carny. Another had him winning a scholarship. Either way, Will missed his brother. The halls of the Highlands house echoed back his own loneliness. He'd spent a week at the Westport boathouse with his father in July, but then it had been a summer in the hot city—his first in years.

"I asked you a question." Gower jabbed Will's shoulder, then elbowed his buddies. "I heard he had a girl with him." Gower's face was sunburnt from spending the holiday weekend at the beach. Tomorrow he and his cronies would attend the colony's end-of-summer dance at the Westport Casino.

"You heard wrong," Will said, suddenly flushed. The "accident" was family business.

"Come on, we all know it was a girl. He had lots of girls." Gower leaned into Will. "What was her name, little man? Maybe I can have a little fun in the fun house."

Will turned and Gower spun him around. "Spill it, or I spill you."

Will had overheard his father once say that he didn't want his boys being raised by nannies and butlers like so many other Highlands children. John Gower Jr., the youngest of five, was such a boy—spoiled to the core.

"Go to hell," Will said.

Gower bumped Will's chest, knocking him back a step. "Say it again, and I'll pop you one." Couples from nearby tables rubbernecked.

"Go to hell."

Gower shoved Will, knocking him to the floor. Will jumped to his feet and raised his fists.

"Where's Helen?" Ray Sheehan stepped between the two, slapping his meaty paw on Gower's forearm and twisting the arm behind his back. Ray stood a head taller than any boy in the hall. Gower's crew tiptoed backward.

Will lowered his arms. "Haven't seen her."

"Well, she's your date, ain't she? Just like Fanny here." He stood arm in arm with Dr. Boyle's daughter, Fanny, a girl stricken with her old man's sandbag jowls. The two had met at Elizabeth Bartlett's funeral. Ray eyed Gower, then Will. "This one of your pals?"

"Oh, yeah. A good buddy," Will smirked. Gower rolled his eyes, and his feet skipped a little dance as Ray tightened his grip.

"The kid slipped," Gower said

Ray wedged Gower's arm up his back. The couples seated around the dance floor stood as Gower's knees buckled. The conductor waved his baton.

Tommy raced across the floor. "You'll dance with him later," he said and punched Ray, who released Gower.

"Cut it out, Ray," Tommy whispered. He tipped his hat—"Hey, Fanny."—and shrugged at Gower as if to say, *There's no controlling this ape.*

"Just doing your job, little brother."

"Then do it with talking next time." Tommy jogged back to the door.

Ray clamped Will around the neck as if his hand were a wrench, dragging him toward his sister's group. "The boy stinks more than his old man."

"Thanks," Will whispered.

The Crescent Orchestra was an up-and-coming ten-piece group Tommy called his find, though the Highlands crowd had heard them at a wedding the previous spring at the Quequechan Club. Will and Helen danced the entire first set. The bandleader called out that the next number was switch-a-partner. Helen whispered to Will that this was her chance to dance with her socially maladjusted cousin Burt, fulfilling a promise to her mother. Will nodded but decided he didn't want to dance with another girl. He watched everybody pair off. The young Highlands girls, the ones in the stylish dresses, stepped forward, knowing they'd be picked first. Then the rest, English and Irish girls, their fathers overseers or cops or fireman, then the daughters of professionals, both lovely and saber-toothed. All had great expectations. All inflated their chests. Once teamed up, the newly formed partners awkwardly practiced a few steps before the music started.

From the refreshments table Will watched John Gower Jr. zero in on a young Durfee girl he'd probably known since diapers. But surprisingly, Gower stepped past her. He continued to the door, where Nellie Zorra sat next to Tommy. Little Doc was on his knee removing an ice bag from her ankle. He jumped up when he saw Gower. He shot Tommy a look, and then the three of them peered down at a beaming Nellie. As Little Doc explained her condition, John Gower patted his shoulder.

"Better stick to horses like your old man," he said, then to Nellie,

"How about I carry you around the dance floor for a number." He extended his hand. "You came all this way."

The bandleader waved his baton in the air, and music erupted, the horn section filling the room with a blast the whole crowd felt in their stomachs. Nellie tried to stand, but stumbled, falling into Gower's arms. Tommy reached forward. Gower snapped, "I got her, paperboy," and scooped her up in his arms. Nellie clasped his neck to hang on. Tommy offered a weak smile to Little Doc, who slammed the bag of ice to the floor, spraying water in all directions. He stormed out of the hall. Each couple Nellie and Gower passed burst into laughter, and Nellie buried her red face in his neck. He lowered her in the center of the floor, and the two turned in a jerky circle like windup toys that had been left out in the rain.

"What did I tell ya." Helen knocked Will's shoulder. "Social-climbing numbskull."

"Where's Burt?"

"Busted his glasses," Helen said.

Will regretted Nellie was being used to get back at him and Ray. "It's my fault."

"I think I'm gonna puke," Helen said. "Where's Little Doc?"

"Outside."

"I'll talk him down." Helen started walking away.

Gower whispered something in Nellie's ear and she laughed, the flush in her as face bright as the dance lights. Will had seen Hollister coax girls with such silliness, girls who normally weren't fooled. That's the part he couldn't figure. Why did they fall for such nonsense when they'd have mocked one of their own for acting so foolishly? Surrendering encouraged Highlands boys to believe everyone owed them something.

Will watched Tommy take a pull from his flask of elderberry wine. It was a blatant violation of the dance rules, but so was stealing another guy's girl, even if she wasn't your girl yet. Tommy wiped his mouth, his left hand turning dice in his jacket pocket. He handed the door counter to a kid he was training and left the hall to gamble with the livery drivers.

The song ended and the couples applauded wildly. Across the room Will heard faint strains of Nellie's snorting horselaugh; it was the type that required a hand to cover the mouth. Gower carried her to the punch bowl. He seemed intent on dragging out the indignity awhile longer. Will searched out Ray to stop it, but the giant was nestled in an alcove with Fanny Boyle, sipping punch. Mary Sheehan would be proud.

Helen burst into the pavilion. She cupped her hands to her mouth and shouted, "They've started!" She waved to Will and ran outside. She was a sucker for a good explosion, Will thought. Beyond the pavilion's plate glass windows white streaks of light blasted out of Mount Hope Bay. Explosions of blue light filled the sky. Everyone in the pavilion cheered. The horizon flashed white again, and then the sky lit up with hundreds of red tendrils of light. Pink stripes reflected off the black water, lighting up sloops bobbing near the barges. The boys without dates raced onto the boardwalk; the rest of the ballroom quickly followed. Will and Helen joined in the crush down to the water, stopping only to peel off their shoes on the beach stairs.

Under the canopy of color, men on a wooden barge a hundred yards out weaved and ducked, lighting the rockets in a choreographic dance. A funnel cloud of gray smoke rose over their works and then leveled out to cover half the bay. The barge was a ghost ship in a fog. The crowd cheered as two large streaks with red tails crisscrossed one another in their ascent. A cascading umbrella of silver stars met as oily reflections on the water. A girl near Will shrieked, and then asked her boyfriend if the boats moored offshore would catch fire. The boy smirked and then lit a cigarette. Most of the couples sat down in the dry sand. Tommy and a cluster of boys stood barefoot in the surf, smoking. The music struck up in the pavilion. "Look there!" a boy yelled. Heads turned as the brass and wind sections of the orchestra marched down the beach stairs in single-file, each man barefoot, their cuffs rolled under their knees, blasting out "When the Saints Come Marching In." The crowd stepped aside as the conductor led the parade to the edge of the water. The drummer had rigged a snare over his shoulder with his belt. More rockets whizzed overhead, sending blue and silver streaks across faces. A few of the older boys and their dates rolled up their pant cuffs and kicked up their heels in the surf. The girls hoisted their dresses. Helen pulled Will into the water. Tommy and Ray and Fanny locked arms and spun in a circle, kicking water onto couples nearby. Will spotted John Gower Jr. dancing with another girl and, on the boardwalk, Little Doc marching toward the car park, Nellie hopping a few feet behind.

Will pulled Helen to the rim of the dancers on the wet sand, but she skipped into the center of the group, stomping in surf. A wave rolled over Will's ankles as a long series of white blasts shot off the barge. A crowd of a few hundred now stood on the boardwalk. The encore of rockets exploded in the sky; the horn players blasted their instruments to be heard over the roar. The cascading white streaks unfurled over the water, riding waves toward the beach. Most dancers stopped to watch the barrage, but Helen kept kicking up the liquid-light dance floor. She held her arms down at her sides, but her wrists flared up as she skipped in a circle in the center of the light. Her ginger-colored hair aglow under the falling final flash. The ragtag band stopped, and the crowd cheered and whistled. The men on the barges took bows, their fuse lighters shining through the thick curtain of volcanic haze that engulfed their ghost ship as an acrid cloud of sulfur permeated the salty air. Under the haze of the boardwalk lamps, the band started marching in place; turning back to the pavilion, they struck up "Alexander's Ragtime Band." Couples tagged on to the end of their parade, grabbing the shoulders of the person in front of them. Folks belted out the first verse:

> *"Come on and hear, come on and hear*
> *Alexander's Ragtime Band*
> *Come on and hear, come on and hear*
> *It's the best band in the land."*

Helen stepped to join the tail of the procession, but Will spun her around, loosening her French twist. Copper-colored in the light, the wisps clung to her flush cheeks and neck.

"Let's go." She tugged at his hand, but he didn't budge. Helen rolled her eyes. She put her hands on her hips and tapped her toe jauntily on the soft sand. "What's it gonna be, Will Bartlett?"

He stepped closer to see her clearly through the haze. The fistful of sweet pickles he'd scoffed down while Helen danced with Burt churned angrily in his stomach. He'd been too nervous about the dance to eat his dinner, and now his pickle gorging was going to ruin everything, perhaps even Helen's pretty new dress. He turned his face as a wicked belch roared from his mouth.

"Excuse me," he hiccupped.

"You gonna be sick?"

"Wait," Will coughed. The music swelled and then softened as the band entered the pavilion. There were just a few songs remaining.

"If I get caught in the undertow I hope you're nowhere near the beach."

"Why's that?" Will dusted sand from his suit.

"Cuz I'd drown," she said. "Now or never."

Will's gut tightened as he suppressed another belch. They'd been assigned to opposite ends of the puberty yardstick for too long, and tonight, goddamn it, he was determined to be the man. He whirred and clamped his arms around her shoulders and squeezed. It was a move he'd seen the other boys attempt. Helen stumbled backward on her heels.

She shook him off and said softly, "Let's try that again."

She anchored his hands to her hips. "Start simple."

He closed his eyes and inched forward. Her warm breath coated his chin. He felt her hand on his jaw, guiding his mouth to hers. His face stiffened. Her lips tickled the tiny hairs on his lower lip.

"Salty."

"Loose lips," she said, and squeezed his cheeks in three quick bursts.

Will craned his head back to get a look at her. "How do you know so much?"

Helen slipped her hand behind his head and pulled his face to hers. "Looser," she intoned from deep in her throat. *Girls' lips are spun from silk—* Ray had told him that earlier that summer at the beach in Westport. He opened his eyes to see if anyone was watching, but gray smoke enveloped the beach. Helen clutched his coat, crunching the cotton lapels between her hands. He heard a soft cry. Was she weeping? He couldn't be sure. Was *he*? He moaned, and she squeezed the lapels tighter. The orchestra began the last set. The smoke thinned down the length of the beach; other couples were going through the same awkward motions. He saw a boy skate his fingers up and down his girl's back. Will unmoored his right hand from her hip and gently stroked Helen's hair. When she didn't recoil, he pulled the pins from the French twist, setting her hair free down her back. Will closed his eyes, surrendering to the weightlessness of the moment.

Helen broke the spell.

"Must"—she panted—"breathe." They doubled over, catching their breath. Will stood wide-eyed, thinking Helen's smile could power half the mills in Fall River.

"Pretty proud of yourself, aren't ya, Will Bartlett?" Helen blushed. She kicked sand on him. "I've been waiting."

"And?"

"Not too bad."

"Not bad? I was great," he said, raising his eyebrows.

"Race you back?" Helen lifted her dress and darted across the dry sand. Will stumbled behind laughing, stopping only to scoop their shoes off the seawall.

PART IV
1918
WOUNDS OLD & NEW

VICTORY ARCH

First Lieutenant Hollister Bartlett crouched in the trench, sucking a long, hot drag. It was a Hun butt taken from a pack of Prinz Heinrichs he'd pilfered from the breast pocket of a dead German hung out in no-man's land. The tobacco was poor, like most Hun supplies at this stage of the war and unlike the comfort of his beloved Chesterfields, but fresh smokes were scarce as the operation moved into its seventh day. Still, the nicotine calmed his nerves before going over the wall. The trench was littered with tin cans, spades, cracked stocks and barrels from discarded Springfields, but no other doughboys. Etched initials and farewells to sweethearts and parents were carved into the wooden supports. To avoid frontal assaults across no-man's land into waiting German machine guns, and perhaps survive the war, Hollister had volunteered for reconnaissance. But his job in Europe's damn war—more important than repelling the Hun from French soil—was getting home alive. Not to Fall River—hell no—but back to Commandant Blunt and a job teaching warfare at White Mountain. Working alone increased the odds of survival.

It had rained the night before, and a shallow puddle inched over the heel of Hollister's leather boot. Down the tunnel, he heard squeaking—probably rats gnawing on chunks of flesh blasted into the muddy walls. Frogs croaked in a nearby riverbed, and the guns in Bouresches, where the Marines were mopping up their victory and turning back another German offensive, shook the earth to the east. In the rush to get there, the American brass had passed by the artillery and machine gun nests in Belleau Wood that had not succumbed to the artillery barrage from the fifty batteries pounding the dense growth of trees. Hollister's mission was to find the tiny forts that the Germans had carved in the rocky strongholds of the oak forest and diagram their whereabouts in the gullies and underbrush for the next round of bombardment. After the howitzers had devastated the forest, the drawings would pass to Fourth Brigade Commander James Harbord to plan the next frontal assault. Hollister was tapped for the mission because he was the best. The French were pushing the Americans hard—Paris was fifty miles to the east. And yesterday, June 6, 1918, had been the worst day of casualties in the history of the Marine Corps.

Hollister licked his fingers and extinguished the cigarette. He stowed the remaining stub for his return to the trench. It had become his ritual. A small reward for another mission accomplished, and the only thing he felt he had going for him. He wedged his boot between two planks supporting the wall and popped his head over the embankment; he turned his ear toward the wood. After a few minutes, he climbed up on the parapet, then tumbled forward quickly so he wouldn't be silhouetted against the first traces of moonlight. He crawled forward through a decimated wheat field and lay on his stomach in a deep shell hole, listening for German voices. He peeked over the edge of the crater, hoping to glimpse a burning Prinz Heinrich. Three hundred yards from the black mass of forest, all he could hear were the owls.

Hollister traveled light; he carried lead pencils and a writing tablet in a cloth wrap, plus his well-oiled Colt, bayonet, gas mask, and two bombs in his pockets in case he chanced close enough to destroy one of the forts. His heightened senses registered each rock and stick jabbing into his torso and knees, even the bead of sweat rolling down the black polish covering his face. He'd learned to control his nerves, but his possible discovery by Hun machine gunners hidden in brush piles or snipers perched in treetops ate a hole in his stomach. Each sound was amplified, but his experience helped him differentiate between a hare darting down a hole and a German's heel dragging across the forest carpet.

He waited ten minutes in the crater and then advanced on his belly to the next one, zigzagging a path behind enemy lines. His long, wiry limbs snaked beneath or between the barbwire enforcements the Germans had haphazardly assembled in their retreat to the woods, though much of the line had been destroyed by American bombs. Closer, he encountered abandoned trenches and mortar positions. What little breeze there was carried with it the sweet smell of blooming lilac. He stopped every few feet to listen. On the rim of a large hole he stopped. Across the pit two German jackboots stood upright in the soggy mud with a soldier's feet and brown corduroy trousers snug inside, but missing the boot's owner above knee; the remaining flesh and bone, ragged like a torn loaf of bread. A blackened steel helmet lay upside down beside the boots. Rainwater collected in the bucket. Hollister swallowed the bile collecting at the back of his throat and rolled down an embankment out of the heart of the field and into a damp creek bed, hoping the frogs would drown out his advance.

After another hundred yards he reached the edge of the wood. He stopped and put an ear to the air. German voices. He undid his kit in a dry clearing beside the creek. The frogs had quieted, the owls too. He'd traced the area before setting out and quickly recalibrated his bearings by touch, finding the blotches of wax he'd melted onto the map. The Germans were holed up in a clump of woods covering a knoll that rose sharply from the wheat field. He'd marked his route, so he had a good idea how far he'd advanced. He jotted down the distance for artillery. Aided by the moonlight, he sketched the locations; he crawled fifty yards forward to the top of a dirt mound and sketched the machine gun nests dug out beneath a boulder.

He heard a German patrol, and he stowed his kit and rolled to the base of the mound. Two—no, three sets of feet. He smelled burning tobacco and heard the soft rap of a canteen against a hip. Hollister slipped his bayonet noiselessly from its leather scabbard and raised the Colt, hoping the men would change course and pass by unaware.

He fired when the first set of boots hit the top of the mound. The German's head snapped back as the slug split open his forehead. His body crumpled to the ground. The others jumped at the blast. Hollister aimed at the next silhouette on the mound and fired. The shot clipped the man's right shoulder. His left hand jerked to the wound as the next round found his chest. The force blew him back down the hill. The last man launched himself off the mound, his short spade reflecting the moonlight. Hollister thrust his bayonet in the air, piercing the German's gut as the spade lopped off the corner of Hollister's shoulder. Voices called from the woods. The bayonet jutted out the man's back; he slid down the blade pinning Hollister to the ground. Blood gushed between them, and Hollister wasn't sure who was dying till the German screamed, his spastic arms batting Hollister's neck and head. Hollister felt for his Colt. He rammed the barrel into the German's temple, closed his eyes, and fired. The man's head snapped left and his body heaped. Hollister pried his left arm free from between their bodies and shoved the dead German into the trampled wheat. He clutched his shoulder. No pain, but blood seeped between his fingers. He bit his lip and pressed the hot metal barrel of the Colt to the wound, hoping to cauterize the blood vessels. Through the ringing in his ears he heard the popping of flare-lights. This surprised him. He had expected to be dead momentarily. But the Germans were cautious, not wanting to shoot their own. Perhaps reserves were low. With his good arm, Hollister threw two hand grenades in the direction of the closest machine gun nest, then secured his gas mask and scurried back to the creek bed as the night sky lit up in red.

Near dawn, a four-man wiring party from Battery F found him on the outskirts of the wheat field, near dead from crawling through the night. He still clutched his kit. The field surgeons at the dressing station in Lucy-le-Bocage removed a slug from his broken right leg and treated the blisters caused by mustard gas, but the poison had entered his bloodstream through the shoulder wound, and by the time he was transferred to England, his vision was failing. He told his friend Michael Murphy that the last thing he remembered was the ripping burst of a machine gun and the cracking sound, not unlike the breaking of an egg, of a gas canister snapping open against the moss-covered rocks lining the creek.

* * *

Joseph received a letter from the army describing Hollister's wounds in July. The English and American doughboys that survived the field dressing stations in France were shipped across the Channel. Hollister spent weeks with other gassed soldiers recuperating from the mustard-colored blisters that appeared on their neck and arms. And unlike many, his leg had been properly set in Lucy. Many boys had to go through the painful process of having their crooked limbs rebroken and reset in England. His son was alive, Joseph thanked God for that. The papers were vague on details except the naming of the dead. But as he reread the letter in the subsequent days, he couldn't shake his guilt. He had given up on the boy all those years ago. Joseph feared that when his time came, neither of his boys would remember him fondly. Now he desperately wanted Will to return to Fall River from New Haven. The boy was his only hope. Hollister's future was unknown, but he'd return a hero. Now that was something.

The second correspondence was postmarked from Dover, but Joseph seriously doubted his boy ever saw the white cliffs. The letter sat in a china bowl on the end table in the breezeway. It was dated August 12. Joseph didn't recognize the handwriting on the envelope.

Dear Sir,

I am writing on behalf of your son Hollister. We met in the hospital and discovered we are neighbors of a sort. My family lives across the river in Somerset. Hollister is making progress and may be home near the harvest. His leg is mending nicely. He's had quite a shock; his memory fails at times. He shouts his mother's name but not much else. Though the doctors believe he will walk soon, there is one other complication. Your boy is losing his sight. That gas is the devil's work. The eyes are near swollen shut, but he suffered a low concentration. He can see shapes and color in the magazines I fetch him. I will mind him on the sail home.

Sincerely yours,
Lieutenant Michael Murphy

When Mayor Kay heard a slew of wounded boys were returning, he commissioned the construction of an arch in front of city hall. Each wave of returning boys would receive a parade and medals. After a review of the town's books, it was decided the arch should span Main Street; trolley cars would pass beneath it. The wooden arch was to be covered with plaster and then painted to look like marble.

By the end of September the tide of the war had turned against the Germans. The wire reports published in the *Evening Herald* described worn-down Hun guns hitting their own troops and American firepower hailing down on badly trained German teenagers, many suffering from starvation, dysentery, and typhus. When Bulgaria signed an armistice the end was near, and the prognosticating mayor set about finding a statue of Winged Victory for the arch's apex and ordered the Italian artisans to change VALIANT atop the arch to VICTORY. But the mayor's monument was behind schedule. Only the wooden understructure was complete when the first wounded soldiers returned.

The city's mills had done well during wartime, and job rolls swelled. Government contracts flowed like the yarn off a spindle. Cloth to clean big guns and rifles. Cloth for leggings and knapsacks. Cloth for bandages and uniforms. Millions of yards of cheap, coarse cloth meant high dividends and paid taxes. Cloth Joseph had chosen not to manufacture. He doubled his niche in fine cloth and silk but contributed to the mayor's memorials and parade committees like the rest. As Fall River's boys boarded a ship for home all the papers sent reporters for the crossing. All the papers ran stories of heroism—Black Jack Pershing had become sort of a folk hero—people had chosen to forget the four hundred thousand killed at Verdun, the horrors of razor wire, mustard gas, daisy cutter artillery, and hand-to-hand fighting in the narrow trenches. The wounded local boys would be the town's first contact with the fight itself.

THE QUEEN OF BOATHOUSE ROW

Before Helen arrived, Will stood on the deck watching the orange sunset reflect across the still water of the Westport River. The slack tide temporarily brought the tidal body to a halt, but soon millions of gallons of saltwater would flow in from the Atlantic, raising the wooden boat docks and floating catboats far above the shallow eelgrass where he and Hollister netted fiddler crabs and minnows. The family's only watercraft, a single-mast beetle cat, sat on its mooring twenty feet off their small dock, which was littered with white seagull poop and bits of crab and lobster shell. The stilt houses lining Boathouse Row were dark, shut up for the winter. Across the channel he spotted a flickering bonfire on Cherry Point. The mild fall weather echoed summer. The water temperature was in the low sixties, spurring talk of a possible hurricane, but nothing came from Buzzards Bay but warm September days and cool nights. The waves gently beat the thick pylons supporting the house. The lighthouse bell at the Point of Rocks, at the mouth of the rocky harbor, rang, and for a moment Will remembered the fun house incident. And now a returning hero. Will shook his head. He had not seen his brother in two years.

"Criminy!" He raced back inside. He'd forgotten that his father didn't visit the boathouse after Labor Day, and Mr. Coggeshall, the local plumber the summer people called to fix everything, had shuttered the house and cut the water like the others. Will had come right from Middletown, stopping only to pick up a picnic basket Evelyn had prepared. He bathed in a shallow tide pool, using a coarse horse soap he'd found in the livery stable at the end of the lane, and changed into a wrinkled gabardine suit that hadn't seen the light since a dance at the casino two years earlier. He'd only had time to uncover the first-floor furniture and make sure the outside privy was serviceable when he heard car tires crunching down the gravel lane. Quickly he set out the picnic on the sideboard and found a blue ceramic water pitcher for the Montauk daisies he'd picked from the roadside. Before opening the door, he poured a capful of water from the canteen into his hands and splashed it across his warm face and neck.

He had seen Helen only once that summer: at Cousin Pete's birthday weekend in late July. He'd come down from his job clerking in Boston, but Helen could only manage the Sunday of the actual birthday away from her job at the Hyannis boardinghouse. The divide between the Highlands and the Flint had finally caught them. Helen studying at normal school, managing the boardinghouse, and disappearing to the Cape, still hammering her socialist politics and endlessly pursuing equal rights—interests sown while he was at Yale.

Late that afternoon, the two swam out to Elephant Rock, just offshore, and lay shoulder to shoulder, drying under the hot sun between the tiny crags of barnacled rock. They were hidden on a ledge the locals called the High Shoulder that looked out to sea. After ten minutes they heard Ray, Tommy, and the rest jostling in the water. Helen turned on her side, her hazel eyes unusually large. He raised his hand to block the glare; her lips curled, and she seemed to be summoning him, but he couldn't make head or tails of what he should do, so he said nothing. In twenty-one years, he'd never had to read her expressions, because her mouth never stopped. When the boys clamored up the rock, Helen whispered something into his ear and then rolled away. He called to her, but she ran and jumped off the head of the Elephant, a peak so steep the boys only attempted it at high tide.

Helen directed Ray's old Model T between the dips in the gravel lane stopping beside the boathouse. She'd just started teaching in Westport and moved in with Ray—he'd finally married Fanny Boyle and left Snell Street. Teaching was one of the few professions in which she'd be independent and exercise her mind, not her back and hands. Ray had taken to defending his baby sister's freedom at family gatherings.

He stepped in front of the car and raised a hand. The headlamps shone on his chest.

Helen pulled the handbrake and turned to Will with the same mischievous expression from the previous summer.

"What's it gonna be, Will Bartlett?"

"Huh?"

"How's the water?" She stepped on the running board. "Don't scratch it," she smirked and kissed his cheek.

"Nice to see you too." He reached for her arm, but she slapped her driving gloves into his hand, hopped down, and skipped into the house. She sashayed over the clamshell walk as if she were the queen of Boathouse Row. He drove to the car park, gnawing at the inside of his cheek on the walk back. He feared the night getting away from him before it had even started. This had been his rendezvous, his date. He dabbed his forehead. He feared he wouldn't say what needed saying.

He found her on the porch overlooking the river. "When your father dies, my mother should come live here," Helen said. She held a glass of João's Portuguese wine.

"Why would you say such a thing?"

"Well, she can't very well move into June Street."

Will walked inside and poured a glass for himself and made two plates from the sausage, cheese, and johnnycakes in the basket. Helen called after him, "You know, your father is a beastly man, and she's no better."

"Does she know you're here?" Will handed her a plate of food, and they settled in two weathered Adirondack chairs he'd wiped clean of seagull shit.

"The less she knows of my life the better. Tommy and Cousin Pete will watch after her."

"Who will watch over you?" Will jumped up. "More wine?"

"Always."

Helen stepped to the railing as the last bit of pinkish-brown light faded to black. Through the salt-sprayed window glass, he studied her. A small pressure pushed against Will's chest, his temperature rising like the incoming tide. The playfulness of their banter made it difficult to know what was true. But this playfulness ebbed each time she caught him staring. He had reached the age where he was allowed to imagine her body without shame. In the past, he'd freeze when she'd nab him, then blabber something about a run in her stocking. Thankfully, Helen had also reached an age where she wasn't embarrassed by his attention, and on the rare occasions when they were alone, encouraged it. Of course, their agreement to gawk had never been discussed, nothing much had, but Will considered her encouragement as a sort of commitment. And though his Yale friends would have read Helen's teasing as an invitation, Will held back, afraid of many things. He had never crept behind the velvet curtain to meet the dancers at the Bowery clubs he visited with his school chums. Others had, and reeked for days, a few scratching rashes before the train even reached Union Station.

He'd overheard his college dates call him big eared, good manned, and well groomed—descriptions better suited to a dog than a man. Perhaps Helen saw something else, or perhaps he was the only dog she'd allow close after her father died. He dumped more wine into his glass, slammed it, and filled it again. When he looked up, she was staring at him. Her elbows perched on the railing, her head thrown back. Her strawberry hair reminded him of his mother. It was braided down the back, between her shoulder blades. A poor man's French twist. High school boys had no doubt enjoyed staring at her full lips and quarter-sized hazel eyes and at that heart-shaped face dotted on either side of her long, ramped nose with inky freckles. John Singer Sargent would kill for such a model.

He studied the crosshatched weave of her plain calico dress—hell, he even knew the pattern: gold trillium. Cleveland Mill hadn't worked with calico in years. She probably owned a week's worth in sweet pea and lavender, dated schoolmarm clothes she'd purchased off discount racks, too proud to allow her family to buy any velvet or linen for the country schoolteacher. Will was beginning to like the calico dress. It ran the length of her long athletic figure, but she'd rolled up the sleeves up past her elbows like her father had back on the shop floor, freeing arms shaped from years of tennis and her new sport, field hockey. Above the tapered waist was the squared front, his favorite part, revealing a wide swath of creamy skin and strong bones that ran from shoulder to shoulder above her smallish breasts—breasts that had shocked him in his father's bathhouse six years ago and which, seemingly, had stopped growing after that summer.

Helen took a deep breath and sat back down. Cutting a sausage she called, "Stop staring. I'm not for sale." She shook her empty wine glass. "Bring the bottle."

"Some sunset," he said, and began pouring.

"So's my dress, evidently—thank you—I'm on a budget."

"That never stopped you before."

"I discovered teenage girls are much braver than twenty-year-old women."

"Or more likely to get arrested."

"Friend, *you* were the only one who came close to that." She tapped his arm with her fist. "No, I'm temporarily retired—that is until my big heist. I'm still searching for a good nickname."

"Right! We were supposed to make one up after that dance."

"Maybe I'll knock over some Fall River banks before all the money moves south."

Will had hoped to avoid any Fall River bashing, but Helen always found a way to tie it in to their banter. It was really a swipe at his father. Helen had made no secret of her suspicions about his charity to her family: Why so much? A lot of workers died in fires. What did he give the two Frenchy families who lost *their* breadwinners? Will shook his head, not wanting to engage Helen's conspiracy theories. The Cleveland fire had been an accident. Everyone had put it behind them—everyone but Helen and her brother Tommy. He poured himself another glass and drank it fast. The sky was starless and growing dark. He could just make out the outline of a few boats, their mooring lines pulled taut by the incoming tide. Will set his hand on Helen's arm; his forefinger traced a scab below her elbow.

"Field hockey," she said. "Some girls use that stick like a tomahawk."

"I'm glad you came." He kissed the scar.

"Ray thinks I'm headed all the way to Middletown to fetch some of João's milk. Did you bring the jugs? He won't expect me till late, as if he has a say in the matter. You know I'm managing his finances again. Just like when we were kids. Fanny is equally as dimwitted." Helen turned in her chair to face Will. She started to laugh. "Oh, wait till Maria sees your brother."

"She won't."

"Those Roses get around now."

"João won't let her."

"But one day—"

"Just don't, please," he said. "The parade is tomorrow."

"The walking wounded. A big mistake."

"They deserve it."

"They deserve a paycheck and medical care. You read the papers? These guys are going to be missing pieces."

"And Hollister's going blind, so just drop it."

She raised her glass. "To the sons of Fall River."

"Little late for that." Will gathered up the plates and went inside. The previous afternoon, while skimming cranberries with João, he'd broken the news of Hollister's homecoming. João assured him all was forgiven—another lie. They'd agreed Maria shouldn't be told.

The screen door creaked, and he turned.

"Sorry," she said. "Pee outside?"

Will nodded. "He's still my brother."

"If it wasn't for his bad eye, Tommy could have gone. I get it."

Will tossed their plates in the basket and opened another bottle of wine.

The first floor of the boathouse was a large rectangle divided by the chimney and the stairwell to the second-story bedrooms. The kitchen and eating table took one half; a large sitting room occupied the other. The interior walls were unplastered, leaving the exposed beams and two-by-six planks. Framed photographs of beach picnics and Cleveland company outings hung on the walls. The air was damp and the room cool without the sunlight. He struck two table lamps with shades painted with a nautical map of the area. The light projected their fuzzy images against the walls.

"My mother should definitely get this house," Helen said, surveying the room.

"This one is mine. She can have the rest," Will said, and poured the wine. "So what did you do all summer? You haven't been home since July."

"I worked. And some Saturdays I took the trolley to Provincetown."

"Never been." He scratched his head. "You go with girls from school?"

"No."

"Really?"

"I have some friends there. Jesus, Will, I raised myself. I have great times with—"

"With who?"

"Are you jealous?"

"You've never mentioned any of this in your letters."

"You really want to know?"

"I know you're a kleptomaniac. I know you skim Ray's earnings. I know you dream of running away. I know you vandalized Sunny's father's Cadillac after she whipped you."

Helen flung a coaster at him. "That fight was a draw," she said. "Anyway, I've met some artists."

"Artists? Who's an artist?"

"Writers, and playwrights, and actors, and theater directors." She struck a haughty pose Will knew well from Yale. "They call themselves the Provincetown Players."

"I've been to the theater. Met actors." He leaned forward in his chair.

"No, silly, not like that. We're friends. They come to the Cape from New York for the summer. They know everybody—Emma Goldman, for Christ sake."

"Come to New Haven, like you promised, and you'll meet people like that."

"You're not listening. This is not a lecture series. We discuss politics, the vote. It's freer away from suffocating city society. Freer thinking. They allow a woman a cigar, brandy—to pour the brandy. We're on the beach, not some stuffy sitting room."

"This past Labor Day in South Park, there was a concert—"

"Jesus. Will you stop harping on about Fall River? Those lily-white men only write about themselves and their society wives, not the ninety thousand workers, mostly yellow and black and brown, whose backs drive their machines. But train those people to read, give them a wage so their kids can stay in school—"

"Dad supports the Children's Bureau."

"Ten-year-olds shouldn't work." Her hands gripped the armchair, flexing the tendons in her muscular arms.

"They don't in ours."

"May there be a place in heaven for you and your father."

Will poured another glass of wine. "Moving on," he said. "Where do you meet such *artists*?"

"They stayed at the boardinghouse one night after a gale forced them off the road near Hyannis two summers ago. This one fella had a trunk full of plays, and we read them through the night and into the morning."

"Fella? What fella?"

"His name is Eugene. He's good."

"You go alone . . .to visit men . . . in Provincetown."

"There are women too. Susan founded the theater, with her husband."

"But there's single men?"

"And once, in August after we painted some of the new theater, we went swimming at night."

"We've done that, right here on the river, two summers ago after Tommy won that money at the pavilion."

"But we were naked and drunk."

Will froze. The smirk on Helen's face tightened and she widened her eyes to imitate Will's shocked mug. "Pour me another glass," she said, "and we might get there ourselves."

Will jumped to his feet. "Enjoying yourself?"

"Immensely." She stood, facing him. "Say it."

"What?"

"The reason you asked me here." She jabbed a finger into his chest. "You still can't. Little Willie Bartlett. He can pound Damian but can't talk to girls. Sad." She turned toward a tall hutch filled with Elizabeth's old collection of cut-glass animals and picked up a unicorn. She ran her finger over the bumps of glue down its back and up to the horn, scratching off the nub of hardened glue at the base with her nail, and then placed it back in the hutch. "I asked you to the Rock last summer because Eugene said I should push the issue. But if you don't love me—"

Will stomped his foot. "You swam naked!"

"You don't get it, the men, most of them anyway, my friends, are fairies."

"They fly?"

"Will, they like men. Not me. Don't you get it? They're homosexual." She laughed, throwing her arms in the air. "It is very liberating."

He clutched her elbow. "What about Eugene?"

"What?" She shook free.

"Is he a fairy?"

"No, he's married to Agnes."

"Do you wish I were like them? These *theater people*?"

Helen set her fists on her hips. "I'm glad you're not a homosexual, Will. Really I am."

"You know, one summer at camp, I played Dogberry in *Much Ado about Nothing*."

"Poor, poor Will," she said, her tone one of genuine pity. She touched his cheek. "Always the fool."

"Shut up," he snapped, knocking her hand away.

"Will Bartlett, don't you understand me at all? After all these years?" Helen walked to the sideboard and poured herself a glass of sherry from a decanter. "My friends, those men—the flyers, as you call them—live these horrible, closed lives, so when I told them there was boy I loved, they asked why I wasn't with him. They convinced me not to waste time with societal nonsense . . . but go get him. You don't know the fear I have of being bossed about like just another girl in the weaving room. Every day, I wish my father were alive, though if he were, I know I'd have been sold off to some rich Highlands boy and locked in some granite prison on the hill washing his shirts. For the first time, I've met people who don't care if I was raised on Corky Row or June Street. There's a world out there besides textiles and that foolish city." Helen stepped to the rolltop desk and picked out a pack of Helmars wedged in one of the cubbies. "This is why I didn't tell you in the letters. I knew you'd never understand." Helen tapped a cigarette against the desk and lit it. She paced the room. Her left arm folded under her right elbow to prop up her forearm. The cigarette smoke rose to the ceiling.

"So better to be a hussy than to rely on a man who might get himself killed."

"You're finally listening."

"But what if I was that man in the big house on the hill?"

"I can't imagine that."

"Why not?"

"You've never issued orders to me, Will Bartlett."

"I don't want to."

"My point exactly. You don't want anything. There's a whole world out there, and you're content to hopscotch between your family's connections like some latter-day prince and snuggle with your New Haven friends when it gets cold outside. Face it, even if I wanted to marry you, you're not ready to tame me."

"Could if I wanted," he snapped.

"Like your brother with those mill girls?"

"That's not what I meant." The growl of a fishing boat returning to the harbor rolled up from the water. The boat, outlined in green and red running lights, cruised downriver past the boathouse.

Helen exhaled two long tendrils of gray smoke from her nose and picked at her front teeth with her nail. "Okay, then like your father does my mother."

"They've just managed best they could."

She jabbed the cigarette at Will. "Oh please, I've seen it."

"That was years ago. Hell, my mother had just died."

"Jesus, Will, what chauvinistic bastard won't you defend?"

"Fatty Arbuckle." Will crossed his arms, pleased with himself.

"Oh please, grow up, will you?"

"Shut up." He stepped closer to her.

"What time is it?" She peered around the room. "I should make tracks."

What's it gonna be, Will Bartlett? He extended his arm, blocking her path to the door. "Take off your dress."

"Excuse me?"

"Swim with me."

"It's freezing."

"So you're objecting to the temperature, but not my proposition?"

"*My proposition?* When did you start talking funny? Just say it. Swim naked with me, Helen. I want to see your boobies, Helen."

"Shut up."

"And when you have the jump on someone, dear boy, you don't ask them questions. What did they teach you down there? My six-year-olds would eat you for lunch."

"Stop it."

"Swim by yourself." She took a slow drag.

Will swiped the cigarette from her mouth and flicked it into the empty fireplace.

"Get me another."

He slapped her face.

Helen rubbed her cheek and rolled her neck. "Finally, some spirit," she said. "Too bad you went soft after your mother died."

He slapped her again, gentler, but hard enough to snap her neck back around a second time. Her cheek burned red with an impression of his hand.

Helen sucked her two front teeth, then maneuvered her jaw. Her bite was off a few centimeters. "Now, about my dress," she started. Will sniffled, on the verge of tears. Her eyes narrowed.

"I'm—"

"If you apologize, I'll never speak to you again, Will Bartlett."

He wiped his sleeve across his face. "I hate you sometimes."

"Good," she said.

He grabbed her shoulders, balling the collar of her dress in his hands, stretching the seams.

"So?" Her nostrils flared. "I can always get another dress."

Will ripped the dress in half, a clean split down the middle seam. He jumped back. She was naked underneath.

Helen smirked. "Eugene suggested this too."

Will clutched her face. "I love that man." He kissed her deeply. She exhaled into his mouth and he swallowed, the silver of warm air filling his chest. He whispered, "I love you."

"Finally."

He swung his arm under her legs. Helen let loose a holler as he mounted the stairs to his old summer bedroom. On the second stair Will took a deep breath of her soapy skin. By the last step, the tickling of her navel hairs against his neck was secondary to the anticipation of his spine shattering through his pelvis. On the landing, he stumbled down the short hall to his room, turned and rested his bottom on the doorknob an instant, then bumped it open with his hip. The door swung and they twirled inside, Helen kicking it shut with her feet. It was pitch black. He stood for a moment, forgetting where the iron bed was, though it was right before him. He registered a musty odor and the old sail bag in the corner.

"You okay?" she said, barely above a whisper.

He grunted and then bent and set her softly on the bed. They both smirked as the bedsprings whined. He exhaled and arched his back; he hoped she couldn't see his strain. It wasn't that she was heavy; he was just unfit. He felt for the heavy drape Coggeshall had hung and tied it back and cracked the window. A bluish glow from the single lamppost on the fishing wharf reflected up from the water, outlining her figure on the bed. He stared at the mound of red hair between her legs.

"I think I drank too much." she said.

"Ditto."

"It's a tad cold." She gathered the bedspread over her body, then wriggled around in the cocoon of fabric before propping up on her elbow to face him. "So?" she said, her tone teasing. "Why'd you rip my dress off? To show me your room?"

Please stop talking, he thought. Another joke, and he'd lose his nerve, or vomit sausage salad. He took in the walnut dresser, the tiny closet, and the pine bookcase housing his boyhood summer library of *Wild West Weekly* and *National Geographic*. Above it hung a pinwheel of blue, red, and white sailing pennants he'd won on the river. A pressure knotted in his chest had collected below his bladder; it was unlike what he'd experienced at the burlesque shows. It bordered on pain; his stomach felt hot, and there was tightening around the scrotum and anus. And was he panting? Perhaps he *was* a dog. Helen laid back on the bed, her eyes closed, the mischievous expression returned. Her trail of breadcrumbs had led him to this cliff. It was not how he'd imagined their first time, but the dog within him wagged its tail. He cinched his shoulders and shook, and his suit jacket fell to the floor. Next, he pinched his heels together and wedged first the left, then right loafer off. He fumbled with the eyes and buttons on his white shirt, snapping two loose. He paused, but there was no sound of them striking the floor. As his undershirt passed over his head, he felt a tugging at his waist and then his belt whip around, the tip zipping through the loops like a mouse through a maze; it snapped at the end and took flight, the buckle clanging into the bookcase. Laughing, Helen yanked his pants down and he flipped forward, arms flexed to catch his weight. His left hand landed beside her head, his right fell between her legs. His hand tensed and inched down her leg, but Helen clasped his wrist, pulling it tight between her legs.

"I like it." She applied pressure to his arm, guiding his movements against her sex. He was glad to finally have some direction; he spread his fingers wide on the mattress for support. She squirmed and he eased off.

"Don't stop," she whispered. "Faster." He quickened the stroke like gently sanding the hull of his boat and felt her body tense but also loosen at the same time. She grew wet. "Faster." She clutched his forearm. Air bunched up in her chest. She squeezed tighter.

He swooped down to kiss her warm neck. He spread his legs and flexed his left arm, making a three-legged stool to support his weight and free his right hand. He drummed his fingers down her velvety skin from her neck to her stomach; between her legs the folds were warm and slick like a skinned red pepper just off the fire. The center swelled against his thumb, and he polished the spot with his index finger. He had never concentrated so hard in his life. And then she released a soft moan and exhaled. *I've finally pleased her.* Helen's lips parted, moving but emitting no sound. Were all creatures so dumbstruck?

Helen pulled him onto the bed. She began stroking his penis with her right hand. The tip bounced off her belly.

He kissed her stomach, and then both her breasts. "All that from my index finger."

"Fireworks in the veins," she said and kissed his forearm. "Closer." She pulled him forward by the penis and stroked him with both hands.

"Helen—"

"Don't think," she said. The knot tying his scrotum loosened, his cheeks burned as a honeyed sensation thundered through his wiry limbs. He gasped as a mild spasm seized his calf and thigh muscles. *Helen.* He came, grunted softly, and collapsed on top of her.

"Wow." His whole body quaked.

"Yeah, sticky wow," she smirked and wiggled beneath him.

He felt his heart beating in his neck, the tops of his feet, his fingertips, his penis.

"We're glued now," she said.

He began to cry. "Finally," he said, and when he looked up, she was also crying.

Her mouth settled against his ear, and her lips popped, the sound like a canning jar sealing shut. "I've waited for you," she whispered.

"Really?" He wiped his eyes on her shoulders. "You seem to know—"

"I read a lot." They kissed. "And now I know you waited too."

"There's no one else."

"Time for that swim."

The sound of tires on the gravel drive outside suddenly filled the house. They perked up.

"That your next girl?"

"Shhh," he said, straddling her. Feet came up the clamshell walk, then a heavy knock at the door.

"The French call it *ménage à trois.*"

"Seriously, shut it."

A keychain rattled, the lock clicked, and the door creaked open. A voice called, "Anybody here?"

"It's Coggeshall." Will hung his head. "I forgot to call him."

Helen bucked, throwing Will to the floor. "You go."

"I go." He groped for his undershirt, and mopped his chest and crotch. "Don't breathe."

Will threw one arm in his jacket, then the other, yanked up his pants, and did the buttons to cover his damp crotch. At the top landing he exhaled, then called, "Mr. Coggeshall, how are you, sir? I'm just taking a nap before heading back to the city."

The two halves of Helen's dress draped over Coggeshall's leathery hands. Will descended the steps and took the pieces, thinking of the linen suit he'd buy Helen. "And I'm cleaning up a bit with that old remnant," he said. "No one wears this calico anymore."

Coggeshall stared at the wine glasses. "No one sent word."

"Sorry about that."

"You father always sends word so I can get her ready."

"Well, I'm not my father," Will said, walking to the stairs. "I'll close her up. Sorry to wake you. Good night."

NO MAN'S LAND

Will leaned against the skeletal wooden scaffolding supporting the Victory Arch and popped a hot nut he'd bought from a peanut vendor at the trolley stop into his mouth. Main Street funneled under the arch, then past a grandstand that had been erected opposite the review platform in front of city hall. Local editorials believed it a patriotic duty to attend the parade, but mill owners kept the looms spinning. The grandstand was half full, mostly with politicians, newspapermen, clergy, and of course the families of soldiers; most of the crowd lined the parade route. Placards proclaimed VICTORY IS NEAR. OUR BOYS ARE HOME. The sky was overcast; rain was expected. A tepid wind came up from the pier, carrying some notes of "The Star-Spangled Banner." Perhaps it was the Cleveland Mill band. For the first time in a long time, Will had to give it to his father.

Will exchanged an expectant glance with the man standing beside him, and tipped the nut bag, but the man shook his head. No doubt a nervous father. He'd received a vague letter from the army, too, and was equally excited and scared to see his boy. Will recognized faces from Cleveland. His father had given the operatives the day off. Not even the Bordens had matched that. He spotted his old man moving through the crowd, surely on some welcoming committee. Will crumpled the greasy bag and walked to the grandstand. He spotted Mary Sheehan, Ray, and Fanny waving flags near the top.

The parade was late. A rumor spread that when the mayor saw so many crippled boys disembark the steamship *Pilgrim*, he ordered the few floats in the procession emptied to give them a ride, and when the boys demanded the right to march, the route was shortened to a quarter mile.

Will found a seat in the second row across from the low platform. It was less than a foot high, so the boys didn't have to take any steps. There were ramps for wheelchairs. The music faded, and the crowd started to rustle.

"They're coming!" a voice shouted. Folks craned their necks down Main Street.

"Where?"

"False alarm." Everyone sat back down. Across the street, the city treasurer walked across the empty stage and whispered something to the Durfee High School music director, who stood and raised his baton. An endless medley of wartime favorites began with "When I Get Back to the USA."

Will surveyed the crowd, hoping Helen might surprise him instead of covertly moving the last of her belongings out of her mother's house. He waved his cap before his face. On second thought, he was glad she wasn't here; Hollister's homecoming was enough for the family. Will rubbed his index finger under his nose, the smell of her was not yet familiar, and he immediately got hard at the first scent. (A week ago he'd have thought it sour, not sweet and erotic.) He held the finger out, as if admiring a ring. Damn, he thought, the power of this little digit. He smiled as he adjusted the crotch of his suit pants. After Coggeshall had left they took their cleanup swim in the dark water and shared a moldy-smelling towel. He dusted off an old dress of his mother's for Helen, but she insisted on wearing some of his old dungarees from the hall closet. Walking to the parade, he'd stopped in McWhirr's to buy Helen a linen suit. The model in the advertisement looked very modern and sporty, leaning her rump on a golf club. He'd had it wrapped and delivered to the house. She'd wear it the next time—the next time . . . perhaps a weekend in New York once Hollister was settled on June Street.

The music stopped, then started again, louder.

"Here they are, Fall River. On your feet," the treasurer announced. "Our Heroes."

The grandstand stood as the soldiers swayed and stumbled in an undulating formation up Main Street, wearing their dress blues with red piping. Three drummers led the procession. Behind them came three rows of limber boys with arms in slings or head bandages, then two rows of strapping, quick-stepping boys on crutches. The next few rows walked unaided but were glassy-eyed, not seeming to register the reams of bunting hanging off McWhirr's or the horde of cheering paperboys and blue-clad bike messengers near the Hotel Melon. Others swayed, their heads swiveling as if they expected an ambush from Touhey's pharmacy. One row shook uncontrollably, as if noodles had replaced their femurs, a volunteer nurse or nun at their elbows to guide them down the street. A few screamed gibberish that the crowd figured for cheers and gave right back. When the entire regiment of eighty men had passed under the arch, the grandstand roared. A few soldiers cowered. Two near the back began running the opposite direction. Wheelchairs jerked out of formation. Will overheard a journalist nearby say the boys had brought the trench home with them. Another said the British had a name for it—they called it "shell shock."

Hollister passed within ten feet of Will, moving slowly with the aid of a cane and a one-armed man at his elbow. His eyes were hidden behind dark glasses. The gold second lieutenant bar on his hat and collar shone. But his breathing was labored, and his dress uniform was two sizes too large. It hung from his shoulders, pulled down by the weight of the medals pinned to his chest. His skin had the pallor of sea salt, except for the blisters left from the mustard gas, which now resembled large spider bites on his neck and hands. Like many boys, around his neck he carried the cigar and match tin the Red Cross had handed out on the boat from New York.

Each man had a Purple Heart pinned to his chest. The severely wounded had oak-leaf clusters pinned to the ribbon, one for every injury. Hollister had one cluster pinned to his, plus the recently established Distinguished Service Cross for his heroism in the field. Many had a cross. One man was missing both feet and walked on his stubs using special shoes and canes; he had no oak-leaf clusters pinned to his medal. Will figured the army didn't count each foot separately. A few were missing their jaws; others had bandages on every joint. Those in wheelchairs varied from three-limb amputees to men who looked like they could jump out of their chairs and dance. This latter group had no medals at all.

Helen's plea echoed in Will's head—*A paycheck. Free medical care*—and then the oft-repeated refrain *When the money stops coming you die*, a Sheehan family favorite. As the more seriously damaged rolled and hobbled past, the parade slowed and the applause tapered. A strained rendition of "I'm Gonna Pin My Medal on the Girl I Left Behind" filled the void. Panic bordering on revulsion swept the grandstand. A woman and her three daughters broke into hysterical sobs as a boy missing both arms walked by in a daze. Who were these deformed strangers imitating their sons? "Like a sack of bruised tomatoes," a man whispered. "What must losing look like?" another replied. The faces that had delivered papers, scooped ice cream, punched tickets, or shoveled walks were unrecognizable.

Nine months from now, in early July, when the sun shone again and kitchen gardens grew thick with herbs, residents of Spindle City would sit in this same grandstand beside the completed Victory Arch and screech their hearts' approval for the real heroes of this "war to end all wars," and a woman would turn to her middle-aged husband and whisper, "What happened to all those wounded boys?" Then a firework would explode beyond city hall and she'd forget the question, unaware that some of those wounded boys sat a few rows below her, their caps pulled low over their missing ears and cheekbones, wanting more than anything to return to the time when their lives meant something, fighting on the Western Front.

"There," a voice called. "He's fallen." Beside the wooden scaffolding, where the crowd was three and four deep, a young private had doubled over, one arm on a streetlamp. He clutched his gut; a wet circle darkened his jacket. The crowd bowed backward, and might have fallen into the Taunton River if not for the tight knot of bodies. Then a freckled Irish girl with red, white, and blue ribbons in her hair popped from the throng like a cork from a bottle and handed the doughboy a tiny Stars and Stripes on a stick. She held out an arm, and he stood and twirled the flag at the crowd; the girl smiled; and—perhaps inspired by the music, the crowd, surviving a war—he pulled her close and kissed her. The crowd gasped, but when the girl didn't recoil but clasped the sides of his head, they cheered; the town had been lonely without their boys. Further on, another soldier stopped and kissed a girl. The roars grew louder. Amid this din, a few soldiers covered their ears and retreated down Main Street.

Mayor Kay stepped to the podium, his tie crooked. "Ladies and gentlemen—" His voice cracked, and he stepped back to clear his throat. "Ladies and gentlemen, our Sammees are back," the mayor cheered, using the French nickname for our doughboys. The crowd applauded. Kay raised his arms. "These boys stood toe to toe with the enemy and spit in their eye."

"A few caught some spit themselves," a boy near Will whispered. His father smacked the back of his head. Others shouted, "The Hun didn't know what hit 'em," and, "Glad they're on our side." The treasurer approached Kay and whispered something into his ear. Kay nodded and then shuffled through his speech, paused, shook his head as if having a conversation with himself, and then folded the papers in half and tucked them into his suit jacket. He shouted, "We bombed the Hun to hell." One of the palsy-suffering boys in the back rows screamed, then stepped off the stage, falling smack on his face. Two medics lifted him up by his arms and legs and spirited him away, but as long as the band played on, no one seemed to notice. Will's hands went numb, but he whacked them harder and shouted his brother's name over the noisemakers.

A local troop of military men in khaki uniforms, really a hodgepodge left over from the days when Fall River had its own militia, stood in a line facing away from the platform to give the boys a twenty-one-gun salute. Their leader—Mr. Grimes, a baker—unsheathed his saber and thrust it heavenward; the men hoisted their rifles.

"Fire!" Grimes slashed down his blade, and the first report blasted. Immediately five men onstage dove for cover. Mayor Kay's jaw dropped. Spectators screeched, pointed at the boys, and gasped, hands covering their mouths. Kay yelled to stop the shooting.

"Fire!" Another ten men dropped. Those in wheelchairs buried their heads in their laps. A few toppled over and crawled under their chairs for cover. Nurses and nuns scurried about. The spectators rushed the stage, but many stopped at the edge of the platform, not recognizing their fathers and brothers. Amputees extended crutches to hoist comrades. An out-of-breath police officer grabbed Grimes's wrist to prevent a third volley. The shooters removed the cotton from their ears. One dropped his rifle and ran into the heap of bodies shouting, "Arly! Where's my boy? Arly!"

Up in the grandstand, Joseph slumped down as Hollister hit the deck. Everything seemed off with the boy. His son's childhood was one large black mark that the military was supposed to remedy, not worsen. Rehabilitation, not annihilation. Joseph buried his face in his hands, but jerked them away, surprised by the stench of his own breath. He had not slept the night before. He hadn't been eating well. His mouth filled with saliva, and he swallowed it, tasting the blood that seeped from his gums. Joseph saw Maria's bruised face in the shadows of the farm coach. With my help, Joseph thought, the Germans had given Maria her revenge.

"That's what you get when you rely on the military to raise your boy," Evelyn had said at breakfast. "Mrs. B could have saved him." The military had become his family, just as Commandant Blunt had promised, and now his family had abandoned him. The stout boy he had seen off eighteen months ago was now broken, and for once Joseph couldn't hire someone to fix him.

Joseph saw a handful of mill agents as he walked to the platform, though most had sent surrogates or checks for the arch construction. Their sons had never enlisted. Others maneuvered out of the draft to stay in Fall River and rake in profits on garbage cloth for the military. There was talk of another cotton celebration to boost morale now that the war dollars would soon dry up. Joseph's stomach ached thinking about such solipsistic folly. He squinted at the unfinished Victory Arch and shook his head.

Will reached his brother a moment before Joseph. Both stood idly by as the man next to Hollister helped him to his feet. Hollister's glasses were missing from his face. The skin surrounding his eyes was scarred and puffy, nearly swallowing his tiny pupils.

"You must be Mr. Bartlett. Michael Murphy. I pray you received the letter?"

Joseph hugged his son and his eyes welled up. Hollister did not return the embrace. Will extended his right hand to Michael Murphy but quickly withdrew it, realizing the man was missing his right arm.

"Good thing I'm a lefty," Michael joked, offering his remaining hand.

The mayor gripped the lectern. "All is well." His voice wavered. "No one panic. There are trained nurses traveling with these boys. Please back off the stage. All is well."

"Come on, Dad," Will said, rubbing his father's shoulder. On the edge of the platform, Will passed Mr. Grimes slumped on his knees. An officer knelt beside him, urging him to stand.

The mayor's face was dripping sweat; he offered a crooked smile to the crowd, waving his outstretched hands for calm. The police mimicked him. When the soldiers retook their seats, the mayor moved quickly to present the individual honors, small silver medallions engraved with the city's seal attached to blue ribbons. The city treasurer stepped to the podium to read off each name. The crowd stood silent. His voice bounced between the buildings. Far off, a whistle blew as another shift in the mills ended. Soon, another would begin.

* * *

They brought Hollister to the June Street house and deposited him in his old room. He hadn't slept there in over seven years, but they were hoping the doctor's hunch was correct—once surrounded with memories, he'd snap out of his malaise. The walls were covered in countless postcards and his school drawings. He'd shown promise with his drawing—the prelude to his mapmaking at West Point and then the army. But these were mostly landscapes and family portraits, the Westport River at dawn and countless couples and girls strolling in South Park that he'd observed from a dark corner of the shelter. There was no reason why some were complete and others mere sketches. One of a mother and daughter at a duck pond had a blue competition ribbon attached to the frame. In it, the solemn mother gazed past the daughter to a café across the pond. The café was full of men, their reflections playing on the water. Above the door, one picture had been removed, leaving a square gap in the patchwork of art. The square of plaster, hidden for so many years, was bright white.

An hour later, Will poked his head into the room. Hollister sat unmoving on a walnut rocker in the corner, his two feet firmly planted on the floor, his posture perfect except for his tilted head. His ears led him where his eyes had before. One doctor had described Hollister's fragile frame of mind as if "a madman were controlling the switch to his brain." During his hospitalization, he had completed sketches of the hospital grounds one day and didn't lift himself out of bed the next. He'd retained some sight. He couldn't pick out a goldfish in a bowl, but he knew it was something quick and orange.

"Bet you'd never figured to be back in your old room, huh?" Will said but was met with silence. "Years ago you'd have told me to bugger off. Yeah . . ." Hollister's head shifted to and fro as if tracking the flight path of a buzzing mosquito. "I'll be heading out after dinner. Gonna see Helen. You remember Helen, right?" Will stared at the scars on his brother's face, then the shiny cord on his shoulder. He wondered if he was indeed missing a chunk of flesh from a German spade. He had read in *Harper's* that the Americans fought with rifle butts and bayonets, while the Krauts preferred the maneuverability of spades. How many men have you killed, big brother? Will stood and exhaled, suddenly embarrassed at his frivolous life.

"Dinner in five, big brother. You need help?" he asked and, after a beat of no response, "Hey, Hollist—"

"I gotta piss."

"Hey, you can talk!"

"Piss, then chow." Hollister stood and shuffled down the hall.

Will called after him, "I assume you can find your dick."

* * *

At dinner, Joseph had set a welcome home card from Commandant Blunt on Hollister's plate. Joseph was still seething at the son of a bitch for not attending the parade. Hollister opened the card, but no sense of recognition registered on his face.

Joseph asked, "May I read you the letter?" When Hollister didn't respond, he turned to Will, who shrugged.

Evelyn backed through the swinging door and set a roasted chicken on the table. "Dinner is served."

Hollister's nose quivered. He felt around for utensils, and Evelyn handed him the carving knife and oversized fork. The gas had vaporized 40 percent of his lungs, so he breathed in slowly and said in a shallow whisper, "Thank you." Next, he ran his finger along the breastbone and then carved himself a thick chunk of white meat and filled his plate with potatoes and beans. He didn't offer anyone a morsel or notice Evelyn holding out plates. When she cleared her throat in an attempt to get Hollister to serve the table, Joseph picked up the serving fork and said, "Pass it here."

Joseph had had Evelyn prepare an extra-large bird, thinking the boy hadn't seen such food for months, perhaps years—and thank heavens for that. After five minutes of continuous swallowing, Hollister paused long enough to take a swig of wine and belch before loading up a second plate full of food. Will exchanged a glance with his father, and then both focused on their own dinners. Joseph had asked Will to postpone his last year at Yale to help his brother adapt. He'd declined. Joseph suggested Hollister might work in the mill office. But doing what? He was far worse off than they'd expected. There was no girl or old pals to welcome him home. It had been a long time since a member of the Bartlett family had required help. Will prayed Evelyn would keep her mouth shut. Thankfully, she did.

When his second plate was cleaned, Evelyn offered Hollister a slice of apple pie. He held up two fingers.

As the others finished in silence, Hollister became preoccupied with cleaning his fingernails with the flatware. He tried each utensil before deciding the salad fork worked best. Once this task was complete, he sat up straight, as if waiting to be dismissed from the table. His head was turned toward a portrait of his mother that hung above the sideboard, but Hollister hadn't changed his posture for some minutes, leading Joseph to believe he had dozed off.

Evelyn bit her left knuckle and exhaled. "Mr. Bartlett, if you please." She cleared her throat.

Joseph nodded.

"God saved you for a higher purpose, dear boy." She began, reaching over the table to take his hand, jarring him from his stupor. "From now on, your life has a higher purpose."

Judging from the way his son dispatched the carving of the chicken, Joseph figured this higher purpose was working as a buffet carver or fishmonger.

"On Sunday, the Father is having a special service just for you boys."

"Evelyn," Joseph chided.

"How about it?" She tapped Hollister's wrist. He grunted, as if he could sense everyone's eyes on him, begging for the story that would explain his injuries, but no one, not even mighty Dickens, could truly communicate the horrors of the trenches.

Hollister jerked free of her grasp, lifted his crystal wine glass, and banged the stem into the center of the bone china plate, cracking it down the middle. Evelyn gasped. Gravy from the chicken leaked across the table, but neither Joseph nor Will made a move to sop it up. Hollister ran his index finger down the jagged edge until it caught on a porcelain sliver. He pressed his thumb to the cut, pooling blood on the tip of his finger, and then dragged it across the white tablecloth in a wavy line.

"Us," Hollister whispered.

"Mr. Bartlett!" Evelyn shouted.

"Shhhh."

Hollister pooled the blood again, and painted another line a foot above the first. "Germans." He set a saltshaker behind one line and the pepper shaker behind the other. "Guns." Between the two he drew a series of X's. "Wire." He scribbled three wavy lines above the wire. "Gas." He kicked back from the table, pointed at the drawing. "War."

His father and brother eased back in their chairs. "And you won," Joseph said. "You're a hero."

Hollister shook his head. "I lost." Suddenly he tilted his head, listening for the mosquito. Joseph never knew what triggered the boy's bloody war demonstration, but the tear that fell from beneath his son's dark glasses was easy to understand. The tears continued rolling down the sides of his face, stopping at the edge of his angular jawbone.

"I'm sorry," Joseph said. "You're home now. You're safe."

Hollister shook his head, and the tears rained off his chin, soaking the battlefield. He put his bloody finger in his mouth and left the table.

* * *

Will squatted between two blue hydrangea bushes in his mother's garden (it would always be his mother's garden), unwinding pesky honeysuckle vines that were slowly suffocating the wooden stems. With a stick, he inscribed HELEN BARTLETT in the dirt. Will needed Helen to help him make sense of the parade disaster and Hollister's return. He'd found Hollister asleep shortly after dinner; his father had returned to the mill office. Will retrieved Hollister's old paints from the cellar and set them beside his brother's bed, thinking that perhaps next time he'd paint the war on canvas. He'd suggested to his father that he might do well on the farm in Middletown and rehashed his conversation with João, but Joseph wouldn't hear of it. Will disagreed, and as he waited for word from Helen, he cooked up a plan to get his brother out of Fall River. He could be late to school.

Will snapped the stick over his knee and looked at his watch. Where was she? His note with the linen suit suggested she join them for dinner on June Street and that they could then return to the boathouse together. She should have arrived hours ago. He brushed his index finger under his nose.

A taxicab whirled to a halt against the granite curb. Helen leapt from the car, cutting sharply across the freshly mown lawn, kicking the grass clippings Wiggins had left for another day. Will dusted his hands and stood. He chuckled when he saw her wearing another square-front calico dress. She made a beeline toward the house, head down and arms swinging wildly, red blotches across her chest and wisps of loose hair stuck with sweat to her temples. That ramped nose now looked pointed, like an eagle's beak. Will feared she'd had a row with her mother. As he stepped to embrace her, he noticed a parcel clutched under her arm. Closer, he noticed her bloodshot eyes. Definitely a row with her mother.

"Where's your father?" she shouted, her red eyes scanning the windows. "He's a bastard."

Will stepped back, dusted off his hands, and finally said, "He may be," trying to lighten the moment.

"I found this in Mother's room." She held out the parcel. Inside were four lace doilies and a letter in a scratchy hand. He flipped the parcel over to inspect the foreign stamps.

"Who's it from?"

"Uncle Charles. Granny died. He sent her antique lace to us kids. Four pieces."

"Sounds right."

Helen lifted the note. "He says, 'The night before Mother passed, she told me to send the four grandchildren her family's lace.'"

"There's three of you and Pete."

"In the next line he calls us, *Mary's four babies.*"

Will yanked the letter from her hand. "Just hold on."

"Remember my mother's trip to County Cork the year after the fire? How no one had heard of any Aunt Meara?"

"Your mom was miserable about her sick sister. I remember she threw up her Christmas dinner."

Helen rolled her eyes. "She was sick from the baby, you dummy."

"But Ray said he'd met her once."

"Ray's a chowderhead. As a boy he thought cow pies were something you ate. Don't you get it? Mom's story of a dying sister—a lie. The story of the sister's deathbed wish to take her infant son to America—another lie."

"And my father's a bastard because he helps support Cousin Pete?"

"Pete is not my cousin; he's my half-brother. Your half brother!"

"Now, wait a second." Sure, Pete did have Grandpa Otis's large receivers, but—

"Then I remembered the night before your mother's funeral. Your father stumbled to our house in the middle of the night." Helen's voice caught in her throat, on the verge of tears. "I think he raped her."

The freckles on her neck began to glow, and she pumped her first. He waved his hands at her to cool down. "What else?"

"Ever notice the scar on his knuckle? That night he knocked the vestibule chandelier. She went to him, and he bull-rushed her onto the study couch."

Will shook his head. "That's crazy."

"First he impregnated her after Dad died, then he kept her warm in his old house—bastard figured he owned her. Owned us all."

"Dad's no rapist."

"Probably little Bartlett bastards in every neighborhood."

"Shut up," Will shouted. "He's given your family everything."

"But why? 'Cause of one little brat?"

"You know how he looks at her. He loves your mother." Will wanted to forgive his father, if for no other reason than for all the hope that was dashed when his mother died. The old man came home every night to her sickness. That had to be worth something. With his wife gone and Tom Sr. buried long ago, God couldn't condemn them.

"Maybe so . . ." Helen acknowledged. The cab driver called up the hill, and Will asked the man to take a lap around the block. "Maybe so, but he forced her to hide his son."

She had a point, he thought. Scandals ruined families. Hogwash—if the Bordens could withstand financial scandal, his father could weather any Highlands society mudslinging. Will handed back the package. "What does your mother say?"

"What's it matter? He's brainwashed her to lie." Helen snorted, then let out a wild laugh. "She deserves better than a man who asks to change the sheets after *he* soiled them with *her*."

Perhaps it was the notion of ownership that set Helen off. No one was free, not the Portuguese operatives, not the Irish cops, nor the skilled Frenchies in Saint Anne's parish; in Helen's mind, all power emanated from the Highlands. Let her try to dismantle the hierarchy, he thought, one stone at a time. Dad was the best friend labor had in this town. And everyone knew it.

He pointed at the package. "Who else knows?"

"What's it matter?" She skipped a pebble down the drive, then another. She looked up at Will, caught his eye, and said, "I'm leaving Fall River."

"Calm down." He set his hands on her shoulders.

She slapped at his arms. "Don't touch me."

"Helen, please," he begged, holding her tighter. "I'm not my father." Will led her by the elbow to the back of the house and left her sitting on the side steps while he fetched a glass of water.

She gulped it and then stood up and squinted at the house, knocking the glass against her palm like a field hockey stick. He looked into her bloodshot eyes for a hint of that hazel swirl. As her breathing returned to normal, the red rashes faded from her chest. She tilted the drinking glass so it caught the porch light. This seemed to humor her, and she smiled—well, sort of smiled—and Will nodded and grinned, remembering last night. But then her face hardened. She reared back and hurled the glass over his head through the kitchen window. A beat later something smashed to the floor. Helen raised her hands to her mouth. Finally she'd shocked herself.

Will stood, dumbly looking between the shattered pane and Helen. A muffled cry came from the house, and Evelyn's head appeared in the hole in the glass.

"Jesus Christ." Will waved to Evelyn. "You okay?" She nodded slowly, looking aghast at her violated kitchen. "I'll be right there."

Helen's chest heaved. "I hate him."

"Don't hate anything," Will said. Hatred was something that couldn't be patched or easily forgotten. "The Lord says—"

"Oh, shut up. You're starting to talk like my mother."

Out of the corner of his eye, Will saw the cab turn the corner toward the house. He stepped toward the street to signal another lap, and Helen snatched up the spade he'd wedged in the ground and raised her arm to launch another salvo. Evelyn shrieked and Will whipped to catch Helen's arm; he spun her around, pinning her against the side of the house. She winced, but he held the arm tight.

"Let me go!"

"Relax," he said. He stroked the back of her neck. The tendons were hard as oak. Yesterday he had kissed the nook of the elbow he now twisted. His stomach churned, and he tasted acid in the back of his throat.

"Typical Bartlett response," Helen sneered over her shoulder. "Did Hollister teach you that over dinner?"

The cab driver shouted something and got out of his Ford. Will said everything was fine and eased off the arm. She'd never before used his brother against him.

"We'll leave—go away and never come back."

"Bastard. You're all bastards." Helen worked her wrist in a circle. His handprint lingered in the crook of her elbow. "I guess I was wrong about you, Will Bartlett. Yesterday you slapped me silly, and today you nearly break my arm. You're finally hoisting the family colors." She charged forward; Will shielded his face. She charged again; he flinched. She jerked a third time, but when he didn't budge, she snapped, "But you'll never be better than me," and kicked his shin with the toe of her gray boot.

"Goddamn, Helen." Will hopped in a circle.

"He gave my mother that house to hold her prisoner. He kept her and his bastard down. All of us down."

Will lifted his trouser leg. A trickle of blood soaked the lip of his sock. "You're talking nonsense. Who got Ray those promotions?"

"Go crawl in a hole." She raked the back of her hand across her wet face. Both sockets were swollen.

He limped toward her. "Don't forget Cousin Pete—"

"*Brother* Pete," she corrected.

"Brother Pete's future. I'm sure they planned on telling him the truth eventually," Will said, though he knew, that ship had already sailed. Highlands folk carried secrets to the grave. He squeezed her forearm. "Come inside. Dad will be back soon."

"Oh, he'll get what's coming to him."

"You're acting like a loon." His father had used the term to describe woman organizers, *loons*.

Helen punched his hand to release her arm. "I must have been a loon to say I loved the likes of you."

"You know you don't mean that."

"And I've been with lots of men."

"Why are you doing this?" Will opened his arms, but Helen backed out of his reach. "Helen, I love you."

"Sure you do, until you lock me away in one of your daddy's slum apartments like some doll, some mistress plaything; force me to produce bastards while your frigid society wife plays house on the hill."

He folded his arms. "You're talking crazy."

"Go to hell." She waved to the driver to start the engine and turned.

"Helen," he shouted. "Get back here!"

"Never!"

"What about last night?"

"That'll never happen again."

"God damn you!"

The slope of the grass carried her quickly into the waiting taxi.

"Helen!"

The door slammed, and the car disappeared down the steep hill.

NEWPORT NEWS

Waiting on the dock in Newport, Tommy Sheehan yawned. The sun poked between row houses on the water as he leaned against a luggage cart, tucking in his shirt and watching the unloading of vehicles from the belly of the *Priscilla*. Near the front of the procession was a converted Model T, a small truck now, with BARTLETT FARMS painted on the sides. Tommy knew Joseph's farm distributed milk in southern Rhode Island, but as far as New York? Not in that truck. The truck came down the pier and idled beside Tommy. The woman in the passenger seat wore a yellow hat with a large ostrich feather; she glanced over his head at the steamship. The driver was clearly Portuguese; he leaned out his window to talk with one of the dockworkers in a denim coverall. The woman looked down at Tommy, and her smoky black eyes met his. She focused on his strawberry eye but smiled nonetheless, and he tipped his hat. She was something, with smooth brown skin and a long swan-like neck, but her nose was bent like Jack Dempsey's, and near her hairline there was a discoloration of the skin from a scar that meandered to the ridge of her left eyebrow. Over the engine noise came shouting, beeps, and the cries of gulls as they stared at each other's imperfections. The truck pulled forward, and the woman's eyes shot open.

"The girl." Tommy yanked off his boater and ran to the middle of the pier. The truck banked left behind a stack of wooden crates and disappeared. What was she doing in a Bartlett Farms truck? A horn blasted. Tommy jumped.

"Outta the way," a dockworker shouted.

Tommy waved and jogged back to the luggage cart. He combed a hand through his wavy blond hair. His mouth ran dry. The fun house. The blood. The glass. The torn frock. Hollister. Tommy could never forget. He'd run down the hill to the centennial carnival and done Joseph's bidding; he'd sniffed Hollister out. Carried the girl out of the shards. It was Tommy who'd explained Hollister's pedigree to the police. It was Tommy who'd suggested that the operator might have had a hand in the girl's disfigurement. Tommy never heard what shenanigans Joseph had pulled to get Hollister out of that mess. Sending Hollister to White Mountain came after the police did not file charges. Muckrakers at the *Gazette* had sniffed around the story, gotten a tip from one of their snitches at the city lockup where they'd thrown the ride operator. But a Boston lawyer nobody had heard of showed up, and the man walked out of the cell the next day before Billy Connelly could pay the carny for his story. The carnival left town, and the girl disappeared with it. All the Sheehans knew the story, and in recent years Helen had ridden roughshod over Tommy for throwing the police off the trail long enough for Joseph to call in favors. Lately, she'd put a bug in Tommy's ear about the Cleveland fire too—another tragedy that, according to Helen, was too easily explained. She'd collected a scrapbook of clippings about the blaze. She figured only two things could have motivated Stanton Cleveland to run into a burning building—a girl or a mountain of money. (Experience had taught her these two were responsible for most bad behavior.) And then there was the question of the security guard. Security guards don't usually slip and drop lanterns. They get coldcocked. She shared these theories with her big brother.

"There's a third reason to run into an inferno," he'd said.

"What? Craziness?"

"Honor, bravery, selflessness—call it what you like. That's what killed Daddy."

"All the more reason for you to help me," Helen said.

"That's old history," he said. "Ain't bringing anybody back. And ain't worth a penny."

"But the truth is worth something."

"Only to you, squirt," Tommy lectured his little sister. "Only to you."

Tommy knew nothing stuck to men like Joseph Bartlett. And now there was word that the Workers' Union was giving him a humanitarian award. Perhaps even their medal wouldn't stick.

* * *

"Anything else?" the waitress said. Tommy was sitting in a small coffee shop not far from the pier. The waitress glanced at his bad eye and shrugged her shoulders as if to say, *I've seen worse.*

Tommy hated telling half-truths to girls, especially blond ones of marrying age wearing cute scalloped aprons with heart-shaped pockets on the hips, but he determined his reputation needed a hot story more than another girlfriend—Journalist Dictum #19: Skirt Chasers Miss the Story. He'd been sitting at the window table for two hours, waiting for any sign of the girl from the fun house. The trail had gone cold at the corner of Scarlet and Merchant Streets. He found the farm truck parked across the way. A small granite corner stone read MANAGED BY BARTLETT PROPERTIES. INQUIRE WITHIN. The coffee shop was the only place to loiter at six in the morning, plus he hadn't eaten in eighteen hours, so Tommy stretched the breakfast out over two hours by ordering everything à la carte: first a poached egg with toast, then cold ham slices, a glass of milk, a cranberry muffin with butter, canned peaches, more coffee, ladyfingers.

His serendipitous stakeout had begun on a somewhat unlucky note. The *Priscilla* had benefited from calm waters in New York Sound the previous night, making it to Newport twenty minutes ahead of schedule. Tommy overslept. A drowsy purser rushed him off the boat minus his satchel. On the pier Tommy flagged down the head purser, Pete Newton's son Patrick, who raced back to the cabin to retrieve it before the boat sailed on to Fall River. Tommy was headed north to Bristol to interview a boatmaker. The assignment was another soft news story to add to Tommy's already mushy clip book of soft news stories. The plan was for Tommy to sail with notable skippers before next year's America's Cup. His editors at the *Globe* wanted a jump on the story, given that the 1914 race had been suspended due to the war. Tommy had complained about the assignment, preferring to dwell in soft civic affairs and Ruth and the Red Sox rather than whisking three feet above the waterline with an egomaniac at the tiller. He epitomized the *Globe* mantra: *We Publish Pictures with Text.* Frankly, he was a poor swimmer, and large fish scared the bejesus out of him.

The waitress said, "Perhaps that eye is worse than I thought?"

Tommy smiled. He liked her already. "You bring me a little more butter for the muffin?"

She turned and sliced the end off a square brick on the counter. "A little goes a long way."

He spread it over the muffin. "Super creamy," he mumbled.

"It's made up the road in Middletown. Rose Butter." Waiting on the dock, Tommy remembered seeing tubs with the name Rose Butter branded into the side of ash barrels waiting to be loaded into the *Priscilla's* belly. "They're moving in across the way there," the waitress pointed outside. The block was a long row of triple-decker, Queen Anne–style apartment houses flowing down the hill toward the Narragansett Bay. Their appearance ran the gamut from what Tommy called Yankee thrift to mild exuberance near the Island Cemetery. Windows of clear glass and solid shingled porch railings gave way to stained glass and railings of turned balusters and turrets. "There's an old mill building behind those houses. Mr. Rose bought himself some newfangled butter-molding contraption; he's gonna run it down there, near the dock. Ship Rhode Island butter up and down the East Coast."

"You like the sound of that, do ya?"

"About time we sold something besides fish and cotton."

"This Rose a friend of yours?"

"Said he'd deliver our tub personally, once he's up and running."

"Is that his truck parked there?" Tommy stood up and pointed. "The one there: Bartlett Farms?"

"That's who makes the butter. Says it on all the wrappers." She gestured toward the yellow brick on the counter. "But what's it to you?" She crossed her arms.

Tommy took out his press card and set it on the counter.

The waitress spun the card around with two fingers. Her eyes narrowed.

Tommy had talked himself out of plenty of sticky situations, most with street urchins he owed money. The key was to believe what you shoveled. "I'm doing some reporting on the economic development of the waterfront. This Mr. Rose sounds like a good man to profile."

She rescrutinized the card, picked it up, then handed it back. "Tommy, is it?"

"That's me."

"I don't know what the man drives."

Tommy kept fishing. "He's a ways from Middletown."

"He's a heck of a ways." The bell on the door rang, and a workman in blue dungarees entered and took a seat behind Tommy. Walking around the counter, she continued, "Born and raised in the Azores. Nice fella, though."

Given the drudgery of what awaited him in Bristol, Tommy was determined (for another hour or so) to eat sponge cake and drink coffee till his blood ran black—Journalist Dictum #4: Stories Lurk on Barstools— if it meant finding out why a Bartlett Farms truck disembarked from the steamship *Priscilla* in Newport, Rhode Island, at six in the morning carrying a Portuguese butter baron and the mill girl Hollister Bartlett had mutilated seven years ago.

The waitress seemed to forget about him during the breakfast rush, but now his three-plus-hour stakeout was generating suspicion. Tommy noticed her pointing his way with a saltshaker and the cook coming out of his hive to investigate. The man wiped his hands down the front of his greasy apron and looked over his shoulder at a clock as the waitress whispered something behind a raised menu.

She walked toward Tommy and set his slip on the table. "You've ordered everything on the menu but me." She winked. She was a tad older than Tommy had originally thought. Creases etched around her mouth as she smiled. Her blond curls hung listless. But her spirit was intact; she placed her elbows on the counter and leaned forward, waiting for some come-on or otherwise smart-aleck comeback. Tommy suppressed it—Journalist Dictum #11: Friends Make Better Sources Than Enemies. She stood up and swept an empty saucer into her palm. "The boss says to kick you out."

He flipped up his sagging bang and tucked it under his boater. He sipped the last of his coffee and set it down on the counter without a sound.

He turned the slip over. "What do I owe ya?" Tommy pulled out a few extra coins for her patience. "This Rose fella a nice guy?"

"Is to me."

"He was driving a woman. Nice dresser."

"Never brought one in, but he wears a ring."

"Right."

"I don't." She extended her left hand.

Tommy stood and smiled. "You work all day?"

"Just me and Ned."

"A family business then."

"Neddy's family business. I just collect tips." She blew a strand of hair out of her face, then wheeled around as the pick-up bell rang.

"I'll see ya next time?"

"I'll be here."

As Tommy set the money down, a letter carrier came in on the first of his three rounds of the day and slid a picture postcard across the counter.

"Here ya go, Sheila," he called.

"Thanks, Paul." Paul saluted her from the door.

A crazy plot metastasized through the circuitry of Tommy's gray matter before the door latch struck. Joseph had taken an interest in Otis's run-down gentleman's farm after the accident, renaming it Bartlett Farms. This newfangled Rhode Island butter dynasty was news to him, but what if? he thought. Who's this Rose? Why a Portuguese partner? What if? A chill shook him. Just maybe. He slipped a sheet of *Globe* stationery from his satchel. He knew the half-truth he'd told Sheila was really a full-blown lie, but it had led him to this place, so he'd roll the dice. The truth was worth something. He scribbled out a note and reached for a three-cent stamp, determined to follow through regardless of the consequences. Envelope in hand, he tore out of the coffee shop and galloped toward the letter carrier as he exited the next building.

"Excuse me." Tommy peered down at the name on the envelope,

suddenly his tone unsure. "Could you deliver—" He stopped midsentence. Could Helen handle the truth?

"Give it here," the postman said, plucking the letter from Tommy's hand. "I'm behind." He tipped his blue cap and continued on his route. Tommy shrank down on his hunches and let out a long whistle. Game on, little sister. Time to ante up.

THE ONLY MOMENT THAT COUNTS

Michael Murphy's father pleaded with his overseer at the Cummings Mill to hire his son, but by the fall of 1918, dual-appendaged women and children were preferred for most unskilled jobs. When Michael's teenage sister took ill with Spanish flu, he sought out Hollister Bartlett. After surviving the best Kaiser Willie could throw at him, he sure as hell wasn't going to let his little sister take him out. Michael moved into Will's old room on June Street in late October.

He found his friend trapped in a minefield of canvas. Hollister had painted himself into a corner; unframed paintings lay three deep. Many were dreadful. Michael believed his friend's mind had what he called black splotches. Evelyn was the only patron to Hollister's gallery. She'd rearranged the pictures by subject—landscapes, portraits, war and death—when he was out walking, and on one occasion, she stole a rare, sunny print of two girls playing hopscotch. The only canvas now hanging in the room was of his mother, vibrant, confident, and rosy cheeked. Evelyn called it his *Lady Agnew of Lochnaw*. He'd torn a picture of the masterpiece out of a photo magazine at West Point and carried it in his rucksack across France until it literally disintegrated between his fingers during a rainstorm outside Paris. Similar to Sargent's model, Hollister had painted his mother sitting in a languid pose. Evelyn couldn't determine the location; neither the June nor

Snell Street homes had such drapery. Elizabeth's face seemed all possibility: the right side of her mouth, flat and pensive; the left, up in a teasing smile; her eyes, slightly widened and inviting. Hollister's love for his mother was palpable, and so, too, Evelyn dared to think, his love of the female form. Unlike his lead sketchings, the oil portrait had taken a week to complete.

Michael convinced Hollister to work in his father's library. Each afternoon, Michael stretched on the sofa, eating ginger snaps and sipping tea that Evelyn replenished every hour, watching Hollister paint variants of the gray afternoon light slanting across Tiffany lamps, a ship's brass bell clock and compass, the complete works of Shakespeare, and his mother's old Minnesota Model A sewing machine. By the third afternoon, Michael moved to a high-back leather club chair behind Hollister, eating cookies and sipping tea that Evelyn replenished each hour, but now he was commenting on light, perspective, and color. Hollister chain-smoked and sipped his tea. On the morning of the fifth day, Michael arranged a vase of blooming burgundy grasses on an end table at a forty-five degree angle from Hollister so he could turn and fondle the grass, then turn back to the canvas a foot in front of his face. By the end of the day, Hollister was drawing with one hand on the grass and his nose nearly touching the canvas. Michael whispered instructions from behind, some Hollister acknowledged with his lead pencil.

Michael hatched his get-rich-quick scheme after Hollister began to solicit his advice on shadows and angles and hues. And the third Sunday in November, he humped Hollister's easel and pencils and paints to the South Park Pavilion. Hollister's only request was that he be home before dark. They wore their army uniforms, thinking that alone might attract attention. He instructed Hollister in the creation of a sign: VETERAN'S PORTRAIT GALLERY. IMMORTALITY GUARANTEED. $2 PER SITTING.

The wind whipped up the hill from Mount Hope Bay, blitzing the open-air shelter with arctic blasts. Hollister camped in a corner, sometimes burning sticks in an old coffee tin set between his feet. The touch-and-whisper system, as Michael called it, had yet to be perfected, and Hollister took a minimum of an hour per canvas. Ladies went numb posing. They sat on a round stool in front of Hollister for the first five minutes—the touch. Hollister ran his hands over the face of each sitter. At first, this scared away all but the most adventurous. Next, the model moved to a stool across from Hollister—the whisper. The women—they were mostly women posing for their doting husbands—sat out of earshot, so Michael could freely detail their God-given endowments and deficiencies to Hollister, who sometimes sat for long minutes staring down the sloping park into the bay. Michael came to accept this as part of Hollister's process; he didn't rush his partner, as long as the pencil returned to canvas. The only sign that Hollister enjoyed the work—the money he handed to the children outside Saint Anne's on his walk home—was his stiff nod and wiry grin when the women gushed over their portraits, many leaning on his shoulders as he signed his name in the lower right corner. A gallery of gawkers standing three and four deep generated attention. Michael arranged for the Troy Store to deliver canvas and frames every week. As word spread, they added Tuesday and Thursday afternoons to the schedule. Michael tried offering smaller dollar portraits, but quickly learned that Hollister's limited sight did not adjust well to quick conversions in scale. (The one small canvas he attempted became known as *Turtle Woman*. The sitter's irate husband haggled the price down to fifty cents.)

In mid-December, the weather turned unseasonably warm, and Michael extended the hours of the Veterans' Gallery through the holidays. He contracted another army pal to sell hot nuts, and a third warm cider. To advertise, Michael hired another pair to walk the surrounding neighborhoods wearing sandwich boards.

The week before Christmas, the Sunday *Globe* ran a photo with a short caption written by Tommy Sheehan: *One-armed sergeant and blind veteran of the Great War make a living painting portraits at South Park.* Michael read it to Hollister at breakfast, and then presented him with a wool beret.

Michael said, "Looking sharp, maestro," and his partner laughed. It was the first time Michael had ever heard Hollister Bartlett laugh.

* * *

Just north of the park, on Dover Street, Joseph sat on the granite steps of Saints Peter and Paul, waiting for Mary Sheehan to finish wrapping the orphans' Christmas presents. Flashes of sunlight poked through a steel-gray sky. The overnight dusting of snow had vanished, and coatless children zigzagged between strolling couples. Joseph slumped over his knees, fingering the brown-stained silk liner of his old derby. Will's letter from New Haven burned a hole in the breast pocket of his greatcoat. Will had left abruptly for Yale the night of Hollister's return, the smashed window unexplained. Throughout the fall, the Sheehan boys hinted at Will's row with Helen, but no one knew the details that had pushed them to opposite ends of New England. Helen retreated to Westport, and her holiday plans in Provincetown were well known. Then this morning, on his way to church, Joseph had found Will's letter hidden behind the porcelain bowl in the breezeway where Evelyn set the mail below the portrait of Otis.

Dear Joseph, it began queerly, *I've applied for a clerkship at a New York law firm. I won't be coming home. I won't be working at Cleveland. I prayed to Grandpa Otis for forgiveness.* The second jolt unleashed sweats that dampened Joseph's skin: *Cousin Pete is no cousin. He's your son. I've seen evidence, you philandering son of a bitch.* What followed were two searing paragraphs that sunk Joseph's heart two levels, like a stalled lift suddenly dropping once, then again. Joseph knelt down in the breezeway. The letter dropped. He stared down at the last line until his eyes blurred. Why did this happen? "The fire," Joseph whispered, "burned us all." He fingered Will's signature. There was no one left to lose.

Absolution had not come the night Elizabeth threw the ledgers, the evidence of Stanton Cleveland's corruption, into the fire. Her consternation simply forbade him from ruining their future, all the while securing him a slot in hell. Without her, the punishment was far worse than any judge's sentence. He reread the letter. Secrets are like a small hole in a boat, you can bail all your life, but the cracks never stop taking in water, and eventually you sink. June Street had cast a green dye in her blood, and no matter his disdain for the establishment, the success of Cleveland Mill had secured his fate. Under Pete's Irish freckles, he had the Bartlett features, Joseph's features—it was plain to see. So why deny it? Joseph had played along with Mary's game, allowing her unspoken sacrifice to hide the boy's true lineage. He realized this now. With Pete's bloodline no longer a secret, he and Mary were the only ones left hiding, and it ate a hole in his stomach. He pocketed the letter and turned into his study and lay on the couch. Mary Sheehan had not a wanton bone in her body. She'd kept Pete a secret; he'd kept the fire. They were far from even.

As a boy, Otis had caught his son lying about breaking a neighbor's window. Joseph had worked Saturdays in the Cleveland cardroom to pay for a replacement. He closed his eyes. He'd heard the haunting voice of his father with each sweep of the broom: "A life built on a lie is sure to crumble."

"Ready?" Mary Sheehan stood two steps below him on the limestone stairs.

The scent of sandalwood incense filled Joseph's nose. "How long have you been standing there?" Joseph said, startled. He donned his derby and scurried to his feet.

"I started walking." She turned her round face toward him and sighed. Her cheeks were flushed, and she gripped the ends of her woolen shawl tightly over her shoulders. "I hope your daydream took you to an exotic place."

"No. Just this place. Spindle City."

"If only those old men in the association cared as much as you for this darn town," she said.

"I don't know how far all that caring has gotten me."

"They'll be sorry when you Bartletts are gone."

I will be the last one, Joseph thought. He bit the inside of his cheek as he remembered the summer he'd booked Will on the Textile Club's annual European tour. While the other boys toured museums, Will searched the textile markets to buy cloth samples for the mill. How did this happen? Joseph knocked his derby against his hip. Helen, he thought, loony bird turned socialist puppet. She's probably delivering babies with Sarah Strong. Helen turned Will against me.

"Something wrong?" Mary grasped his elbow.

Joseph scratched the hair on the back of his neck, tipping his hat forward over his eyes. The phrase "philandering son of a bitch" taunted him. "Wrong? God no." He straightened his hat and said, "Perhaps we can teach young Pete to carry on the tradition."

Mary bit her lip. "I . . . I hadn't considered that."

He said, "Pete's a smart boy. Ray can show him around when he's ready."

"But what of Will? I thought he was next in line."

"His love of Fall River is waning." Joseph shook his head. "They have no idea what we've done for them."

"Young people today." Mary's voice faded.

He set a hand on her shoulder. "I'd like to speak with Helen when she comes back."

"No," Mary said, her voice gaining strength. "She's not coming back. I raised her to take care of herself. Had no choice but to get her out of those mills. I'm saddened, but regret nothing since Tom died."

"Nothing?"

"Nothing."

"I miss my boys," he said.

"It's our lot as parents. And there is nothing we can do but love them anyway." Mary turned down the stairs. "Are we going to walk or not?"

Joseph bit his cheek again.

She tugged his sleeve. "Is something wrong?"

"Where's Pete?"

"At the neighbors'."

"I'm his father."

"That'd be news to Meara," Mary quipped, as if she'd been expecting the question for years.

Joseph hesitated. Why didn't she trust him? They shared holidays, Sunday dinners, and on the rare occasion, a bed. He peered down at her, focusing his energy between her eyes, willing her to tell him the truth. A pressure grew inside him, and he struggled to be still, thinking that if

Mary didn't tell him this instant, he didn't deserve to know. But if we lie to protect those we love, is it really love? And whom are we protecting? Joseph had worked tirelessly to protect his workers. Perhaps they were his real family.

She said, "The child is happy. I like a happy boy."

"And that's enough, is it?"

"We raised the older children to think, so let them think." Mary waved to two women leaving the church. "Now, are we walking or not?"

He had a strong desire to kiss her on the church stairs, secretly hoping Father Curley was spying on them from the vestibule. But he doubted it would close the distance that would always exist between them.

Mary stomped her foot on the stair. "Take me to South Park this instant."

They walked to the Middle Street trolley. At the Broadway stop, a crowd had gathered around an assembly of suffragists in their white hats with yellow ribbons. Two women stood in the back of a Buick playing trumpets. Joseph expected to see a few on horseback. Stepping off the trolley, Mary whispered, "The Providence posse is back." Unlike Fall River, Providence housed a storefront suffrage headquarters that outfitted ladies in marching outfits. The women waved the Stars and Stripes with their VOTES FOR WOMEN pennants and passed out buttons and pins. The mother hens, Joseph called them. There were a few chicks like Helen in the ranks. Most were well-to-do ladies trying to recruit middle and immigrant classes to the cause. They'll get their vote, Joseph thought. Wilson wanted it, and after winning the war, he'd get anything he wanted. A woman extended a button to Mary. She shooed her away. "Baloney," she said, and directed them around the bottleneck. "Can't we have one day of peace?"

The park consisted of two large rectangular tiers bisected by Broadway Street. The pavilion sat in the lower, larger rectangle on the esplanade that ran downhill toward the water. Joseph thought it best they keep moving. He led Mary down to Bay Street, then turned back up the hill. The weather had emptied houses; a large crowd was out. Mary smiled to the passing couples. Joseph focused on the ground before him as always. He'd walked the park hundreds, perhaps thousands, of times and cared little for its charming detail; he didn't grasp the craftsmanship of Frederick Olmsted's design. Of course he had never visited the man's greatest works in Chicago or New York. Joseph took the boat to New York every other month, but he'd never walked Olmsted's parks or been to the Met. He knew he must before he died in a mill fire.

Mary turned up a serpentine path toward the esplanade. "I have grown used to your long silences," she said. "But for some reason, I need you to speak. Did the Protestants have service today?"

"I think it was canceled." Long ago Joseph had accepted his damnation, while Mary believed her fate was still negotiable.

Mary stopped and squinted at the sun. "On account of the nice weather."

"That was the rumor."

"Father Curley considered that, but said we Catholics never get a day off."

"Sounds about right."

Mary pinched Joseph's arm, and he trotted ahead. When she caught up, she said, "Now, bore me with details of the mill."

"You find the mill boring?"

"All except the profits."

"After all these years, you're showing your true colors," Joseph said.

"I thought you would like that." Mary laughed. "Long ago, even before Tom died, I lost interest in the whole enterprise." She looped her arm around his. "But I know it's in your blood."

"Yes, my blood." Joseph stopped, squinted at the sky. "I've gotten farther than any of them. And now it's over."

"You're not dead yet." Mary squeezed his elbow and they continued down the path. "Let's stroll by the pavilion."

"Fine," Joseph said, then thinking of Hollister, his spirit improved. He hadn't seen much of his boy. Hollister was either at the park or in his room. Evelyn provided room service for food, cigarettes, and art supplies. "I've yet to see the portrait enterprise I financed. I'm told it's become quite the entertainment."

"We won't join the fray," Mary cautioned. "I've learned to let them think they're on their own, no matter their age."

They found a bench near the start of the slope that led to the water. The pavilion was fifty yards off, but a crowd had gathered, and they couldn't yet see inside. The air smelled of hot nuts and cider. Suddenly the pavilion shook with applause and laughter. Moments later, a woman with her hands in a muff burst from the crowd, followed by a man holding a square canvas. He paused at every step to display his wife's new portrait. Onlookers nodded their approval. The man beamed.

Joseph swiveled to face Mary on the bench. He felt his lungs constrict and forced himself to breathe. "There's one more thing."

"You may not have my portrait painted," Mary chided. "Will you look there? It's Tommy."

"Where?"

"There." She pointed. "No, there. Darn. There are too many people. He's walking into the pavilion."

"Don't see him."

"He said he was working on something important today. When I asked him what could be important enough to skip Mass for the last month, you know what he said? 'If I'm right, and I hope I'm not, you'll see me every Sunday from now on.' Now isn't that a funny thing to say?"

"It was a nice thing he did, writing about Hollister."

"We'll let him be. He likes playing detective once in a while. Gets him off those boats."

A boy screamed. People whirled. The child laid facedown, sobbing on the cobblestones. The other children hovered over him. One boy held an orange ball. Then a man emerged from the crowd, pushing a baby carriage. He dropped beside the fallen child and hoisted him to his feet. He brushed the boy's knees and fanny and pushed him back into the game. The man had his back to Joseph, but the shock of black hair was familiar. And the children, they were Portuguese. João. That was his boy. His daughter was farther off with pink ribbons in her hair. A white christening gown flowed over the edge of the baby carriage. Where was Maria?

Joseph jumped to his feet. "Will you excuse me? There's a man from the mill I need to speak to."

"See, it is in your blood."

Joseph flashed a nervous smile. "Won't be a moment." Before Mary could reply, Joseph darted across the green. The frost-covered grass crunched under his feet.

* * *

In October, Tommy had returned to the coffee shop in Newport to meet with João. Sheila's replacement, the ornery Patty, didn't take kindly to Tommy ordering à la carte and frowned when he displayed his press card. She hadn't seen João in a few weeks and, after two hours, asked Tommy to leave or said she'd flag down a cop. Either Tommy's letter requesting an interview didn't make it to João, or he didn't want any publicity. Tommy guessed the latter. Outside the café he followed the street behind the Bartlett building to the loading dock where João's farm truck had parked during his last visit. Tommy hopped up on the dock to peer in the window. As Sheila had said, there was some sort of installation going on. And empty Rose Butter barrels stacked in the corner. But why? The question had nagged Tommy the entire summer and fall. Why does a Highlands gentleman adopt a Portuguese laborer?

In the library he found the city directory for the year of the fire. In the *R* listings he discovered *João Rose, Steep Brook, Cleveland Mill.* No listing appeared the subsequent year. He picked up the 1911 directory. In the *M*'s he found *Maria Medeiros, Flint, Cleveland Mill.* There was no listing for 1912. On a brick of Rose Butter, he discovered the company was established two years after the fire. He nosed around Steep Brook and another Portuguese neighborhood, "Below the Hill." No one would talk to him. He found Maria's family in Flint and followed her father to the Pocasset mill. He worked in the dye house. Tommy thought marching through the gates of the Bartlett farm would get him fired, and ignite his mother's ire, so he placed a call to friends at

Pocasset, and retreated to the *Globe* to reread the archives on the Cleveland fire that killed his father.

> At 10:37 p.m., Box 18 was struck for a blaze that started in the Cleveland Mill office building at the corner of Anawan and Washington Streets. The roof is almost gone, and the second story is ruined beyond repair, although the first-floor walls remain quite solid. The insurance on the building was $50,000. Fire Marshal Davol determined a security man mishandling a lantern in the second-floor office started the blaze. Why mill owner Stanton Cleveland ran into the building is somewhat of a mystery. Engineer Thomas Sheehan is said to have entered to save Mr. Cleveland. Neither man survived the blaze. Mill agent Joseph Bartlett, who left the mill prior to the alarm being struck, expressed sorrow at the loss of life.

In November, Tommy got a call from an overseer at the Pocasset mill who owed him money. Maria's father was overheard talking about his granddaughter's upcoming christening.

* * *

Tommy stood on the ledge of the pavilion, shoulder to shoulder with a silver-haired man watching the watchers watch Hollister. The corner portrait studio had become an attraction, a stop on couple's Sunday walks like a nickel peep show. From Tommy's angle Hollister was hidden behind his easel across the pavilion. He hadn't so much as gotten a flash of him between portraits. Only his scuffed brown boots, coated with a light dusting of cigarette ash, were visible. Occasionally a lead-stained hand emerged to retrieve the cup of cider from the ledge or a puff of gray smoke floated over the canvas. The line for portraits snaked down the stairs and into the green. Maria was next. Tommy had been staking out the ten o'clock Mass, the christening Mass, at Santo Cristo for three weeks straight.

"She's beautiful," Tommy whispered.

"Thank you," said the silver-haired man standing next to Tommy. He nodded toward his wife.

"Not her," Tommy said.

"Watch yourself," said the silver-haired man. Tommy was gripping the man's shoulder. The man shook, and Tommy jerked his hand away nearly losing his balance.

The man pointed to Tommy's bad eye. "What happened to you?"

"Shark attack."

The man screwed up his face.

"You should see the shark."

"Wise guy, huh?"

"Piss off," Tommy snapped.

The man turned away.

Tommy loosened his collar; nearly forty degrees, and sweat coated his back. For the first time since discovering them in the fun house, he'd caught Maria and Hollister in the same frame. Over the years, usually on his knees at Saint Anne's, he'd asked forgiveness for not reporting to the police what he had found in the fun house.

Tommy turned away from the scene to face the park and took a deep breath. At the time, he had blamed Maria, as if her brown skin had somehow encouraged the beating—no Irish girl would be so stupid. No Irish had to be, he thought. Family responsibility and an allegiance to Joseph Bartlett had blinded him. That was clear to him now. Helen has been right about that much.

"These are new shoes," the silver-haired man said. "Don't get sick on them."

Tommy shook his head and spit yellow bile into the shrubs. He popped a Necco wafer in his mouth. He spotted Joseph striding up to João. João smiled as Joseph approached, but as Joseph spoke, João's face turned to stone. Joseph pointed to the pavilion. João pointed and then João spun to the man next to him and called his son. The man's wife grasped the handle of the baby carriage. João tore toward the pavilion. Joseph gave chase.

"We thank you, madam," Michael Murphy's voice bellowed inside the pavilion.

A woman with a blue-feathered hat stood to accept her portrait.

Michael spoke loudly for the crowd to hear. "Surely we'll accept an extra fifty-five cents if you think the portrait is worth it."

"Give it to him," she instructed, pointing to Hollister. The crowd laughed.

Michael plopped the coins into the tipping tin on the ledge. "A tip for the maestro." He lifted the canvas with his one arm and handed it to her husband. Hollister sat with his head down, wiping his hands with a rag. The creases between his fingers were black. He reached for his cider, and Michael set a new canvas on the easel. Tommy hopped down and cut through the throng to the opposite side and jumped on the ledge. João and Joseph pushed up the stairs, against the tide of onlookers. The woman in the blue-feathered hat and her husband bumped into them. A little dance commenced between the men and the new portrait.

"Are you next, madam?"

Maria nodded.

"Do you know how this works?"

Maria met his eye and shrugged.

"The maestro here first needs to have a look at ya. And aren't you lovely. Well, he doesn't see very well, so he is going to touch your face so he can transpose your beauty to the canvas. Is that fine with you? That he touch you?"

Hollister raised his head.

Maria reared back on her heels, falling into the well-dressed woman behind her.

"Well, I never," the woman roared, then stopped. Her mouth formed a large O, either disarmed by Maria's beauty or shocked by the sight of such a finely dressed Portuguese woman. Michael steadied Maria. Her hand latched onto his forearm for balance.

"Madam?" Maria's face rapidly lost its walnut color. The thickening crowd pushed forward like a giant wave. Michael flashed them a tight smile as he stooped down to whisper in her ear. "If you'd rather wait, we'll hold your spot in the line."

Tommy leaned forward. Holy crap, he thought, she's gonna let him do it.

Maria peered over her shoulder. João elbowed forward.

Maria turned to Michael and shook her head, her breathing suddenly labored. She slid two bills from the sleeve of her blouse.

"Fine then." He winked at the Yankee woman. "Allow me." Michael scooted the stool in front of Hollister with his toe and guided Maria down with his arm. "This here is the maestro." Hollister sharpened a pencil with a pocketknife. "And you are?" When she didn't answer, Michael asked again, "Madam, your—"

"Stop!" João barreled into the tight corner, the veins in his muscular neck pulsing. His wrists hung below the cuff, exposing lean tendons that twitched as he clenched and unclenched his fists.

"May I help you?" Michael asked, forcing a smile.

João's nostrils flared, and Tommy thought he saw the portrait barker's knees shake. The crowd hushed; more craned toward the pavilion. Tommy had heard stories in the newsroom about men going berserk, men so consumed with rage they could lift an automobile.

"Sir?" Joseph appeared behind João. Michael caught his eye. "Friend of yours, Mr. Bartlett?"

João said, "My wife." He stared at Hollister sharpening the pencil.

"Fine," Michael said, his voice strained. "But we only do solo portraits."

Maria watched her husband as his face, slowly draining of color, took on a look of pity. He whispered something in her ear.

Maria pressed one of João's fists to her lips, and held it there until his breathing slowed. She glanced at Joseph, nodded, then turned back to João and kissed his palm. Joseph stepped forward and put his arm around João.

"It's okay, Michael. Make it good one." Joseph steered João back to the green.

Tommy clapped his hands knocking off the hat of the man below him. "I got it," he shouted. "João was there." Tommy took out his notepad and began writing.

Maria sat down on the stool. Hollister hadn't moved, his glassy eyes unchanged.

"Let's start again," Michael said. "You are—"

"Ma-ri-a," she said slowly, punching each syllable. Hollister's expression didn't change. Her chest heaved. How many times had she imagined this moment? Dreamt of her revenge? But sitting before her was a different man. His shirtsleeves were rolled over his elbows, revealing scarred and nicked forearms. There was a heaviness about him, his face pudgy, as was the belly that hung over his trousers. His movements weren't quite labored, but slow. He had a look of weariness only war can etch in a man.

"Very well, Ma-ri-a," Michael mimicked. "Will you be wearing your hat?"

Maria wore a medium-brimmed hat trimmed with a draped purple scarf and a large buckle. She removed it and set it by her feet.

"She's ready for you," Michael said.

Hollister tipped forward, balancing the stool on two legs. Maria bent back into Michael.

"Relax," Michael said. "He won't hurt you." He tilted her stool flat. "Maestro, time's a-wasting."

Hollister's black-streaked fingers joined at the top of her head and walked down her cheeks until his palms met under her chin. He repeated this motion up and down, as if shaping a snowball, then moved to the canvas and sketched the shape of her head with a lead pencil. He leaned close, the tip of his nose brushing against the canvas.

"Can you see me?" Maria whispered. Her face, already warm, flushed.

Hollister continued to draw. When finished, he placed his fingers under her eyes and ran them down her cheeks.

"Can you—"

"Very little," Hollister said. He turned to the canvas, made a mark, then looked back at her. "And only very close."

He set his right thumb and forefinger on either side of her nose and traced it. He got to the bend and stopped. Maria bit her lip. He retraced it and stopped a second time.

"You had an accident," he said, and leaned back on the stool and made another mark. "But I'll fix it."

Maria picked up her hat and began to fan herself. A bead of sweat formed on her temple.

Michael said, "The maestro could write a person's history from their face."

"Does he know what happened?"

"The past is the past." Michael nodded toward his missing arm. "The past has not been kind to some of us." He craned his head over the top of the canvas. "Just a minute more. Looking lovely. Then you move across the way there."

Hollister poked and probed her ears and nostrils. He brushed her thick black hair and stroked her neck.

"Ready?" Michael asked.

Hollister nodded, his face pressed close to the canvas.

"Wait," Maria said. "Give me your hand." She placed Hollister's index finger at the top of her forehead, near the hairline, where the scar began. She traced it up and down. "Also from the accident," she whispered.

"He can make them go away," Michael said.

"No," she said. "He can't."

Hollister closed his eyes and bowed his head. His expression had not changed through the entire process, but now he paused. She dropped his hand, and he scratched his left cheek.

"Remember?" Maria asked. When he didn't reply, she whispered, "Spider."

Hollister looked off over the granite ledge into the park. He lit a cigarette and dropped the match into the tin can at his feet.

Michael rolled his eyes and shot a tight smile to the next women in line. "Come here, now," he snapped at Maria. He hoisted her to her feet and led her by the elbow to the chair across from the easel.

She sat down, but as Michael turned, she grabbed the tail of his coat.

"What now?" He winked at the next woman in line.

"If he doesn't remember, does that make it real?"

"Oh, he'll remember, and it will be a memorable portrait."

"Just a portrait?" Maria's eyes welled up.

Michael crouched down and set his one hand on the chairback. "Do you have similar portraits in your house?"

She shook her head.

"Well then, this is the only moment that counts."

"But—"

"No buts, Maria." Michael stood up. "The past is the past. When you die, this is how you'll be remembered. Young and beautiful. So dry those tears, and smile. The maestro loves to make people happy."

PART V
1919

To hearken what I said between my tears, . . .
Instruct me how to thank thee! Oh, to shoot
My soul's full meaning into future years,
That they should lend is utterance, and salute
Love that endures, from Life that disappears!

—Sonnets from the Portuguese, Sonnet 41
by Elizabeth Barrett Browning

MAKE LIKE A BIRD

Howard Borden trampled through the deep rough on the ninth hole of the Fall River Golf Club, whacking down poison ivy and rugosa rose vines with the wooden head of his driver. The late summer day was a scorcher. A small yellowthroat warbler squeaked out a song. A caddie in a white cap lifted a ball out of the brush. "Silver King 4?"

"Not mine," Joseph called. He stood under a maple tree. It was two days past his fiftieth birthday. He removed a deer tick from his forearm as the three other men shagged for his slice. Joseph hadn't played since last summer, and he was embarrassed when the head caddie didn't recognize him. The caddie returned with pro Willie Dow who explained that Joseph's bag was one that had drowned in the spring floods. Dow suggested Joseph take his sticks, but Howard cobbled together a set from his other two bags. Proven irons, he assured Joseph, though the putter never worked as advertised.

The caddie tossed the ball to Howard who pitched it into the fairway. "Hit it anyway. Yours is a goner. You know, Bartlett, I've never seen a man lose so many balls in nine holes."

"I do have a knack for it."

"I don't remember you being such a duffer. Dad always enjoyed playing with you."

"He enjoyed taking my money." Joseph rolled the ball under his foot.

"Elizabeth teased me for being so bad." He took a practice swing. "How far from here?"

"Hundred and fifty yards. Lay a nice six-iron to the front of the green. Keep your head down." Joseph loosened his grip, glanced at the hole, exhaled. The swing was fluid, but he topped it. The ball bobbled down the fairway.

"Another worm burner." Howard laughed. "Watch it." The ball scooted between the two sand traps guarding the front of the green, caromed off a rake, catching air, and landed within ten feet of the cup.

"Whatever works," Howard said, walking to his ball. His caddie handed him his nine. "Watch and learn." Howard took an easy, compact swing, a motion practiced during winter holidays in Florida. He had just returned from a trip to the Carolinas, or was it Alabama? Joseph wasn't sure. Somewhere visiting cotton growers was what Howard had told him last week at the Q Club. The Borden juggernaut, the Iron Works, had remained vital to almost every mill in the city except Cleveland and a few other specialty outfitters, but the special relationship the two mills had shared was all but forgotten in the years since Matt Borden's death.

Howard hit behind the ball, shaving a divot the size of a hundred-dollar bill off the fairway. He froze, the club wrapped around his neck as if he were posing atop a trophy. The ball arched high in the air, cleared the front traps, and landed with a thud in the middle of the soft green before trickling backward toward the cup, stopping a few rotations inside of Joseph's ball. Howard dropped the club over his shoulder and started walking toward the green. His caddie unsheathed his putter and extended the grip into Howard's path. He snapped it out of the air without breaking stride.

Joseph tipped his cap back and said, "That's what I was trying to do."

"Maybe on the next hole," Howard said. He stopped in the fairway and pointed his putter at Joseph. "You know, down south, a man can golf twelve months a year. Think about that. That's the ticket."

"That's a small fortune in golf balls."

"You'll make it up in lower wages and taxes."

"I'm making plenty right here."

Kicking a divot on the fairway, Howard said, "That will soon change."

That morning Evelyn expected she'd have to pry him out of bed to make the tee time. But when she swung open the door, the bed was empty. She found Joseph at the breakfast table nibbling toast. The Bordens had always buoyed him. The invitation had been a surprise, but when a Borden summoned you, you accepted. Joseph hoped Howard was channeling his father's business acumen, and he would use his leverage to propose a new initiative, a postwar Fall River plan, to help shake off his recent malaise. (Behind his back Evelyn called him Mr. Bumble.) The Manufacturers' Association's half-baked Put Our Boys to Work initiative, which guaranteed returning soldiers a job—was a publicity stunt. And nonmembers, like the Iron Works and Cleveland, were singled-out in bogus editorials as unpatriotic for not helping the vets. Joseph's lieutenants, who ran the Cleveland day-to-day operations, were the ones in the line of fire. The agent position Will was supposed to fill remained vacant. And Mary Sheehan skipped Sunday walks to devote herself to church charities. Joseph feared that Father Curley's decades-long disapproval of their relationship had finally worn the woman down. In the spring, Joseph spent weekends at the farm, but soon realized it was João's to run. His claim to Otis's farmhouse had passed. In May, Joseph bought more farmland and Newport real estate with his mountain of profits. After the shareholder checks were cut, he received a letter from Saint Augustine on orange stationery. Hannah Cleveland thanked him for the high returns and invited him to join her in Cuba the following winter. During his afternoon nap, he found temporary solace in dreams of orange groves.

* * *

As they made the turn to the back nine, Joseph was down thirty-five dollars, and he had not yet brought up business, preferring instead to concentrate on being outside. The fresh air somehow energized him; perhaps this sudden lightness was to blame for him believing his golf game was up to snuff. He had wrongly agreed to the princely sum of five-dollar skins after sinking his first two practice putts. Now, after shooting fifty-four on the front nine, he was resigned to losing all seventy dollars. He hadn't given anything to the game and, after his first round in nine months, didn't see it giving him anything in return. The graybeards playing ahead disappeared into the rough. Golf courses are where young men hide from their wives, and old men come to die, he thought. Otis never had the patience for the game. Joseph spat on his ball and wiped it down his knickers. There was a streak of red in his saliva, and he ran his tongue around his porous gums. Joseph motioned for his driver and joined Howard on the tee box.

"I'm sure you've heard the rumors that we're unpatriotic."

"I wouldn't worry about it." Howard leaned against his club. "I've contacted the army and plan my own announcement during their Labor Day party. It will be in all the papers."

"No one seems to remember that I hired the men that came home with Hollister. Deformed and mentally damaged boys. Good workers, though. Their minds don't tend to wander."

"That's why you get awards, Joseph, and the rest of us just fat profits." The operative newspaper, the *Labor Standard*, recently announced they were honoring Joseph with an achievement award for "a lifetime of dedication to the wealth and welfare of mill operatives" at next week's Cotton Week Celebration.

"But that, too, will soon end," Borden said. "War profits like this come only once a lifetime."

"Let's hope." Joseph paused. "About the wars."

"I heard about your boy Hollister. Matter of fact . . ." Howard stopped walking. "My daughter had her portrait drawn during her last visit. Not half bad."

"Off and running, he is."

"He'll make a killing next week."

For some, the city-sponsored Cotton Week over the Labor Day holiday was a flashback to the successful centennial festival eight years prior, and the chamber of commerce billed it as such. But to Joseph, it lacked the legitimacy of the centennial; it rather stunk of a manufactured event designed to reassure the choir how well they could sing. Though, this time around, there would be no Horse Show, no Auto Parade, no daredevil aviators at Sandy Beach, no visit from a sitting president, and no carnival midway. Thank God for that, Joseph thought.

There were rumors of a postwar tension between local banks and the mills. Cotton Week organizers gave in to Central Savings' pressure to put the recently financed millinery on the governor's tour schedule; a new fuel oil factory made the second page of the program. THE LARGEST IN NEW ENGLAND, read the headline. There were new beaus at the Cotton Ball.

A cloud blocked the sun as the foursome ahead emerged from the woods and walked out of Howard's range. As he bent over to tee up his drive, he said matter-of-factly, "Eighty percent of Fall River mills will be out of business in ten years." He reared back and smacked a drive down the middle. For a moment, he stood on the tee, admiring the shot. "Boy, I'm slugging it today. You know, Joseph, down south you can golf twelve months a year."

Joseph's hand shook as he jabbed the tee into the turf. He aimed to the right of the fairway bunkers. His hands choked the grip. The forearm tendons bulged and reddened. The club whipped around his neck and back. The ball sliced right, vanishing into the woods. Howard lurched forward, listening for a knock, and then watched the fairway, thinking the ball might ricochet free. There was no member's bounce this time. Joseph pounded the club head into the turf like a sledgehammer.

"Right postage, wrong address," Howard joked. He tossed another ball at Joseph's feet. "If you break that club, you're buying it." Joseph teed up the second ball. A bead of sweat fell from his forehead to his right toe. His heart thumped in his chest. He torqued the club so far around his head he nearly grazed his left knee; the club head snapped back around, smacking the ball. It launched deep into the woods.

"Goddamnit!" Joseph hurled the club over his head. It cartwheeled down the fairway.

"Lateral hazard," Howard called, already tramping down the fairway.

"What the hell is that supposed to mean?" Joseph charged down the front of the tee box, cutting him off.

"It's a stroke penalty. I'll let you forget about the first one. Call it a mulligan."

"I'm not talking about the stupid ball. The mills, Howard. All failing?"

"Eighty percent, I said—eighty percent." Howard's caddie held out a five-wood and Howard motioned it away. The sun returned as the four-some on the ninth green looked up from their putts. Howard waved to the men and then motioned for Joseph to walk.

"Not in front of the sheep, Joseph. They find comfort in their ignorance," Howard whispered. He spat and adjusted his knickers. "Living in New York allows me the long view," he said. "Twenty-one percent of Fall River's mills use modern Northrops to seventy-plus in South Carolina alone. You know it's cheap to operate—the labor, taxes, construction. New England can't compete. All the New York banks are committed down there. You know as well as I what Father preached, what a capitalist's hard-on the Southern states were. Heck, you said as much ten years ago when you went away from printcloth. Listen, friend, I've always respected your efforts to keep the city honest, but this flood is too big for you to contain, and the association never learned to swim. The war is over. In one, two years, imports will return. Profits will bottom out against the competition. The association's antiquated mills will follow. The market's boot will bear down on the city's windpipe. It's time to make like a bird and head south. Now watch out." Howard grabbed his five-wood, then effortlessly lifted a shot down the middle of the fairway.

Joseph dropped in the middle, not bothering to go look for either of his drives. He was six to Howard's two. He remembered the night on the steamship *Commonwealth* when Matt Borden had asked him to watch out for his boys. Oh, how he had failed Uncle Matt. Joseph smacked a five-iron a few feet above the ground, then dropped the club where he was standing, afraid he might sock Howard across the ribs. Denial. I am not in denial, he thought. Astonished, yes, but blinded? No. Howard's math was wrong. Ten years maybe, but there was time to turn the ship around. He kicked his ball forward, waiting for his caddie to catch up. He bladed a seven-iron across the grass, but this time the ball found a bunker. Denial was pretending your operatives weren't human. Denial was thinking you could abandon your city without getting any blood on your hands.

Howard's approach also hit the sand. Golf wasn't the only thing on his mind, either. Joseph wondered if Howard was just realizing the prophecy his father had first shared with him when he had mentored with the old man at J. and E. Wright and Company. Joseph knew that if the shrewd bastard were alive, this shift in thinking would have taken place the day after the Paris armistice. But this didn't comfort him. Awash in bubble profits, 30 percent or more, it was widely known the owners had poured little capital back into the shop floor, even though the South now matched New England's fine-cloth output. The Fall River system resisted product diversification. No new mills had been constructed in over ten years. A new oil factory might employ a few hundred, but a new mill fed thousands.

Waiting on the fourteenth, Howard told the caddies to wash all the balls in his bag. He motioned Joseph to join him on the tee. Joseph noticed Howard's boyish face, nearly forty-two and still the same sandy blond hair and smooth cheeks. The man ruled via telegram from New York, Florida, and Europe, never troubling himself with the details of workers' lives, while Joseph toiled in the factory din. Perhaps Joseph worked for Howard, too, keeping the peace on Main Street. Joseph sat on a bench, dumbstruck; he had rarely considered his role in the larger print of the textile world. He suddenly realized why the establishment had never accepted him. It wasn't his breeding or lack of formal education but that he didn't think large, like Howard's ilk—men who dreamed, like Vanderbilt, Carnegie, and Morgan; men who believed themselves giants on this earth. But what have they done for the people of Fall River? Where are the libraries bearing their names?

Over the scratching of the ball washer, Howard said, "There's more. I've charged my man down south to start pricing land. I'm keen on Tennessee. Within eighteen months, perhaps longer, we'll lay the cornerstone for a new Borden mill."

"The Southern menace has won."

Laughing, Howard waved his finger at Joseph. He called, "Ball," and his caddie tossed him one right from the washer. Howard bent over and stabbed his tee into the turf. "It'll house about a thousand operatives, a hundred thousand spindles, and two thousand looms. That's a ballpark. The Iron Works will continue, but I'd guess we'll be out of Fall River by the end of the next decade."

"You might as well engrave RIP on that cornerstone."

"Don't be so dramatic."

"She'll go faster than the *Titanic*."

"You can lay this at my feet, but I'm going to jump right over it." Howard hopped to his right.

Joseph walked up to the front of the tee box so Howard couldn't address the ball.

Howard stepped away. "You think I should use an iron?"

"The tax base will plummet." Joseph threw his hands in the air. "There'll be no other industry."

"Well, let's see." Howard stroked his jaw. "Whaling is harpooned, and fish stocks are trending down. We don't make automobiles or guns or appliances or refine oil. I got it—those new hat factories everyone is so keen on. There's your future."

Joseph kicked Howard's ball off its tee.

"Was that necessary?" Howard's caddie came running up with the ball. "I'm a businessman, Joseph, not Jesus Christ. Anyone with his head not up his ass can see what's coming." Howard nodded, and the caddie set the ball back on its perch. "We've known each other a long damn time, Joseph. I'm telling you this because Daddy was fond of you, loved your old man. Now don't ruin his memory by getting loose in the jaw about my plans. There's nothing left to discuss. We'll keep in touch and, perhaps, see what I can do for Cleveland down there."

Joseph stepped to the side. He removed his cap and squinted down the fairway. "In 1900, we set the market for cotton in this country."

"I'm nostalgic, too, Joseph. But it's over. Our boys will run mills in the South."

"Maybe yours." Joseph motioned for a club. "And in the meantime?"

"I'm no hypocrite. Our band will march in their damn parades; we'll pay our taxes. In fact, I pity the city for its myopic ignorance. They've done better than most. Take Lowell, for example, but now they'll get what they've sown and rot on the vine." Howard paused. Joseph's head dipped between his shoulders. Drops of sweat—or was it a tear?—fell to his shoe tops. Howard squeezed his elbow. "Sorry, old friend, your award is well deserved, but I fear it is a swan song, an achievement for past wars fought, and not a star on the horizon. And I can bet you those pesky unions will think you owe them a favor nonetheless. Now watch and learn." Howard set his feet and swung, driving the ball down the middle of the fairway.

* * *

Joseph settled his golf debt and paid for the putter snapped over his knee on the eighteenth green and hopped the trolley back to town. Wiggins was only too happy to get back to his gambling behind the caddie shack. Joseph jumped off on Main Street near the Granite Block. The heat had broken. The streets were choked with people and wagons and trolley cars. People enjoying the Sunday afternoon. He missed Mary. Near city hall the businesses had dusted off their red, white, and blue bunting. Long yawns of the stuff were draped over the completed Victory Arch. Folks streamed from the downtown hotels and lined up outside the restaurants. There was laughter and friendly joking between couples waiting outside the Savoy for the next showing of Lon Chaney in *The False Faces*. Joseph thought Fall River every bit as cosmopolitan as Boston or Chicago—he passed Sheedy's Vaudeville at the Academy of Music and a packed dining room at Charlie Wong's—yet, she was a one-industry town and unable to survive without her mills. He saw the idle chimneys dotting the horizon. The future. Au revoir, free dental care. Adeus, libraries. Arrivederci, city pharmacy. An emptiness filled his stomach. Howard's proclamation would come to pass: grass would grow up Plymouth Avenue. "My land will be better used for grazing livestock than producing prints," Howard had said as they parted. "The big mills have no choice, and the smaller ones never followed your lead."

Joseph paused by the front window of a new ice cream parlor, the Dairy Bar. Inside, hundreds of multicolored lights hung in streamers from the ceiling. A boy plucked a chocolate-covered cherry from a tulip-shaped dish and dropped it in his sweetheart's mouth. Perhaps Howard was right, and the town would blow away after the mills left, brick and granite, steel and glass swept into Mount Hope Bay on the wake of the departing Fall River Line. But what of the people? Such hard workers. He thought of the baby, now a little boy, born on the wood floor of a tenement in the Cogsworth slum. The future prince of a shuttered city. Joseph was sorry he would live to be a part of it. The transition would be devastating. Inside the parlor, Joseph sat at the counter before a large marble soda fountain like he had as a boy each Saturday afternoon on the walk home from the mill with his father. He ordered the same malted milkshake with an egg. Soon folks wouldn't have enough money to keep the place in business. He wanted to shout that the end was near but instead slurped his shake. The cream soothed his upset stomach. Howard's word, "hypocrite," had caused the indigestion. At a recent Textile Club luncheon, Joseph had laid out a rosy picture of the future, but it was the hyperbolic jolt his audience—politicians, mill agents, and newspapermen—needed to hear. He saw one banker shake his head at the projections. The upcoming Cotton Week would bring merriment to streets as the centennial had years before. But the day was coming when shipping coal from West Virginia, cotton from the Deep South, and then turning around and shipping finished products west was drawing to a close. Cotton Week revelers wouldn't know the celebration was a wake.

* * *

"I'm home," he called from the vestibule, as he did each day, but there was no answer. He dropped his key in the crystal dish below Otis's portrait. Today the old man's expression was stern, a streak of late-afternoon sun turning his eyes red.

"It's over, old man."

How could you give up so easily? old Otis seemed to ask.

"I've tried."

When there were no markets, we made them from scratch.

"There's nothing left to do." Joseph lifted the frame from the nail and set the portrait in the hall closet. The old fart is right, Joseph thought, but he couldn't do it without the boys. He exhaled and swallowed a mouthful of metallic spit. He went into his study and locked the door.

He sat behind his grandfather's old oak desk. Beneath an early draft of his acceptance speech for the labor award was a contract to supply

Marshall Field & Company with premium bedding. He signed it and put it into an envelope addressed to his second at Cleveland. He dug under his yellow fingernails and bit two of them. He picked at the dry skin around his thumb with his index finger and then tore off a nub of skin with his teeth and rolled it over his tongue. The thumb began to bleed, and he sucked it. He noticed the perfectly squared blanket draped over the couch, his books organized by subject matter, and the three logs stacked in a neat pyramid in the fireplace. Nothing was out of place. He sat for the rest of the afternoon, picking and biting in hope someone would call for him. He was about to strike the lamp, when a crushing sense of failure came over him. Eventually he fell asleep at the desk. He woke an hour later to the ticking of the old clock; nothing had changed except the light.

"Time, sir," Evelyn called from the hallway. "Mr. Bartlett?"

"Time for what?"

"Dinner, sir. Have it in my arms." It was then that he smelled the baked scrod and lemon.

"Yes, it is." Joseph clicked on his banker's lamp. "Time, indeed."

"Can you manage the door?"

"No." He blinked and slapped his cheeks with his hands.

"Sir?"

"Come back at half past."

He stretched his arm across the desk and swept everything to the floor. He fetched a clean sheet of stationery and began a letter to Will. After that letter was sealed with wax, Joseph took out another sheet and began a long-overdue letter to Mary. He found Tom Sheehan's fine glass pointer and held it under the light. A tiny rainbow of color danced across the leather blotter. He folded it into Mary's letter and sealed the envelope.

Joseph stood and pushed his gun cabinet away from the wall to reveal a safe embedded in the plaster. He twirled the dial back and forth through a series of clicks and then cranked the handle down. He set the letters on top of the cash he kept on hand. Evelyn knocked. He locked and hid the safe and then opened the door. She set the dinner tray on the desk and busied herself collecting the papers.

"Leave that for later," he said. "Thank you for this." He tipped his wine glass. Tomorrow he'd send Evelyn and her sister on a two-week holiday to the Cape.

Evelyn straightened her apron and marched out. Joseph stepped around the desk to the old phonograph in the corner of the room and dusted off Lizzy's favorite Hungarian waltz. He cranked the turntable to life; the record warbled and the speaker hissed. He sat on the floor beside the player and ate his dinner. Outside, he heard fabric rustle in the hallway.

* * *

He spent the days before the festival walking the city. He fell down from the Highlands at a quick clip. He found himself in the Cogsville neighborhood, standing before a pile of rubble where Sarah Strong's tenement once stood. A dark-skinned scavenger boy dragging a scrap sled rumbled past.

Joseph said, "What happened to this building?"

"Burn down." The boy's accent was thick, clearly Italian.

Joseph noticed the charred frames of the adjacent apartments. He set his hand on the boy's threadbare jacket. "Anyone hurt?"

"A lady, her baby. Wouldn't jump."

The boy mopped his runny eyes with a crusty rag. Joseph jerked his hand off the boy's shoulder. He reached into his vest for his handkerchief. He tossed the boy a coin.

The boy's eyes beamed like two torches on his dirty face. He said, "More questions?"

"How old are you?"

The boy held up two hands.

"That's ten," Joseph said. "Tell your mother to take you to the free clinic." The boy shrugged and went about his work.

In Globe Village, Joseph attended a service with the Lebanese at St. Anthony of the Desert. In Steep Brook, a dark Patagonian man in a bright yellow shirt driving an ox stopped him to ask the time. Down south, he walked the Portuguese cemetery, visiting the Sousas and the Silvias and the Aguiars. He spent a day at Beattie's quarry watching the men blast and drill granite blocks from the earth. Stone bound for carts, then trains out of the city. Up the Flint, he bought corned beef at Brady's and was given free cabbage. He passed hulking mills, their oil-soaked floors ill-suited for many other northern industries. He watched greasy-faced sweepers and doffers and spinner boys—leaving the Gower Mill at dusk, their dark overalls, and probably their lungs, were coated in cotton lint. Their mothers and sisters stopped at the corner for the waiting tin peddlers, eager to trade clothing scraps for tinware. On the stairs of the textile school one evening, he passed a knot of Italians in white undershirts eating grilled eggplant and yellow peppers. Later, he watched drovers hauling cattle and swine across the Slade's Ferry Bridge while the city slept.

On Wednesday night, the eve of the festival, he left the house through the kitchen door. The night was cool; summer was over. He'd crisscrossed the city in the last three days, meeting many hardworking men and women, but none, he figured, could turn the tide. Earlier in the day, he met with his overseers and approved their plans to produce artificial silk; he mailed João a five-year farm plan, and instructed his lawyer to transfer the deed to João's children.

Joseph walked down Columbia Street, through the smell of chowder and galvanized pork, carrying a leather briefcase. It was a foggy night, and balls of sticky light encased the streetlamps. He kept off the trolley route and spoke to no one, not even the newsies who stuck late editions in his face on every corner. Near the Pocasset mill, he turned on Anawan Street and followed the thundering roar to the falls, where the Quequechan River tumbled four stories over granite rock into Mount Hope Bay. Out in the bay, one of the floating palaces of the Fall River Line blew its whistle as it neared the wharf. Joseph imagined mill agents sipping brandy in their staterooms as the second-class dreamers, fresh from Ellis Island, stood along the starboard railing, staring wide-eyed at the city on a hill. Below, in the hold, sat the five-hundred-pound cotton bales they would spin into cloth.

At the end of the lookout, Joseph climbed on the parapet. He sat down on the wooden planks, overcome by the unbridgeable gap between the intensity of his failures and his desire to make things right. For a moment, he regretted that he had not measured his worth in dividends like his peers. This last act would go misunderstood in their drawing rooms. He stood and climbed over the railing for a bird's-eye view of the cascading water that gave the city its name. The end of the line. He spread his arms. Warm spray struck his face. It tasted of coal ash and metal. The crush of water seemed to jump from the cliff, separating into unique drops before reassembling into a thick block to smash into the rocks and surf. Joseph feared that the mighty river that had powered Colonel Durfee's first mill would gradually disappear as generation after generation paved over the life source that his had so badly spoiled.

PEACEMAKER

The night before the start of Cotton Week, Helen lay awake in her tiny room off the kitchen in her brother Ray's modest cottage. His snores vibrated the shade on her bedside lamp. The jug of beer Helen had contributed to dinner enhanced the loud blasts. How could Fanny stand it? Helen figured the girl's soft brain extended to her ears, but the beer had done its job. At one in the morning, she tossed off the covers, fully dressed—boots too. She eased the window open, stood on her desk chair, and jumped over the blueberry bush into the moonlit grass. She walked the two miles to the Hartwell farm in twenty minutes. The slaughterhouse was near the road it was the farthest outbuilding from the barn. She found the gun wrapped in an oil-stained cloth on the warped shelving, behind coffee cans full of rusted nails. On an egg run last summer, Hartwell's oldest son had shown off the weapon, a Colt Single Action Army, which had belonged to his dead uncle—a lawman, the boy claimed. Helen asked if he'd ever killed anyone. Lots, the boy smirked. They call it the Peacemaker. The name amused Helen still, and she chuckled as she handled the gun, inhaling its stale oil aroma. She stepped toward the barn door, changed her mind, and whirled. She lined up the bloodstained slaughtering table—*bang*. The tool shelves—*bang*. The window—*bang*. The moon—*bang, bang*. The gun fell to her side. It was heavier than she remembered, and the thick grip didn't fit her small hand comfortably. She had hoped to conceal it in her jacket, but the long barrel stuck out of the pocket like the rat's nose. Back in her room, she wedged the gun under the mattress and dressed in her bedclothes. She desperately needed rest, but Ray's snoring was relentless. The vibrations cut though the house as if the plaster, bearing beams, and even the brick chimney and clapboard were conductive. This snore current, as Helen called it, electrified the frame of her iron bed, shocking her very bones. She lay awake, praying Fanny might sock him one. Helen pulled Tommy's letter out from under her pillow, the paper had begun to tear from all the handling. She skimmed it again. This time, not tearing up when she came to her father's name. She hid the letter and lay still, staring at the ceiling. The lampshade shook. Helen made a finger gun and aimed it at the ceiling. Perhaps she'd shoot Ray first. She needed the practice.

* * *

João Rose returned from the cow barn as the sun peeked over the horizon. He set a metal jug of warm milk on the kitchen counter. He carried the smell of the barn, a musty, earthy odor of hay and manure. He removed his muddy boots and then walked across the sitting room in Otis's old farmhouse, passing beneath Hollister's portrait of Maria over the fireplace. She came down the stairs in her bedclothes to fill a bottle. She removed the metal cap from the jug. The warm steam smelled of earth and grass. João pulled down a small leather-bound journal from the mantel and knelt on the hearth. As he thumbed through the pages, a sketch he'd made of his grandmother twenty years ago slipped out and he wedged it back in the center. He propped the book against the andirons and spread out his arms and bowed his head.

"Joseph Bartlett, in the name of the Father and the Holy Mother, I bless you. If you have quebranto from an evil eye of a man or woman, or the way you work, I bless you, that it goes to the ends of the ocean, where nobody ever hears the crow of a rooster. In the name of the Father, and the Son, and the Holy Spirit. Amen."

João lowered his arms, exhaled, and sat back on his haunches.

"On the trip back, buy the cod-liver oil," Maria said.

João nodded. He closed the notebook and set it back on the mantel.

"Take one of the children," Maria continued. "But I need to stay with the baby."

João shook his head. "I'll go. I will tip my cap and return."

"What of the soldier?"

"I said I will deliver your message," João said, his voice rising.

"He will sleep at Kitty's and paint in the meadow overlooking the bogs. The fresh air will do him good."

João stood. "You owe him nothing."

She touched her forehead. "The scars have faded from this old face."

"I don't want him near you."

"I know," Maria said. "But it's my wish."

"He'll paint where I tell him."

"And, sweet husband," Maria said, her voice softening. "Say a blessing for yourself." She turned up the stairs, leaving a milky vapor in her wake.

* * *

The steamer passed the Bristol Ferry Light into Mount Hope Bay as the morning sun climbed over Fall River, catching the gold crosses atop the twin spires of Saint Anne's. From the top deck of the *Priscilla*, they shimmered, seemingly floating over the bay. Farther on, the observatory at Durfee High School came into view. Its round dome slit open like a giant eye watching over the city. Seagulls swept over the boat, dive-bombing toward their breakfast, only to bank up at the waterline into twisting S curves around the steamer's two black smokestacks. One bird waddled down the white railing toward Will, stopped an arm's-length away, and shifted his head side to side as if recognizing him from Bliffin's Beach, then darted off to join a screeching funnel cloud of birds chasing a passing lobster boat. Two tugs motored toward the *Priscilla*. Will descended the starboard stairs, the Labor Board's invitation poking his ribs as he walked. At the gangway, he checked his watch. The luncheon started at eleven thirty. He had plenty of time. He spat on the lapel of his suit jacket and used his nail to scratch the mustard stain from yesterday's lunch. He had gone from his law office to the North River pier for the overnight trip. He licked his mustard-stained finger. He pitied his father, but had come to accept that textiles were in his blood, too, and so did the partners at his new law firm. He wondered if he should have cabled his father. They hadn't seen one another in nearly a year. At the Borden Flats reef the lighthouse bell rattled and the *Priscilla*'s steam whistle blasted a reply. The boat slowed, and an alarm rung deep within her steel hull. The boilers rumbled and the floor planks vibrated beneath Will's feet as the paddle wheels reversed. Across the bay, the brick smokestacks passed clear air. Will removed his hat and leaned over the railing, hoping the rumor about Helen being engaged was false. Hard to tell with that girl. The cloudless blue sky stretched to the horizon.

* * *

Hollister sat in the pavilion shelter gazing out over South Park thinking he had someplace to be, as Michael haggled with a Frenchy about Roger's depiction of his wife. Since Michael's sister succumbed to the flu, he'd been in a sour mood, convinced he'd contract it soon. Time was Michael's enemy. But the Frenchy had a point; Roger's portrait wasn't much. Michael had discovered Roger outside the Fall River Evening Drawing School, a novice for sure, but a vet with a talent for quick caricatures. Confusion reigned Roger's first month. Folks weren't sure who painted what, though the sign clearly stated one-dollar caricatures to the right; three-dollar portraits to the left. Michael had also added a food stand and a souvenir cart for Cotton Week. Earlier that summer he'd moved out of June Street into his own rooms; he'd dedicated half to housing Hollister's *real* paintings, one of which he'd shipped to Robert Dunning's former dealer in Boston. Though Hollister's paintings didn't have the bright colors of the Fall River school, they were still lifes nonetheless—the type of detailed characterizations that had put Dunning on the map.

"If you want a portrait," Michael shouted, "the line starts there." Frenchy shook his head. "Well, then take this and scram." Frenchy pushed the canvas away, and Michael waved over two thick-armed vets. After the Christmas crush, he'd hired security to keep the peace. Folks believed the men had real authority in their uniforms. They lifted Frenchy off his feet and carried him into the grass. His plump wife waddled close behind.

Michael waved his hand before Hollister's face. "Couple more to go."

"I have to be somewhere."

"Where?" Michael's patience for Hollister's moods was wearing thin.

"I can't remember."

"Here's the deal. You paint a few more, and I'll tell you where you have to be. Now grab your pencil. You've got plenty of time."

* * *

George Pierce's wife, Mildred, lifted lint from her husband's suit jacket with a strip of tape. He'd been tapped to present Joseph with his humanitarian award at the luncheon.

Mildred said, "Why haven't you told him? I think you should have told him already. He'll be angry if he hears it from someone else."

Pierce continued to comb his mustache. "Why? Because at the end of the day, he's not one of us."

"He wasn't one of you when he helped divert the strike last year?"

"No."

"Didn't your fathers work together to pass the Saturday half holiday?"

"Enough of that."

"Here." She handed him the labor union sash he wore at banquets and parades. She thumbed the silk. "Didn't Mr. Bartlett's slogan win you a seat at the AF of L Congress?"

"'Diplomacy Not Defiance' wasn't liked by all the members."

"Merging of unions was Mr. Bartlett's mantra." She kissed her husband's bearded cheek. "Tell him your plan."

"It was everyone's idea." Pierce brushed her hand off his shoulder and shooed her away. "Even the great Samuel Gompers said it behind closed doors."

Mildred choked up. She bowed her head, snorted. then said, "He sent dinner after Timothy died."

Pierce sighed. "Come now, sweet." He motioned to embrace her, but she stepped out of his reach.

"You speak to that man," she said sternly. "And don't touch the ale until after your speech."

"Enough of that," Pierce quipped. "I have a meeting." He snapped up his hat and walked to the door. He pulled the knob, paused, and then turned back to his wife. "We needed to have someone on the inside, didn't we? If it weren't Bartlett, it would've been another Highlands knob."

"He was a friend."

"Nonsense."

"You play dirty pool, George Pierce."

"It's the American way," he said, and slammed the door.

* * *

Mary Sheehan had signed Pete up for the footraces at the Cotton Week field days, but the boy woke with a fever, and she decided to keep him out. Perhaps he'd compete in tomorrow's events. She sat in her sitting room drinking the last of her Earl Grey from one of Hannah Cleveland's old orange-patterned teacups. The tea tin had been last year's birthday gift from Joseph, delivered from the Troy Store in a red velvet box. She maneuvered her oversized sewing scissors around page five of the *Herald News*. The scissors were ill-fit for the job, but they were all she could find. She took the clipping and accompanying photograph of Joseph, whose location she couldn't place, and pasted them into a family scrapbook she kept hidden in the bottom drawer of the rolltop desk. The book held clippings from before Tom's death, along with steamer tickets, Tommy's clips, and theater playbills. With her thumb, she pressed down a stubborn crease that ran between Joseph's eyes, but that only made it worse. Now it split his face. "The two halves of Joseph Bartlett," she said aloud. The hall clock chimed. In a few hours, the town would celebrate him. Deservedly so, she thought. She wanted to see it. She shut the book and tucked it beneath a mound of letters. She sipped her tea and sucked her teeth. The dregs of the tin were bitter. The doorbell rang, and she jumped to her feet to answer it before whoever it was woke poor Pete.

"Good morning, ma'am," said the blue-clad messenger. His head rose just above Mary's hip. "Are you Mary Sheehan?"

"Well, indeed I am."

"The man said to give this to you—only you." Mary recognized the handwriting on the envelope. "Care not to drop it. Something's in there."

Mary tapped her thumb over the long object inside. "I'll be careful." She plucked a nickel from her apron pocket and held it out to the boy. "For your trouble."

"No thank you, ma'am. The man tipped me triple. He said to give your money to Pete."

"Did he, now. And where is this man?"

"Up the Highlands."

"What did this man look like?"

"Older gentleman. Wild beard, curly hair. Spoke kindly of you."

Wiggins. "Smelled a bit of booze, did he?"

The boy hesitated until Mary smiled. "Yes, ma'am. A bit."

"Did he say anything else?"

"Ma'am?"

"How old are you?"

"Eleven."

"Did he have other messages to pass along?"

"No, ma'am." The boy pointed. "I'm guessing that's why he wrote the letter."

* * *

Before Michael could say, "Who's next?" Helen plopped down on the stool in front of Hollister. Michael searched around for a trailing husband.

"It's just me," Helen sneered. "I've got plenty." She rubbed a five-dollar note between her thumb and forefinger.

"Extra special service for you." Michael plucked the bill from her fingers. "You know how this works?"

"Does he really not remember anything from before the war?"

"He remembers long enough to transfer what I tell him to the canvas."

"Good," Helen said. "Put this in the portrait." Helen removed the Colt from the canvas sack at her feet and laid it across her open palms like some sort of offering. "Paint it like this," she said.

Michael dropped his hat over the gun. "Let's not call attention to it." This was their first gun. They'd had requests for oranges, lobsters, drums, and one frying pan, but never a gun. "I will describe it for him," Michael said.

"It's called the Peacemaker."

"Peace to the one still standing."

"Just include it."

Michael whispered, "He knows guns." And then shot a nervous smile to the next woman in line.

"I heard he was good."

"You won't find a better soldier."

"I meant at painting."

"Oh, he's top notch." Michael glanced at Hollister's glassy eyes. "Guaranteed immortality."

"Then I came to right place," Helen said as she rolled the gun into the folds of her skirt.

* * *

Mary sat on the leather couch, opening and closing the translucent arms of Tom's retractable glass whatchamacallit. United States patent 792,432 lay on the end table beside Joseph's letter and a tear-soaked handkerchief. It had been so long since she'd had any physical contact with anything to do with her husband. She'd loved his analytical mind. The small invention—one of many created in the company workroom, but now officially recognized—staked claim to a kernel of history and, in a small way, created a sort of immortality for Tom Sheehan. The simplicity of materials, glass and brass; the wizardry of the hinges, sewn together with catgut; and its beauty, the way it caught the light and spilled out color—it was stunning. Mary twirled it between her hands. She had known Tom—the man held no mystery; but for his children, robbed of their father, it was this very mystique that drove their passions. She set the pointer on the end table and looked about the room for a suitable hiding place. For the time being, it would be her memory alone.

* * *

"What's the time?" Hollister asked.

"Ten minutes since the last time you asked," Michael snapped. He forced a smile toward the woman seated across from his partner. "Pay attention. You're almost done."

"I want to go."

"Finish this one and you'll make it."

"Something's wrong."

"It looks fine." Michael winked at the woman. "Keep going, then lunch."

Hollister set down his brush. "Done."

"There's no background."

"Finish later. She can go."

Hollister stood up and groped for his cane. Michael lifted the canvas and set it beside the frame of the crazy woman with the gun. She'd said the police would probably come for it. Total loon. Said it would make Hollister famous. One of the thick-armed vets took Hollister's elbow and escorted him into the park. "Sorry, folks," Michael called to those waiting in line. "Maestro is off to the toilet. We'll open again after lunch. Visit the snack truck while you wait."

* * *

George Pierce rose from his seat at the luncheon when the editor of the *Labor Standard* introduced him to present the humanitarian award. Other honorees sat with gold medals dangling from their necks on red silk ribbons. Pierce knocked the empty chair beside him with his knuckles, and then patted Will's shoulder as he made his way toward the podium. He knitted his brow as he passed. A messenger sent to Cleveland had returned empty-handed. Wiggins had chased off the boy sent to the house. Mill operatives and their families picnicked in the green outside the white tent; Cleveland workers were handsomely represented. Will recognized the faces of a few overseers. Farther back, he spotted an ashen-faced Mary Sheehan standing beside Dr. Boyle, fatter and more stooped since the last time Will had seen him. Pete slouched against Ray's thick shoulder. Fanny rode his hip rocking a baby. Tommy stood to the side, hunched over, reading something Will couldn't make out. Near a back tie-down he spied João Rose fiddling with his hat. No sign of Hollister.

"It's a great honor to present Labor's first lifetime humanitarian award to Joseph Bartlett. Though I've only met the man a few times, I know much of his good deeds for the workers of his shop and many others. Sadly"—Pierce pointed to the empty chair on the dais—"Mr. Bartlett couldn't be here today, but his son Will, just in from New York, will accept the award in his stead. But first, a few words about the man we honor here today."

As Will waved to the crowd, Tommy's neck snapped up. He folded the letter and hustled off, disappearing into the park.

"I'm sure many of you don't know that Joseph Bartlett lost half of his pinkie on the job."

João pulled his hat tight over his head and peeled off into the sea of Sunday walkers and baby carriages.

"Crushed by a cotton bale. His father, Otis, made him work in each department before climbing the ranks."

Mary whispered something to Dr. Boyle, and he took her arm and led her away.

"Cleveland's mill store is famous for its low prices, not to mention, time-and-a-half birthday pay."

Where the hell is he? Where are they all going? Pierce shuffled the pages of his script—three to go. Will saw no escape from this old anarchist's glorified biography of his father.

* * *

The ocean breeze propelled Will up Cherry Street. A front had blown in from the west, and the wind carried damp air up from the bay. A light mist coated his shoulders. The neighborhood was quiet, what with the events in full swing, except for three boys tossing a ball in the street. Will recognized Dr. Boyle's Ford parked on the street. Behind it was a Rose Butter truck. Approaching his father's house, he spied a pair of legs dangling from the old tree fort in the corner of the lawn. He smiled, thinking some local boys had discovered his old haunt, but closer, he recognized his brother slumped on the platform at the top of the wooden ladder. He stopped on the sidewalk next to the iron gate surrounding the house. Up in the lawn Ray, Fanny, and Pete played croquet. Ray waved his mallet.

"Hollister, what are you doing? It's Will. Down here."

Hollister peered down between his legs.

"What are you doing up there?"

Hollister stared.

Will jumped on the granite ledge and grabbed the bars of the fence. "Hollister, say something."

"Dad's gone," Hollister called.

"Where?"

Hollister straightened up. He pointed toward the house. "Ask them."

The front door was unlocked. Light leaked from the study. Will bound in and the conversation stopped. João, Mary, Tommy, and Dr. Boyle froze as if caught in the middle of burglary.

"So, where is he?"

They glanced at one another.

"Tell me what the hell is going on."

Finally Dr. Boyle said, "Letter for you, on the desk."

Beside the envelope sat the remains of a bound Cleveland accounts ledger. Most of the red leather front was charred black. The pages inside, except for the edges, were not burned. Yellowed, but decipherable. He didn't recognize the handwriting. The bottom of each page was initialed with the letters *SC*.

"What the hell is this?"

Dr. Boyle nodded toward the envelope. "Read the letter."

"Aloud," Tommy snapped.

Will shot him a look and sat down in his father's chair. As he read, his chest ticked steadily forward until his head nearly touched the desk. He whispered, "Is this true?" No one answered. Will unbut-toned at his collar; his face flushed. After a beat, he jabbed his middle and index fingers into his eyes and rubbed vigorously. Deep down he had always suspected some nefarious plot had catapulted his father to the front of the line. But party to a murder? His mother's people must have pulled a string or two. Quickly, his anger turned to melancholy. He pictured young Tom Sheehan, handsome and strong. His father always spoke fondly of the man. But hadn't Dad acted reluctantly? Wasn't that worth considering? His intent had been noble—even en-couraged by Boss Borden, if the letter was to be believed. Dad had held the truth to his chest to protect everyone: the operatives, Mother, João, even the Sheehans. Without him at the helm of Cleveland, the mill would have followed the association's whims. But his silence brought a weight too great to carry, Will thought. Perhaps these letters had re-leased the pressure.

"Where the hell is the bastard?" Tommy shouted.

"Watch it, mister," Mary said.

Will opened the ledger slowly with his index finger. The puzzle piece that had been hiding under the cushions for twenty years. He flipped its pages, skimming Stanton's scribbled figures, knowing it would take a lot more study. He shut the book and slowly his color returned to normal as a sense of relief came over him. He leaned back, his hands planted firmly on the desk. He looked over the group. What must they think of his father? And yes, where the hell was he?

The front doorbell rang. Dr. Boyle nodded to Tommy to answer. They heard voices in the vestibule, and then the front door shut. Tommy reen-tered with Patrick Newton. He was dressed in his purser's uniform and carried a tweed trench coat over his arm.

"You all know Patrick," Tommy said. They all nodded. Patrick gave a short wave. "Tell them what you told me."

Patrick's head dipped down between his shoulders. He started to speak, then stopped, and removed his cap. "Like I said to Tommy here. I worked the *Priscilla* over and back, you see. Yesterday morning, in New York, one of the maids brings me this coat for the lost and found. Said she fished it out of the salon rubbish. Well, it's a fine coat for someone in the salon to be wearing. I poke around the pockets, for a name or card or something, and I find this, plain as day." Patrick held the coat by the shoulders. Stitched in script between the middle seams was the name *Joseph Bartlett*. "I stowed it and figured to drop it on my walk home today."

"Let me see that." Will raced around the desk and rifled through the pockets. Empty. He slipped the coat on—he was about his father's size—and crossed his arms. It was his Dad's all right. He tossed it to Tommy, who turned the pockets out yet again.

"Did you see him on the trip?"

"No."

"But you could have missed him, right? It's a big boat."

"That's the funny thing," Patrick said. "See, I checked the passenger manifest, and he wasn't listed."

"A simple oversight," Dr. Boyle said.

Patrick shook his head. "Don't think so, sir. They're mighty careful since the Newport fire. Need to account for everyone."

"But the coat could have been on board since his last trip?"

"We clean and sweep after every leg, Dr. Boyle. Had to be the night before last." Patrick paused. He looked around the room and studied each face. Watching João fiddle with his hat in the alcove between the bookshelves, he said, "You have a break-in or something?"

"Thank you for dropping it off." Will patted Patrick's back. "I'll be sure to tell my father. Tommy will see you out."

As the two turned toward the door, Will said, "One more thing, what's the water temperature these days?"

Patrick looked out the window, then to Will. He shrugged, "Oh, with summer just past, around sixty."

"Thanks." Will shut the door behind them.

"My God," Mary said. "You think?"

Tommy returned. Will pointed to Dr. Boyle, leaning over an armchair. "Is it possible?"

"He could last a few hours, but he'd need someone to pluck him from the water. He wasn't much of a swimmer."

"Fucking coward," Tommy snarled.

"Thomas Sheehan!"

"You watch your mouth," Will snapped.

"Save it." Tommy sucked his teeth. He began to pace the room. The veins in his strawberry eye swelled with each step. "Even if he did jump and wanted to survive, you got to know what you're doing. Those paddles draft a ton of water."

"He's right," Dr. Boyle said. "There's only one reason to jump."

"Screw your father," Tommy said. "Is that burnt ledger for real? Did my father die because of Highlands greed? Because if that's true, I'm gonna burn down this house."

"Calm down, son." Dr. Boyle touched his shoulder as he passed by.

"I want the truth." Tommy whirled, knocking Dr. Boyle into an armchair, and then swiveled round and bull-rushed João into the corner bookcase. He pinned his forearm over João's throat. "Say something, you idiot. You were there. Did it happen like he said?"

João remembered the tremendous heat of that night—every footstep, every scream. And the story remained the same. Tragedy has no need for hyperbole. Mr. Bartlett knew this. João nodded his head slowly.

"Get the hell off of him," Will shouted.

"Please, Tommy," Mary pleaded. She knelt on the carpet. Her hands rose over her head. "Release the poor man."

Tommy pounded the books above João's head with his fist. He grabbed a brown hardcover and flung it across the room, nearly striking his mother.

Dr. Boyle walked slowly toward Tommy, his palms up. "Nothing good can come of more violence."

"Really?" Tommy lurched forward on his toes, and Dr. Boyle recoiled.

"Good attempted to save bad, and they both lost," Dr. Boyle said.

Tommy sneered. "The Bartletts didn't lose."

Will's fist connected with Tommy's chin, then continued into his shoulder. Tommy fell to the carpet. Will hovered over him, his arm cocked for another salvo, when João tackled him to the floor.

"My father suffered his entire life," Will shouted from his knees. "He wanted none of this." He glared at João, jumped to his feet, and walked to the window, rubbing his elbow.

Tommy sat up slowly. His eyes blinking open and shut. His face blanched. Mary knelt at his side but he brushed her away.

Dr. Boyle stood between the two men, his arms outstretched. "Everyone calm down."

Tommy stood. His thin legs wobbled. He grabbed the doorknob and jabbed the air with his finger. "This is not over." He raised his right knee to step, then thought better of it. He inhaled then exhaled a large quantity of air. He bounced to test his balance. Satisfied, he opened the door. "Let's go, Mother."

Mary fingered the glass pointer hidden up her sleeve. "I'm staying," she said.

"Fine." Tommy jabbed a finger Will's direction. "You and me," he barked. He slammed the study door. A moment later, the front door rattled.

The room was silent. João retreated to the alcove. Dr. Boyle paced before the hearth.

Will moved quickly across the room. "Wait a second. João, give me a hand." Will and João lifted the gun cabinet away from the wall, revealing Joseph's safe.

Dr. Boyle whistled.

"The combination." Will drummed his fingers across his lips.

"Nine-thirteen-sixteen," João said.

"Shit," Will whistled. The group stared.

"He had me memorize it."

Will knelt before the safe. The others huddled around.

"What did he keep in there?" Mary asked.

"A reserve of cash, company documents. I suppose that burnt ledger. There." Will cranked the handle and pulled the door. He rattled his arm around inside. "Nothing now."

Dr. Boyle knelt down and flung his arm into the safe. "Where's the cash?"

"The bank?" Will paced the room. "I haven't seen inside in a few years."

Will nodded at João. "How about you?"

"Second time here."

"Wait a second," Dr. Boyle said. He swiveled on his knees, a small origami bird resting on his palm.

"What's that?" Will said.

"A paper bird." Dr. Boyle scratched his chin. "Huh."

"Hand it here." Will plucked it off Dr. Boyle's palm and whirled it in the air. He smiled.

"A what?" Mary asked.

"An albatross," Will said.

"Or a gull," Dr. Boyle said. "Hard to tell. Mary?"

Mary slumped back on the couch. "Never seen it."

Will knelt before her. He felt a sudden tenderness for her. "Please read me the last lines of Father's letter."

She slipped it from her sleeve. Dr. Boyle, still on his knees, removed an envelope from his jacket and unfolded a letter of his own.

She read: "*Goodbye, dear. I am leaving you, the three boys, Fall River. My time has come. My heart has stopped.*" They spoke the last line in unison, "*My new journey begins today.*"

A bird with a long wingspan, Will thought. He rubbed his hands over his face. "Dr. Boyle, call the chief of police and report a suicide. Ask him to come personally. It's in his best interest to keep this quiet." Will tossed his letter on the end table.

"Okay . . ." Dr. Boyle hesitated. "But, but there's no body."

"Talk to the sharks in Long Island Sound."

Mary began to weep.

"It was a full life," Dr. Boyle said. He walked to the small bar in the corner of the room. And poured scotch into four short glasses. "Let's toast to his memory."

"None for me," João said. He backed toward the door. "Past time for me."

"You knew him better than anyone," Will said, taking a glass. "Was it his time to go?"

João shrugged, then sniffled. "He was good to me."

"Go home." Will walked over and embraced João and led him to the door.

"I forget." João pivoted back. "Bring Holl—your brother to the farm next week."

Mary wiped her eyes and stood up. "Ask your wife."

"Her wish." João looked around the room, pausing on the books. "She reads like Mr. Bartlett. Knows about things. Love. War. Forgiveness." João tipped his cap and left.

The three stood in the center of the room and raised their glasses. "For a great man."

"For Dad."

"For Joseph."

The scotch stung Will's throat. He set his hands on his father desk and let out a deep breath. When the money stops coming you die, he thought. But what if the money kills you first?

The sound of shattering glass filled the room.

"Who's upstairs?"

Mary and Dr. Boyle exchanged glances. Finally, peering over his round glasses, Dr. Boyle said, "She was the first one here."

Will shot out of the room and up the stairs. Glass shards from a hurricane lamp sprinkled the landing. He smelled tobacco and followed the vapor trail into his old room at the end of the hall. He pushed the door open and stood on the threshold. Helen sat on the foot of the bed, a cigarette tapping her knee.

"I wanted more light," she said.

"Then open the drapes."

"No," she said, exhaling. "There's too much commotion on the street."

Will stepped to the window. Indeed, a small crowd of neighbors stood at the front gate. Ray Sheehan stood below Hollister's tree house jabbering about something. Will turned and perched the paper bird on the dresser.

Helen walked to the dresser and took up the bird. She fingered its long neck. "What's this?"

"Dad's bird."

"Does it fly?"

"Over great distances." He grabbed her elbow.

"I won't hurt your new toy."

"You're not wearing your calico schoolteacher dress." He rubbed the label of her linen jacket between his fingers. "Fancy suit on a teacher's wage."

"I stole it," she said, the cigarette hanging from her lip. She tucked her hands into the pockets of his suit jacket and squeezed his hips.

Will snatched her cigarette, took a drag. Exhaling, he said, "You were always good at taking things that didn't belong to you."

"Better than you." She removed her hands from his jacket, and twirled around. "You bought me this. Remember."

"Just wanted you to say it."

Helen rolled her eyes. "Men are so dumb."

"Perhaps." He tucked a loose curl behind her ear. "Why are you here?"

"You've made every other boy inadequate."

"Very funny." He handed her back the cigarette and walked to the bureau, removed his suit jacket, and tossed it over the desk chair. He stood in the middle of the room. "Now, why are you here?"

"To see you." She sat on the bed.

"But no one knew I was coming."

"I guessed." He reached for the cigarette, and as she extended her arm, he grabbed her wrist and yanked her to her feet.

"Why are you here?"

"Finally some pep."

"I'm serious." He twisted her wrist. Helen grimaced and he eased off.

"Time I came home," she said.

"To my father's house?"

"He's always been good to us."

"You're crazy." He dropped her arm, and the cigarette fell to the carpet.

She snatched it up and walked across the room, rubbing her wrist. "So where's your father?"

"At the bottom of Long Island Sound."

"Oh God!"

"That sounded awful."

"Yes."

"I'm sorry. I don't know what to think right now." Will glanced at the paper bird. *Where are you?*

A car horn honked, and she peeked out the window. "Drowning. Dreadful. Even I have sympathy for that." She turned, her voice trailing off. There was a row of gapers bumper-to-bumper down June Street. Ray shook his croquet mallet at the gathering crowd. In the distance a siren wailed. Down the lawn she saw Hollister pacing the tree house. The leaves on the old oak were just beginning to turn. She followed the phone lines down the hill until they disappeared into the fog rolling up from the bay. She let the drape fall and took a drag. Exhaling, she said, "You're an orphan now."

"I was hoping to surprise him at the awards ceremony, then apologize for what happened between us. I just ran away."

"That's something we have in common."

Will sat on the corner of the bed. His shoulders shook. "And he's left me to hold it all together. The mill, the operatives, Hollister. I don't know if I'm mad or sad. Jesus Christ."

"He must have known you could do it."

"All I ever did was what he told me to do." His eyes glistened as he blinked back tears. "I can't do it alone."

Helen slipped a hankie from his suit jacket and handed to him. "Hey," she said. "Maybe it's time we made something of this two-bit mill town, don't ya think?"

He shook his head. "Then we gotta trust one another."

"Seems that's the only way." She dropped the cigarette in the glass of water on the bedside table and stood before him.

"But first this orphan is gonna be sad for a night." He blew his nose into the hankie and threw it across the room. "I'm gonna miss him." She pulled his head to her chest and kissed the top of it.

"Rest. We'll dominate the world tomorrow."

"Promise me no more stealing."

"I'll try."

There were footsteps on the stairs, and a voice called up; Helen pressed a finger to her lips. She turned and locked the door. Will fell back on the bed. Helen knelt down and removed his shoes and socks. She brushed street dust from his trousers, and then lifted his feet to the bed. Will rolled over, squeezing his body into a tight knot. Helen found a green wool blanket in the bottom of the chest of drawers and spread it over him. She removed her shoes and jacket and snapped off the bedside lamp. She wedged her knees inside his and pressed her forehead to the nape of his neck, hoping he didn't feel the gun stuffed under the mattress.

EPILOGUE

What follows is a partial audio transcript. The estate of Helen S. Bartlett donated the recording, along with other mill documents, artifacts, and her own personal diaries, to the Plymouth State University library following her death on September 26, 1984.

Date of Recording: August 12, 1964

To: Cleveland Mill Employees

From: William D. Bartlett, Company President

In the memory of Colonel Jefferson Cleveland, Hannah Cleveland, Stanton Cleveland, Otis Bartlett, and my father, Joseph Bartlett, I stand before you with a heavy heart. In one month's time, the Cleveland Mill will cease operation. Rumors that the white knight of Omaha might purchase Cleveland, as he has our friends down Route 6 at Berkshire Hathaway, are incorrect. Though phone calls were exchanged, he has kindly passed on our offer. As you know, since the

war, we have started new lines, trimmed budgets, and
attempted all kinds of maneuvers to keep the Cleveland name alive, but now the banks, but mostly my
heart, tells me the time has come to close our doors.
We have outlived hundreds of competitors and beat
back the Southern menace. We survived the Great Depression, recessions, two World Wars, and the lure of
overseas production. On behalf of my wife, Helen; my
brother Peter; and the entire board of CCM, I want
to thank you for your service. You are the sons and
daughters of Fall River.

All of you know the story of my father's . . . [re-
cording garbled, loud bang in background] . . . as we
used to say, "Loom up," and listen as the ghosts of
Fall River bid you farewell. They are all around us,
operatives of past glory. They are of all creeds and
colors. Men, women, and, regrettably, children. From
Steep Brook to the Flint. From the Watuppa Ponds to
the bay. They drink from the Quequechan River buried deep below our feet. And sleep on the oil-soaked
floors of shuttered mills, waiting for the next great
industry that will once again make our city the crown
jewel of New England.

ACKNOWLEDGMENTS

Given you have your whole life to write a first novel, I've accumulated a long list of friends and readers to thank, but the book started with the real-life stories of my family. I'm grateful to my great aunt Helen and uncle Thomas Sheehan and my grandparents Mary and Thomas O'Donnell—my Fall River heroes, Spindle City natives who lived and worked and are buried in the city. I started recording our conversations much too late. From their tales of triumph and tragedy, I spun my fictional narrative. My apologies for the liberties I have taken to tell this story.

I am grateful for the help of Michael Martins and Dennis Binette at the Fall River Historical Society for opening their door on Rock Street and allowing me to wade through the archives.

I am indebted to the following editors and authors, whose books assisted me in my early research: Philip T. Silvia Jr., *Victorian Vistas: Fall River, 1901–1911*; Mary H. Blewett, *Constant Turmoil*; William Moran, *The Belles of New England*; Carmen J. Maiocco, *The Granite Block*; Daniel Georgianna, with Roberta Hazen Aaronson, *The Strike of '28*; Joe Thomas and Donna Huse, editors of the miraculous *Spinner* anthologies; and finally, the Cotton Centennial Committee for leaving behind a rich paper trail.

I'm grateful for early feedback from my old Chicago writing group—Ed, Mike, and Kevin—who sometimes moaned when I showed up with more pages from "the Fall River book."

Thanks to my writing and artistic communities—readers, friends, authors, and fellow teachers who were quick with comments and encouragement—from Columbia College Chicago, Central Connecticut State University, the Yale Writers' Workshop, Redmoon friends, Roar Reading Series, the Writers WorkSpace, Novel Generator, ERB authors, Westport and B-town friends, and Muddy Feet. A special note of thanks to the thousands of writing students I've had the privilege of sharing a semicircle with, and to the Ragdale Foundation and Ox Bow Arts for their generous support and for quiet confines to write in during the early years—yes, years—of writing the novel.

Thanks for acts of kindness go to: Sergio Troncoso, Mary Collins, Jacob Appel, Patty McNair, Randy Albers, Christopher Morris, Victoria Rinkerman, Amy Davis, Tanera Marshall, Janet Burroway, Sarah Desjardins, Dena Cushenberry, Suzanne Sturgeon, Uncle Anthony, Jim Wilson, Mr. Mann, Bud and Mary Davis, Rose and Leo, and Brett, Jake, Lindsay and big sister Elizabeth.

The final edits of the manuscript were completed in March 2020, the day after the US recorded the most coronavirus cases worldwide. I write this note holed up in my home office not knowing what the future holds for the world, for you, for me, for this book.

I want to thank everyone at Blackstone for their steadfast support, particularly Megan Wahrenbrock. Also a big thank you to my keen editors Madeline Hopkins and Michael Krohn. It was a pleasure to work with designer Kathryn English on the cover and map design.

Special thanks to my agent, Mark Gottlieb, for his persistence and kindness.

Thanks to my parents, Leonard and Sheila Burrello, for their unflagging love and support no matter the project or harebrained idea. Thanks for showing me the value of hard work, and for taking care of my boys.

Thanks to my three boys—Atticus, Miles, and Baby J.—whose genesis and maturation paralleled the writing of the book. Thanks, guys. (And stay off Dad's computer.)

And finally, to my wife, Kristin: Thank you. Your encouragement and love make everything possible.